INCA MOON
CHRONICLE II

P.H. Carmichael

First issued as Eye of the Condor
Cover illustrations: Adapted from 17th century drawings by Felipe Guamán Poma de Ayala

Order this book online at www.trafford.com
or email orders@trafford.com

Most Trafford titles are also available at major online book retailers.

Printed in the United States of America.

ISBN: 978-1-4669-4870-9 (sc)
ISBN: 978-1-4669-4871-6 (e)

Trafford rev. 07/31/2012

www.trafford.com

North America & international
toll-free: 1 888 232 4444 (USA & Canada)
phone: 250 383 6864 ♦ fax: 812 355 4082

*

INCA MOON CHRONICLE II
Translated from the original

Crónica de la India Qori Qoyllur

Biblioteca Español – Manuscritos Tempranos de las Americas

Acquired from the Whiteacre Collection with the generous support of: Academia Nacional de Historiadoras; Fundación María Mendoza de Pérez; The Postmodern Symposium of Latin American Historiographers; and the John J. and Charlotte Armstrong Foundation for the Humanities.

Author: la india Qori Qoyllur
Scribe: Doña Catalina de Quintana de Betánzos

Note to Readers

The remarkable events described herein took place long ago in Ecuador and Peru, when those two nations were one under the Inca emperor Wayna Qhapaq. In Europe it was 1511, the year Pope Julius II founded the Holy League with Venice and Aragon to drive the French out of Italy, Henry VIII reformed the Royal Navy, Erasmus began teaching at Cambridge, Leonardo da Vinci planned the Trivulzio monument, and Diego de Valasquez settled Cuba. None of them knew golden empires waited in the Americas, for this was ten years before Cortez conquered the Aztecs, and twenty years before Pizarro invaded the Andes. The narrator of this account, the Inca woman Qori Qoyllur, related her tale in later years to doña Catalina de Quintana de Betánzos, who dutifully served as scribe.

While the words are Qori's taken down verbatim, the chapter headings are doña Catalina's. In the style of her contemporaries doña Catalina often includes trivia and omits the salient—at least from our perspective. Her tone is disapproving, but how could it be otherwise? Every sixteenth century book required a royal license conferred by archbishops and high courts representing the king. She merely displays the political correctness of her time.

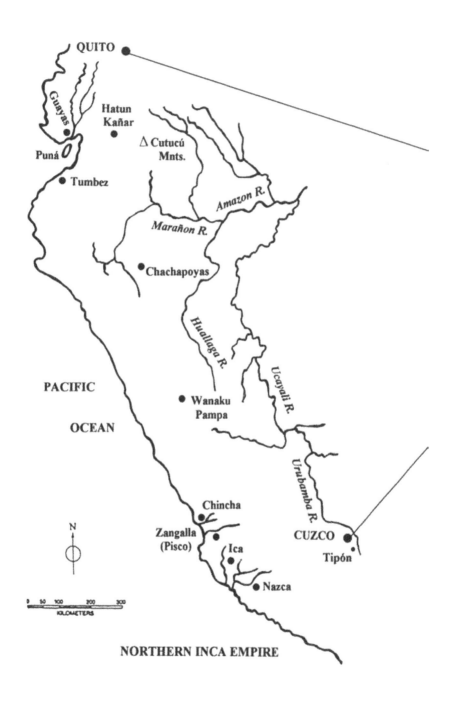

QUITO

Guayas

Hatun
Kañar

Puná

△ Cutucú
Mnts.

Tumbez

Amazon R.

Marañon R.

Chachapoyas

Huallaga R.

Ucayali R.

PACIFIC

Wanaku
Pampa

OCEAN

Urubamba R.

Chincha

Zangalla
(Pisco)

Ica

CUZCO

Tipón

N

Nazca

0   50   100   200   300
KILOMETERS

NORTHERN INCA EMPIRE

Pronunciations

For those who wish, the following examples will help approximate the sounds of foreign words in Eye of the Condor. Do not be thrown off by word appearance; if you sound it out you will come close.

X is sounded like h
I is ee
LL is ya
Q is similar to a hard K
U is oo
An apostrophe in a word is a glottal stop like that hidden in 'bottle' (bot'tle).

Aquixe (a-kee-hay)
Choque (cho-kay)
Cuzco (cooz-co)
Ica (ee-ca)
Illap'a (ee-yap a) puma (poo-ma)
Qolla (koy-ya)
Q'enti (k en-tee)
Qhari (kar-ee)
Qori (kor-ee)
Qoyllur (koy-yur)
siki (see-kee)

Contents

I

In which appears the Hand of Death

It was the heart of the dry season when warm days give way to brilliant nights, and the stars send down frost. I left my compound early that morning while the cobblestone streets of Cuzco still dozed in shadow, but thatch roofs glistened under a wakening sun. The sharp mountain air tingled my cheeks and turned breath to vapor. Warm smells from a thousand hearths met my footsteps, and the hollow moan of a conch shell trumpet called priests to worship. A cur wagged its tail and approached with head lowered, then pricked its ears at its master's call and scampered off. The holy city, my beloved city, welcomed another day.

Not even my maids knew of the charge being brought against me that morning. If all goes well, I thought, the incident will never be known outside the royal council. And if it doesn't go well the whole city will know soon enough.

A girl bent under a load of firewood entered the narrow street. I saw at a glance she was a Chupaychu native from the province of Wanaku, for her people's clothes and coiffures were as distinct as any of the hundred other nations that made up the Empire. When the girl saw me she went to her knees, head bowed. She was obviously new to the city, and awed by the great temples and palaces of those who ruled the world. Her humble reaction to my passing was overly polite. I wasn't accompanied by an honor guard with banners, or by maids shading me with feather parasols, nor was I carried in a hammock. Perhaps the girl wasn't yet aware of these distinctions, but

1

if nothing else she should have noticed I wore the silver jewelry of secondary nobility. A polite bow in passing would have sufficed, but the need for showing respect to her Inca masters had been impressed on her, and she took no chances. Another day I might have passed by with no more than a bemused smile, but seeing her that morning loosed a flood of memories that brought me to a halt. The ashlar walls of the House of Chosen Women rose behind her. I stared at the scene in silence.

I was this girl's age when I first came to holy Cuzco from a distant province, as ragged and wide-eyed as she. Within the House of Chosen Women I spent years learning to be a proper Inca woman, and as full of wonder and hope as she was now. It was so long ago; I hadn't thought of it in years. From the House of Chosen Women I went in marriage to a minor noble, but by my own merit and daring I earned the gratitude of the Emperor. Now I had maids of my own and wealth beyond count. Royalty befriended me, they curried favor, and they trusted me. But would they come to my aid this morning?

I am Lady Qori Qoyllur, I thought, and I have earned my place among them. They should know I do not accept humiliation. I would rather die than live with their sneers. Will this day end with my execution before jeering crowds? Lift your chin high, and never let them see a furrowed brow.

The girl lowered her eyes, unsure what was expected as I stood before her. I extended my hand and she looked up in surprise. I nodded. She took my hand and I helped her to her feet. An old treasure came to mind, the copper shawl pin they gave me when I entered the House of Chosen Women, which always accompanied me as a talisman. It lay in the bottom of my bag. I fished out this cherished memory of hope and innocence, and fastened it to the girl's shawl. "Its name is Qori," I told her.

I emerged from the street into the sudden openness of the great plaza. Royal compounds of fitted stone framed three sides of this vast expanse, and at the lower end the cobble pavement continued all the way to the stone bridges over the Huatanay River. Across the river another plaza opened for the commoners, surrounded by the mud brick residences of provincial lords. Cuzco flexed under a warming sun, nestled in its basin at the head of the Huatanay Valley, and watched by grass-covered mountains now yellowed by the season.

Squealing children dashed by lost in an early morning game of chase, their voices echoing over the expanse. Soon the plaza would come alive, but as yet no more than a hundred strolled there, making the place seem empty. I inhaled the peace of another perfect morning, and if it was to be my last there was no place I would rather greet it. The stone façade of Emperor Wayna Qhapaq's palace compound faced me across the plaza, its high-peaked roofs layered with thatch waist deep. The great hall towered over all, and within its cavern I knew lords and ladies from the ten royal houses already gathered, eager to hear the verdict of the Son of the Sun. But the council couldn't start without me.

While crossing the plaza I spotted two provincials squatting together, intent on something at their feet. I knew what the rascals were up to, and veered from my path to stand over them, arms crossed. One glanced at me nervously, but the other continued prying up cobblestones. They were pilgrims to the holy city, and sought a handful of earth from Cuzco's great plaza—the centre of the world. The devout placed tiny figurines of gold or silver in the hole before replacing the cobbles, but this annoying custom left the surface of the great plaza uneven, and that wasn't right. My city deserved better. I waited, tapping my foot, until the despoilers restored the stones properly.

"Lady Qori?" I turned to find a grandfather at my elbow, hunched near double with age and wearing the garb of a foreign lord. Gray hair hung beneath the cloak covering his head.

I bowed politely, and then with a start realized it was Zapana in one of his disguises. As head of the imperial spy web he never appeared in public as himself, and few knew his true identity.

He spoke in a loud, accented voice for everyone to hear. "I was just about to send my chamberlain to find you. The sarsaparilla root you prescribed for my aching joints eased the pain. I hope to get more."

"Of course, Lord, I have some here in my bag." Zapana stepped closer while I searched the musty packets of herbs and roots. My yellow healer's bag with its line of red llamas was ragged and soiled, and it didn't match my outfit, but it was my badge of station and I never walked the streets without it.

When Zapana met my eyes I saw a sparkle of mischief, and the knowing look that made me blush and duck my head. Being a widow I am accustomed to wishful glances, or outright leers, and it annoyed me to find that Zapana, even in disguise, could still heat my cheeks. But then, I wasn't expecting him. Zapana gazed around the plaza in an unconcerned manner, while I made a show of searching my bag. We conversed in private tones.

"I spoke with the Emperor, Qori, and reminded Him of all you've done for the Empire." Zapana's voice was serious now.

"I didn't ask you to interfere," I said. "Besides, what do you care?"

Zapana flinched as if I'd slapped him. "Qori, I'm doing all I can for you. I didn't come to fight about us."

"You didn't come to fight about us? As if there ever was an 'us'."

Zapana looked so miserable I almost relented, but he only got what he deserved. "Very well," I said, "you spoke with the Emperor. What did He say?"

"He remains torn. He says you are precious to Him, one of the few He can trust, and He would give you anything you ask . . . anything but this."

"If I'm so precious, why doesn't He refuse to hear the charge?"

"You know He can't do that, not now. Soon He departs to inspect the southern provinces, and He will be away from Cuzco for years. The holy city must be left united. He needs the support of every royal house, and in front of the council He must appear impartial."

"He's throwing me to the scavengers."

Zapana squeezed my arm. "Don't, Qori. He needs us, all of us, and He will still do what He can for you, but He can't over-rule the council and risk splitting loyalties."

"Then I stand alone?"

"That's never stopped you before."

"Three youths! Three innocent, defenseless boys. She had them slaughtered, Lord, and stood there gloating while their throats were cut." A gasp rose from the assembly in the Emperor's great hall. Captain Atoco paused for effect, his arm outstretched and finger pointed at me. I followed the finger back to its owner, a lean man with a narrow face and tiny, nervous eyes, his lipless mouth set in outrage. He had waited long to make this charge, and he was well rehearsed.

A hum of disgust filled the cavernous hall and stares pinned me from every side. The Emperor sat on His imperial stool atop a dais covered in jaguar pelts, attended by concubines poised to serve with feather fans and golden drinking vessels. Wayna Qhapaq's face remained impassive. He knew this was only the opening gambit.

I stepped forward and lowered my eyes. "Lord?" The Emperor's hand twitched, signaling his willingness to listen.

I spread my arms showing open palms. "Son of the Sun, those who died were young, it's true, but they were Chachapoya rebels, Lord. If I hadn't ordered their execution—"

"Execution?" Atoco shouted. "It was murder!" The nobles standing with him howled their agreement and waved fists.

It had all started the previous year during the Chachapoya campaign. Atoco felt humiliated when the warlord Chalcochima placed me in command of the raiding party. "But, Lord," he had protested, "Lady Qori Qoyllur? Do women lead Inca warriors? It's impossible, Lord. I won't follow a woman, and I don't need her help on this mission."

Chalcochima thanked me with a look for keeping my silence. I pulled my cloak tighter and lowered my eyes. The argument was expected. Mist clung to forested, jagged mountains behind which a pale glow marked the approaching dawn. Another troop hurried into position for the diversionary attack.

"We discussed this last night," Chalcochima said. "I told you I would be sending a senior person with you."

Atoco's hands went to his hips. "A senior person, yes, but a woman?"

"Not just a woman, Captain Atoco. Lady Qori is a royal physician, and she has the Emperor's confidence. Before troubles erupted in this province she made a healing mission among the Chachapoyas—unaccompanied and at great risk to herself, I might add—and she knows every trail beyond those mountains. She's the only one who can lead you safely to the bridge."

Atoco sighed. "Very well, as guide, but why place her in command?"

"Because that's what I've decided. You know what's at stake. The entire province is in revolt. If we don't deal with these rebels others will be inspired to rise against us. How many victories have you delivered to the Emperor thus far?" In answer Atoco examined his feet. Wayna Qhapaq's father conquered the province of Chachapoya, but it is far to the north of Cuzco on the eastern flank of the Empire. This rolling land of forest and mist received little notice until the Chachapoyas slaughtered their Inca overseers, delivering the first serious challenge to Wayna Qhapaq's reign.

Chalcochima knew what Captain Atoco and everyone below the rank of warlord didn't—Lady Qori Qoyllur, royal physician, was also the imperial spy Inca Moon. If Atoco's mission wasn't critical, I thought, the Emperor wouldn't be sending his best agent.

Atoco stared back at Chalcochima. "We'll smash them this time, Lord. I swear it on my life."

"It may cost your life," Chalcochima replied, but he looked at me when he said it.

"Our southern army is ready?" Atoco asked.

"Yes, and counting on you, as are we all. The Chachapoya host has gathered in a valley where it can be surrounded and destroyed— *if* we can prevent reinforcements from reaching them. What stops us from severing their northern reserve forces from the main body is that fort," he said, indicating the walls on the ridge above. "We've tried for days to take it at enormous cost, but it can't be stormed. Their armies move with impunity behind that line of mountains, and when our attack begins in the south the Chachapoyas will send runners up here for reinforcements. If those messengers get through our southern army will be flanked and slaughtered."

The warlord fell silent. I glanced at the men and saw their jaws set. Shadows hurrying through the dark around us took on the outlines of men. Sunrise was about to illuminate the ridge above, and a thousand Inca warriors muttered prayers and prepared to meet their ancestors. It would be another hopeless assault, men throwing themselves against sheer walls while boulders smashed heads, spears disemboweled, and arrows lodged in chests, or worse, in backs. All this to provide a diversion while I led Atoco and his ten men through a hidden pass and down to the river crossing on the far side of the ridge. The river plunges through a narrow gorge for a great distance, but in one place huge logs provide a rough bridge. This is where the Chachapoya messengers had to cross when the attack began in the south, and this is the place I chose to stop them. Chalcochima wanted to send a hundred soldiers with me, but that number would have been detected. Stealth and surprise were our best weapons. Besides, the plan was to silence the solitary runners, not engage the Chachapoya army. Still, I needed every one of Atoco's men to secure the bridge.

"My prisoners!" Atoco shouted to the nobles around him in the great hall. "They surrendered to me. It was my duty to keep them safe. And now my honor, and that of my entire lineage, is smudged."

Insults and taunts erupted from both sides of the hall, sending startled birds darting among the rafters. Wayna Qhapaq remained motionless, never blinking. The royal fringe of emperorship draped his brows—a hand's breadth of red tassels set with gold tubes, and earspools encrusted with precious stones framed his broad face. He sat on a black stool carved as a snarling puma, inlaid with turquoise and sacred red shell; His stocky form layered in brilliant garments. Though still young, He conducted proceedings with the aloof dignity expected from the Lord of the Four Quarters. We stood barefoot before Him.

A ripple began at the rear of the crowd and moved forward, with people turning to look and quickly stepping aside. A path opened. Lady Q'enti glided forth stealing the breath of those in her wake: a vision of copper beauty with huge, doe eyes, her slender neck erect and midnight hair cascading to her waist. Q'enti raised her voice to the assembly. "Peace. Calm yourselves my brothers and sisters. Remember we are in the presence of our holy father the Emperor, Shepherd of the Sun. Quiet please," she said, imploring both sides with open hands. The commotion subsided when she raised her arms high, providing the men with a better view of her generous figure, and the women a chance to admire her finery.

My veins ran cold. What's she doing here? I wondered. This only concerns Atoco.

Q'enti turned to the dais. Eyes down, she performed the much'a to the Emperor, bending low from the waist with arms stretched forward, palms up, then bringing her fingertips to her lips in a reverend kiss.

Wayna Qhapaq blinked once. He hadn't expected to see Q'enti either. We both knew her arrival bode ill, but what did she want?

Q'enti addressed the assembly. "Brothers and sisters; let us not cloud the issue with anger. It's true Lady Qori deprived Captain Atoco of his captives by ordering his men to dispatch them. She was in command, and she alone bears responsibility for the deaths. Captain Atoco is justified in his protest." Q'enti exchanged a nod with Atoco. "And it's true these captives were young men," she added, "bound and helpless when they were sent to meet their ancestors. But, on Lady Qori's behalf let it be said, the circumstances were unusual . . . indeed, desperate."

Of course you'll appear to take my part, Q'enti, I thought. You're such a 'sympathetic' creature. Let them all remember how the magnanimous Lady Q'enti pleaded on behalf of poor Qori Qoyllur. What's your real game?

I had led the raiding party safely through the pass, never stopping to look back on the slaughter below the fortress walls. We slipped through the dripping forest like shadows, bent low and silent, knowing the receding clamor of battle had been our best cover. Every step took us deeper into the lands of savage hordes where detection meant death for us, but worse, the annihilation of our southern army if the Chachapoya messengers got through. The snap of a twig brought us to a sudden halt—one of our men again,

I exhaled slowly—and then off we went in a crouched run, hoping not to startle birds or blunder into an enemy patrol.

The game trails wound through bush-choked forest down to the gorge, and as the sun rose I hurried the men along, fearful the offensive would begin before we secured the crossing. Atoco insisted on staying at my heels, though I would have preferred him a stone throw behind. He and his men were alert to sight and sound, but they were too preoccupied with their surroundings. My senses projected ahead to the unseen and unheard. Then with a shiver, a familiar sensation tingled the back of my neck like the touch of a cold hand, and I thrust my arm up to signal a halt. The men stopped in stride, eyes searching the forest.

Nothing moved. There should have been birds flittering and chirping among the trees, but the forest lay deathly still. Atoco tapped my shoulder and gave me a puzzled look. He didn't hear the silence or sense the danger ahead. I signaled for him to wait while I went on alone.

The cold hand tightened its grip when I reached a fork in the trail. I cast my senses up each branch. Danger lurked in both directions, but was strongest on the path ahead. No time for hesitation. I raced forward, bent double and ready to drop behind cover. After a distance I paused for breath, jumping off the trail to crouch behind a tree and feel my surroundings. The careless thud of feet ambling up the forest trail reached my ears. I listened and counted. How many men? Four? Three? No, two.

They came into view; two tall, light-skinned men clad only in loincloths and cloaks, and daubed with Chachapoya war paint. Barely awake, they strolled with heads down and unstrung bows dangling at their sides. Before setting out I warned Atoco not to engage the enemy before the river crossing, because I didn't want a trail of bodies marking our passage. I would have preferred to let this sleepy patrol go on its way, but they were headed toward Atoco, and we couldn't risk even one cry of surprise. Atoco's men were hardened warriors, but they weren't taught to deal swift and silent death. That was my duty.

I was well trained as an agent and had 'removed' my share of adversaries over the years, but it's easier to kill when there isn't time to think about it. My muscles tensed as I watched the Chachapoyas, and a rancid taste entered my mouth. The hilt of my dagger felt slippery. I held it in my right hand, blade down, and clenching my fist around the handle I used my left hand to press the fingers into a grip. Forcing myself to take deep, slow breaths, I prepared to spring.

The lead Chachapoya stopped and gestured to a side trail. I shrank back but kept my eyes on them. His companion shrugged, and then the two of them wandered off in a new direction, away from Atoco's men. I lay back with a deep sigh, heart pounding, and after a moment used my left hand to pry my fingers from the dagger hilt.

With the Chachapoyas safely gone I started back, but then up a head war cries split the morning air. Atoco's men! I ran for the screams.

The fight had been brief but deadly. Atoco grinned when he saw me; his spear still dripped gore. Ten Chachapoyas lay sprawled in the bushes, and three others—the youngest of them, hardly more than boys—huddled together on their haunches, hands covering their heads, whimpering. Atoco's victory had cost him three of his men—three more than I could afford. I questioned him with a look. The exchange that followed was in hushed tones.

"It was over in an instant," he said trying to look modest. "They hardly got off a shout."

"I heard them."

He shrugged, and then looked about innocently. "No Chachapoyas. They don't know we're here."

"I told you, no fighting until we reach the river."

Again the shrug. "They came down that other path, and walked right into our ambush. They were so close I could smell them. Besides, I think they were just pretending not to see us so they could return with more warriors. I decided to finish them."

"But you didn't." I raised my chin at the captives.

"They surrendered."

"And what are you going to do with them now?"

Atoco looked unconcerned. "Bind and gag them, and leave a man to stand guard. We can pick them up on the way back."

I knew Atoco. He was only interested in the prisoners as booty.

"No guard. We were few enough to begin with, and now you've lost three. We need every man for the river crossing. I won't have this mission jeopardized further for the sake of your war trophies." Atoco's eyes narrowed. I added, "And I won't argue about it. I'm in command."

Atoco exhaled loudly, then swallowed hard. Staring me in the eye he said, "Very well, Lady Qori, then we'll bind them tight and hope they're not found."

"Can't risk it."

"Then what do you suggest?"

He saw the answer on my face and said, "But . . . but I protest."

I ignored him, and caught the eye of a soldier as he finished tying the prisoners. When I flicked my thumb under my chin the man looked to Atoco. "Do as Lady Qori orders," he said between clenched teeth. Then he brightened. "Let it be on her head. Obviously she's forgotten the Emperor's decree."

Now, standing before Cuzco's elite, it was Lady Q'enti who reminded the royal council of the Emperor's decree.

"Yes, the situation was desperate," Q'enti said imploring those around her. "Consider what was at stake. Consider those brave few deep in savage territory. Consider the outcome." Q'enti paused dramatically, and such a silence filled the hall that a bird could be heard fluttering in the dark rafters above. "But, it's also true that our Emperor in His wisdom had previously decreed that all rebels who surrendered would be spared." A murmur rose from the audience. "With due respect to Captain Atoco, here lies the heart of the matter. Are there no circumstances under which the Emperor's orders can be disobeyed?" A rumble swept the hall in answer to her question.

In spite of myself I admired Q'enti's deftness at delivering an indictment while appearing to plead for mercy. It was brilliant, really, elevating an argument over war captives to a charge of treason. Q'enti savored every moment like a puma playing with a rabbit.

We took the river crossing. There were few guards on either side, and they weren't expecting us. I had Atoco's men wear the clothes of the dead sentries, and take their positions. The messengers suspected nothing when they sped onto the bridge, but none reached the other side. Their bodies vanished in the churning gorge below, and the Chachapoyas never knew of our southern offensive until it was too late.

At the Emperor's camp I shifted all credit to Atoco, then I bathed at a waterfall, donned court dress, and sat demurely with the ladies. It didn't matter to me. The important ones like Chalcochima and Wayna Qhapaq knew it was Inca Moon who delivered the victory. To the rest of the court I was simply Lady Qori, who served as guide to the brave Captain Atoco. I was certain Atoco's vanity wouldn't let him reveal I was his commander, and the incident of the Chachapoya prisoners would be forgotten.

After such an overwhelming defeat the Chachapoyas surrendered. The men, fearful of retribution, melted into the forests. Their families might have been massacred—Wayna Qhapaq was still furious over earlier losses—but a Chachapoya woman who had been his father's concubine begged mercy for her people, and Wayna Qhapaq the All Merciful relented. He satisfied himself with moving some Chachapoya villages to the Cuzco region, and replacing them with loyal colonists to guard the frontier and keep an eye on the locals. Many Chachapoya girls, mostly the daughters of chiefs, were sent to the House of Chosen Women in Cuzco, and a new Inca governor came to rule the province. The Chachapoyas considered these terms fortunate, and Wayna Qhapaq had a military victory to celebrate when He returned to Cuzco—the first of His reign.

Atoco received a gold disk to wear on his chest, and promotion to captain of five hundred. A few days later he went north to Quito, and I went home to my beloved Cuzco.

Wayna Qhapaq reaffirmed His control over other provinces, and then returned to Cuzco in splendor. The crowds in the great square thundered when He walked on the backs of defeated chiefs in the victory parades. But Atoco, determined to share the honors, also came back to Cuzco for the celebrations. Soon after, an official came in private to my compound and delivered Atoco's charge. Why would Atoco wait until we were both in Cuzco, and then insist on a hearing before the royal council? He lacked the patience and cleverness for such a move. I should have guessed someone else was behind it, and I cursed myself for not having seen this coming. Who could persuade him to acknowledge I had been his commander? There was only one person in Cuzco with that power, the one who now revealed herself as Atoco's patron—Lady Q'enti.

Q'enti wasn't Atoco's patron in any official sense—it could be said she was patron to half the men of Cuzco—but he craved her notice and she cultivated his lust, snaring yet another eager participant in her endless schemes. I could handle Atoco, but Q'enti was a power unto herself, and even the Emperor thought twice where she was involved.

It was now only days before the Emperor set forth on an inspection tour of the south; the perfect time for Q'enti's ambush. In the midst of all this activity Atoco's charge might have been a petty annoyance, but Q'enti elevated it to treason on the eve of an important expedition. Were the Emperor's orders subject to circumstance? Could commanders choose to interpret His decrees as they wished? By her own admission Lady Qori Qoyllur had ignored the Emperor's proclamation. The discipline of vast armies now depended on Wayna Qhapaq's verdict.

Q'enti played conciliator before the royal council in the great hall. "Please, friends, let us not judge our sister Lady Qori too harshly. She acted for the good of the Empire." But Q'enti herself had already spoken the critical charge, and her pleas were drowned amid shouts and fist shaking.

"She insults our Emperor, and through Him all of us."

"No one disobeys the Emperor's orders. Never."

"Traitor. Gut her here and now."

"Flay her alive."

"The House of Beasts. Send her to the House of Beasts."

At mention of the House of Beasts the crowd hushed, but heads nodded grimly. It was a noblewoman, one of Q'enti's admirers, who suggested this punishment. I knew then Q'enti had rehearsed them all, though she murmured, "No, no," her hands clasped in pleading for poor Qori Qoyllur. Wayna Qhapaq sat erect and motionless as always, his gaze fixed at the far end of the hall.

It wasn't death I feared, or even the means of death, but . . . disgrace? Those Chachapoya boys were an unfortunate incident—Atoco's fault. I did only what was necessary, and I did it for my Emperor. No, Q'enti, I thought, I won't surrender. I won't let you win. You'll never defeat Inca Moon.

"Lord of the World," I addressed the Emperor, "the order to end those rebel's lives was given to ensure your victory. Have I not served you faithfully in many ways?"

He knew what I meant, even if those gathered did not. I spoke as Inca Moon, the agent who worked quietly among His friends and His enemies, gathered information, thwarted coups, saved armies, and, yes, 'removed' those who threatened the peace of the Empire. He needed me.

For the first time Wayna Qhapaq looked at me, and spoke. "The healer Lady Qori Qoyllur has served us well." He returned His gaze to the distance. Splinters worked my belly.

Q'enti gave an almost imperceptible nod to one of her followers, a man who said, "Yes, she has served the imperial family faithfully, until now. No one counters the Emperor's orders."

Shouts rose again.

"It's treason."

"Stone her."

"Break her back."

"Bury her alive."

"Tan her skin for a drum cover."

"The House of Beasts."

Q'enti motioned Atoco with a twitch of her shoulder. His acting was poor, but he tried his best to sound forgiving. "Hear me. Lady Qori is guilty by her own admission and she must be punished, but in consideration of her past services I will be satisfied to see her head displayed on a spear."

It was a generous concession. A beheading is at least quick, though the display brings shame to the victim's family.

Before anyone could respond Q'enti spoke again, this time summoning tears to her eyes. "Wait, please, anything but death. I implore you!"

This was the signal her accomplices waited for, and the moment she was leading up to, for in truth she didn't want me dead. That was too easy. She wanted to watch me suffer to the end of my days.

A man at the back called, "Then let her continue to serve the Empire, as a soldier's whore. She can line up her troops every night."

Coarse laughter erupted, but it wasn't dismissive. The noblewoman spoke again, her tone flat and final. "Our sons march with the army. She will not defile their honor. Put her in the brothel outside the city. Let the peasants have her."

Stunned, I begged Mother Earth to swallow me. Q'enti's face showed horror, but I saw in her eyes maniacal laughter. Yet still she wasn't finished with me.

"There is one other alternative," Q'enti said.

My mouth fell open. What more could she do to me? The nobles shifted in confusion. Atoco looked puzzled.

Q'enti waited for silence. "Our Lord Emperor, Lover of the Poor, has subdued those who rebelled in Chachapoya. But Captain Atoco has just returned from farther north, from Quito and beyond, where he heard stirrings of rebellion among the northern tribes. How long will it be before they rise against us?"

Q'enti paused again, basking in the attention. Not even the birds in the rafters moved.

"Lady Qori is guilty, it's true," Q'enti said, "but if she can secure the allegiance of the northern barbarians for all time, wouldn't that be worth postponing the sentence?"

I noticed she said 'postpone' instead of 'suspend,' but it seemed irrelevant in the moment.

"Yes, of course," Atoco replied, "but . . . but how?"

"By delivering into the hands of the Emperor the one thing the northerners won't fight without—the Eye of the Condor."

The assembly held an incredulous gasp, and then burst into laughter. I almost joined them. For a moment Q'enti had everyone convinced she was serious, but it was a cruel jest.

Wayna Qhapaq didn't share the amusement. He remained stone-faced, staring over the heads of the assembly. He stood suddenly, and this unexpected motion brought silence while everyone held a bow.

"Lady Qori," Wayna Qhapaq's voice came loud and firm, "do you accept the quest for the Eye of the Condor?"

This is a trick, I thought, why is he asking the impossible? "But, Lord," I replied, "it's a jest. The thing doesn't exist."

"Do you accept?"

My thoughts whirled. Q'enti wouldn't have suggested such nonsense unless it was another of her traps. "Lord, I . . . I . . . ."

Wayna Qhapaq blinked twice. He never waited longer than that for an answer.

"If Lady Qori agrees to the quest I will postpone her sentencing," He announced to the court. "If not, I will pass sentence on her five days hence." Without another word He strode from the hall.

II

Of the Hidden Valley and its Feared Lord, and of those who practice the Abominable Sin.

The Tipón sentries snapped to attention. I paused to exchange a nod with them and catch my breath. Far below where my climb began, kitchen smoke from the village of Qispikancha curled through treetops, and beyond lay the Huatanay Valley, its river and red fields glowing in the late afternoon sun. From this height the peasants in those fields were specks, now trudging home to their villages after a day of planting early potatoes, and unconcerned with the fate of Qori Qoyllur. I often pitied their droll lives, but today I wished I were one of them.

I turned to view the royal estate of Tipón in its high valley. Massive stone terraces step the valley bottom, and above on the far side stand the hall and palace buildings. The terraces near the palace are pleasure gardens arrayed with every kind of tree and shrub and flower in the highlands, and water gurgles endlessly in stone channels fed by springs above. All this is invisible from below in the Huatanay Valley, hidden behind folded hills, and visited only by those summoned on official business. No one in Cuzco dares mention Tipón, or its lord.

Zapana sat on a blanket beneath a tree in the terrace garden, flanked by servants poised with food and drink. When I saw him my pace quickened and I felt a smile spread, then I held myself back. He will think I've come to see him, I thought. Well, I'll soon put an end to that notion. I straightened my dress and smoothed my hair, then approached at a stately pace.

The lines on Zapana's face had deepened over the years, but those piercing eyes and sensuous mouth would never change. He sat erect as always, broad shouldered, his cloak draped back showing the corded muscles of his arms. He saw me and leapt to his feet, dismissing the servants with a wave. They bowed and backed away.

"Qori!" he shouted, arms open as if he expected a hug. I kept my distance.

"You look surprised, Zapana. I'm only here to see Qhari. I assume he told you I'd be coming?"

"Yes, of course, it's all arranged," he said dropping his arms. "It's just that it's good to see you at Tipón again."

I gave him a cool look. "And why would I bother coming before, Zapana? I'm only here now because Qhari insisted on it. Where is Qhari?"

"He hasn't arrived yet," Zapana said, and gestured for me to be seated. "Won't you share my blanket?"

"I don't share your blankets anymore, Zapana, and I'm comfortable standing."

Zapana's head dipped. I'd left all his invitations to Tipón unanswered, though I missed this place dearly. It was on these same terraces that Zapana taught me the skills of an imperial agent, in the days when his father still commanded the Emperor's secret forces. Now Zapana had that post, but he didn't have me.

In the silence that followed I examined the flowerbeds, and wished Qhari would arrive to end this awkwardness. Zapana stepped closer as if to say something, then thought better of it. My head barely reached his shoulders, making me intensely aware of him. His dark red tunic hung to his knees, and today he wore a band of colored fringes on each muscular calf—a new style favored by the young men of Cuzco, which the girls thought dashing. For me? I wondered.

"That's a stunning dress you're wearing," he offered.

It was. The thin alpaca was of the finest weave, sun yellow, with bands of green, purple, and orange at the hem, and a shawl to match.

My maids dressed me three times that morning before I settled on this outfit for Tipón. "Just a gift from the House of Chosen Women," I replied. "The Empress is having one like it made for Her."

Zapana grinned. "Qhari told me about your clothes. He said if you could wear the gold jewelry of royalty, no one would be able to tell you apart from a princess. He spoke truthfully."

I stifled a smile. "Qhari talks a lot. Besides, people are always giving me things. My storehouses overflow, and yet more gifts arrive. I have to wear the clothes at least once to please those who send them."

"And now you have lands of your own," Zapana prompted.

"Oh, a few fields here and there. They keep me so busy at court I've never seen most of them. I have the harvests sent to Cuzco."

"Indeed, my Lady, I hear the Empress keeps you at Her side, when you're not busy giving victories to the Emperor."

I couldn't help but smile at this reference to my brilliant work in Chachapoya. But more telling was that he had kept himself informed of my appearances at court. "Lord Zapana, have you been spying on me?"

"Spying on you?" he said holding up his hands in disavowal. "My Lady, please, there's no need to spy, your fame precedes you."

"You're flattering me."

"No indeed, my Lady. There's no need to embellish the obvious."

I shook a finger at him. "Yes you are, you scoundrel."

Zapana looked to the side with a grin. He always liked it when I called him 'scoundrel.'

I'd let him soften me more than I wished, or he deserved. "What's to be done about this ridiculous charge?" I said. He heard the edge in my voice and his smile vanished. Our eyes met. He said, "I spoke with the Emperor again, after Atoco laid his claim before the royal council." I sensed the weight of this meeting in the pause that followed. Messengers were used to communicate routine matters—indeed, nothing happened in the Empire without Zapana knowing about it even before the Emperor—but the two seldom met face to face. I suppose I should have been flattered to be the cause of such a rare meeting, but they both owed me.

"And?" I prompted.

"And we weighed the alternatives. Qori, we did our best to prevent Atoco from bringing that charge."

No doubt by threat and bribe, I thought. But in the minds of some men Lady Q'enti has even more to offer.

"But," Zapana continued, "Atoco would not be moved. The charge is now before the council, and your guilt established." He held up a hand to silence my protest. "Yes, Qori, your guilt. Of course Wayna Qhapaq understands the circumstances, we all do, and I wouldn't have acted any different in your place, but you disobeyed the Emperor's decree. He has no choice now. You must be punished."

"It's the doing of your friend, Q'enti."

"She's not my friend."

"Every noble in Cuzco knows about it."

"No they don't, anyway, there's nothing to know. It's old gossip. When are you going to let it be?"

I knew Zapana would never be part of Q'enti's schemes, but I also knew a man didn't have to like a woman to bed her. Besides, everyone had seen him with Q'enti.

I decided not to scratch this old wound. "Well," I said, "this charge against me *is* Q'enti's doing."

Zapana softened. "Yes, we know, but *you* know there's more at stake here than Q'enti, or you."

It was true, and it went to the heart of what made us great—and vulnerable. There were ten royal houses in Cuzco, each claiming descent from a former emperor, and each with a voice in the royal council. The first five lineages belonged to Lower Cuzco, and the others to Upper Cuzco. A line through the city united these two opposites in the great plaza. Upper and Lower were like halves of a circle—neither complete without the other, and both parts had to act in accord. Frequent jealousies were smoothed over and intrigues forgiven. No wound could be allowed to fester between the Upper and Lower divisions, for without unity among those who ruled the world the Empire was lost. Q'enti had aligned the Lower Cuzco houses against me, and Wayna Qhapaq needed their support.

Q'enti was a master at brewing trouble between the Upper and Lower parts, though she always directed from the shadows. Her whispering campaigns and intrigues too often delivered the results she sought. Nobody wanted to risk a split between Upper and Lower Cuzco, and a compromise favouring Q'enti's real motives was always reached. She was from the most ancient lineage of Lower Cuzco, but her devious influence spread to all the imperial houses. Even royal ladies, eager for acceptance in the gaudy swirl of court society, flocked to her circle where she played on their dreams and nightmares. As for the men, one of Q'enti's smiles was enough to set their knees trembling.

When Zapana spoke again his words came softly. "Qori, Wayna Qhapaq offered you a way out, accept it, and in time all this will pass."

"What, this ridiculous quest? That wasn't Wayna Qhapaq's idea, it was Q'enti's. She only proposed it to make me appear the fool, the butt of jests throughout the Empire."

"Yes, but what have you got to lose? It buys time."

"Time for what? For Q'enti to enjoy my humiliation? Do you think I'll ever bow to her? I expected more from you, Zapana."

Zapana lowered his head.

A guard called along the terrace, "Lord, the Steward of K'allachaka approaches, Qhari Puma."

Zapana brightened. "Just in time for the evening meal."

"Yes, Zapana, and I expect he brings news that will surprise even you. Do you think you're the only one who can *arrange* things?"

We both spread our arms to greet Qhari. He sprang along the terrace, grinning and waving, and when he came up he took both of us in a single embrace, forcing us to share his laughter.

Qhari wagged a finger at Zapana. "My Lord, it is too long since you've invited your humble servant to dine. But you look splendid!"

Zapana chuckled and grasped Qhari's forearm in greeting. "Nonsense, you're welcome here whenever you can spare the time from running my grandfather's estate. You know that."

Qhari beamed at me. "And you, sister, look at that exquisite dress! What have you prepared for supper?"

"*Me* cook for you, Qhari Puma? Ha! It will never happen. Now give your sister a proper hug."

He looked well, and far younger than his years, but then he is my twin. And he never changed. His eyes perpetually sparkled with some private jest, and he was forever making those around him share his laughter. Long ago he was a messenger, and he still had the lean, hard body of a runner.

"And now, sister," he said releasing me, "am I to expire of hunger in this garden of plenty?" He turned to Zapana. "My Lord I beg you, though I am a less-than-nothing by the wayside, feed your servant."

"At least this lout knows who he is," I said to Zapana.

Zapana laughed. "Food and drink it shall be, but first you'll wish to freshen in your rooms." He clapped twice and servants appeared to usher us forth.

The hall of Tipón sits atop a ridge overlooking the terraces, and the palace structures are on a hill behind. The ascent is by way of a huge stone staircase leading to the uppermost terrace. But when we reached the foot of the stairs Zapana gestured to the left, and we followed him to a set of buildings crouched near the end of the valley, below the hall and palace. They were newly built with plastered stonewalls and high thatch roofs, and at first I thought he only wished to show them off.

"Your private residence," he said indicating the complex with a flourish.

I said, "You mean for Qhari?"

"No, for you and Qhari," Zapana said.

Qhari stepped between us. "And a fine residence it is, fit for royalty. Qori and I will be most comfortable. Thank you, Zapana."

I looked at Zapana over Qhari's shoulder. "I'm not welcome in the palace?"

Qhari pressed my arm. "No, Qori . . . Zapana was just thinking of our privacy."

"The last time you were here, Qori," Zapana reminded me, "you said it was presumptuous of me to assume you wished to sleep near me."

The memory still rankled. I turned up my nose. "Yes, and it was presumptuous. I'll not be taken for granted, Zapana."

"No indeed, my Lady," Zapana said, "and therefore I had these apartments built especially for you. I will be pleased to see you in the palace, or anywhere else whenever you choose. This building," he indicated the largest structure, "is reserved for you, permanently. If the servants I've assigned don't please, take any of the others. Tipón is at your service."

Devious fox, I thought. And I suppose you think I'll scurry through the night like some maid and beg to share your bed.

Before I could reply a messenger approached, puffing after the steep run up from Qispikancha. He caught Zapana's attention and waited at a distance, bent double with hands on his knees. Zapana excused himself with a bow.

Qhari lowered his voice. "Qori, you know Zapana is only trying to please you. Look," he said gesturing at the new complex, "he had this built for you, so you can come and go as you please without obligation."

"He had it built for us, brother."

"He only said that because I'm here. It's for you."

"You always take his side, don't you?"

Qhari looked away.

"Besides," I said, "what makes you think I want to be at Tipón, or anywhere near Zapana? It's presumptuous of him to assume—"

"Stop, Qori," he said sharply. "I know you're angry with Zapana, but you have no reason to be. Those old rumors about him and Lady Q'enti are just gossip. There's no truth in it, believe me."

"Oh, and I suppose you have that on good authority from Zapana? You're so naive, Qhari. Men always stick together. And now Zapana thinks he can buy me back with a hut?"

"No, he doesn't. These buildings were my idea. You only live at court these days, and I thought a place in the country would be good for you, away from all those sniveling lords and ladies. I admit this is a bit abrupt—I had hoped you two would get to know each other again first—but under the circumstances . . . ."

"So this is why you insisted on meeting me here today, to show off Zapana and his huts?"

"They are not huts! Zapana had the best masons build them for you. But, yes, I wanted you to see what's here for you."

"Very well, now I've seen, and I'm not interested."

Qhari's shoulders sagged. I didn't like to disappoint him, but he had no right to interfere. Besides, with the treason charge pending there were more important things to worry about. Wayna Qhapaq and Zapana had abandoned me to the council, but I knew I could rely on Qhari to find a way out. He had told me he was working on something, and said he'd have a plan ready today.

I said, "Well, Qhari, now that you have me here, what's your solution to this foolish charge against me?"

Qhari stared at his feet and scratched his neck. Finally he said, "Let's discuss it later. I think that runner is delivering the news I've been waiting for."

Zapana still listened intently to the messenger. Why would Qhari have access to Zapana's couriers? I wondered. Though the two were close friends, Qhari was only an estate manager. He had nothing to do with the imperial spy web, unless . . . "Qhari, are you spying for Zapana?"

Qhari tried to look modest. "I help in small ways. Some information here and there. Come, sister, don't look at me like that. You've been away, and things change. Don't worry, I can look after myself."

"I do worry. You're not trained for this work, and I don't want to lose you. You're the only family I have left."

Qhari cleared his throat. "I'm not the boy you remember on those long ago beaches."

"Perhaps not, Qhari Puma, but you still blunder around corners. I'm going to speak with Zapana about this." Qhari released an exasperated sigh, but he knew better than to argue with me.

"Qhari," Zapana called.

Qhari gave me a reassuring look and hurried to join Zapana.

We sat on blankets under the night sky in a courtyard attached to the palace, staring into the coals of a brazier. Qhari insisted on seating me next to Zapana, and Zapana now stretched his legs contentedly and leaned back, placing a hand on the ground behind me. His arm pressed my back. Qhari, sitting cross-legged on the other side of the brazier, pretended not to notice.

The air was crisp and still, and being the dry season we chose to take our meal in the open. The servants had laid out rush mats with blankets and pillows, and lighted torches. Zapana might have provided a twenty-course banquet, but I was pleased he ordered simple food served in clay bowls. The beer, potent and brewed from the best maize, warmed my insides. I looked forward to the look on Zapana's face when Qhari announced he had found a solution to my predicament, but during the meal neither of them mentioned the messenger. I decided to be patient and let Qhari choose the moment.

Qhari eyed a bowl of lucuma fruit, and in a familiar gesture swept his hair back over his shoulders while pondering his selection. I smiled to myself. He was terribly vain about his hair. True, it was as thick and glossy black as my own, and hung past his shoulders, but men with long hair usually wear it braided or tucked under a turban. Zapana wore his in the Inca fashion, cut straight across his forehead and no longer than his ears.

"Thank you," Zapana said to his servants when the meal was done, "you may leave us now, but do congratulate the cook for me."

"But, my Lord," the chamberlain protested, "you will need me to serve the beer."

"And me to stoke the brazier," a maid added.

"Another blanket, Lord?" a third asked. She turned to me hopefully. "For you, Lady?" When Qhari also shook his head, she set about fluffing pillows.

Zapana chuckled. "Thank you, we'll be fine. Yes, put that jar of beer by me. Oh, and extinguish the torches so we can see the stars. No, nothing more. Good night, and thank you."

Zapana, being a lord, did not have to thank his servants or even notice them, but that was his way, and they responded with devotion.

"I must leave for a moment," Qhari said, indicating he was off to relieve himself. I nodded, and leaned back against Zapana's arm. I shouldn't have, but the beer summoned warm memories.

"I have a confession to make," Zapana said in a low voice, arching his head close to mine.

"Indeed, my Lord, and that is?"

"I was the one who convinced Qhari to meet you here. I wanted to see you, and I knew you wouldn't come if I asked."

"Very well, I'm here. What is it you want to say?"

"Its lonely at Tipón, Qori. The days are filled with meetings and reports, but I wish I had someone to share my nights, to share my life."

I tensed but did not turn away. Like me he was a widower, and though he could have his pick of the Empire he had never taken another wife. The law forbade women to marry a second time, so he couldn't offer me marriage, but I could be honorably recognized as his consort. Still, it was a foolish thought.

"You always wanted to be Lord of Tipón, Zapana, and you got your wish."

"That's true," he conceded, "but I've found it a hollow victory."

With languid motion he brushed my hair, and brought his lips to my neck. A delightful shiver ran through me.

I shook myself and sat up, feeling the night coolness on my back where his arm had been. I'd let this go too far. Zapana sighed and folded his arms around his knees.

I said, "I have my own life to live, and you have yours. Besides, Zapana, the Emperor needs me, and He keeps sending me here and there, and—"

Zapana broke in, "Yes, yes, and the Empire would fall apart without Inca Moon."

I sniffed. "You're jealous because I answer directly to the Emperor. I'm the only imperial agent not under your command, Zapana. If you could handle everything yourself the Emperor wouldn't need Inca Moon, but He does. That should tell you something."

"You could operate from here," he replied sullenly.

"So you could keep an eye on me?"

Our eyes met, and we both realized this argument was over a future that, given the charge hanging over me, might never be.

Zapana studied his hands. "You know, I could arrange for you to be exiled here to Tipón."

"What?"

"It's been discussed with Wayna Qhapaq," he said looking entirely too satisfied with himself. "Banishment might still be an option."

"You talked about it with the Emperor behind my back? Exiled to Tipón? So that's what all this is about. You might deign to keep me as your bed warmer, is that it, Zapana? Another pretty toy for your collection? Qori Qoyllur is no man's trophy!"

Qhari announced his return by tripping like a jester as he emerged from the shadows. I didn't laugh. He'd been eavesdropping, I knew, and it suddenly occurred to me that he and Zapana had planned this entire evening. My own sweet, faithful brother had conspired with Zapana, and the two of them were determined to have things their way.

"Chilly night," Qhari remarked, squatting by the brazier to warm his hands. His smile wasn't returned. He looked from Zapana to me, then, dropping all pretense he said, "Qori, exile to Tipón was my idea. I had it suggested to the Emperor through my friends at court, and that messenger came to tell us His response was favorable."

Qhari's 'friends,' I knew, were like him, and one didn't ask their names. The punishment for men caught being intimate with men was death, or worse, loss of all titles and banishment. There were women of this kind also, and no less among the nobility, but no one ever spoke of them. These people had their own ways of recognizing one another, and since no one wanted scandal, especially among royalty, they were left alone as long as they remained invisible. Qhari even hosted gatherings for them at the estate of K'allachaka near Cuzco, where Zapana insured their safety. Who these special friends of Qhari's were I didn't know, nor did I want to know, but I knew they had family influence over the highest officials in the land, even reaching the Emperor's ear. Zapana found Qhari's associates useful for information not available from the usual sources, and I confess, so did I.

"It was your idea to have me banished?" I said to Qhari in disbelief. I gave Zapana a sour look. He ducked his head. "So, Qhari, this is it? The best you can do is have me exiled? Q'enti would love to see me entombed at Tipón. I should have known better than to trust your kind."

I hadn't meant to be cruel, but Qhari ignored the barb.

"I tried, Qori," Qhari protested. "I persuaded my friends to take your part—they see the injustice of this as clearly as anyone—but what can Wayna Qhapaq do? The charge is before the royal council, and soon He must leave for His inspection of the south. Fair or not, you broke the Emperor's decree, and every warlord is watching to see how He will respond. Those of Lower Cuzco are especially interested."

"That's Q'enti's doing," I said. "Atoco is only her minion. It's Q'enti who planned all this."

Qhari nodded solemnly. "We know," he said exchanging a look with Zapana. "But what's to be done? Wayna Qhapaq has no choice. The most we can hope for is a lenient sentence. Surely banishment is better than—"

"Than death?" I snapped.

"Or life in a brothel," Zapana said quietly.

"Or the House of Beasts," Qhari said. "Some are even demanding that."

Zapana shifted uneasily. "Once the Emperor passes sentence there won't be any further negotiations, Qori. His word is final. You won't have any choices, and there are those who will ensure the sentence is carried out."

The silence of the stars descended on us. Inwardly I fumed at Zapana and Qhari. That I had given in to Qhari's demand for a meeting at Tipón was humiliating enough, but now they both wanted me to surrender. Zapana would even condescend to let me be his plaything.

"What about the Eye of the Condor?" Qhari finally asked.

"It's nonsense," I said. "I already told Zapana it's not worth considering."

"It would postpone the sentencing," Qhari said. "I thought it was a generous offer from Wayna Qhapaq."

"From Wayna Qhapaq? It was Q'enti's idea. She wants to laugh at me chasing smoke. No, she'll never have that satisfaction. Only a fool looks for a fart in a dark house."

This old saying earned grins, but I didn't reciprocate. Zapana refilled our drinking vessels, and the three of us sat back to contemplate the sky.

The night canopy, cloudless and sharp, glittered like crystals cast on a black cloth, and on such a night the stars seem so close you can reach out and pluck them. I found the fertility star for llamas, and nearby the twinkling patrons for guinea pigs, birds, pumas, bears, and serpents, for all creatures have their guardian in the sky. The Celestial River flowed across the heavens in a great band of white, taking its life-giving waters from the ocean to a place in the east where it goes below ground, and emerges to replenish rivers which return to the sea, thus completing one cycle and beginning another.

"It's supposed to be as big as a squash," Qhari said, never taking his eyes from the heavens.

"What is?" I asked.

"The Eye of the Condor," Zapana replied.

I snorted and settled back.

Qhari joined two upturned palms in front of him. "Imagine," he said in wonderment, "an emerald this big."

"Surrounded by six cat's-eye emeralds, each this size," Zapana added, making a circle with finger and thumb.

"Cat's-eye emeralds?" Qhari asked.

Zapana shrugged. "That's what they say. I saw a cat's-eye emerald once. Very rare. Of course, this one was only the size of a thumbnail.

The six big ones around the Eye of the Condor are said to represent the six directions: north, south, east, west, underworld, upperworld."

"And there are baskets and baskets of smaller emeralds in the Condor Temple," Qhari said, still studying the sky.

I added, "And if you're very bad and don't go to sleep the condor priests will come for you."

The men chuckled. Zapana tipped a bag of dried llama dung over the brazier. Qhari coughed and waved the smoke as if he was about to expire. Then he grabbed a blanket and fanned the smoke at Zapana, smothering me too. I threw a pillow at Qhari to make him stop. He shrieked and, still on his knees, buried his head under the blanket, leaving his siki upward and directed at us.

"A pretty bottom," Zapana remarked.

Qhari, head still under the blanket, wiggled his siki in invitation. Zapana laughed, and I reddened.

"You shameless harlot," I scolded. "Now sit up and behave, Qhari."

Qhari sat up reluctantly, casting doe eyes at Zapana. It wasn't entirely in jest. In private Qhari never hid his love for Zapana, and I sometimes wondered about Zapana. He was too sophisticated a man to be shocked by anything, and he liked an occasional spicy dish. Qhari felt that by not pursuing Zapana, at least not seriously, he left Zapana to me, and this was the most precious gift he could offer. I loved him for it.

Our breath steamed in the crisp night air. Zapana wrapped an alpaca blanket around me. "You know, Qori, those baskets of emeralds are real," he said. "I've seen them. The natives on the far north coast worship emeralds, and bring them as offerings to their temples."

"Have you seen stones like the Great Emerald?" Qhari asked.

"You mean the Eye of the Condor? No, only small stones are on display now. It's said the Great Emerald, their most sacred wak'a, vanished when Wayna Qhapaq's father entered the north. No Inca has ever seen it, and the natives now deny it exists. But others believe the condor priests spirited it away to a hidden temple, and even now they have a secret fraternity to guard the Great Emerald. Every tribe in the north still pays homage to it. Wayna Qhapaq is right;

if we could capture this stone the northerners wouldn't dare rebel. Atoco reported the truth—I heard it from my own sources—there are rumblings of revolt in the north. If the tribes ally there will be war. But with their most sacred wak'a as our hostage none would dare stand against us."

Zapana was right. A wak'a is a sacred place or thing, and every nation has many of them, some more powerful than others. They may be mountains, fields, tombs, or buildings, statues, boulders, or stones, but each contains a life force that cares for its devotees. Some are worshipped only by a lineage, others by an entire people, and the most powerful by many nations. It was the privilege and duty of every subject nation to send an important wak'a to Cuzco each year, where it was honored in our temples and allowed to converse with the Inca gods, before being replaced by another the following year. Since the well being of a people depends on its holy things, the wak'a sent to Cuzco was really a hostage ensuring allegiance, for control of a wak'a is control of its people. A wak'a like the legendary Eye of the Condor demanded the obedience of multitudes, and no rebel armies would dare march with such a prize in our hands.

"You mean *if* the Eye of the Condor exists," I replied. "You said yourself, Zapana, no one has ever seen it. It's a legend, nothing more."

"I said no Inca has ever seen it."

"Then what makes you think it's real?"

Zapana scratched his ear in contemplation. "I'm not sure it does exist, Qori, but what if it does? Think of the lives saved and the security it offers."

Qhari said to Zapana, "Tell her about the condor dust."

I snorted at his foolishness. "Oh Qhari, I've heard that part of the tale, also. Like the stone itself, the dust is legend."

They exchanged an incredulous look but I knew them, and it was clear they'd rehearsed all this for my benefit.

Zapana ignored me and spoke to Qhari. "Condor dust is the most insidious poison ever devised." Qhari nodded as if hearing this for the first time. "Only the condor priests know how to make it, and only they have the antidote. It's said to be a powder, so fine that when a pinch is blown in your face it's hardly noticed, and when slipped into food or drink it's tasteless. You never know when it's administered, or feel any immediate effect. It takes months to work, but gradually you grow weak with symptoms that could be any number of illnesses. The poison consumes your insides, and eventually you die in agony."

Qhari's face held dread.

"I'm a healer," I said. "I know plants and I know poisons, and I can tell you that such a thing as this 'condor dust' doesn't exist. It's a story to scare children like you." I gave them a look of reproach.

"You're frightened of it," Qhari shot back. "Everyone is terrified of the condor priests and their poison. Maybe the dust is real and maybe it isn't, but the legend keeps the curious away. You're afraid too, aren't you Qori." It was an accusation. The edge in his voice left me open-mouthed.

Zapana said, "She's right to fear it, Qhari. The very thought makes the bravest men tremble. To go against such horror . . . ."

"Is that what you think, that I'm afraid? Me, Inca Moon?"

For an instant they had me, but then I saw Qhari's face relax. "Oh, I see, you're challenging me," I said. They shifted under my glare. "Do you two really think you can trick me? I have a question for you, both of you. It was Q'enti who suggested this ridiculous quest. Why, because she wants to stop bloodshed? She's not capable of compassion. Then what's in it for her? Only one thing—my humiliation. Let's send the Emperor's favorite off chasing shadows; that will keep them laughing long in Cuzco.

"Never, Qhari. Do you hear me, Zapana? *Never!*"

I slept alone in my new quarters at Tipón that night. My room was well appointed with its own brazier already glowing, jars of water and beer, a basket of fruit, and a sleeping platform covered by a maize husk mattress layered with alpaca blankets. Bouquets of wild flowers in the wall niches mingled with the earthy aromas of fresh plaster and thatch. A maid had covered the windows with weavings to keep out the night, and the wicker door cover was set firmly in place. The lighted wicks in bowls of fat cast flickering shadows as I lay on my bed staring up at the roof beams. Zapana built this for me? I wondered. He must have ordered it while I was still in the north. Does he really want me, or is he just feeling sorry for me?

Zapana's problem is that he's too handsome by half, I thought. He could have any woman he wants, even if he wasn't Lord of Tipón. And me? In truth, I'm not the sort men stop and stare at. What does Zapana want with me?

I felt the room welcoming me. It was elegant enough for country quarters, but rustic compared to the palaces of Cuzco. I was born in a hut—little more than a hovel, really—and there was a time when I thought a stone cottage luxurious. I felt comfortable here. There was something about the formalities of court life that left one never quite at ease.

But then there's the excitement of court, I thought, ambassadors coming and going, receptions and late night feasting, delicious gossip, and all those handsome courtiers. Why would I trade all that for one man on a country estate? There's no call here for my finery; what would I do with my wardrobe?

My thoughts turned and a flood of rage gripped me. How stupid to even consider Zapana after what he did to me—and with Q'enti!

At dawn Zapana came to my room. "You're leaving?" he asked.

"Yes," I replied without turning. The less said the better. I continued sorting through the things laid out on the bed and packing them into my shoulder bag.

Zapana leaned in the doorway watching me. "You're returning to Cuzco?"

"Yes."

"You don't want to see Qhari before you go?"

Qhari spent the night in a cottage next to mine.

"Let him sleep."

"He's awake," Zapana said quietly, turning his gaze to the yard.

I finished packing my things. If Zapana wasn't blocking the door I could have left. I picked up my bronze mirror and studied my hair.

"I don't want Qhari involved," I said without turning. Zapana knew I referred to Qhari's new role as an informant in the spy web.

"Qhari insists," Zapana said, "and I keep him out of danger. Don't worry about Qhari."

"I won't have it, Zapana."

He fell silent. Then, still looking out the door, he said, "You don't have to go today. Stay until tomorrow."

I sighed and began twining braids in my hair. "I'd like to but I must get back."

"Will you come again before . . . before your sentencing?"

"There won't be a sentencing, Zapana. I know others I can count on." I hadn't meant it as a rebuke, but he flinched. I softened my voice. "I'll return when I can."

Zapana whirled to face me. "No you won't."

"What do you mean?"

"There won't be a next time, Qori. The charge against you isn't going to melt away because you will it. Why won't you let me help you?"

I gave him a sour look and showed my back. He had to make a scene. Why wouldn't he just let me go? I heard him exhale behind me.

"There's no time for this petulance, Qori." His voice was toneless, defeated.

"What do you mean?"

"You know what I mean. You're so accustomed to having your own way you can't believe anyone would dare upset your plans, least of all a worm like Atoco."

"It's not Atoco, it's Q'enti, and I'll never bow to her."

I heard him sigh again. "You never accepted any of my invitations to Tipón," he said in a low voice. "You never even replied. I waited for you."

"Did you wait for me, Zapana?" I turned and fixed his eyes. "Tell me, honestly, how many women have shared your bed since me?"

"And you've never slept with another man?"

"Never," I lied.

"This isn't about bedding, Qori."

He could have his pick of the Empire—the most accomplished harlot or virgin beauty—the Emperor would deny him nothing. I would never allow myself to believe he could be mine alone, and Qori Qoyllur doesn't stand in line. He probably just felt sorry for me, or if there was more it was because I was Inca Moon. But Inca Moon travels like the wind, she belongs to no one.

"Did you enjoy her?" I asked.

"Who?"

"Q'enti."

"I told you, it never happened."

"Then all those people who saw you together lied?"

Zapana sucked in his breath. "It's true I attended a feast at her compound. One of the guests was a foreign prince whom I needed to meet alone, but the councilors his father sent with him wouldn't let him out of their sight. I went in disguise, but Q'enti recognized me, and so did a few others. Yes, Q'enti hovered at my side all evening. I didn't encourage her, but it was useful because she so enamored the councilors I was able to have a private word with the prince." Zapana paused and looked at me. "It went well. That prince now rules his people as our loyal ally."

"And you spent the night with Q'enti."

"I passed the night at her compound. Alone."

As if any man could say 'no' to Q'enti, I thought. I'm not a fool, Zapana.

"I'm going," I said, slinging my bag over my shoulder.

"If you leave now, no matter what happens, I won't wait for you. I mean it, Qori."

I shouldered past him.

III

Concerning events in the Great Square of Cuzco where multitudes gather, the one called Son of the Sun appears in heathen splendor, and the fate of Qori Qoyllur is sealed.

The morning of the Emperor's departure—my judgment day—dawned cool and clear over Cuzco. My city sparkled with streets scrubbed, walls freshly plastered, and roof thatch repaired to honor the Emperor's departure. The great square looked festive with clutches of reeds, flowers, and live birds set out to mark the occasion, its pebble pavement smoothed and swept. Thousands gathered to glimpse Wayna Qhapaq, Father of All, and hear His final decrees before He set forth to inspect the provinces. The journey would last years, and it was paramount that holy Cuzco be left in harmony.

I slept well the night before knowing the warlord Chalcochima would snatch me from Q'enti's claws, and I looked forward to seeing her face when she realized I'd beaten her again. It was a gamble leaving this scheme to the last possible moment, and springing it in public, but the timing and setting were also the brilliance of my plan.

Chalcochima was in charge of the Emperor's train, and I'd come early hoping to find him in the square overseeing final arrangements. I sought only a look of reassurance—if he played his part nothing would go wrong.

I peered down from the terraced hillside above the city, surveying the square and the throngs lining its perimeters in respectful, orderly fashion. The royal viewing platform near the center of the plaza was still vacant, but beside it priests poured libations to the gods on a gold-sheathed boulder to insure the coming ceremonies. Storytellers harangued the crowds, expounding in heroic poems the deeds of past emperors and the glories of Wayna Qhapaq's reign. The people always listened intently to these public tellings of the official histories, though an elder could always be seen shaking his head when he realized that history had once again been rephrased to suit the current emperor.

The Empire is divided into four parts with Cuzco at the center. To the east is Antisuyu, and to the west Kuntisuyu, both of which are small compared with the vast domains of Qollasuyu to the south and Chinchaysuyu to the north. Each suyu has many provinces, and every province was once an independent nation. We called our realm Tawantinsuyu, meaning 'the parts that in their fourness make up a whole,' and that morning I saw our whole world gathered around the great plaza. In the front rows stood the nobles—those of Upper Cuzco lining the north and east sides, and those of Lower Cuzco bordering the west and south. Behind them people arranged themselves according to their suyu and province, so those from Chinchaysuyu stood on the north with people from adjacent provinces at their sides. It always made me smile to see the order my people brought to a chaotic world of many nations.

The towering stonewalls of the House of Chosen Women rose on one side of the square. This compound was an entire city block in length—though a slender block, with the only entrance in the narrow end facing the square. Inside, the warren of dormitories, kitchens, patios, work stations, storerooms, and shrines served the chosen women—girls ten to fifteen years of age, high born, physically perfect, and exceptionally beautiful, carefully selected from all parts of the realm. Once chosen, they belonged to the Empire, and their families had no further claim on them. Some became priestesses married to deities, and remained cloistered virgins throughout their lives; a few might be offered as temple sacrifices, and live in paradise forever; many were awarded as wives or concubines to men who distinguished themselves serving the Empire; and one or two might even become concubines to the Emperor, their offspring providing the imperial bureaucracy with a steady supply of secondary princes and princesses for administrative posts and marriage alliances. But while the chosen girls passed their days hidden from male eyes and learning to become exemplary Inca women, they also wove fine cloth for the Emperor to use as gifts, and brewed urns of strong beer for His feasts.

I was once a chosen woman, though it happened under unusual circumstances having to do with a powerful person who wanted me safely tucked away. Where better than the House of Chosen Women? The girls are confined inside the compound for years under the constant supervision of priestesses called Esteemed Mothers, and men are forbidden entrance to this world of women.

Sumaq T'ika was my best friend in the House of Chosen Women. We were as close as two who are one, but when our graduation came I was sent into the world—married to a secondary noble and soon widowed, while Sumaq was married to Illap'a, god of thunder, weather, and war, and remained sequestered. As a wife of Thunder, she had the freedom to attend her husband's nearby temple each morning, but at night she returned to the House of Chosen Women.

Sumaq was now high priestess of Illap'a, and Most Esteemed Mother of the House of Chosen Women. She knew I had something to do with both promotions—well, as I confided to her, perhaps I had whispered in the ear of my good friend the Empress, but eventually Sumaq would have attained these positions on her own, anyway—and I was pleased to help her career as I could. Indeed, in my role as imperial spy she often helped me, for she was privy to the concerns of noble women and warlords alike. It was Sumaq T'ika, principal wife of the god of thunder and war, who arranged my secret meeting with the warlord Chalcochima, and encouraged him to assist my plan for escaping Q'enti's snare. The idea came to me while I strolled back to Cuzco from Tipón. Upon entering the city I went straight to the House of Chosen Women where I found Sumaq taking her evening meal.

Sumaq greeted me with mocking tone and laughing eyes, the easy banter of an old friend. "Oh, of course, you *would* turn up on the night we have roast guinea pig with peanut sauce. You could even smell it under a lake, couldn't you? It's been months since you've bothered yourself with me, but cook a guinea pig and watch her come running." She knew perfectly well this delicacy made me drool, and it was my good luck they happened to be serving it just then. Had it really been months since I visited Sumaq?

Sumaq sat on a folded blanket in her private patio, another thick alpaca blanket across her shoulders against the evening chill, and looked at me over a small plate she held to her mouth. Long, graceful fingers selected another choice morsel smothered in brown sauce. Sumaq T'ika had been the prettiest girl in the House of Chosen Women, and she was now the most beautiful woman. My eyes fixed on her full lips, and my cheeks heated at the memories. I knelt before her, as one does when seeking an audience with the Most Esteemed Mother, even if she is your oldest and dearest friend. Then my gaze drifted to the contents of her plate, and my mouth watered.

Sumaq T'ika watched me and snickered. She arched a finger to beckon me for the kiss that would free us from formality. I leaned forward and pecked her lips, then quickly licked a spot of peanut sauce on her cheek. "Oh, you . . ." she said blushing and touching her cheek. Then she patted the ground at her side. "Now, sit and behave yourself."

With a wave Sumaq summoned the girls who served her, ordering blankets and another plate of roast guinea pig for me. "Bring a double portion," she told them. "Lady Qori is greedy and most unladylike. You must not turn out like her." The girls giggled, and having delivered the requirements they departed. Sumaq and I were alone in her snug patio.

She watched me lick sauce from my fingers as I devoured a meaty hindquarter. While my thoughts were fixed on the food—the peanut sauce had the savory tang of hot peppers—Sumaq's indulgent smile faded, and she looked off into the night.

"I know what happened in the royal council," Sumaq said quietly. "Q'enti, again." She said it as a statement, and spat the words. "Will that demon bitch never leave you alone?"

"No," I replied, and continued eating. It was a simple fact, and there was nothing to be done about it. Sumaq acknowledged this with a quiet nod.

Sumaq T'ika knew what Q'enti did to me years earlier, and what I did to Q'enti in return, and she knew the hate between us would fester as long as we both lived. It happened when I was with child for the first time, before my belly showed. In those days Q'enti was barely a woman, and I knew nothing of her. Her revenge on me for what she regarded as meddling in her affairs was a savage kick—a kick that stole my unborn child's life, and left me barren. Later, I took what she valued most—her flawless beauty, removed by the flick of a blade on a soft cheek. Thereafter, Q'enti kept the scar well covered with makeup, but the imperfection gnawed at her vanity. A royal decree forbade us from harming one another further, with the aggressor's life forfeit should anything fatal happen, but that never stopped Q'enti from tormenting me through others.

Sumaq T'ika sniffed and bristled at her thoughts. "This charge of disobeying the Emperor is ridiculous, and Wayna Qhapaq knows it." She said it with anger on my behalf.

"Yes," I managed, while spitting out tiny bones.

Her tone became hopeful. "Will you accept Wayna Qhapaq's offer and seek the Eye of the Condor?"

I stopped smacking my lips and fixed her with a look. "That was Q'enti's idea," I said dismissively. "Besides, it's a child's tale—the Great Emerald doesn't exist." Sumaq saw from my expression the subject was closed. She nodded to herself, accepting it, for she knew better than to argue with me.

"Very well, but Wayna Qhapaq has been maneuvered into having to punish you in some way. Have you considered His alternatives? I've heard Q'enti's friends are demanding the brothel, or even the House of Beasts." Before I could reply she hurried on. "Qori, I've been thinking, there is a way we can save you." Sumaq turned to me earnestly, excitement rising in her voice. "Qori, we could make you a priestess of Mother Moon, and you'd never have to leave the House of Chosen Woman. Men are forbidden to set foot inside these walls. If Wayna Qhapaq tried to extract a servant of the Moon

Goddess, every woman in the Empire would howl on her behalf, beginning with the war god's principal wife," she said tapping her chest. Sumaq's huge, gorgeous eyes shone, and she leaned closer placing a warm hand on my knee. "Wayna Qhapaq won't even try, and everyone will understand. You'll be safe here with me, Qori."

"What, entombed behind these walls?" I sneered. Sumaq turned away as if I'd slapped her. She withdrew her hand from my knee and straightened her back.

I set down my empty plate and wiped my fingers. "Look, Sumaq," I sighed, "I know you're trying to help, and I'm sure this is a good life for you, but I couldn't be locked up like this. I need a real life."

Sumaq kept her face turned away. "Is that what you think, Qori, that I don't have a 'real' life worth sharing?" She said it in a small voice that made me ache inside.

"Oh, my poor darling, I've hurt you again, haven't I? Come here, put your head on my shoulder." She resisted, but she never could stay angry with me for long, and after more coaxing she allowed me to put my arm around her. We both wore our hair long and loose, and when our soft, black cascades mingled, Sumaq sighed as she did when we were girls, and rested her cheek on my breast.

When our hearts beat as one I told her of my plan to escape Q'enti's trap with Chalcochima's help—though Chalcochima didn't know about it yet. At first Sumaq didn't like the idea, or the part she was to play in delivering Chalcochima to me, but before I left that night she agreed to everything, and begged me to return to her soon.

Movement among the crowds returned my attention to the great square below. From my perch on the terraces overlooking the city, I watched imperial guards with spears held crossways open a path in front of Wayna Qhapaq's palace compound. This was where the Emperor would enter the square to take His place atop the royal viewing platform. What troubled me was that I couldn't spot Chalcochima's feather headdress among the officials. He must be busy elsewhere, I decided, though he should be out here overseeing the preparations. I glanced at the sun. Midmorning approached and the ceremonies would begin soon. Don't be late, Chalcochima, I muttered under my breath.

I hurried down to the plaza, elbowing my way through the crowd. At times like this short stature is a blessing, for while others turned to contest their places with new arrivals, I merely lowered my head and swam through. They hardly noticed my passing. Still, it was an indignity having to do this. I should have been with the nobles in the Emperor's train. That, however, would be Q'enti's last view of me, standing with the Empress again where I belonged.

I reached the ranks of the Upper Cuzco nobles where heads nodded politely and moved aside, servitors bowed low, and salutations followed me to the front row. I returned the customary Cuzco greeting, "Ama llula, ama sua, ama kella—Don't lie, don't steal, don't be lazy." Glancing around I noticed the women commenting on my attire. I submitted to my maids' whims when dressing that morning—well, most of their whims, except the garish trifles so favored by the lower classes—and they did their lady proud. My silver bracelets and garment pins gleamed, and my dress and shawl were bright blue with purple and red trim. The girls even tied blue parrot feathers in my hair. No lady, I saw with satisfaction, was more splendidly garbed. Then one arrived who was, but of course she would be.

Q'enti, studded in gold jewelry, greeted her Lower Cuzco kin. Her dress was palest silver and clung like a second skin, and she wore her shawl folded back to expose the soft skin of her arms and, most dramatically, her proud bosom. The wide, golden belt rested on womanly hips but cinched a girl's waist. Court ladies fluttered around Q'enti, and she held hostage the eyes of every man in view. The entire gathering focused on her, but of course she pretended to be unaware of the stir she caused.

I stared like the others, entranced in spite of myself, and then she turned her huge eyes on me. Not even I could look away from the perfection of high cheeks, sensuous lips, and flawless honey skin. Flawless, that is, except for the scar I placed on her cheek long ago. She kept it artfully hidden with makeup so no one noticed, but she and I knew the scar was there. It was the first thing she saw each morning when she looked in her bronze mirror. She touched the scar absently as she looked at me. Watchers saw her eyes full of concern and pity—dear Lady Q'enti came out to defend poor Qori Qoyllur yet again—but I saw the eyes of a snake.

The kindest thing I can say about Q'enti is that she was utterly mad, twisted and demented beyond any semblance of humanity. Zapana, Qhari, Wayna Qhapaq and the others recognized her ruthlessness, yet no one but me knew the true depths of her insanity. They thought she schemed for power alone, but power was never Q'enti's ultimate goal; she used that power to destroy others, especially men, in the cruelest ways imaginable and for no other reason than her own amusement.

Qhari appeared at my side, probably the only man present immune to Q'enti's charm, and giving Q'enti a cold look he turned me away. "Where's Chalcochima?" he said, brows furrowed. I had seen Qhari the day before and told him about my savior.

"Don't worry," I said with more firmness than I felt, "Chalcochima won't desert me. He must be on his way here now."

A wave of cheers flowed through the plaza announcing the arrival of Wayna Qhapaq's ancestors. "The Emperor won't be far behind," Qhari said. "Chalcochima had better hurry."

In reply I turned back to the plaza and nibbled my lower lip.

Wayna Qhapaq's parents and grandparents came to see Him off, as was fitting. The royal couples floated on their litters above the crowd. The four mummy bundles had new feather headdresses for the occasion, and the throng fell to its knees as the bearers made a circuit around the viewing platform. Though the imperial ancestors were long dead, a portion of their beings remained behind to look after their heirs. Their attendants now spoke on their behalf, reciting old victories and extolling Wayna Qhapaq to go forth and do His duty to the Empire.

My mind wandered to the arrangement with Chalcochima. He owed me for his victory in Chachapoya, and for many other services that secured his rise to warlord. I had reminded him of this when I approached him in the temple of Illap'a, god of thunder, weather, and war. Sumaq T'ika, speaking on behalf of her divine husband, had summoned Chalcochima to the temple as I requested. But the warlord didn't know why he was called until Sumaq T'ika positioned him by the altar, then departed, and I quietly stepped up behind him.

"What you say is true," Chalcochima had conceded. "But I've already spoken to Wayna Qhapaq on your behalf. What more can I do?"

We spoke in hushed tones. I appeared in the guise of a native Qolla woman, wearing a tent-like dress and shawl with ample padding underneath, and a detached hood that extended half way down my back. I wore the hood forward to shade my eyes and stood behind Chalcochima. We didn't look at one another. It is said the walls of Cuzco have ears. Q'enti had her own spies, and her own ways of dealing with those who threatened her plans.

"There is an old custom, Lord, never used since Wayna Qhapaq donned the royal fringe, but known in his father's time. The Royal Rememberers will remind Him of it."

"I knew the old emperor," Chalcochima said. "To which custom are you referring?"

"That a warlord who has delivered a great victory may beg a lifetime gift from the Emperor."

Chalcochima nodded slowly. "That is so. I saw it once when I was a boy. It's called a lifetime gift because once granted the petitioner can never ask another favor."

"You delivered the victory over the Chachapoyas, with my help. You could beg a lifetime gift."

Chalcochima shook his head, and then spoke using my code name. "Wayna Qhapaq can't pardon you, Inca Moon. You've served Him well, and this charge is unfair, but He can't risk a split between the royal houses of Upper and Lower Cuzco, especially not on the eve of His departure. You know that."

"Indeed, Lord, but I don't ask to be pardoned."

"What then?"

"Only that I be turned over to you for punishment, and my punishment will be to serve you for five years."

Chalcochima stared up at the statue of Illap'a while he considered this. The god's image was that of a man, full size, wrought of pure gold and clothed in royal garments. Chalcochima reached out to touch the golden litter on which Illap'a stood, and then his shoulders shook in a deep chuckle.

"So, Inca Moon would be my personal agent, and accompany me in the Emperor's train during His tour, which will probably last five years. Clever. Yes, very clever."

"But you must not ask this in private," I said, "or give the Emperor time to think about it. It must be done in public without warning. That is your right, and Wayna Qhapaq will know the other warlords—from both Upper and Lower Cuzco—will be watching closely. The Emperor must be generous with His army, and honor the old customs before the people."

Chalcochima chuckled again. "I see now why many fear the name of Inca Moon, even those who don't know she is Qori Qoyllur. Most assume Inca Moon is a man, a very cunning man."

I smiled to myself. "That is as it should be, Lord."

"Indeed. Very well, I'll do it, if only to see Wayna Qhapaq's face."

Relief washed over me. "Good, but one more thing—tell no one, absolutely no one about this. If Lady Q'enti gets word she will find some way to stop you."

"Lady Q'enti? I'll have nothing to do with her, but I must make sure the other warlords are there to witness this."

"Tell no one," I repeated, meaning it. "Remember, you owe me this."

Chalcochima turned to face me. "I will use my lifetime favor to save you, Inca Moon, but know this: I do so out of honor and rightness, not from personal debt. Everything we do, we do for the Empire. Never forget that."

A silence brought my attention back to the great square. The attendants finished speaking on behalf of the royal ancestors, and the crowd now turned to Wayna Qhapaq's palace. The Emperor's entourage came into view. At the head of the procession walked the Napa, a snow-white llama draped in a red blanket and wearing gold ear tassels, symbolizing the first llama to appear at creation. Leading it were two priestesses, or Esteemed Mothers, who carried beer and coca leaves. The Napa had been taught to drink beer and chew coca, and the essence of these offerings flowed to all its kind, returning in the form of abundant flocks.

Next came three splendidly dressed lords bearing the royal insignia on poles: in the center the imperial standard—a small but brightly painted square of stiff cloth, and on either side star-shaped mace heads of pure gold trailing colored tassels.

Following the Emperor's emblems came one hundred men of the Lucana nation in their blue livery, sweeping the ground over which the Emperor traveled, and behind, a hundred of their fellows carried the royal litter, and another hundred followed in close formation. This was the principal tax paid by the province of Lucana—the provision of royal litter bearers—and their men vied for the honor. They were trained to walk at an even pace and shift the noble palanquin from one set of shoulders to another without stopping or causing the slightest jostle. The Emperor appeared to drift over the crowds.

Wayna Qhapaq sat beneath a roof of parrot feathers on His gold-sheathed litter. He held his golden mace, and wore a magnificent tunic of intricately woven squares filled with tiny checks, diamonds, and crosses in brilliant colors, the sole privilege of royalty. Behind came two more litters, one bearing the Empress, and the other a younger brother who was to rule Cuzco in their absence. Some of the Emperor's favored consorts followed behind in hammocks slung on poles.

Warlords marched on either side of the emperor's litter. I stood on my toes looking for Chalcochima, and then sucked in my breath when I realized he wasn't there. Qhari gripped my arm.

The procession came to a halt at the foot of the royal platform, and silence swept the square. With precision the bearers turned as one and lowered their burden. While Wayna Qhapaq and his entourage ascended the platform, Qhari and I stared at one another with eyes bulging.

"Where is Chalcochima?" Qhari demanded, squeezing my arm with both hands.

For a moment I couldn't breathe.

A herald announced the Emperor would deliver His final proclamations and judgments. This was the signal for those pleading cases to step forward. Qhari tightened his grip on my arm. My breath came in heaves. "Don't worry," he said collecting himself, "I'll go and find Chalcochima. I'll be back before . . . ." He gave me a quick hug and vanished in the crowd.

With unsteady feet I walked forward to stand with the others before the platform. Atoco appeared at Q'enti's side and, together with their followers, they took their places nearby. I kept my eyes averted.

With the Empress and high lords gathered behind Him, Wayna Qhapaq calmly surveyed the multitudes and then raised His arms high. Everyone bowed.

"Let it be known here before all assembled, that I, Wayna Qhapaq, Shepherd of the Sun, Lover of the Poor, and Lord of the Four Quarters, declare my brother will rule Cuzco and govern its affairs in my absence."

The prince knelt to receive the headband of governorship, and the title 'He Who Speaks For The Lord.'

My breath came easier. The swearing-in would take awhile. I stood on my toes looking for Chalcochima, expecting to see his feather headdress weave through the crowds. Then I noticed Q'enti watching me. You won't have the satisfaction of seeing me concerned, I thought, and closed my face like a statue.

After the transference of power Wayna Qhapaq made two more proclamations; He recited a long list of men promoted to offices in Cuzco and the provinces, and he decreed that a new village of sandal makers be established to provide the army. The Empress then proclaimed that henceforth every House of Chosen Women in the land—there being at least one in every province—would contribute all cloth and beer production to the military stores. Roars of approval followed these pronouncements, which insured the loyalty of the army while the Emperor was away.

The judgments began. Three governors were demoted for incompetence, and a man found guilty of murder by poison was sentenced to death along with his entire family. A poor man who stole food was reprimanded, but since his need was great there was no further punishment, except the lord who should have been looking after him was fined. A married woman accused of adultery was brought forth. If found guilty she would be stoned to death, but since the charge could not be proved her accuser received the sentence instead. Finally, there was only one case left to settle. Atoco stepped forward triumphantly.

Qhari reappeared at my side heaving for breath. "I can't believe it," he gasped, "Chalcochima is too sick to get off his pallet. They wouldn't even let me see him."

"What?"

"The healer said it was something he ate last night. He's not even in his right mind. Qori . . . he's not coming."

I stared open-mouthed at him. Those around us glanced at this unseemly disturbance before the royal platform. Qhari ignored them, gave me a determined look and, standing fast at my side, lifted his chin. No one saw his hand slip into mine.

Chalcochima isn't coming, I repeated to myself, trying to grasp the consequences. He's sick from something he ate? Q'enti! Oh yes, this has her hands all over it. Chalcochima must have spoken to someone, perhaps another warlord, and enough got back to Q'enti for her to piece it together. Damn her and her poisons!

I couldn't help glancing at Q'enti, and when I did I found her staring at me. She bit her lip and quivered with mirth.

"In the matter of Captain Atoco and Lady Qori Qoyllur," the Emperor said, "I will defer judgment if Lady Qori will agree to search for the Great Emerald of the North, so it may reside here in Cuzco."

Wayna Qhapaq paused, awaiting my response. Q'enti grinned straight at me.

"My Lord," I said, "the thing does not exist."

"Silence!" Wayna Qhapaq's face grew dark and the crowd shrank back. "We are not here to debate. I offered this assignment days ago. You've had time to think on it. Now, give me your answer, yes or no."

I locked eyes with Q'enti. No, you bitch, I thought, you will not have your way. Never. And before I realized it my thoughts took voice and came out in a loud, clear, "NEVER!"

The crowd gasped. No one spoke to the Emperor this way. But Wayna Qhapaq knew my reply was directed at Q'enti. Q'enti's face fell. She'd lost! This alone was worth whatever might follow.

After a pause of astonishment, angry voices rose on all sides.

"Beheading."

"Stone her."

"Flay her alive."

"The House of Beasts."

I knew them, the men and woman gathered there. I tended their aches and sat up with their sick children. I shared their food, accepted their gifts, and even attended their family gatherings. Many of the cold stares directed at me came not from Q'enti's followers, but from those who only days earlier were proud to call me friend. Now they joined in demanding my life, or worse, my humiliation. It was the blood lust of the crowd, and I would not forget a single face.

Q'enti dashed forward. "Wait, please. Lady Qori's crime is great, but not death, please, not that."

She looked frantic, her huge eyes darting from side to side, hands imploring, and this was not a performance—she was genuinely terrified her prey would be snatched away by a quick death.

Atoco stared in bewilderment. He hadn't been briefed for this eventuality. "The brothel," he suggested addressing himself to Q'enti. Q'enti didn't reply. I could almost see her mind pulsating, grasping and weighing alternatives in a blink.

"The brothel," someone joined. "Make her a peasant's whore." Many heads nodded.

Wayna Qhapaq had no choice now. I wished I had accepted Qhari's plan of banishment to Tipón, or even Sumaq's offer of becoming a priestess, but those chances were lost. I trusted Chalcochima and even he failed me.

The Emperor raised a hand for silence. "Captain Atoco," He said, "do you consent to a judgment on Lady Qori that does not require death?"

Atoco exchanged a look with Q'enti. "Yes, Lord," he responded. Wayna Qhapaq gazed at the audience and raised His voice. "And do your kinsmen in Lower Cuzco agree?" Heads turned, then nodded. "And do all the royal lineages agree?" the Emperor asked, opening his arms wide. As one the throng bowed low.

Wayna Qhapaq nodded to himself, letting the moment hang. A cold wind blew through the plaza setting the standards snapping.

"Qori Qoyllur," He announced, "you have been charged with breaking my orders, and you have admitted your crime. Captain Atoco and his relatives beg leniency, and I respect the wishes of Lower Cuzco. But atonement there must be! Therefore I pass the following sentence: banishment from Cuzco, loss of all titles and privileges, confiscation of all wealth, servants and lands, and exile to the province of Wanaku. The Son of the Sun has spoken."

IV

In which are met the Filthy Ones, Qori dispenses boiled potatoes, debates with the governor, and receives an unexpected visitor bearing tidings of a most threatening nature concerning the Steward of K'allachaka.

A downpour hid the morning sky over the city of Wanaku Pampa, and hurried my steps to shelter under the eaves. I heaved my bundle against the wall and pulled the shawl from my head, shaking off what hadn't already soaked through. An icy rivulet trickled between my breasts, making me hunch and draw my shawl tight with crossed hands. Two paces in front the runoff cascaded from the eaves like a waterfall. I could have entered the warm hall instead of shivering outside like a peasant, but I was a peasant, and I was in no hurry to see the inside and be reminded of all I had lost.

Wanaku Pampa is higher in the mountains than Cuzco and much colder, sprawled over a windswept plateau at the base of rounded hills where only stiff grasses grow. At this height the sun scorches while chill winds blow, and when weather sets in the dampness grips your bones. That morning clouds hung in a gray mass over the thatched roofs of the city. Looking across the great plaza I could see no farther than the royal viewing platform at its center.

"So, witch, you came after all."

I turned to see the chief of Pachacoto approaching under the eaves, his retainers behind him hugging the wall to stay out of the rain.

"My Lord," I acknowledged with a slight bow.

"I told you. I warned you," he said behind a waggling finger. "I'll not have you corrupting my people."

"Indeed, Lord, and so it was I moved from Pachacoto to Warapa."

"That village is subject to me also, and what you've done there is worse! You shall pay for your crimes. Oh yes, the governor listens to me." He straightened himself and inflated his chest.

"The governor has summoned you, too?" I asked. It's a three-day walk from the new settlements to the provincial capital, and it pleased me to imagine this bulky little man struggling along the mountain trails. He must have heard I was called to appear before the governor, and hurried to attend the spectacle.

"Summoned me? My friend the governor invited me. All the principal lords attend his councils."

I knew he lied. "Even those who rule a mere one hundred families? Is that common, Lord?"

The waggling finger appeared before my face again. "Pachacoto is senior to all colonies. The old emperor sent my ancestors here from Cuzco to guard against Chupaychu rebellions, and bring His light to the savages. This we still do, and though there are few of us we are the only beacon of civilization in this province outside of Wanaku Pampa."

I lived in his village for a time and endured this diatribe often. Like the other colonists, his ancestors were country folk from the Cuzco region, but to hear him talk you would think they were royalty. The amusing part was hearing this provincial cur speak archaic Inca with a Chupaychu accent.

"If you are still the only beacon of civilization, Lord, have you failed in your mission to enlighten the Chupaychu?"

"They're barbarous. Can't be taught a thing."

"The people of Warapa are also colonists from Cuzco, and they appear to get on well with their Chupaychu neighbors."

"Warapa? Those people not only speak Chupaychu now, they marry them. They ignore my commands and give you haven. This will stop today. The governor will back my demands for a new chief at Warapa, and your filth will be dealt with."

I knew he had been complaining about me, but the imperial officials usually ignored him. When I arrived from Cuzco I had to present myself to the governor at Wanaku Pampa, because no one travels without permission, and officials must know precisely how many people reside in their province and who these people are. As Inca Moon I had wandered the realm with impunity, so this formality was yet another indignity of my new non-status. The meeting was fraught with contempt. The governor and his court expected me, and after satisfying their curiosity—even the guards sneered at a royal physician in disgrace—I was given directions to the colonies and sent off on my own. I had no wish to see Wanaku Pampa again. The chief of Pachacoto now wanted to believe my return to the city was his doing, but the governor's summons made no mention of him. Still, he was a complication I hadn't foreseen, and his complaints could be a convenient excuse for a fatal outcome.

I swallowed and addressed him with head lowered. "Lord, if I have offended you I humbly beg your pardon."

"Too late. You, woman, are a disgrace to our people. This day will see you stoned to death." He pushed by, retreating with his followers into the warmth of the hall.

My crime, I realized now, was returning his contempt from the day we met—he knew I was an exile from Cuzco—and in doing so I made myself a convenient target. He needed an excuse to bully the other colonies and I, foolishly, provided it for him.

He was also jealous of the new prestige Warapa enjoyed as the home of an Inca healer. I hadn't felt kindly enough towards those of Pachacoto to reveal my healing powers, but I could not stand by and watch the gentle folk of Warapa suffer their ailments. Before they knew I was a healer they welcomed me with no thought of benefit to themselves, and later they built a cottage for me of rough stone on the edge of their settlement, and even cleared some ground for a garden. The village is spread along a ridge overlooking a plunging valley with a fast-flowing river. The climate is similar to Cuzco so the valley is cloaked in bush and trees, while behind the village are higher, grass-covered hills for grazing.

News traveled, and soon the sick from other villages began arriving at my door. My clients were poor but they insisted on sharing what they had. They kept my roof thatch in repair, and I never lacked firewood or food or pottery, nor any of the simple needs they produced with their own hands. Two harvests passed in this tranquil backwater before I was forced once again to confront the authorities at Wanaku Pampa.

Another delegation hurried across the plaza and disappeared into the hall. The rain now came at a slant, backing me against the wall as it leapt from the ground to splatter my dress. The hall would be crowded and warm . . . and full of sneering faces.

The royal road runs north from Cuzco up the spine of the mountains, and Wanaku Pampa straddles the highway so that all traffic must pass through its great plaza. Wayna Qhapaq's father built the provincial capital here, there being nothing on this spot before the Inca walls rose, so the city is well planned with its own House of Chosen Women, thousands of buildings to house travelers, officials, and work crews, and hundreds of storehouses dotting a hillside above to provide their needs. It's an odd city because no one really lives here; workers rotate seasonally, and officials are stationed for a term, but everyone calls some other place home.

My thoughts strayed again to my beloved Cuzco; I couldn't help torturing myself with the memories. They followed me through my days and filled my nights, growing ever fonder with the passage of time. I always saw Cuzco under a bright sun amid green hills, the familiar streets bustling with gaiety. Yes, it rained in Cuzco too, but it was a warm, gentle rain.

If I thought hard I could remember every paving stone on those blessed streets, and see myself strolling from welcome to welcome at the palaces, the Empress Herself filling my beaker with sweet Cuzco beer, servants bowing as I passed, court ladies whispering in envy. I had bales of dresses, so many I could change every day of the year and never repeat. More than they owned, those haughty mistresses of Cuzco, and mine all gifts from the Empress and Emperor, from warlords and wizards and governors and priests.

I looked down at myself shivering against the wall. It was well no one saw me as I was now. My dress, the better of two I owned, was of coarse brown llama hair, mud splattered and frayed. The shawl didn't even match, and my dress pins were copper. Well, at least I wore my clothes in the Inca fashion, not like the shapeless bag-dresses of local women, and I had sandals even if they were straw. My healing bag with the red llamas still accompanied me wherever I went. It was the last vestige of my former self.

My former self? Which self? The little girl who ran barefoot on the ocean shores and didn't know she lived in the empire of Tawantinsuyu? The wide-eyed peasant girl who found herself in the Cuzco House of Chosen Women, and was given in marriage to an Inca? The young widow who learned healing ways from her mother-in-law, and was secretly trained for the imperial spy web? Inca Moon, the master spy whose true identity remained a mystery, but whose exploits were legendary? The royal physician Lady Qori Qoyllur, personal friend of the Empress, court favorite, possessor of wealth beyond count? Yes, these were all my former selves, once, long ago in a world that no longer existed for me. It was gone, all of it, like wisps of smoke in a cloudless sky.

Now I stood lost in my misery staring blindly across the great plaza of Wanaku Pampa, waiting to see the governor. The rain lessened and the clouds lifted, but it was shouting and a woman's shrieks that broke my reverie. She ran toward me, a rag clad skeleton chased by a gang of boys pelting her with clods, the boys yelling taunts and eager to corner their prey, she pitifully shielding her head and sobbing. I had warned her to stay out of sight. If my audience with the governor didn't go well she would be stoned this very day.

I pulled her behind me and thrust my chin at her tormentors.

"Give her to us," their leader shouted. "She's a Chachapoya, a stinking rebel, hand her over."

"Filthy One, Filthy One," the others chanted.

In reply I placed a stone into my sling.

The oldest boy pointed a finger at me. "Don't you dare."

In a blink I twirled the sling and let fly. I could have shattered his skull but I contented myself with a warning, glancing the stone off his shoulder.

"That's not fair," he whined, "I'll tell my father."

I fitted another stone. They ran.

Turning to the girl cowering behind me, I placed my arms around her and closed my nostrils to her stench. She whimpered and clung to me. It wasn't only the cold that caused her to shiver uncontrollably. Had she not sought me by name they would have killed her long ago.

What the boys said was true, she was a Chachapoya, and her people's costly rebellion was still a fresh sore, but that had nothing to do with this girl. Her crimes were being caught wandering away from her home province without permission, and worse, being a Filthy One. If I hadn't arrived the previous night I doubt she'd have lasted this day. No one would feed her, and she was covered with bruises and welts.

My own troubles slipped away. No one could be more miserable than this poor creature. When I opened my bundle to reveal a nest of boiled potatoes and gestured for her to eat, she fell to her knees with a sob and began shoving them in her mouth with both hands.

A guard emerged from the hall and looked around. "Are you the woman from Warapa," he demanded of me. I nodded. "Then get inside, they are almost ready for you." I motioned to the girl but the guard cut in, "No, leave that filthy bitch out here." He covered his nose and stepped back.

"And you will guard her, Captain?" He was a common soldier, but I never met one who didn't mind being mistaken for an officer.

"Not me. I'm not standing out here in the rain."

"Please, Captain," I begged, "if she's left alone she will be attacked again, and there's no place for her to hide."

"No doubt," he sneered. "Who wants her around?"

"Perhaps you will accept this in return for your kindness," I said, holding out a tiny obsidian knife given me by one of my patients.

"Hmmm. Nice blade. Very well, but be quick."

The hall was one of a pair fronting the east side of the plaza. It usually served for feasting and bedding travelers, but today the governor used it as his seat of judgment. It was puny compared to the great halls of Cuzco, and this day crowded with tribal chiefs and their attendants from all parts of the province. As I shouldered my way toward the governor's dais at the far end I saw a tall, hooded figure, alone, leaning against the wall and trying to be inconspicuous. No one else seemed to notice.

A herald stepped in my path. "Are you the Warapa woman?" I nodded and bowed. "You will be dealt with next," he said. "Stand over there."

'Over there' was a hushed group of supplicants, some looking pensive and others fearful, all awaiting judgments on their petitions or crimes. The governor sat on his ceremonial stool, a carved wooden seat one hand high. A tufted feather rose from a gold crescent on his forehead, and a standing collar of eagle feathers framed his face. He was a new appointment, and not the man I faced when I first arrived in Wanaku.

"No argument," he shouted at the chief bowed before him. "You will provide your traditional quota of workers for the Emperor's fields like everyone else, and for the same number of days. If your work force has diminished due to deaths, then you are not looking after your people. How many days each year are they obliged to work for you personally?" He didn't wait for an answer. "Just reduce the service they owe you and they will have plenty of time to pay their labor tax to the Empire. I have spoken." He dismissed the man with a wave.

In every province there were lands set aside for the Inca temples, and others for the Emperor, but the local chiefs and their people controlled the largest share. Taxes were always paid in labor; workers tilled, sowed, tended, and harvested the fields of the Empire, and delivered the produce to centers like Wanaku Pampa. In lean years the imperial storehouses were opened so none went hungry, and in good years all was repaid. While fulfilling their service the workers were housed and fed, so nothing but their labor was asked, and this on rotation so no household was unduly burdened. Some tended the

Emperor's flocks, spun wool, and wove cloth, and others maintained the roads and bridges in their province, constructed new buildings, irrigation canals and farming terraces, or contributed to military levies. The people paid a similar labor tax to their local chiefs, but most of the year they were free to look after their own needs. Still, a benevolent Inca governor makes allowances for his charges as circumstances change. This one ruled with arrogance.

The herald announced, "The woman Qori from Warapa." I stepped forward and bowed, but before I could speak the governor exploded in a sneeze. He groaned and wiped his nose on his cloak, regarded me through watery eyes, then sneezed again. There wasn't much of a nose to blow. Such a tiny, upturned thing, it must have stopped growing when he was a boy. His brow glistened. My old teacher always said herbs in a steaming bowl held to the face alleviated these symptoms, but no one believed her because everyone knew illness is caused by sin or sorcery. The governor groaned again and held a hand to his temple, setting his headdress on a tilt. It made him look ridiculous, but he was either too miserable to notice or too arrogant to care. For a moment he seemed not to recognize his surroundings, then his eyes focused and a look of disdain settled on his face.

"And who are you?" he demanded of me.

A portly official repeated the question in the local Chupaychu dialect for my benefit. They didn't recognize me, or notice I wore my clothes in the Inca fashion, but more telling was the governor's reliance on a translator. Every official of quality took the trouble to learn the language or languages of the province in which he served. The Inca tongue, Runasimi—Human Speech, was the official language of administration throughout Tawantinsuyu, and most native lords spoke it, but the common people retained their ancestral dialects. I was fluent in five languages and had passable knowledge of many more, including Chupaychu.

I replied directly to the governor in eloquent Runasimi, "I am the healer Qori from the colony of Warapa, Lord, and I attend at your summons."

The governor was taken aback when he heard me speak, as were those around him, but the captain of the guard nodded and said, "She is an exile from Cuzco, Lord. I remember now. She arrived soon after I was posted here. Banished by the Emperor, as I recall."

The governor twisted his mouth in disgust. "She must be very evil. Why did we summon her?"

The captain replied, "It's the matter of the Filthy One, Lord, the Chachapoya girl caught wandering in this province without leave. She claimed to be looking for Qori of Warapa. We received complaints before about this Qori woman. She provides shelter for two other Filthy Ones, a Chupaychu and a Wamali."

Before the governor could reply he was taken by another sneezing fit. I looked away while he further soiled his cloak.

The first one, the Chupaychu girl, was a surprise. She simply appeared at the door one day begging my healing powers. Her stench announced her problem, and a puddle spread on the ground between her feet. She stopped her entreaties and followed my gaze, then lowered her head in shame and sobbed into her hands.

I had seen Filthy Ones before; it's rare, but it happens to women of all nations, even Incas. They have no control over the urine that trickles out of them day and night. Since they can't change clothes often enough they go around in wet dresses, reeking. The cause is a mystery, but it comes to some women who endure days of labor in difficult childbirths. Only one thing is certain—there is no cure. People believe such women are either possessed by an evil spirit or have brought this upon themselves by committing a terrible sin. They are cast out of their families and shunned by their communities, left to wander in shame and starve.

I felt sorry for these women but there is nothing any healer or priest can do for them, so when I encountered one by the wayside I simply closed my ears to her wailing and passed by. At least I didn't throw stones like others. I was trying to shoo this girl from my door when she jerked the pin from her shawl and held it up. "Qori," she whined. "Qori, Qori, Qori!" The copper pin was old and bent, and her clenched fist trembled as she held it before my eyes. At first I thought she offered it as payment, surely the last thing of value she had left in this world, and I was touched. Then suddenly I understood and the memory came rushing back. It was the Chupaychu girl I passed outside the House of Chosen Women in Cuzco, on the morning Atoco denounced me before the royal council. She had fallen to her knees when I approached, burdened under a load of firewood. What made me stop and raise her to her feet? Why did I give her this old dress pin and tell her its name was Qori? I suppose she reminded me of myself at that age, a peasant girl from the provinces with eyes full of the wonders of Cuzco, and I wanted to show her kindness. It was kindness she sought again now.

While gulping the first meal she'd had in days, she told me she was in Cuzco when we first met to serve her lord during his yearly residence in the holy city, and later returned home to Wanaku with him. She soon married a boy from her village, as most girls marry at age fourteen or fifteen, but after days of labor her first child was stillborn, and the dribbling curse began. She became an outcast, but having heard there was an Inca healer named Qori living at Warapa she thought it might be the same great lady who showed such kindness in Cuzco. No, I assured her, I was not the same great lady, but I was the same Qori, and though I couldn't heal her she could bide with me for a time. After all, we were outcasts together.

The people of Warapa were not pleased to have a Filthy One living on the outskirts of their village, but when I threatened to leave they resigned themselves to her presence. Much to my relief the girl insisted on building herself a hut on the far side of the garden, and refused to enter my cottage, thus sparing me and my patients. She stayed away from the village, and fetched water only in the evenings when others weren't around. I gave her every scrap of cloth I could spare, but there was never enough because she needed to change ten times a day. Still, at least she was diligent in washing her meager belongings, and her stench lessened. My garden was never so well tended, and each morning I found a fresh jar of water outside my door.

The Wamali girl appeared some time later, also unannounced, having heard a Filthy One was allowed to live at Warapa. Her story was the same—after a terrible labor the dribbling curse began, and she too was driven from her people to die alone in the high, cold lands. But she had the courage to seek us out, and my Chupaychu girl so glowed at the prospect of company that I couldn't deny the new arrival.

A few days later I was startled to hear the two of them giggling. How could they? Surely they were the two most miserable creatures in the world. It was a puzzle that haunted me.

The Warapa folk sighed, but tolerated this addition to my family, and we might have been left in peace had the Chachapoya girl not blundered into Wanaku seeking me by name. She was arrested, and a runner arrived with a summons for me to appear before the governor at Wanaku Pampa.

"Lord, the woman Qori," an aid prompted. The governor finished cleaning his hands on his cloak and looked up in bewilderment. "Who? Yes, well, what have you got to say for yourself?" he said, trying to pick up the thread.

"Lloque," I replied.

"What?"

"The lloque shrub, Lord. Have your chamberlain brew the bark and leaves. Drink some, and with mantle drawn over your head breathe the steam from the bowl. This will relieve your symptoms."

A priest replied sharply, "The Lord Governor has said prayers and made offerings at the temple. The gods will soon relieve him. He doesn't need a sorceress."

I looked at the governor. "I once prescribed lloque for the Emperor, Lord, and He said it worked very well."

The governor cast a hopeful look at the captain of the guard who replied with a shrug, "She was once a royal physician, Lord."

"Fetch this lloque for me," the governor barked at a servant, who vanished instantly.

"Now then, Lord," I said, "it seems this unfortunate Chachapoya girl has come looking for me. I wish to spare you any bother, so I will take her off your hands and we can be done with the matter."

"Wait," the captain said. "Lord, this girl was caught wandering in your province without permission."

The governor, now more kindly disposed toward me, offered an apologetic look. "It's true," he said, "and we cannot have people just strolling about wherever they please. There would be no order. No, this won't do. I'm afraid I must have her executed to discourage others."

"Of course, Lord, that is wise and just," I said. "We certainly can't have people drifting from province to province at their own whim. But, with respect Lord, the girl has broken no laws because she's not a person."

"Not a person?"

"No, Lord, she's a Filthy One. She's been disowned. Her family and lord won't acknowledge her, and like a dead person she's already been removed from the counts in her home province. Therefore she doesn't exist, and what does not exist cannot break laws."

The governor squinted his eyes. "Well . . . I . . . that is . . . ."

The captain intervened. "Lord, the girl is a Filthy One, and we received complaints about other Filthy Ones this Qori woman has living with her."

"Filthy Ones living with her? Is this true?" the governor asked me. I nodded. He made a face. "And who lodges these complaints?"

The captain gestured and the chief of Pachacoto stepped forward with a flourish, his moment come. "Most Fortunate and Just Lord," he addressed the governor in his quaint Runasimi, "I am Chief of Pachacoto, and your faithful servant always. The old emperor entrusted my ancestors to maintain this land for Him, and I continue to guard it in the name of our sovereign Wayna Qhapaq, Lover of the Poor, Shepherd of the Sun, Bringer of Light, Lord of the Four Quarters."

He had a great deal more to say, especially on the subject of his ancestors, but the captain hurried him to the point.

"Yes, Lord, as I was saying, this woman harbors Filthy Ones in Warapa, a junior settlement under my care. This is a disgrace to me, and all our people. The chief of Warapa—who must be replaced, Lord—has refused to expel them from his village."

"And what harm have they done you?" I interjected.

"What harm?" he blustered. "What harm? They are evil, and so is anyone who consorts with such filth. They are an abomination to Mother Earth and the mountain gods. Our crops will wither, our children go hungry, and our wells run dry."

"And have they?" I asked.

"Have they what?"

"Have the crops withered or the wells run dry? It seems to me you've had exceptional harvests of late."

"That is not important. The gods bless us because we sacrifice lavishly to them, and now we do so more than ever because of the Filthy Ones, but if this continues we will be impoverished and the gods will turn away. Ruin! Only ruin and death can follow."

I knew he made no more sacrifices than usual, but the governor listened attentively. I tried another approach.

"Tell me, great lord of Pachacoto, why are these women evil?"

"Because they are Filthy Ones."

"Ah, yes, and why are they Filthy Ones?"

"Obviously they committed terrible sins and are being punished by the gods." He looked satisfied with himself.

"Indeed." I turned to the governor. "Lord, many believe that sin is the cause of illness, is it not so?" Everyone looked about and nodded, the priests most vigorously, and the governor replied, "It is so."

"Indeed it is, Lord, but sometimes illness is visited upon the innocent by evil sorcerers. Is this not so?" I looked to the priests who shrugged. "Yes, it is so," I said, "and our own beloved governor is proof, because such a virtuous man could not possibly deserve poor health, and therefore his ailment is the work of a sorcerer."

A priest shouted, "All the more reason why he should forget your foolish herbs and return to the temple." Those around him nodded wisely.

I allowed them their moment and conceded a bow, then turned to the governor. "Lord, like you these poor girls have been bewitched. Their presence does not harm the crops, nor do they infect others. Look at me; am I not whole? There is an evil one who wanders these domains casting spells on innocents. I wish to rid your province of this menace, but to catch this sorcerer I need his victims to help me prepare more powerful spells. That is why I keep these Filthy Ones, Lord, to aid me in my duty to serve you."

The governor looked favorable but the chief of Pachacoto sputtered, "But . . . but I won't have Filthy Ones living with my people. They should be stoned. And this . . . this woman," he pointed at me, "was disgraced and banished from Cuzco. We don't want her amongst us either. She should be stoned, too."

I replied to him, "Calm yourself, Great Lord. What I do is for our beloved governor, and to protect the good people of Pachacoto. I would never dream of troubling you with the presence of Filthy Ones, which is why I went to live among your poor cousins in Warapa. Let them put up with the stink." I gave him a conspiratorial wink. "But if you will allow me to continue my labors for the benefit of all, I am sure the governor will reward you."

The governor sat up. "What?"

"Yes," I continued, "he will reward you with a personal gift to mark his friendship and gratitude, something you can wear proudly for all the world to see—his very own cloak."

"What?" the governor said.

I turned my back to the chief and winked at the governor. He blinked in uncertainty, but when I raised my bottom lip and nodded over my shoulder at the chief he understood; he and I knew how to deal with these dull-witted provincials.

"Your cloak, Lord," I said holding out my hand. He grinned and complied. I held the slim-coated garment with two fingers and presented it to the chief, who beamed and, ignoring the slimy streamers, threw it around his shoulders.

I left the hall feeling satisfied with my morning's work. The governor was pleased, the chief of Pachacoto was delighted, and my girls were safe for now. It was time to collect the Chachapoya girl and put some distance between us and Wanaku Pampa.

The rain stopped and the clouds parted to reveal a warm sun over the golden roofs of Wanaku Pampa. The Chachapoya girl made a great fuss of prostrating herself and kissing my feet. When I finally got her to stand she insisted on shouldering my bundle and walking behind. Well, the poor thing had to show her gratitude somehow.

We were on the outskirts of the city when a man's voice came from behind, "Lady Qori."

I spun around to find the hooded figure I noticed when I entered the hall. "No longer 'Lady,'" I replied.

The Chachapoya girl looked from me to him, then curled her fingers and crouched ready to attack.

The man raised a hand palm outward. "I mean no harm, only a word, in private." I recognized the voice.

"Go and wait for me over there," I said to the girl, pointing up the road. She was reluctant to leave. "It's all right, I know him." She moved away then, but never took her eyes from us.

The hood slid back revealing a handsome face.

"Lord Zapana, what are you doing here?"

"I'm on my way north—more reports of rebellion brewing there." He said it flatly with a neutral expression, watching for my reaction to his presence.

"Oh?" I replied, my feelings diving in every direction. "The situation must be critical to require your presence."

Zapana shrugged. A moment hung, then he added, "There have been poor reports on our Wanaku governor, and since I'm passing through I thought I'd see for myself."

"This governor leaves much to be desired," I said, relieved to have a safe topic while I gathered myself.

Zapana looked pleased to agree. "Indeed, he was a poor choice. Never mind, he will be gone soon." Then he looked at me quizzically. "I heard you defend the Filthy Ones. Why have you taken them in?"

"I'm not sure, but they are harmless. The people should leave them alone."

"But what use are they?" He caught my look and hurried on, "Very well, I cannot order people to change their customs, but I will tell the next governor to leave those at Warapa in peace."

I thanked him with an honest smile.

Zapana lowered his eyes. "I also came to see you, Qori."

"I thought you didn't want to see me anymore?"

"Did I say that?"

"The last time at Tipón you said you wouldn't wait for me. That was presumptuous. I never asked you to wait for me."

I thought he might at least be contrite, but he spoke calmly. "No, you didn't ask. I was only telling you that I had been waiting for you, but my patience was at an end."

"Fine. Then what are you doing here?"

"I wanted to tell you that I'm sorry for what came between us. I should have told you myself about passing a night at Q'enti's compound. You were away at the time, and later I forgot. I'm sorry you heard it from others first."

"Does it make any difference who told me? It happened."

"Yes, it happened, but not the way others tell it. I spent the night there, as did many guests. Nothing happened."

"And now you want me to forgive you?"

"No, I'm not asking forgiveness, I'm telling you how it was. I tried to tell you before but you wouldn't listen."

"I suppose you think I should have come crawling back when you gave me a hut at Tipón. Now you've come to gloat."

"I came to see you, and Tipón is always there for you."

"As if it does me any good now."

Zapana looked away, working his fists. When he turned back his voice was cold. "I have heard of your bitterness. Oh yes, I have my sources. They said you had become a dried potato, and now I see it's true. Qhari knows about it also, and he grieves for you as if you were dead."

I was stung; he might just as well have slapped me. Zapana looked away, surprised by the force of his words, but no apology followed. I couldn't look at him.

Zapana sighed and gathered himself. When he spoke again his words were even, but still frosted. "Some news about Qhari caught up with me a few days ago, and I thought you should know."

"Qhari? Has something happened to him?"

"Apparently, but first you should know about the emerald."

"The emerald?"

"Yes, a cat's-eye emerald this big." He joined his thumb and second finger in a circle. "It arrived in Cuzco just before I left. No one's ever seen anything like it. It was a gift from the oracle of Chinchakamaq."

The shrine of Chinchakamaq is near the ocean shores in the province of Chincha, a fertile coastal valley and the center of sea trade with the north. Though the temple is wealthy nothing this spectacular had emerged before.

"Where did such a thing come from?"

"A trading raft arrived bearing a man from the north. He was ill and made an offering of the emerald to Chinchakamaq in hopes of a cure. The priests sent the stone to Cuzco. That's all I can tell you."

An ache of foreboding rose within me. "And what does this have to do with Qhari?"

"The messenger said Qhari is headed for Chincha in search of the man who brought the emerald."

I fumed inwardly. Stupid brother. Yes, the legend says six cat's-eye emeralds surround the Eye of the Condor, and I suppose you think this is proof the Great Emerald exists. You're such a fool, Qhari.

"By whose permission does Qhari travel?" I asked.

"He travels without authorization. Simply vanished one day. One of my people recognized him in Zangalla, then lost his trail, but I'm sure he's headed for Chincha." Zapana let this sink in, and then added, "Qori, he will lose everything if he's caught."

"Can't you find him?"

Zapana blinked. "With the Emperor in the south and rebellion brewing in the north, do you think I have time to chase after Qhari? No, Qhari is on his own, and I don't mind telling you I'm not pleased with him, either. Suddenly abandoning his duties . . . what would make him do such a thing?"

I suspected the answer but kept it to myself. "What do you expect me to do? I'm not allowed beyond the borders of Wanaku."

"That's true, and officially the decree of banishment can't be rescinded. But there's something more you should know." The warmth returned to his eyes and he placed his hands on my shoulders. "Qori, Lady Q'enti also knows about the emerald from Chincha, and she too has set out to search for the man who brought it. You can guess what will happen if she finds Qhari alone."

V

Of the Despicable Vice and how it was indulged, and of the Coastal Valleys where Qori seeks and is sought, and finds herself in a tree.

The great trading rafts of Chincha rode at anchor only a sling throw from the beach, and overhead gulls cried in a cloudless sky. I paused to remove my sandals; the sand felt good between my toes, the air fresh and salty. Lizard-eyes stopped when I did and pretended to examine bales of dried fish. I studied him without turning. He had the shape of a stump, but the muscles on his bare arms and legs were taut; his expression closed but eyes darting. A green lizard draped over his shoulder, its pointed tail hanging to his waist behind, its face mirroring his. That alone wouldn't have drawn my attention, for people from all parts of the Empire wandered the rows of cargo and exotic creatures—indeed, I thought the lizard a nice touch, as if he had nothing to hide—but he stayed exactly twenty paces behind and stopped when I did, and with this last pause as a test I knew he was following me.

Qhari was a fool to abandon his duties and run off chasing emeralds. If caught he would be executed, but if I could get him back to K'allachaka without incident he might be forgiven. What worried me more was that Q'enti was on the same trail, and if she found him she would do her worst just to spite me.

Zapana arranged for a guard to deliver my Chachapoya girl to her sisters at Warapa, and ordered them left in peace. He didn't want to hear my plans—there was no need, he knew what I would do—but he had the storehouses of Wanaku Pampa opened for my selections. He squeezed my hand once, then left for the north.

I departed Wanaku in the guise of a grieving Lupaqa widow returning south, having lost her soldier-husband on the frontiers. Where a branch of the highland road leads down to the coast I became a Lucana grandmother on pilgrimage to the coastal shrines. That disguise should have taken me to Chincha, but I descended by way of the Zangalla Valley where Puka Tampu—an imperial rest station constructed since my last sojourn in the region—straddled the road at the head of the valley. It couldn't be avoided, and the new garrison was too efficient in checking travel permissions. So I plastered my hair under a colored netting, darkened my skin and hardened my features with paint, bound my breasts, stuffed my sandals, dawned loincloth and knee-length tunic, lowered my voice, and became a man of the Charka nation.

"What did you say your name is?" the guard asked, then added, "Never mind, I can't pronounce it anyway. You should learn proper Runasimi. I can hardly understand your accent."

I nodded humbly.

"Now then, you claim to be a servant assigned to . . . who did you say your lord is?"

I made up a suitably royal Inca name and titles. All the great lords had servants contributed from nations throughout the Empire.

"I see," he said with a sigh. "And you are delivering a message to him from his wife. Where is he now?"

I listed the coastal shrines.

"But you think you'll find him in the Ica Valley? Well, perhaps, but you must wait here until we confirm your story."

Keeping my head bowed, I spoke firmly.

"Yes," he replied, "of course it's urgent, everything is but . . . Of course I know who your master is . . . Speak clearly, I can't understand you. My name? Why do you want my name? His wife will do what to me?"

The Charka disguise worked so well I decided to keep it, but instead of turning south to Ica I went north to Chincha, seeking my fictitious master whenever the need arose. Being a slender woman the binding of my breasts was not a bother, but the loincloth chaffed my thighs. I've never understood why men insist upon it, except for the sake of modesty when they remove their tunics to work. Though men's clothes are better for running and fighting, feminine dress is infinitely more comfortable because it doesn't require undergarments. Nonetheless I endured, for to play a role successfully you must be the role, and think and dress accordingly. I even padded the front of my loincloth, swaggered, and sat cross-legged.

Lizard-eyes and his green twin still drifted twenty paces behind. I pressed my shoulder bag to feel the reassuring outline of my dagger, ready when needed, but first I wanted to know who followed me and why, and whether he had friends nearby. I quickened my steps and Lizard-eyes followed.

Across the cotton fields behind the beach stood palaces and temples, rising like immense hills from the flat plain of the Chincha Valley. Made of mud brick plastered white and red and yellow, they shimmered in the distance like sleeping giants. The long outline of Chinchakamaq dominated the north, the platforms and ramps of the palace leading to one towering block—the sacred shrine. And behind the shrine, lower down and tucked at the end of the complex, stood the Inca governor's compound—by comparison a small, unobtrusive annex, and the only sign of Inca presence in the valley, but nonetheless strategically located. The Lord of Chincha knew who his lord was, and as long as he took directions from Cuzco he was free to rule his people as he chose, and continue his lucrative sea trade, the benefits of which I now inspected while Lizard-eyes trailed behind.

Stacks of cargo lined the beach, ready to be loaded on lighters and ferried to the big ocean-going rafts rolling at anchor, their single masts spiking the sky. Cargo was being landed farther along, and everywhere men hurried and strained amid shouts; idlers gawked, dogs slunk, and birds glided overhead on the fresh sea breeze to swoop at opportune morsels.

I had Lizard-eyes strutting fast to keep up with me. Then I turned and walked back as if distracted by something, forcing him to keep his stride and pass by, his face directed elsewhere as if unaware. I knew I wasn't dealing with an amateur. Ahead of me now, he paused beside another man who admired a pile of fishnets. They didn't speak but I caught an exchanged glance, enough to tell me Lizard-eyes had a partner. The second man was a head taller, and the bronze ring through his nose hid his upper lip. They stroked the feathered amulets at their throats while considering the fishnets.

I had made inquires before coming to the landing, and that's how they must have spotted me; they'd been on the lookout for anyone asking those questions. But, I thought, you don't know who I really am, and there lies my advantage.

My first stop in Chincha had been a small temple up valley. Qhari told me about it years before when he had only heard of it himself, but it was his fervent wish to visit there one day. I knew he wouldn't miss this opportunity. Here, the locals raised some boys to be girls, who dressed and acted like priestesses, and served as temple harlots on feast days. It's abhorrent to Inca beliefs and contrary to our laws, but in subject provinces where it's an ancient custom we don't interfere, providing it's not flaunted and no Incas are corrupted. Qhari had been entranced by the notion, so I visited the temple in my male disguise hoping to learn his whereabouts.

"Did you come to worship?" she said coyly, indicating with long fingers a private room off to the side. In reply I simply stared, speechless.

I say 'she' because he was a she in every way, except for being flat chested and having a bump in her throat. She wore the clothing of coastal women, a loose top leaving the midriff bare, and a short, wrap-around skirt, but the local women never wore them so provocatively. The blue outlining her eyes and red on her lips was perfect. Pleased at my reaction she swept her hair over delicate shoulders and posed invitingly.

"I seek a man," I said in the coastal tongue.

"Yes," she said smiling boldly.

"No, not you, another man."

She pouted. "If I'm not to your liking I have sisters. Shall I call them for you?"

"No, you will do, I mean . . . I'm looking for a man not of this temple. I was hoping you had seen him."

"I see many men."

"Indeed, yes, I suppose, but I think you would remember this man. He's not unlike you."

She tossed her head and giggled. "Oh, one of those."

"Well, yes. He likes men too."

"And you, my handsome suitor, don't like men?"

"Me? Of course. That is, no, of course not. I'm a man." I planted my fists on my hips and tried to look indignant, but she was so fetching I half wished I was a man.

"Ah yes," she said, "I understand. You don't like it but you will condescend to my ministrations. Very well, my hero, come and let me show you the ways of worship." She took my hand and led me to her chamber. The wicker door slid shut behind us.

What was I to do? There I was, a woman pretending to be a man, with a man pretending to be a woman. In truth, there was something strangely erotic about it.

She turned sultry eyes on me. "How does my hero want to worship? Don't be shy. Would you like to lie down, or stand?" She fingered the knot binding her skirt and gave a winsome smile. "Or shall I remove—"

"No," I said holding up my hands. "Thank you, but what you can do is tell me about the one I seek. His name is Qhari, and he's my twin brother."

"Qhari," she said opening her eyes wide. "That's why you seemed familiar. You are Qhari's brother? He said he had a sister but . . . ."

"Then you have seen him? How long ago? Where was he headed?" She caught the urgency in my voice.

"A week ago, maybe more. He was full of questions about that big emerald. I told him to ask the herb man at the landing; he's a special friend of mine, and he told me the story. He even knows the man who brought the emerald from the north." She stopped fidgeting with her skirt and looked at me intently. "Qhari's fond of me, too," she said wistfully.

I patted her cheek. "So am I."

I went to the landing and inquired after the herb man, friend of he who brought the emerald, but I must have asked directions once too often because Lizard-eyes and Nose-ring soon picked-up my trail. I had them both in front of me now, pretending to examine a pile of fishnets.

Are there more of you? I wondered. Are you after Qhari, or me, or the Great Emerald? Well, you know where I'm headed so let's go and see the herb man together.

I walked past them with my head turned to watch some monkeys tethered to a pole, but when I was twenty paces ahead Lizard-eyes and Nose-ring fell in behind me. They were good, but too predictable.

Eventually I found the herb man bargaining with a sailor. The two squatted beside an open sack, examining its contents, and arguing over the number of copper ingots to be exchanged.

The herb man slapped his bald forehead. "But that's twice as much as before, and you were robbing me then."

"It's not my fault," the other protested. "Our rafts don't land at Guayas anymore—Tumbez is as far as we go—and so we must deal with the Punáe traders."

"You go to the Island of Puná?" the herb man asked.

The sailor balked. "I've been known to take risks, but I'm not mad. The Punáe are lying, thieving pirates, besides being the most degraded savages in the north. Land on Puná? They'd bugger me blind and have me for supper. No, I wait for them to bring their goods to Tumbez, then we trade."

The herb man held up a handful of dried roots. "But you can't seriously demand ten ingots for this."

"You can find sarsaparilla for less, but not of this quality. It's from the Island of Puná, and you know it's the finest you will ever see."

Peering over their shoulders I saw the root was indeed the best, and Puná sarsaparilla is renowned among healers for all manner of ailments. I also knew the Chincha herb traders received thirty ingots for every sack they delivered to the mountains. Behind me I sensed Lizard-eyes and Nose-ring moving closer.

The traders stood, the herb man with hunched shoulders and palms open. "But I can't possibly give you ten ingots. I'll be ruined. My family will starve. Please accept five, and I will give you two more the next time you come."

"Ten, or I'll take it elsewhere."

The herb man sighed heavily. "It's piracy, but you leave me no choice. Very well, ten it is." They each clapped their hands once to signify the deal was made, and the mariner left with a bulky leather bag.

"It is the finest quality," I observed.

The herb man noticed me for the first time. "Indeed, and what do you know about sarsaparilla?"

"Only that the best comes from the Island of Puná, and the mountain healers will give you thirty ingots for it, or a few emeralds."

He frowned. "Emeralds? They come from the north, and my brother traders move them southward where they fetch even more than this root."

"How interesting. A mutual friend of ours, a beautiful young *lady* at a certain temple, told me you met the man who brought the famous cat's-eye emerald to Chincha. Is it true?"

At mention of the priestess the herb man reddened. I winked at him and said, "The *lady* is a friend of mine, too."

"Well, in that case," he said giving me a knowing look, "yes, yes indeed, I know the man well." He puffed out his chest, and without further prompting launched into the story. It was an oft given recital of the kind that grows with each telling, stressing a great friendship based on one or two meetings. But I quickly learned that a man named Asto fled the north with a bag of emeralds, and arrived by raft in Chincha. He gave the great cat's-eye emerald to the temple of Chinchakamaq in hope of a cure for a strange illness that plagued him. While the herb man animated the tale with excited gestures, I noticed Lizard-eyes and Nose-ring, their backs turned, edging closer to overhear.

"Was Asto cured?" I asked.

"No," he sighed, "my poor friend still suffers, and now even worse than before. He offered emeralds to every shrine and healer around here, but the evil that possesses him won't let go."

"Where is he now?"

"At his estate, I suppose. Chinchakamaq gave him fields on the south side of the valley, at the foot of the hills in the new area they are trying to irrigate."

"Has anyone else come asking about him?"

"About Asto? Many come to hear the story of the emerald."

"What about a man named Qhari, who looks like me?"

The herb man peered at my face, then ran his eyes over me. "Qhari? Yes, I met a Qhari, but he wasn't a Charka. Still, you do look like him." He stepped closer. "Would you care to have a meal with me?"

"Where is this Qhari now?"

"Oh, he went off to find Asto. Here, take this," he said presenting me with a handful of sarsaparilla. I accepted without moving my gaze from his face, and slipped the precious root into my shoulder bag.

"Has anyone else come by, an Inca noblewoman perhaps?"

His eyes lit up. "Qhari's friend, Lady Q'enti you mean? Why yes, she was here a few days after Qhari." He pressed my arm. "I have fresh fish and strong beer. Please join me tonight."

"His *friend* Lady Q'enti?"

"Indeed, an exquisite woman. She asked after Qhari and Asto. I think she hoped to find Qhari at Asto's estate."

Lizard-eyes and Nose-ring were almost back-to-back with me now. "Have you met my friends?" I said stepping aside and gesturing with a flourish. Lizard-eyes and Nose-ring spun around in surprise.

The herb man bowed courteously. "No I haven't, but I saw them come ashore yesterday. Welcome to Chincha." He bowed again, then inclined his head toward me. "These fine men can tell you about emeralds." Lizard-eyes and Nose-ring took a step back. "Don't be alarmed," the herb man said, "there are no thieves here. We are honest traders. But word has spread that you carry emeralds, and have been most generous with them. Perhaps I can interest you in some tobacco? It makes good snuff to clear the head, and is an excellent charm against snakes and jaguars."

The pair regarded me with boiling eyes, then turned on their heals and vanished.

"My master isn't at home," she said.

"Where has he gone?"

"Away. If you are another of those traders you will find no jewels here. Lord Asto took them with him."

I assumed *lord* was an honorary title, for in spite of his fabled wealth Asto lived like a peasant. His *estate* consisted of a few wattle-and-daub huts on parched ground at the base of barren hills, and the lone servant before me was threadbare.

"It's unfortunate he's left," I said, "because I am a Charka healer and I bring powerful herbs to cure him."

"A healer? Poor Lord Asto has tried many cures. He is of the Kañari people, who have powerful healers, but they failed, and none here can chase the evil from him."

"I see. Perhaps you could describe his symptoms?"

She screwed up her face, hand at her mouth. "Oh, it's terrible, he suffers so. His insides burn, his strength fades daily, and I can hardly get soup into him."

It didn't sound like anything I knew of, but I bobbed my head knowingly. "Exactly as I thought. We have the same malady in my land, and it's easily cured with this." I held out the herb man's sarsaparilla root. He had looked hurt when I left without accepting his invitation to dine.

The woman peered at it and sniffed. "What is it? Will it cure him?"

"It's a common remedy among my people. If I could only get this to him I'm sure he would recover, and be ever so grateful to you."

"Do you think so? Well, it's worth a try, but he ordered me to guard his house. If you took it to him I am sure he would reward you, too. He can be very generous." She looked sincere, and hopeful.

"Very well, mistress, as a favor to you. Where will I find him?"

"He's gone to consult the Seer of the Lines in Nazca."

"How long ago?"

She shrugged. "Two weeks, more or less."

"Has anyone else come looking for him? A man named Qhari, perhaps?"

"No one by that name, but there was a woman named Qori."

I leaned forward. "I have a sister named Qori. Tell me, did this woman look like me."

She studied my face. "Why, yes, she did, but she wasn't a Charka, she was Inca like Lady Q'enti."

I sighed and rubbed my eyes. "Lady Q'enti was here, after Qori?"

"The day after, and such a beautiful lady! She stood right there, right where you're standing, and she talked to me. And she had servants and llamas, and her dress, you should have seen her dress!"

As I departed Chincha on my way south to Nazca, I looked back to see two men following in the distance.

It didn't surprise me to learn Qhari wore women's dress. He needed a disguise and taking my name seemed natural, even flattering. He probably got the idea from his priestess friend at the temple in Chincha, and the clothing from her, too. The first time I saw Qhari dressed as a woman was when I attended one of his private gatherings at the K'allachaka estate.

"Sister!" he had beamed, gliding toward me across the patio. I didn't recognize him at first. He wore a bright yellow dress bound with a broad belt, and women's slippers. His hair, parted in the middle and brushed back, was laced with parrot feathers, and paint outlined his features.

"Qha . . . Qhari?"

"Yes, it's Qhari," he said striking a pose, "your very own sister. What do you think?"

I knew he was a man-woman, a lover of men, but I had never seen him dressed like this before. I was speechless, and a little awed. He looked beautiful.

He said, "I see you're surprised, well, never mind dear, you'll get used to it." He took my arm with the propriety of a hostess. "Now come along and meet my friends." I allowed myself to be led through the gathering.

His friends were from Cuzco, but I doubt I'd recognize any if I saw them on the streets. Many of the men were dressed like Qhari, though I had to look closely to assure myself they were men, and they fluttered around others who were very definitely men, but dressed in the costumes of other nations. There were other men present too, who were really women if you looked closely, and they paid court to delicate women in feminine attire who giggled behind their hands. The patio breathed with laughter and music and the buzz of animated conversation, while attendants circulated with platters of delicacies and urns of beer. Heads nodded our way pleasantly as Qhari led me past.

I whispered to Qhari, "How do you tell the boys from the girls?"

Qhari grinned. "You don't. Just be whomever you want to be."

There would be beheadings if the authorities knew about this gathering, or at the very least titles would be revoked, wealth confiscated, and the culprits shunned if not banished. But the authorities didn't want to know. The disgrace of so many noble families would be shattering. Qhari and his friends were discreet in public, and since K'allachaka was outside Cuzco, Zapana made sure they weren't bothered during these one-night festivals. I knew such gatherings took place, but this was the first time I'd been invited.

Qhari introduced me and chattered at my side as if it was all perfectly normal. He spoke in a higher pitch, his gestures feminine. I began to relax and accept that I stood beside my sister.

When Qhari left for a moment a man who had been eyeing me came over. He was very handsome, with large eyes and graceful features. I tried not to stare while he chatted amiably, and though his voice and posture did nothing to betray him, I suddenly realized he was a woman. If I looked closely I could imagine him as a woman, but he made a more attractive man. He offered to fetch me a fresh beaker of beer, and invited me to join him in the dance lines! I blushed. I don't know why, except I felt like a maiden being courted for the first time. Then Qhari returned to save me from my dilemma—I think I might have gone with my suitor out of fascination—and my beautiful woman-man released me with a wishful look as Qhari led me away.

"You looked like you needed help," Qhari said.

"What? Oh, well, that man . . . I mean that woman was just being nice."

"Indeed, and getting ready to eat you up on the spot, no doubt."

"Oh Qhari, it wasn't like that. I mean I'm not . . . I'm not . . . ."

Qhari smirked. "Well, he's very handsome. If you change your mind you can find him later."

Qhari led me out to see the night sky from a terrace. Having recovered from my initial shock I realized he trusted me with an intensely private part of himself. He knew I would accept it, but he also knew no words could have prepared me. It was strange to see him now as my sister, and remember the times he'd fought beside me as a warrior. He was a good fighter, though often I had to rescue him while he was trying to rescue me, but his courage was formidable, especially where I was concerned. Tomorrow he would put on his tunic again, and if the need arose he would be just as fierce. How could there be two persons living in one?

"Qhari, did you always want to be a girl?"

He looked surprised. "What, me? Never."

"Then why . . . ?"

He chuckled. "Why this dress? It's a jest. We're all pretending tonight. Didn't you ever want to try something different, just for a night? Tomorrow everyone will look like they're supposed to, but isn't it delicious breaking the rules? Besides, some men like me in a dress."

He always said things like that to shock me.

"Does Zapana know . . . about the dress I mean?"

Qhari wiggled his eyebrows mischievously.

The gnarled branch was uncomfortable, but it was thick enough to support me, and it hung directly over the trail. I stretched out full, adjusting myself to its contours, and settled in to wait. Lizard-eyes and Nose-ring would be along soon. Nazca was only a day's journey away, and Q'enti would be trouble enough without those two at my back. Had Q'enti found Qhari yet? She had asked for him by name in Chincha, obviously expecting him, and now she knew he traveled disguised as me. But she didn't know the real Qori was close behind, and as soon as Qhari was safe Inca Moon would rid the earth of Lady Q'enti. I should have done it long ago, but now I had nothing left to lose.

The forest in which I hid covered the south end of the Ica Valley, a long and broad expanse of green surrounded by desert browns. I was born here . . . well, not in the great valley, farther west where the Ica River emerges on the shores of the ocean. But Ica is the province of my birth and I felt its sun drenched land welcome me back, the memories of childhood coming so thick I had to brush them from my eyes. Only days earlier Qhari must have walked under this very tree, dreaming the same thoughts of long ago innocence.

The forest birds came alive, twittering and darting from tree to tree. A pair of foxes ran past. Foxes in the daytime? I raised my head to look about. A tawny shadow slunk by, a puma hurrying in the same direction. Within moments a herd of deer approached nervously, following the puma. Surely they smelled it? Distant shouts and the beating of drums reached my ears. My heart sank. Lizard-eyes and Nose-ring hadn't appeared, so they were still outside the ring of beaters. Only lords could order hunting surrounds, and they executed poachers.

I was about to drop to the ground when the foxes, puma, and deer came racing back, all mixed together but ignoring one another, then turned and frantically dashed in another direction. It was too late, the ring had closed, and with a frightened puma circling below I felt safer in the tree. The animals returned and milled around my perch. Somehow I'd managed to pick the tree in the center of the surround. The great cat stretched itself up the trunk and growled at me.

VI

Concerning that which transpired in the Forests of Ica, after which Qori meets a Wizard, walks on the Mysterious Desert Lines, and drinks the Devil's Brew.

From my roost on a branch overhead, I heard the great cat scream as it twisted through the air. It landed on its side, snapping the feathered dart. The broken shaft protruded behind the front legs. It twitched and emitted a growl that ended in bloody foam, then lay still.

"A perfect kill," someone shouted. Another voice joined, "Look, Captain Atoco took a puma." They spoke the dialect of Ica.

I looked also, but no longer at the cat. Captain Atoco emerged from the trees with a line of beaters. The men encircled my perch still pounding their drums, and others held yelping dogs on leases. Several hunters stepped through the line and fitted long, obsidian-tipped darts in their spear-throwers. Their tunics bore the fish and bird designs of Ica. Atoco smiled at congratulatory nods. I tried to melt into my branch.

It was only the first kill of the slaughter. The deer, eyes frantic, leapt and stumbled into one another, darting back and forth while men shouted and waved cloaks. Dust rose to my nostrils, and darts hissed through the air. The Ica lords laughed and slapped one another on the back, then fitted more darts.

A man I hadn't seen in a long time now stepped up beside Atoco, Lord Aquixe himself—the native Great Lord of Ica.

"You use that better than my own men," Aquixe said, indicating Atoco's spear-thrower. It was a glossy black shaft, fingertip to elbow in length, with a hook at one end to fit the hollowed butt of a fletched dart—these being as long as a man is tall. They were the favored weapon of the coastlands, never adopted by Inca warriors who preferred mace and sling, but they launch fearsome projectiles with great accuracy. Atoco, spear-thrower in hand, was humoring them, but what was he doing here?

Atoco tried to make little of Aquixe's compliments, though he was clearly pleased with himself. "An interesting weapon, my Lord. I've always wanted to try one, but there's nothing like a good mace for smashing heads at close quarters. I like to see my enemies piss themselves before I split them open. But for hunting animals, yes, these spear-throwers are useful."

"Indeed, men like us don't need them on the battlefield," Aquixe squeaked, "but they're good for sport." The two spoke in Runasimi, the Inca language. Though Aquixe was the native lord of Ica he spent as much time in Cuzco as possible, and attended every gathering whether or not he was invited. Except for heavier jowls he hadn't changed much, a short, chinless man with the eyes and shoulders of a fish, draped in gaudy clothes and wearing too much jewelry. His remark to Atoco made me smile; I knew Aquixe had never seen a battlefield.

"Now, my Lord," Atoco said, "with your permission it's time for some real sport." He pulled his dagger, eyes flashing wickedly.

Aquixe nodded. "By all means, Captain Atoco, show these lords of mine how it's done. I would join you but I've forgotten my blade." He offered the remaining animals with a sweep of his arm.

A few deer were still on their feet, and several thrashed on the ground. The Ica lords in their finery looked at one another, then unsheathed their daggers and followed Atoco into the blood pot.

I closed my eyes and became the tree. Enough time passed that I began to think they were not going to notice me, but then someone shouted, "Look, there's a man on that branch. You there, come down."

Another called out, the blood lust still in his voice, "Lord Aquixe, we've caught a poacher!"

I would have come down on my own, and in a much more dignified manner, but they leapt at my perch like dogs on a stag. I was knocked to the ground, then dragged on my knees before Aquixe. Atoco stood beside him. I kept my head lowered hoping neither would recognize me.

"A poacher in my forest," Aquixe announced to Atoco. "He looks like a Charka—my people know better." Aquixe next spoke to his men in the Ica language. "Bring a rope. We shall string him upside down and use him for target practice."

Atoco said, "Yes, a Charka, but what's he doing here? Ask him by whose permission he travels."

Without waiting for the translation I said in courtly Runasimi, "Lord, I am a messenger sent to contact Lady Q'enti." I hoped my voice was masculine enough.

The men stirred. I could feel them looking at each other but I kept my head bowed, heart thudding. Aquixe's lords gathered around seeking new sport.

"He lies," Aquixe said, but it was more of a question directed at Atoco.

"Why should we believe you?" Atoco said to me, his voice like cold bronze. "And why are you dressed like that? You're not a Charka, are you?"

"No, Lord," I replied, "it's a disguise. I am Inca, but I was ordered to travel secretly."

"Why and by whom?" Atoco demanded.

Aquixe tried to imitate Atoco's tone. "And what were you doing in my tree?"

"I was resting, Lord, out of sight. I seek Lady Q'enti of Cuzco, but I cannot reveal the one who sent me, or the message I bear."

Aquixe said to Atoco, "Shall we take him back to my palace, or just leave his carcass here for the condors?"

"Stand him up," Atoco said. Aquixe gestured to his men and strong arms jerked me to my feet. "Look at me," Atoco ordered, staring into my face. "If you don't tell me what this is about, I'll turn you over to my friends for target practice, after I cut off your balls."

He thought the stunned look I returned was fear, but in truth I couldn't believe he didn't recognize me. But then, he and Aquixe were not expecting me. "Lord," I said, "do as you will, I cannot reveal my mission. But there is an Inca in this province who can speak for me, Captain Atoco by name, who is a friend of Lord Aquixe, Great Lord of Ica."

Atoco and Aquixe exchanged a look. "Who told you to ask for Captain Atoco?" Atoco said.

"The one who sent me," I replied. Atoco watched me shift my eyes to Aquixe, then back to him.

Atoco turned to Aquixe. "Let me speak with him in private, Lord."

"But Lady Q'enti is a friend of mine too," Aquixe whined, never wanting to be excluded, "and this is my forest."

"Lodge a complaint," Atoco replied flatly. He grabbed my arm and marched me a few paces away. Aquixe simmered.

"I am Captain Atoco," he said to me.

I showed relief. "Captain Atoco? My Lord, save me from these provincials. I must get through to Lady Q'enti. Is it true she's gone south to Nazca?"

Atoco grinned like a fox, a very stupid fox, and lowered his voice. "Yes, she has gone to see the Seer of the Lines. You bring news of the banished healer Qori Qoyllur, don't you?"

I cleared my throat to buy a moment. "You are wise, Captain. Yes, the healer Qori Qoyllur has left her exile in Wanaku and is now in Chincha."

Atoco slammed his fist into his palm. "Just as Lady Q'enti said she would."

Still absorbing this I said, "Have you been waiting long for this Qori woman?"

Atoco shrugged. "As soon as Lady Q'enti heard that Qori Qoyllur's brother was on his way to the coast, she predicted Qori would not be far behind. As always she was right, but we didn't expect Qori so soon. It's a good thing you arrived. I thought I had a few more days to hunt, but I better start watching for her."

"You will kill her?" I asked enthusiastically.

Atoco looked askance. "Kill her? Certainly not, nor must anyone raise a hand to stop her. I'm to send a runner ahead as soon as she appears in Ica, then follow her south." He leaned closer. "That brother of hers, Qhari Puma, is only a day ahead of Lady Q'enti, and he travels disguised as a woman!"

I chuckled with him, trying to bring the sound from deep in my throat. Qhari probably thinks his disguise is brilliant, I fumed.

Atoco's expression hardened. "What disguise is the healer using?"

"She travels as a Lucana grandmother visiting shrines."

Atoco smiled knowingly. "I will watch for a Lucana grandmother, but this Qori is crafty, she may change disguises." I nodded in awe of his wisdom. "And she is quick as a viper," he added, "I've seen her in action myself." I looked impressed.

"I will tell Lady Q'enti of your vigilance," I said.

Atoco raised his chin and nodded wisely. "You go on ahead. I will wait here another day, and then join you in Nazca. Oh, and since Qori is on her way, tell Lady Q'enti that Qhari Puma can be disposed of now."

The ropes holding the load on my back bit deep, tearing my shoulders. Another stone dug into my sandal, making me stagger sideways. The bindings broke leaving one foot bare.

"I'm not going another step," I shouted at him.

Ten paces ahead the Seer of the Lines turned to see me with hands on my hips, puffing. He said, "You have been telling me that all afternoon. I told you to leave the tumpline over your forehead, it makes the load easier."

"It was pulling my head off."

"Yes, well, we are almost there."

"That's what you have been telling me all afternoon."

We spoke the coastal language.

The seer straightened his considerable bulk and pointed ahead. "Just over there," he said, and walked on.

I looked where he pointed and saw nothing but more flat, stone strewn pampa, indistinguishable from what we traversed all day. The sweat on my face began to dry, and I felt a tang of coolness in the air. Having suffered through shimmering heat I wasn't sorry to see the sun dip behind me, but the desert night would be cold.

Up ahead the seer stopped and lowered his pack. It was half the size of mine. I sighed and limped over.

"Why does a woman come dressed as a man?" were his first words to me when we met the day before.

"I am a man," I had replied in a deep, indignant voice.

He chuckled. "There are men with women's spirits, and women with men's spirits, but you are neither. Your body and soul are female, yet you dress like a man. Why?"

He was a big man with a huge belly, wearing only a loincloth, but one look at his smooth, round face showed he was entirely comfortable with his size and it was of no importance to him. He wore his hair in a long knot on his forehead, like a turned-up tusk, bound with an embroidered band. His eyes, oddly slanted, pierced me without waver or blink. In spite of his good humor he was not a man to be trifled with.

"I am in disguise because I travel without permission, seeking a man named Qhari Puma."

He nodded. "The man dressed as a woman calling himself Qori."

"You've seen him? How long ago? Where is he now?"

The seer laughed and held up a hand, then with a flourish indicated his hovel in a grove of desert huarango trees beside the river. "Come, we have much to prepare."

He made clear my urgency was not his. Beyond acknowledging he knew the emerald man Asto, and Qhari, and Q'enti, he ignored my questions. I gave him the herb man's sarsaparilla root. The seer knew what it was and gave it an appraising sniff, then set it aside without even a word of thanks. What a waste, I thought. He won't be bribed.

"It's been most interesting watching this story unfold," he said. "I've seen all of you coming, being drawn to me, and you are the last one, but this story and your journey are far from over."

His hut consisted of reed walls and a flat roof of branches, through which the sun cast shadowy light into his meager home. I recognized the stack of pottery and mound of clothing as gifts from grateful clients, but the seer took no interest. When I remarked on this wealth he shrugged and said, "People keep bringing me things. Help yourself, it's of no use to me." There were Inca women's garments among the clothes. I longed to let my hair down and be rid of the Charka costume with its uncomfortable loincloth, so I exchanged what I wore and became a woman again. The Seer kept his back turned while I changed and combed my hair. When I finished he nodded approval.

"They fit you as well as they did Qhari," he said.

"These were Qhari's clothes?"

"Yes, he decided to dress as a man again."

I sniffed at the shawl and drew it closer.

The seer removed four slender, spineless cacti from a basket in the corner. He took an obsidian knife and cut slices, dropping them in a pot of water.

"What is it?" I asked.

He paused and turned his face to me, the knife still poised in his hand. "The sacred cactus some call achuma." He put the knife down and held a cactus reverently, drawing a finger down one of its ridges. Excitement edged his voice. "Look, it has four ribs. I use the seven-ribbed variety for most seekers, but this is the rare, four-ribbed kind—very lucky, matching the four roads and the four winds—and they come from the hills below the mountains where the most powerful achuma grows. I've been saving them."

"I'm flattered, but I don't have time for a meal."

He laughed. "Go and gather fire wood."

Dismissed like a servant, I wandered the huarango grove gathering branches, and trying to think of some way to elicit the information I needed and be on my way. Q'enti might already have Qhari in her clutches.

He set the pot of achuma to boil, then began a simple conversation, all the while watching me. In spite of the innocent chatter I had the unsettling feeling he was sifting my thoughts, aware of every question and answer locked inside. His movements were few and languid, but deliberate, and all the while he sat cross-legged before me, his smooth bronze skin and huge belly on display, the tusk of hair on his forehead pointed at me. But soon I found my gaze fastened on his broad face, and then only on his eyes, narrow but deep as wells.

He said his name was Qhawachi, though it must have been a title because he claimed to be the fortieth Qhawachi, and the word, meaning 'make them see,' also applied to the ancient mounds by the river near his hut. Here, water flows year round, only ankle deep most of the time, but enough for sustenance. Farther up, where the narrow channel winds across the desert plain, water flows on the surface only a few months of the year, and below Qhawachi the water vanishes underground again. All around are low, rolling hills and pampas, dun colored and gravel strewn, in places littered thick with dark stones, a parched and naked land. With springs seeping from the valley sides at Qhawachi you would expect a town here, but aside from workers coming to tend fields in the river bottom the place was empty.

Later, Qhawachi took me out among the ancient mounds, now gently sloped and sand covered with hardly a trace of the terraces which once stepped their sides.

"Can you feel them?"

"Who?"

"The ancient ones, my ancestors. There are thousands of them sleeping beneath the ground in every direction. Can you *see* them, *feel* them, row upon row, slumbering in their burial shrouds but ready to aid us when we call."

I couldn't *see* his ancestors, but I could imagine them. The deserts of Ica and Nazca are so dry that nothing rots. Maize cobs chewed by the ancients look as if they were dropped yesterday, and when by chance a tomb is exposed the occupant is still seated with hands on knees drawn against the chest, brittle brown skin stretched over the bones, hair long and black, and garments still rich in color.

"This was their city?" I asked.

"City? Only some shaman-chiefs and their families lived here long ago. But people from many villages gathered for great festivals each year. They built the mounds, brought their dead, prayed and danced and feasted together, and honored their ancestors. There were many powerful seers in those days. People came from distant valleys to consult them." He sighed and looked off across the desert. "Now I'm the only Qhawachi."

"Some still come," I said. "Asto sought you out."

The seer shrugged. "Sought me out of desperation. It is an old religion, an ancient way of *seeing*, still potent but mostly ignored. The lords don't come anymore. Most of them worship Inca gods now." He snorted.

Night fell fast on the pampa as I struggled up behind the Seer and slipped from my bindings, letting the load drop. He hurried over and righted the bundle. "Be careful or you will break something," he admonished. I sank to my knees and sat back on my heels, bone weary, watching him.

Qhawachi untied my bundle, first removing the pot of achuma brew and reverently setting it aside, then piling the firewood, blankets, bags, and gourds of water nearby. His own bundle consisted of two blankets. He usually had helpers and several patients when he ventured onto the pampa, he had explained when he loaded me, but tonight was for me so it was only fair I should carry the weight. I didn't think it fair—the man was bigger than three of me—and I hadn't asked for this night on the bare desert, indeed, I had argued against it, but he insisted he would take me to Qhari, and that alone kept me following his steps. Now, looking around the pampa, there was still no sign of human life.

"We are camping here? I said.

"In a manner of speaking."

"Where's Qhari?"

"You will see him. Now, put a blanket around yourself and rest over there. I need silence while I prepare."

He laid a blanket on the ground, which he called his 'altar,' and from the bags I lugged he withdrew an array of objects: seashells, animal bones, bits of ancient pottery, feathers, seeds, pebbles, and handfuls of herbs, muttering lovingly and placing them with great care in rows on the blanket. Then he produced several short, wooden staffs, each carved with animals and symbols, and stood these upright along the altar facing him. Among these he inserted a maqana, a club of hardwood shaped like a two-handed sword. The pot of achuma and another small vessel rested on the right side of the blanket.

Qhawachi sat back contentedly and surveyed the rows of curios on his altar. "Lay a fire," he instructed without turning, "but do not light it."

I obeyed with a sigh, determined this was the last time I'd be his maid. As I lay the sticks I enquired over my shoulder, "When is Qhari coming?"

"Soon. But first I must bring my altar to life."

"What are all those things?"

"Power to those who understand them. Each has its own spirit to guide and assist us. Those on the left of the altar are death and darkness, those on the right are life and light, and these in the middle," he indicated with a gesture, "will mediate and balance the forces of light and darkness."

"Why do you have things of death and darkness? Are they for casting spells?"

"Death and darkness are part of the world. You cannot ignore them. Darkness is necessary to balance light, to make a *whole*, just as death is necessary for life. Without one the other does not exist. The forces of darkness *are*, and therefore must be controlled. Those on the left help me *see* evil, and know its source."

"What's that?" I pointed to a small pot with a chamber like a ball and two spouts set on top connected by a bridge. Painted hummingbirds hovered on the sides, their needle beaks poking a white flower set between the spouts. It looked nothing like the pottery now made in the region.

"Ah, the hummingbird," he said fondly, placing the tiny vessel in the palm of his hand. "The ancients made this, and it carries their power." He raised a finger. "The hummingbird moves so fast it hovers between worlds. Those you see in this world can be messengers bearing news from far away, sometimes announcing a death. The hummingbird is also the spirit of wizards who suck evil from their clients, just as these birds suck from the flowers."

I knew such wizards. They slip things into their mouths and pretend to suck them out of their patients, revealing the illness was caused by a stone or bone, sometimes a worm or toad, and with its removal the person is supposedly healed. The odd thing was that in believing themselves cured their symptoms often disappeared.

"But," Qhawachi continued, "in order to remove evil one must first *see* it, and this the hummingbird helps with also, not just evil, but all causes of distress." He cocked his head. "You will *see* the hummingbird tonight."

He replaced the vessel and picked up a deer's foot. "This will help me too when I journey with you. The deer is swift and elusive. He warns me of attacking demons and aids in exorcising evil spirits."

"When you journey with me? Are we going somewhere tonight?"

A smile spread on the seer's face. "Oh yes, we are going to see Qhari Puma. We will also need the dog staff." He pointed at a black shaft with a seated canine carved at the top. "Because of his keen smell and tracking sense the dog finds stolen objects, and people. He will lead us to those you seek."

The horizon faded into darkness, and the first stars appeared. I regarded the unlit fire longingly, then sat by the altar. Qhawachi outlined his eyes with black paint, and from the corner of each trailed two lines back toward his ears. "Falcon eye markings," he explained, "to help me *see*. Now it is time to make the altar come alive."

"Will it move?"

"Of course not. Bringing the altar to life means calling the spirits of the things laid on it. When they are present we may begin."

Three times he sipped maize beer and sprayed it from his mouth over the altar, then he knelt before it and shook his rattle, swaying and chanting in a mysterious tongue. Occasionally he stopped to utter what I took to be prayers, and sometimes he rose to shuffle back and forth while whistling to the shake of his rattle. A few times he poured a dark liquid into a clamshell, and this he drank through his nose!

Finding Qhawachi wasn't difficult. Narrow valleys cross the desert plain, and from the valley north of Nazca a road runs straight to the ancient mounds. This road was made by sweeping aside loose stones on the pampa surface, leaving a low ridge on either side. When the dark stones are turned the ground below is a lighter color, so the roadway is easy to follow. But as the journey progressed I encountered other paths crossing over my road, these running straight from one horizon and vanishing into another, all constructed in the same fashion. I realized these were the Desert Lines, and the *road* I trod was one of them.

I learned about the Desert Lines in Ica. They cover the plains around Nazca, but no one remembers who made them or why. Besides the straight lines which seem to run forever, it's said there are trapezoids and rectangles, and even the sinuous forms of giant birds and animals and fish, though when standing on the flat pampa one sees little but bare, gravel strewn desert. Such a place is full of spirits, and no one wanders there at night.

As I walked behind the seer that afternoon we passed more of these lines, and some we walked on for a distance; he seemed to know exactly when to follow them and when to step aside, as if the entire pampa was etched in his mind. Without him I would have become hopelessly lost.

Throughout the Empire other seers wandered alone in desolate places, many of them here in the coastal deserts. They went about naked, eating only the wild plants of the earth, and stood all day in the cold and the heat staring at the sun. Though lean and filthy they enjoyed perfect health and lived to fantastic ages. Qhawachi was different. He always lived in his hut by the ancient mounds, bathed himself in the river, and according to his belly ate hugely from the fields nearby. I had never seen another seer like him, and I was prepared to believe he was indeed the last of his line.

I had pretended not to know what achuma was because I hoped he would dismiss me as one of no consequence, and send me after

Qhari to be rid of me. But I knew about achuma, and I knew about wizards. Though I had never imbibed achuma, once, long ago, the Wizard of the East took me into a jungle clearing and made me drink a brew of ayawaska, the dead man's vine. I journeyed into the spirit world and saw fearsome creatures, yet I survived and was stronger for it. It was not the demons of the spirit world I feared now, but those I knew grew within me.

The seer refilled his clamshell from a small jar, and added a few drops of achuma, then beckoned me to rise. I faced him and he offered the shell to me.

"What is it?"

"Falcon tobacco. There is wild tobacco soaking in there," he said indicating the small pot, "and I added some achuma to rouse the spirit. This will clear your mind and speed your thoughts toward the end you seek. Now, drink it through your nose."

"Why?"

"Because that is the way of things."

I placed a finger against one nostril and tilted the shell to the other, inhaling the liquid down my throat. It burned. I handed the shell back to him, coughing and swallowing hard. He watched me for a moment, then nodded to himself and bid me sit. Again he returned to whistling and chanting at his altar, muttering a prayer as he touched each curio.

Black night descended, the air cool and still. Qhawachi's invocations carried across the pampa. I lifted my eyes to the world of stars above.

Atoco had made it clear I was expected. Was Qhari only bait? Qhari probably thought he acted on his own, but somehow Q'enti anticipated what he would do and that I would follow, and it suited her plans. What plans? Why did she want me here? My stomach tightened as I felt myself once more drawn into Q'enti's evil schemes. But she wouldn't win, not this time. As soon as Qhari was safe Inca Moon would deal with Lady Q'enti.

"Drink."

"What?" I looked up to find the seer holding out a bowl.

"Drink," he repeated.

"More falcon tobacco brew?"

"Achuma."

I stood and faced him. "It's dark, and cold. Shall I light the fire?"

"Not yet. I will do it later. Now, drink."

"Up my nose again?"

"No, this you may swallow through your mouth."

I took the bowl but hesitated. "Why must I drink this tonight? Let's wait until tomorrow."

"The achuma cactus only blooms in the dark. At the mid point of night its fragrant white flowers open. It will help you unfold like a flower."

"But I don't want to unfold, or *see*. I want to find my brother, Qhari Puma. He is in danger. Just tell me where he is. This is the only reason I came to you."

The seer chuckled. "Is that what you think? Then you are mistaken. You seek your brother, you want to save him, and he is in danger, that's true. But you won't succeed unless you are prepared, the real inner *you*. I sense that you were strong once, but weeds have grown in your fields. You must purge yourself to be strong again. Only then can you hope to defeat what lies in store for you."

"Weeds? What are you talking about? Just tell me where to find Qhari."

"You know what I mean, oh yes, you know very well. But you won't allow yourself to think it, and so it festers in the dark places of your soul." He paused and searched my face. "Inside each person there is a bag of memories, feelings, thoughts, which your waking mind won't allow you to examine. The achuma will help you jump out of yourself, and open the bag of memories where lies the roots of your distress."

"I have no distress, except finding my brother."

"That's not what I see. You are weak because you are full of pride and bitterness."

"I am not! I don't need you or your magic brews. Where is my brother?"

He looked at me placidly. "Don't worry, I will go with you tonight. Together we will make you strong again."

"I don't want to go to the spirit world."

"I thought you weren't afraid of anything? The achuma will heighten your senses, especially your inner sense, and shoot your spirit into supernatural realms. There you will do battle with your demons and jump through the barriers of time and distance. You will fly, and *see* with true vision."

"Fly? Will I sprout wings?"

Qhawachi rolled his eyes. "Your body will remain here. It is your spirit that flies. Now, cease stalling and drink. Do you want to save your brother? He needs you more than you know."

"Do you promise I'll see Qhari?"

The seer nodded.

I gulped the noxious potion straight down.

At first I felt a slight dizziness while I sat listening to the seer drone over his altar. Then I realized I was sweating. A foulness rose from my stomach into my throat. The nausea thickened. I swallowed hard but it built like a flood against a dam. I scrambled on hands and knees away from the altar. The contents of my stomach shot out of my mouth into the darkness, again and again, while my body quivered and heaved, obeying its own commands. I felt helpless and disgusted with myself.

The seer watched me crawl back. He nodded to himself and returned to his altar.

The weakness passed. I found myself sitting with head up and back straight, a slight numbness in my body, but my senses clear and sharp. I knew a fox slunk nearby, curious at the seer's chanting, but the night was too thick to see her. My fingers brushed a rock next to me, stroking it like a dog. I lifted it with one hand. Its weight felt good, and it liked me. I set my rock beside me.

Red and yellow sparks swam in and out of my vision. They spun around, and spinning faster became a yellow spiral with red dots racing around the loops to the center, where they vanished and emerged again at the start. The spiral became a whirlpool of light. I did not know if my eyes were open or closed.

I looked at the ground. Flecks of gold scurried over the stony surface like insects. The desert, so barren in the day, pulsated with life. The gold flecks covered me and I breathed as one with the pampa.

My eyes fastened on the blackness of night where the horizon should have been. There was nothing. Panic built and I felt I would be swallowed by the darkness. I tilted my head to the sky. Stars thudded like heartbeats, assembled themselves into birds and fish, then shot off in all directions leaving trails of blue and yellow, only to reappear as animals, spin, and vanish again.

My rock, patiently lying beside me, grew to a mountain. I gazed at its towering cliffs. It was beautiful and mighty, as different from all other stones as one person is from another. I apologized to it for thinking it was just another rock, but I don't know if the words were spoken or in my head.

Qhawachi knelt and peered at my face. Points of golden light twinkled in his hair and eyes. The hair-knot on his forehead was a tusk. I sat up and studied him.

"Take this," he said folding my hands around another bowl of achuma. I drank, feeling the liquid run through me but tasting nothing. When I lowered the bowl I saw painted on the inside a hummingbird with two heads. It seemed to hover there. Qhawachi retrieved the bowl and filled it for himself. I vaguely remembered him drinking from it earlier. When he turned his head toward me again half his face was bare bone, a skull, the other half alive and wholesome.

Life and death. Death in life. Two sides of one. Each needed by the other.

I became a dog vomiting, my sides rippling. Then I was a worm, a hollow tube with liquid gushing out my mouth.

Light engulfed me. Qhawachi had lit the fire. In the flames I saw a friendly serpent, coiled and shining, spreading its glow through the night.

Qhawachi asked me to tell him about my life and the people in it. The story I told became its own life pouring from me as if I was but the vessel, an unstoppable flood with no thought of what was right or wrong, or what Qhawachi might think. I don't remember what I said, but the telling left a vile taste in my mouth.

Qhawachi stood and grasped the hilt of his maqana with both hands, then flailed wildly at a creature beyond my vision. He paused, filled his mouth from a gourd bottle, and sprayed the space before him three times. The maqana blade came up again, slashing the air. The demon must have been ferocious to withstand such punishment, but I knew Qhawachi would be victorious. Next, he performed seven somersaults in a cross pattern to shock the demon into leaving, and then he settled down to his altar again.

I turned my head and stared into the darkness. I didn't realize I was looking away from the fire and thought the light had vanished. I was alone. It was black.

I saw Zapana sitting beside me. My heart raced to him. You're handsome, Zapana. You admit you're lonely sometimes. Why show me that? It makes you weak. It makes me weak. You force me to reveal my inner places. You make me love you. That becomes dependency, and dependency is weakness. I come and go as I please. I have any man I want. Your love would steal that from me. Feel the ache inside me. You cause that. You make the hurt that won't go away. I'm a healer, yet I don't know how to stop this pain.

Ah, Qhari, look at you, you're ten years old. Father told us not to go near the sea cliffs, but mother will forgive you when she sees that basket of tern eggs. You don't press me like the others. You don't demand from me. You're just you. As constant as a spring. You let me draw from you and ask nothing in return. I love you. You never make me say that. I don't have to say it with you. Why the frown? I feel your worry. For me? No, don't be afraid, I'm Inca Moon. I'm strong. It's true. Isn't it true?

I felt myself coming up like a sunrise, and then I realized the seer had taken my hand and raised me to my feet, turning me to the fire. In the firelight a carpet of red and yellow jewels stretched off across the pampa. Qhawachi spoke to me. I followed his directions and leapt over the fire four times to shape a cross.

Qhawachi picked up a flute and moved around the fire. He played blue and purple music that drifted away like tendrils of mist.

Then he led me by the hand out on the pampa. It was dark, but I saw the pampa through the blackness. A breeze danced like feathers over my skin. Qhawachi held my hand tight, drawing me along behind him, his other hand shaking a rattle to a low chant.

I realized we were walking on a line that seemed to emerge from the desert floor. Not a straight line. It was sinuous and narrow. We followed it in one direction, and then it curved back on itself, looped around again and took us in the first direction, around, back, each circuit shorter.

Qhawachi let go of my hand. It was good. I heard him just ahead of me, or beside me, chanting quietly, the shake of his rattle guiding my feet. He was close but I walked alone. Golden insects scurried away from my steps.

The path turned back, and after a few paces reversed itself. Back and forth, some long, some short. Leading where? After some time—I know not whether it was a long or a short time—I became aware I had been on this path before. Not this exact path, but one that turned in the same way, except the first one was over there and pointed in another direction. Two the same that formed one.

In my mind I retraced my steps, the turnings this way and that. A red light followed my progress, but stayed, marking a trail behind me. Then suddenly I *saw* the whole image, and realized I stood on the head of a hummingbird!

A rush of wind. Far, far below lay the outline of the hummingbird on the pampa floor. Qhawachi looked up at me with his falcon eyes and smiled, his forehead tusk shooting sparks. Somewhere over the horizon dawn stirred. I had to return before the dawn. Qhari. You search for Asto. Where's Asto? My hair streamed loose behind me.

I looked down on a tiny oasis in a sea of sand. I hovered over a shelter on the outskirts of a village and saw a man huddled alone inside. Asto? Yes, I feel you. You're weak. You are going to die soon and you know it. You whimper for your mother. I don't sense any good in your life. Where's Qhari?

Another rush of flight across the night sky. Another oasis, this one larger and up river from the first. A cluster of huts. There is Qhari curled in a blanket, sleeping. He dreams. He dreams of . . . Zapana?

Qhari you scoundrel! He's mine. Oh, there I am too. Zapana and me. Now you, you're with us also. You're safe for the moment. Where's Q'enti?

A short flight to where two rivers meet. Another hut. There she is, sleeping. Yes, Q'enti, that's you. And there are your guards and servants outside. No, I don't want to know your dreams. I'd never escape from inside your head. But look at that beautiful scar on your cheek, that angry red gash I put there. It ruins you. Ha!

Your men are stirring, beginning to rise for an early march. Qhari still slumbers, but he's not far away. Qhari, wake up!

VII

Of a perilous journey through a naked land, and gnawing truths denied.

Sand blasted my face. Peering through my fingers I watched the horizon vanish in a blur of grit and dust. But the wind had not yet reached its full fury. Another gust hit and I stumbled; the arm I held out for balance being blown back over my shoulder. I could no longer walk into the mouth of the gale, but where was shelter? Dunes of white sand, the only relief on the desert flats, migrated across the hardpan.

It was late afternoon of the day following my spirit flight, and I struggled alone in the desert wastes. I knew where Asto was, and I knew Qhari, followed by Q'enti, would reach him soon. There was no time to lose. I tried another step but was blown backwards. In despair I yielded and collapsed on the stony ground. I lay on my side arching my back to the wind and drew my knees under my dress, then pulled the shawl over my head and wrapped myself in a blanket. The wind howled past, but the sand still searched every fold as if intent on suffocating me. I kept my mouth and eyes shut tight and a hand over my nose.

There is a wind most days on the desert. It begins on the morning shores and gusts inland through the afternoon. Often it becomes a true gale with sand whipped like rain, and sometimes it strikes as it did this day, a tempest no creature can withstand. When these scour the pampas there is no telling how long they will last. Stories are told of a dune shifting to reveal its core—some hapless traveler wrapped in a blanket who vanished years or generations earlier. But there was nothing I could do, except try to keep from smothering under my wrappings and stay awake. Sleep could be permanent.

I awoke that morning on the bald pampa somewhere near our overnight camp, though there was no sign of it or the seer. It was late and the sun roasted the desert pavement. I found myself alone, wrapped in a blanket with a gourd of water beside me, lying at the base of a line shooting off to the southwest. There was no sign of Qhawachi ever having been there, only a memory. Was he real? Did my spirit flight really happen?

I sat up and tried to collect my thoughts. The sensation of wind in my hair and looking down on the oases came back to me. I saw Asto and Qhari and Q'enti, yes, and then returned to find Qhawachi kneeling beside me, speaking, asking questions, his face and the tusk of hair on his forehead still traced in golden points of light. We walked, sometimes on lines and sometimes not, but for how long and in which direction I have no idea. Eventually the points of color faded leaving me thirsty and weak, but Qhawachi led me on and as we strolled he interpreted my visions.

"The hamlet where you saw Asto is in the last oasis on the Great River before it reaches the sea. I sent him on a pilgrimage to shrines all over the Nazca desert, and the river mouth is his final destination. He will reach it this morning."

"Qhari is close to him?"

"Yes, only a day behind. He will find Asto tomorrow morning. I told Qhari about the first stop on Asto's pilgrimage, the white mountain called Moich, and he has been following from shrine to shrine."

"And Q'enti is following Qhari, but she's near to him. How close?"

"As your vision revealed, very close. She might overtake him today."

"You could have just told me the route."

The seer shrugged. "I didn't know how far the thief had traveled until you saw him."

"Asto's a thief?"

"You felt inside him. Do you think a spirit so crude could possess sacred emeralds? No, the stones weren't his, but they caused his sickness."

"He confessed this to you?"

"He came to me seeking a cure, and I flew with him to divine the cause of his distress."

"You weren't able to cure him," I observed.

"For him there is no cure but death. His insides have rotted. I saw what time he had left and gave him what I could—hope. He will be dead by sundown tomorrow."

"Did Qhari drink your achuma?"

"Yes, it was most interesting. His search for Asto is on your behalf."

"On my behalf? But I didn't ask him to—"

"No, but he is trying to save you."

"To save me?"

"From yourself."

I changed course. "Did you fly with Q'enti also?"

"With Lady Q'enti? Certainly not. I know evil, and I've done battle with rare monsters, but Lady Q'enti . . . no, not willingly would I look into the abyss of that soul. I told her Qhari went to seek Asto at the white mountain of Moich, and sent her on her way. She has been trailing him, drawing ever closer."

"Will she harm Qhari?"

"If she can, yes. But I saw you coming and this matter is between the three of you."

I baulked. "The great Seer of the Lines can't deal with Lady Q'enti, but he expects me to."

Qhawachi's eyes never wavered from mine, nor did his tone change. "I don't have to, that's your purpose."

"I see. Then what's your purpose?"

"To strengthen you. Last night you journeyed well. You've become a potent force because the achuma made you see your weaknesses. Now you can expel them and be strong again."

"My weaknesses? Lord Seer, you don't know to whom you are speaking."

He chuckled to himself, making me angry.

I said, "I don't remember everything I told you, but I was in the grip of your achuma. I probably spoke nonsense."

"It made sense to me," he said, "especially the last part of your story when you were stripped of your titles and wealth."

"What of it?"

Qhawachi heaved a great sigh, made all the greater by the sheer bulk of him. "I always allow my patients a day to rest, and then we spend many more days sorting through their visions. But time is short for you. Very well, I shall tell you, and though I doubt you will accept it now at least the seeds will be planted.

"Pride blinds you. Consider your actions when the charge was made against you in Cuzco; you turned to those you love, but you didn't approach them with love, instead you demanded repayment of favors and then ignored their advice."

"It wasn't like that. Besides, their suggestions were unacceptable, and I was determined."

"Ah yes, determination. A good thing when reasonable and just, but determination also sees the truth of things. You showed willfulness, which demands that we get what we want now, the way we want it, ignoring truth and the will of others."

"I don't agree."

"No, of course not. That would be admitting you were wrong, and such an admission would drain this well of self-pity in which you dwell."

"But they owed me; Wayna Qhapaq, Chalcochima, Zapana, all of them."

"Do you always keep a tally? Tell me, when you stand before your gods will they count your wealth and titles, or the good works you gave freely to others? You don't seem to understand, Qori, we only keep what we give away."

"Then what about my girls, the Filthy Ones? I ask nothing from them."

"True, you act from compassion, and that is good. This is how you should treat all people." He placed a hand on my shoulder. "I did not say you are all bad, Qori. There is much good in you which shines through in spite of your pride, but in some matters you've strayed.

"As for this man Zapana, you seem to want him, and not want him." He held up a hand to silence me. "I know you have your reasons for treating him as you do, but look hard at those reasons, Qori. There is more behind them. Ask yourself what it is you fear?

"Then there is the wealth and titles you speak of so often. Did you lose them, or was their burden lifted from you?

"Strength is what you need to face these truths, and for strength you should look to your brother Qhari."

"Qhari?"

"Indeed. Any man who dresses as a woman cannot take himself too seriously, or worry much about what others think. He has freed himself. Draw strength from his example."

"If I do as you say, will I rescue Qhari and dispose of Q'enti once and for all."

"Perhaps."

"Perhaps? But you said—"

"I said you are a potent force, stronger than when you came to me, but not even I can see to the end of this."

"Then tell me this much, will Qhari live?"

"Possibly, if Q'enti doesn't overtake him first. Even so, we all die sometime."

"I must find Qhari quickly."

"I agree, but after you rest. You have journeyed all night and my patients usually take a full day to recover from the achuma. I had thought you would have time for that, but Qhari and his shadow Q'enti moved faster than I anticipated. Still, if you rest this morning and then go straight across the desert you should reach Qhari by tomorrow morning. He follows Asto's trail along the dry channel of the Great River, as does Lady Q'enti. This path is cooler walking and there are oases to pass through, but the channel twists like a snake across the desert, so it takes much longer. The distance is shorter and easier walking if you stay on the flat above the river valley."

"Good. I'll leave now."

"No, I said after you've rested. You don't realize how exhausted you are, and crossing the desert is not for the weak. There are dust storms and serpents, and the desert has a way of confusing the unwary. Some enter and never leave."

Qhawachi stopped. We had reached the base of another line, this one five paces wide with a ridge of pebbles marking either side. With the sun rising behind us the lighter soil in the line seemed to shine against the dark surface of the desert. Qhawachi followed it with his eyes to where it vanished in the distance. He nodded to himself. "This is your line," he said. "Follow it to the end, then continue straight on and you will find the river mouth. But, first you must sleep until the sun is high. Don't worry, unless you get lost in the desert you should still arrive ahead of Q'enti."

Those were Qhawachi's last words to me, or all I remembered. Somehow he calmed my panic and made me lie down to sleep, and when I awoke there was nothing but the line I slept on and the blanket and water gourd. Was it all a dream? There was no time to search for Qhawachi and convince myself otherwise. "This is your line," he had said. "Follow it and continue straight on to the river mouth."

Now, alone on the pampa and curled up against the wind, I craved sleep again. My mind slowed and my body demanded complete rest: blissful nothingness, every limb at peace, my head a stone, no thoughts. See the hummingbirds whirring around the flower, poking it with their needle beaks. One by one the hummingbirds vanish like extinguished lamps, slipping into another world. My quilt is heavy and warm. Quilt? It's a blanket. Why is it so heavy? I can't move!

With a start I forced myself to sit upright. I peered through narrowed eyes, sputtering and spitting grit. My lower parts were under sand, and soon my burial shroud would have been complete. I held out a hand to test the air. The wind continued but only carried dust now, no stinging sand. The storm subsided.

The sun dipped on the horizon, a pale glow behind the settling dust, but there was still plenty of light to travel. With luck Mother Moon would illuminate the desert night. There was still much ground to cover.

Summoning all my strength I forced myself to my knees, then dragged myself upright and shook the blanket aside. I spared one handful of water to wipe my crusted face, and a second for my parched throat. It tasted so sweet I could have emptied the gourd in an instant, but it was a small bottle and the desert still stretched ahead. After shaking out my clothes as best I could, and thinking longingly of a bath, I heaved a sigh and set out once more.

During a windstorm everything on the desert that can move, does. Dunes shift and reform, silhouettes change, vistas open or close, rocks emerge or are buried, and dry shrubs blown out of the river oases rearrange themselves over the landscape. You can't trust any moveable feature. Only sparse rock formations jutting here and there offer guides to navigate, but they too are full of tricks. Looking at them from different views as you pass they alter shape and remind you of outcrops seen earlier. Their muted colors are just as deceiving, for they change with the light. The blinding midday sun sucks the colors from the land, leaving hazy whites and yellows and grays blending into one another, but at dawn and sunset the colors sharpen, adding rich gold and purple, blue, green and red. I fastened my eyes on a notch in the hills ahead. There was no sense in looking behind, the view was the same, and the line-path I started on ended long ago. I fought down the gnawing fear I was disoriented after the windstorm and now headed in the wrong direction.

For those who live here every place on the desert has a name and story. Qhawachi told me about the white sand mountain of Moich behind the town of Nazca, where Asto went first on his pilgrimage. "Moich was wife to the high mountain Illa-kata, sender of water to the coast," Qhawachi had explained. "But Moich was seduced by Tunga, spirit lord of the warm coast lands. He convinced Her to run away from Her husband's cold heights, but when Illa-kata discovered She was gone He roared thunder, and Moich feared Her husband would overtake them. Tunga hid Her under a pile of maize flour and fled. But Illa-kata saw Tunga running to the sea and turned Him into a mountain. You can see Tunga frozen where He stood, and Moich still hidden under Her white cover." I wished Qhawachi were with me now to name the hills and keep my feet on the right path.

The dust settled just before sunset, allowing the land to don its evening mantle of purple and red and stark white. The hills before me grew, framing the distance on right and left, and the stony hardpan gave way to gravel, then coarse sand. I staggered on, longing to rest but unable to stop, my legs refusing to break stride. The ground remained warm long after sunset, while a cool wind dried the sweat on my brow.

On a moonlit night you can see far across the desert, though everything around you is cast in silvery sheen. But luck was not with me that night. A pampa of clouds split the earth from the heavens; the stars never appeared, and Mother Moon remained hidden. On such nights darkness falls thick, consuming the land and those who walk it. Unable to see beyond an outstretched arm I finally halted, breathing heavy, my head throbbing. I turned around, looking this way and that for something to guide me, but there was only blackness. I turned again, and realized I had lost all sense of direction.

A cold breeze roused me from sleep. I drew the blanket closer and shivered, distantly aware that my head rested on soft sand. Not the desert hardpan, or gravel, but yielding white sand. The wind carried a hint of salt. I jerked upright. The sun already climbed the horizon, though a chill still hugged the ground.

I leapt to my feet, then staggered and sat down heavily, my tongue thick and stomach rumbling. The ocean, close enough to smell but not yet visible, beckoned. I tried to collect my thoughts. Full morning. I've already missed much traveling time. This is the day Qhari will find Asto at the river mouth, if Q'enti didn't overtake him yesterday. She and her men were at his heels. There's a small oasis near the river mouth where I saw Asto on my spirit flight. Now, where is that oasis?

Looking around I saw the place where I'd collapsed in the darkness was between two ranges of hills. The sun was at my back, the cool breeze from the ocean on my face, so the Great River and its last oasis lay behind the hills on my right. I stood, drained the last of my water, and set out in haste.

Fear chased me up the barren hills. Atoco said they didn't need Qhari anymore—he could be disposed of now. Qhari is the bait, I thought, it's me they want. Very well, Q'enti, I am here, but if you've harmed my brother . . . .

By mid morning I stood panting, looking down on the oasis. The Great River meanders in its narrow channel far below the desert plain, but now and then the desert retreats to allow fertile oases, the only swatches of green in a parched land of sand and rock. It never rains in the coastal deserts, or, when it does briefly, perhaps once every few years, the fat drops fall widely and vanish without trace. So the Great River, fed by the snowcapped mountains to the east, is the only source of water, and its annual flood soaks the oases. But the channel is dry most of the year, and some years the floodwaters fail to arrive. Still, oasis farmers cling to the hope of the good years when their fields of maize, quinoa, squash, and cotton produce abundantly.

The oasis I looked down on, the last on the river's tortuous journey through the waste lands, was tiny and checkered with fields on either side of the dry river channel. I could see the peasants planting in anticipation of the yearly flood. Hearth smoke drifted over the only village, and the shouts of children at play rang across the basin. From my vantage the entire oasis and its inhabitants were in view.

Was Qhari somewhere below, or had he already set out for the river mouth? I looked to where cliffs sealed the west end of the oasis, except for a steep gorge winding through to the ocean shores. That would be Qhari's route. A chorus of barking swung my gaze to the opposite end where the river first enters the oasis. Peasants already walked in that direction, their dogs racing ahead of them. A column of people and pack llamas emerged from the gorge to the east. They were only specks at this distance but I didn't need to see them clearly—the local dogs already identified them as strangers. Q'enti had arrived.

I raced down the slope, sliding in soft sand to my knees, tumbling, running, sinking again; then rolling like a log to the bottom. When I sat up and brushed the sand from my eyes I found myself at the feet of a small girl. She stood perfectly still, eyes wide, staring at me in disbelief.

"Good morning," was all I could think to say.

Her eyes darted from me to the hilltop and back. "Are you a mountain spirit?" she inquired innocently.

"Not quite," I said, standing and brushing the sand from my clothes. "I'm a traveler, seeking a man."

"Then you're another stranger," she stated.

"Have there been others?"

"Oh, yes. More than I have seen in my whole life. Strangers everywhere. But you're the first woman," she nodded encouragingly.

"How many other strangers came here recently?"

"Two!"

"A veritable horde, indeed. And where are these strangers now?"

Obviously pleased to have the answer she said, "The sick one, Lord Asto, went to the river mouth yesterday, and Lord Qhari, who arrived last night, set out to visit him this morning."

"*Lord* Qhari? Well, it seems he has promoted himself. How long ago did he leave?"

"Just now."

"Following the river channel?"

"Yes, through the gorge, there," she pointed.

"Good girl. Now, don't tell anyone you've seen me."

"But I *have* to tell my sister," she pleaded.

"Very well, your sister. Now hurry to where the dogs are barking and you will see another lady and many more strangers, but don't tell them about me, it's our secret."

She hunched her shoulders and giggled behind her hand.

The gorge cuts deep on its last stretch from the oasis to the sea; the entrance framed by a towering cliff of gray stone on one side, and a steep hill of white sand on the other. The bottom is level and a sling throw in width, through which the dry riverbed loops from side to side. It's easy walking. The channel is fine white sand laced with rounded pebbles, and the flats are covered in grasses and thorn bushes. Having crossed the desert it seemed to me a garden. But I wasted no time. Qhari was just ahead and Q'enti close behind. With luck the oasis dwellers would delay Q'enti long enough for me to collect Qhari and escape.

"Sister!" Qhari exclaimed when he saw me. He had been ambling along gawking at the canyon walls and I was almost upon him before he noticed. He swept me up in his arms. I was relieved to see he wore men's clothing.

"Yes, it's me, you fool, now let go."

He did, but still held me by the shoulders, his eyes shining. "You came," he said. "I thought you would. Did Zapana tell you?"

Mention of Zapana brought an ache. "He did," I managed. "Now, all that matters is getting you out of here and back to Cuzco. Zapana said you left your post without permission. Qhari, how could you?"

Qhari dismissed this with a wave. "I'm doing something more important. Qori, the Great Emerald, the Eye of the Condor, it's real! A man called Asto brought a cat's-eye emerald from the north—one of the six that surround the Eye of the Condor—and he's at the river mouth now. You've arrived just in time."

I said, "I know about Asto and his emerald, but one green stone proves nothing. The Great Emerald is a myth, Qhari, a story, nothing more. You left your post without leave, you wander through the provinces without permission—Qhari, do you realize how serious this is? If you return immediately and beg forgiveness—"

"I'm not going back," Qhari said, letting his hands slip from my shoulders. "I am going to find Asto, and then I am going to find the Eye of the Condor. Besides, what are you doing here? By whose permission do you travel?"

"Qhari, Lady Q'enti is right behind me. There's no time to argue."

He looked puzzled. "What's she doing here?"

"I suppose she thinks the Great Emerald is real, too."

There seemed little point in telling him he was the bait and I was the one Q'enti wanted. He thought he was the only one trailing Asto, and didn't realize how close he'd come to falling into Q'enti's clutches.

Qhari said, "Then that's all the more reason to hurry on to the river mouth and question Asto before Q'enti gets to him." He turned and walked on briskly.

I caught up, but he didn't break stride so I fell in beside him.

"Qhari, this is foolish. Why are you risking your position and your life chasing shadows?"

"To find the Eye of the Condor."

"Even if it exists, what do you want it for?"

"To buy your freedom."

"My freedom? You mean this is about me? Qhari, that's sweet of you, but please stop this now. I'll speak to Zapana, and I'm sure he'll—"

"I am going for the emerald, Qori, with or without you."

Qhari set his jaw and kept his eyes forward. There was no sense arguing with him when he was like this. Very well, I thought, I will go with you, and if Asto is still alive he can tell you himself he knows nothing about the Great Emerald, and then we can get away from here.

A tiny owl landed on a thorn bush nearby. She was brown and white like the desert, and above her in the cliff face was the fist-sized tunnel marking her nest. She watched us pass with huge, curious eyes.

I said, "You traveled through Chincha and Ica dressed like a woman?"

Qhari brightened and ran a hand through his hair. "Yes, and you should have seen me, I was beautiful."

"You promised me once you wouldn't do that except at K'allachaka."

"Did I? Well, I've seen you dress like a man."

"That's different. It's one of my disguises."

Qhari glanced at me sideways. "Yes?"

When I looked away in exasperation he chuckled. "You must admit I'm very pretty in women's clothes, and you should have seen the men in Chincha looking at me."

He was leading me again. "Don't you ever wonder what people think of you?" I said.

Qhari shrugged. "Should I? I know who I am, and they can accept me or not."

"People know you are my brother. Don't you ever think about me?"

"Often. That's why I'm here."

"What about Zapana? What would he think if he saw you in a dress?"

Qhari's eyes lit up. "Oh, he has, in Cuzco when I was following an ambassador. Zapana was in disguise, too. He says I look like you. I think he likes me better in a dress."

I feigned shock, but it didn't surprise me when I thought about it. Qhari had always been in love with Zapana, truly in love, and Zapana, I knew, could be enticed. Qhari had at last found a way—by being me. He'd even taken my name in Chincha. I didn't want to imagine what it was like for Qhari pretending to be someone else to attract the love of his life, yet always denying himself that love so another could have it.

Had I pretended to be someone else, and then forgotten I was pretending? Had Lady Qori Qoyllur become a person neither she nor others recognized? I thought people liked me that way, expected me to be so, but did they? Did I?

Silence surrounded us for a distance. We passed a folded section in the canyon wall, one side tan with red layers, the other a dark massive with gray streaks running at opposite angles. Qhawachi will know a story about this place, I thought.

Qhari stared at the cliff face, then his eyes wandered to me. "You look terrible," he remarked.

"Don't I please you, brother dear? Could it be because the Seer of the Lines made me drink achuma to find you, and then with hardly any rest I had to cross the desert and endure a sand storm, spending two nights in the open?"

Qhari ignored my sarcasm. "You met Qhawachi? Interesting man," he said with brows raised.

"Interesting indeed. But I could have done without the delay."

"What did he tell you?"

"Nothing for your ears, Qhari Puma."

Qhari grinned to himself. After a pause he said, "I told Qhawachi about myself."

"You mean about liking men?"

Qhari glanced at me sideways. "Is that the only thing that comes to mind when you think of me?"

"Well . . . ."

"You like men too, but is that all there is to Qori Qoyllur?"

"No, of course not."

"Don't you have hopes and dreams?"

"Yes, but—"

"Tell me, sister, what do you want in this life? What do you dream of?"

I pressed my lips together and walked faster. Qhari lengthened his stride.

Once I had everything a woman could wish, I reflected, but they took it from me. Now I only dream of how things were.

Qhari listened to my silence and said, "I think you still live with what you lost, not what could be."

"What could be? Dreams are for children, Qhari. I've seen too much of the world."

"Have you? Is there nothing you truly want?"

"Things are as they are, and there's nothing anyone can do to change that."

"I can."

"You can what?"

"I can't change the world, but I can change me."

"Are you still full of Qhawachi's achuma? You're talking nonsense. Very well, Qhari Puma, what do you dream? What does Qhari want?"

"I want to be a sailor."

"What? A sailor? Have you gone mad?"

Qhari thought for a moment. "I don't think so."

"That is ridiculous."

"Why?"

"Because you've never even been on a sailing raft. You don't know anything about it. Besides, you're Qhari Puma, steward of the royal estate of K'allachaka."

"I've made up my mind, Qori. I've wanted to sail since we were children and watched those big rafts gliding past our shores. When I went through Chincha seeking Asto I saw the great trading vessels straining at their anchors, eager like me to be off across the waves. I promised myself my time had finally come. First I am going to find the Eye of the Condor and buy your freedom, and then I am going to be a sailor."

He was serious. I looked at him open-mouthed. "You never told me you wanted to be a sailor."

"You never asked."

"Well, it's a childish notion, Qhari Puma. Look at you. You're a grown man. You have obligations, in case you've forgotten. People depend on you."

"You mean people at K'allachaka? Yes, they do depend on me, and I was happy there, but it's time for a change."

"Time for a change? You should hear yourself. As if you can simply walk off one day and do as you please. You have duties, responsibilities."

"Qhawachi said my first duty is to myself."

"Qhawachi's achuma has tilted his mind. Now you listen to me, Qhari Puma. We started as peasant children, you and I, and you have risen to steward of a royal estate. You're not going to throw all that away for a foolish dream. You will lose everything. Sailors have no wealth."

"But they are free."

"Free to be poor."

"Yes, but it's because they don't have wealth to worry about that they are free."

"This is nonsense. Anyway, you forget that you are a servant to Zapana's lineage. You belong to them and you need their permission to leave K'allachaka."

"Yes, but Qhawachi says if you are truly committed you can find a way to make anything happen."

I withdrew into silence. With Qhari being so unreasonable there was nothing more to be said. He could be so stubborn.

After a distance Qhari said, "There's more to my dreams."

I sighed.

Qhari cleared his throat. "I want to see you at Tipón with Zapana."

"I'm not discussing Zapana, Qhari."

"Why not? You love him as much as I do."

"I do not!"

"Of course you do. I've thought about it, and I don't think you are as angry as you pretend over that rumor about him and Q'enti. I think it's an excuse. What are you really afraid of?"

"Just because you trust Zapana doesn't mean I must."

When Qhari spoke again there was an edge to his voice. "Do you know how many pleas Zapana and I launched on your behalf? No, you don't. They all failed, it's true, but we kept trying. Now you're consumed with bitterness and self-pity. You're not the Qori we love. She's gone."

I looked at him. "I am not gone, I am right here. And I came to save you from Q'enti. Self-pity? You sound like Qhawachi. They will have heard by now that I broke my exile and left Wanaku. Do you know what that means, Qhari? All I have left is my life, and I've risked that for you."

"As have I for you," he said quietly.

The salt breeze grew stronger, and as we rounded another turn the estuary opened before us. It seems broad when you first step from the confines of the gorge, but in truth it's hardly more than two sling throws wide, and short enough to see the gray-green swells straight ahead. Grass and shrubs edge a shallow pool of warm water—the only water I'd seen in the Great River—and a wide sandbar separates the pool from the sea. In flood the river must break through to the ocean, indeed, great piles of driftwood litter the beaches demonstrating it's so, but in this season the dry riverbed stops short of its goal. We climbed a hill for a better view and scanned the river mouth for Asto.

A line of hills separates the desert from the oceanfront. On the north side of the river these hills are covered by gray sand showing patches of white and red, which drift down to a terrace and then fall away to broad beaches. But on the south side a headland of black rock juts into the sea.

Qhari's hand slid into mine and together we looked out on the ocean vastness. Anyone who has just emerged from the desert cannot help but stand and stare. My skin drank the moist air, my hair cooled to the touch of breezes, and my eyes feasted on broad swells breaking white along the beaches. I knew what Qhari was thinking. We were raised on such a beach not far from here. Qhari and I didn't know what sandals were then. We were free like the sea birds gliding overhead. Standing on those shores again with Qhari I knew a part of me would always be there.

"Yes," I replied to his unspoken question, "I remember." He squeezed my hand.

"Look," Qhari said. I followed his pointing finger to a driftwood hut. It stood across the river mouth from us at the base of the black headland. Smoke still curled from the hearth in front.

VIII

In which the Fated Confrontation takes place, and matters
Culminate in Utmost Evil.

His face was swollen and purple, and the rest of him beneath the
blanket was like a bloated seal. The stink forced us to breath through
our mouths in the confines of the tiny hut. His eyelids fluttered. The
parts of his eyes that should have been white were red. He didn't
seem to be aware of us. Fresh blood seeped over encrustations at
the corners of his eyes and nose. A gurgle came from his throat, the
only evidence of breath in this lump of rotting flesh that was once
a man. Qhari and I exchanged a look and retreated outside to the
sunshine.

Qhari exhaled loudly. He said, "It must be Asto, I suppose. I
heard he was sick but I never imagined . . . . Have you seen this
before?"

"No, never." When we entered the hut I studied Asto's symptoms
and ran through every ailment known to me, those of the mountains
and jungles and coastlands, but never had I witnessed such festering
devastation.

Qhari sniffed the air and made a face. "It's a disgusting way to
die. If I'm ever afflicted with what he has, do me the favor of ending
my life before I reach that stage."

I nodded, and we moved farther away from the stench.

"Well, Qhari, are you satisfied? Can we go now?"

Qhari stared at the sand and shook his head slowly. Then he looked at me. "We came this far, we must try. Maybe Asto can still speak."

"He doesn't even know we're here. He'll be dead before sunset, maybe sooner."

"But we have to try, Qori." He tugged my arm. "Come on."

Asto's maid had said her master was of the Kañari people, who dwell in the province of Kañar in the far north of the Empire. It is a large and wealthy highland province, and Kañari was one of the principal languages I learned as a girl in the House of Chosen Women. I knelt beside Asto and spoke to him in his native tongue.

"Asto. Asto," I called warmly.

His eyelids moved. I said his name again.

He answered without opening his eyes, his voice a thin whisper, "Mother?" Qhari gave me an encouraging nod.

"Yes Asto, it's mother. Why are you sick? Tell me so I can help you."

Asto only whimpered. Qhari leaned over me impatiently. "Ask him about the emerald."

At the sound of Qhari's voice Asto spoke. "Pisar?"

I pushed Qhari back. "It's mother, Asto. Who is Pisar?"

". . . brother . . ." came the labored reply.

"Does your brother Pisar know what's wrong with you?"

". . . yes . . ."

"Can he cure you?"

". . . Pisar knows . . ."

"What does Pisar know? Does he know where you got the cat's-eye emerald?"

". . . yes . . ."

"Where is Pisar now?"

". . . Guayas . . ."

I glanced at Qhari. Guayas is a port in the far north, at the mouth of a great estuary that empties into an ocean bay of the same name. But it was outside the Empire's boundaries and inhabited by savages. Qhari sighed heavily.

"Asto, tell mother about the Great Emerald, the Eye of the Condor. Does it exist? Have you seen it?"

A shadow blocked the door. Before I could turn there was a dull '*whump*' and liquid sprayed my face. Qhari cried out. I wiped my eyes and saw a pole rammed through Asto's distended belly—which had burst and drenched me—and Qhari outside struggling with a man. Then a hand seized my hair and dragged me outside.

He hauled me along on my back and I couldn't see him as I twisted attempting to free myself. I reached over my head and dug my thumbs into his wrist. He let go and I rolled over, then sprang up, hands extended for battle. It was Lizard-eyes; I'd almost forgotten about him. His companion, Nose-ring, lifted Qhari over his head and dropped him with a thud on the sand. Qhari groaned and tried to pick himself up, but collapsed. Nose-ring snorted at him and grabbed a driftwood club. Lizard-eyes grinned wickedly at me and drew his dagger. He went into a crouch, blade extended. Nose-ring hefted his club with both hands, aiming at Qhari's prostrate form.

I dove at Nose-ring's legs trying to throw him off balance, but it was like running into a tree. He kicked me aside. I came up on my knees. Lizard-eyes plunged his dagger at my head, but I caught his wrist with my right hand, then shot my left under his tunic and grabbed his privates. He shrieked and fell back.

Nose-ring forgot Qhari and swung his club at me. I ducked and leapt at him, catching his throat in a claw-grip. His tongue came out when I dug into the cords of his neck. He dropped the club and tried to tear my hand away while sinking to his knees. He was too strong for me. I let go and knocked him flat with a knee to his face.

Lizard-eyes charged from behind with a roar. Without turning I collapsed in a ball and he tripped over me, sprawling face first on the sand. I dashed to the hut where I'd left my bag. Asto stunk worse dead than alive. In disgust I realized the slimy contents of his belly were still on my clothes. I turned to see Lizard-eyes and Nose-ring back on their feet. They looked at me with new respect.

I drew my knife from the bag. They glanced at each other, then set their eyes and came on.

I faced them in a crouch, my eyes fastened on their eyes. They were both too slow for me and they knew it, but while I dealt with one the other could do his damage.

Lizard-eyes lunged first. I dodged and came back with blade slashing. Lizard-eyes howled when I opened his cheek, but before I could stab him Nose-ring flung his arms around me crushing my face to his chest. He shouldn't have done that; it was the wrong move in a knife fight, but for that reason he caught me off guard. And it was a sacrifice move because I could finish him easily, but not without leaving myself open to Lizard-eyes. These two didn't care about their own lives, and you seldom defeat men so determined. But in the instant this flashed through my mind I heard a thud, and out of the corner of my eye I saw Lizard-eyes collapse face down. Qhari stood behind him holding the driftwood club.

Nose-ring, still crushing me to his chest, lifted my feet from the sand and swung me around to see what had happened. When he saw Qhari he flung me aside and charged.

I sat up gasping for breathe and saw Qhari land a solid blow to Nose-ring's shoulder, but it didn't matter to Nose-ring. He closed his great hands around Qhari's neck and lifted him. Qhari dropped the club and clawed at the hold, his feet kicking wildly in the air.

"Leave my brother!" I cried. I threw myself at Nose-ring's broad back and plunged my knife. The blade seared through flesh and lodged in bone. He grunted and let Qhari crumple at his feet, then whirled on me ignoring the knife still protruding behind, his lips curled in fury. His left arm hung useless, but his right paw seized my hair and twisted viciously. I tried to fasten a claw-grip on his throat, but he shoved me back and my hand came away clutching his feathered amulet. Nose-ring instantly released me when I threw the amulet aside, his good hand darting to his neck where it had hung. He knelt to retrieve it and I landed a sidekick to his head laying him full out.

I ran to Qhari and helped him rise. Color returned to his face, but bruises from Nose-ring's grip marked his neck. He pressed them gently, and then turned with a start. Nose-ring and Lizard-eyes were on their feet again. Nose-ring stuffed his amulet under his tunic, while Lizard-eyes removed his and did the same. They moved calmly and with purpose, like men determined to finish a difficult task but planning carefully. After exchanging a grim nod they both produced daggers and came at us.

"*Who are* they?" Qhari said, shaking his head. Our blows would have silenced ordinary men, but these two were unstoppable. Qhari and I rose together, our hands empty.

I stepped in front of Qhari. "Run, Qhari," I whispered. "Run up the beach and keep going."

"I'm not leaving you," he said moving to my side.

"Do as I say," I hissed, trying to push him back. But he wouldn't budge. Lizard-eyes moved to my left and Nose-ring edged to Qhari's right, preparing to spring.

"You won't have your way this time, sister," Qhari said cheerfully. "These two are mine." He shoved me aside.

Lizard-eyes and Nose-ring moved as one with a speed I hadn't thought possible. Instead of charging they flipped their daggers to grasp the points and threw hard. Lizard-eyes stood closer to me but he threw at Qhari, while from the far side Nose-ring sent his blade at me. I had never seen this move, and though it happened in a blink I admired the cunning.

A blunt jab on my shoulder knocked me back—Nose-ring's throw wasn't true, his knife struck hilt first—but Qhari cried out and collapsed. I fell to my knees beside him, my right arm numb and useless, and saw the dagger stuck clean through his side. It wasn't a mortal wound, but the blade had to come out. I seized the handle and jerked. Qhari grimaced and covered the punctures with his hands.

Lizard-eyes grabbed me from behind, one thick arm like bronze at my neck cutting off my breath, the other twisting my good arm up my back. Nose-ring closed a crushing grip on Qhari's throat. I struggled to help my brother but I was powerless in Lizard-eye's grasp. Qhari let out a hoarse gurgle, his face turning from red to blue.

Then a shouted command came from behind, "Don't move."

Lizard-eyes let go of me and I rolled to Qhari, gasping for breath. Nose-ring had freed him, too, and the pair stood over us with hands open at their sides. Qhari coughed and took short, deep breaths. He looked at me as if to say, What happened? We sat up slowly. Warriors hurried into line not forty paces away, their spear-throwers armed and raised. I exchanged a glance with Qhari and froze. More warriors arrived and fanned out to form a half circle around us. Lizard-eyes and Nose-ring looked on in bewilderment. Then, stepping out in front of his men, Atoco appeared. He took in the scene and nodded, looking extremely satisfied with himself. My one thought was for Qhari—Atoco had said he could be disposed of now. Atoco shouted, "Kill them."

I didn't have time to say good-bye to Qhari, but my hand found his already outstretched and we closed our eyes together. I held my breath. There came the whistling of fletched darts in flight, and the hollow thud of shafts impaling their mark. I waited, expecting obsidian points to tear through my flesh in the next heartbeat. Nothing. I opened my eyes to find myself unhurt, and still holding Qhari's hand. Qhari stared back at me and blinked, then examined himself in amazement. We were untouched, but Lizard-eyes and Nose-ring lay behind us, each with a thicket of darts in his chest. Their bodies convulsed, then lay still. The warriors re-armed their spear-throwers.

Atoco stood over the bodies admiring the marksmanship. "Aren't they good?" he said conversationally, giving his men an approving nod. "That fool Aquixe lent them to me." Then he straightened and turned cold eyes on us. Qhari and I still sat upright holding our breath. "Kneel," Atoco ordered. We glanced at each other and I knew what Qhari was thinking—our chances had been better with Lizard-eyes and Nose-ring. I helped Qhari to his knees while he kept his hands over his wounds.

"Well, well, Qori Qoyllur," Atoco gloated, "absent from her exile without leave. What will I do with her?" He strutted around us with hands on his hips. Qhari stared at Atoco with eyes that could burn holes. I laid my hand on Qhari's knee.

"I need to bind Qhari Puma's wounds," I said.

"Not necessary," Atoco replied. "That one isn't needed anymore. He is your brother, is he not? Would you like to watch him die before I give you to my men?"

"Stay away from my sister!" Qhari shouted. Under the circumstances it was a pathetic threat, but Qhari meant it.

"Oh, a fighter," Atoco chuckled without mirth. "Maybe you will give us more sport than I'd hoped." I didn't want to know what Atoco considered 'sport' but he told us. "You're a man-woman, aren't you?" Qhari looked away. Atoco sneered. "Perhaps I'll cut your balls off, or make you scramble on hands and knees to see which of my men can put a spear up your ass first. You'd like that, wouldn't you?"

I swallowed hard. "Leave my brother out of this, Atoco, it's me you want."

Atoco flared. "*Captain* Atoco to you, and you're just Qori, another peasant. Haven't you learned not to cross me?"

I bit my lip to stop the invective that swelled within. Atoco was full of bluster, but capable. This was no time to goad him.

Qhari said, "Let my sister go and you can do what you want with me." The words came in an even, calm voice that made Atoco pause. I looked at Qhari and saw that he meant it.

Atoco pointed at Qhari and shouted to his men, "Get him on his feet. I'll show you how to make a man-woman squeal."

Before the men could respond a commotion erupted behind them. Heads turned and the line opened. Q'enti appeared with a maid bearing a feather parasol hurrying behind her. A stone formed in my belly.

Q'enti paused when she saw Atoco standing over us. She sent the maid off and came to Atoco's side. He bowed and took a step back. Q'enti looked fresh and composed, her hair and dress immaculate as always. I knelt in my stained traveling clothes covered in Asto's filth. Q'enti sniffed in my direction and turned up her nose, then settled her eyes on the bodies of Lizard-eyes and Nose-ring. She turned to Atoco in fury. "I sent you ahead to secure prisoners, and I said there were to be no deaths until I arrived."

"My Lady," Atoco replied, head lowered, "you told me the physician was to be unharmed, and those men were trying to kill her."

"Trying to kill her?" Q'enti said. "Why? Who are they?"

Atoco shrugged. "Thieves? They were on her when I arrived."

Q'enti looked unsure, then turned as if noticing me for the first time. She smiled pleasantly and nodded to the bodies. "Who are they, my dear?" By her manner you'd have thought she was inquiring about guests at a banquet.

"I don't know," I said quietly. Qhari was about to speak but I nudged him. He pursed his lips and lowered his head. Q'enti observed this and nodded to herself. "Well, we will soon find out," she said.

"Shall I torture them?" Atoco offered hopefully.

Q'enti gave him an icy stare and he shrank into silence. She looked down at us. "You may rise," she said regally.

We struggled to our feet and faced her. My knees wobbled, and Qhari's face drained. He kept his hands over his side, but he was too proud to show his pain in front of Q'enti. "He has been wounded," I said, "I must tend to him." Q'enti shrugged. I removed my broad belt and used it to bind Qhari's wounds. Qhari tightened his lips but made no sound. Luckily there was little blood, the blade had gone straight through but severed nothing vital.

Q'enti looked around the river mouth while I tended Qhari. She pointed at the driftwood hut. "Asto is in there," she announced as if winning a guessing game.

"Yes," I replied, "but you are too late. He's dead."

Q'enti's face fell. She hurried to the entrance, glanced inside to see Asto with the stake through his stomach, and turned on us. "Who did this?" she demanded.

"Not me," Atoco replied hastily.

Qhari nodded to the bodies of Lizard-eyes and Nose-ring. "They did," he said.

"Did you speak with Asto before those two arrived?" Q'enti asked him.

Before Qhari could answer I stepped forward. "No, we came just after they killed him, and then they attacked us."

There was a long pause while Q'enti studied us. Finally she said to me, "You're lying, I can see it in your brother's face. No, Qori, you questioned Asto, and you know where to find the temple. Now, tell me."

"Temple? What are you talking about?"

Q'enti shifted her weight to one leg, folded her arms and raised a finger to tap her teeth. In this pose she considered us at length. Her left eye twitched rapidly, but she was unaware of it.

Q'enti stopped tapping her teeth. She closed her mouth and her lips paled as the thoughts took hold. Atoco swallowed hard and edged away when Q'enti lowered her arms. She was seething, and even Qhari and I leaned back from her.

Q'enti stared at the bodies of Lizard-eyes and Nose-ring again. "I know who they are," she said between clenched teeth. "Atoco, you fool!"

"My Lady, what are you talking about?" Atoco protested, taking yet another step backward.

"I will show you what I'm talking about," Q'enti said. She pointed to the body of Nose-ring. "Expose the shoulders on this one." Atoco hurried to comply. Q'enti didn't watch but turned her eyes to the sky. "There is a small tattoo on his right shoulder," she said prophetically. "It is a solid red circle surrounded by six red dots."

I looked. The tattoo was there as she described.

"You will find the same mark on the other one," Q'enti said, "and if I'm not mistaken on Asto, too."

Atoco checked Lizard-eyes and nodded, then went to the hut. He came back to announce, "My Lady, Asto has the six dots on his right shoulder, but not the red circle."

Q'enti shrugged. "He must be a novice, then."

Atoco looked mystified. "My Lady, how did you know?"

Q'enti gave him a devious look but remained silent. It didn't surprise me—if anyone would know about the secret marks of assassins it would be Q'enti. Atoco appeared frustrated but pressed, "Then who are they, Lady?"

Q'enti snapped, "They are condor priests, you fool." Atoco shrunk back. "As I suspected, Asto was also, or at least an initiate, and he stole one of the cat's-eye emeralds surrounding the Eye of the Condor." She gestured to the bodies. "These two were sent to recover the emerald and silence Asto. The condor priests don't like people knowing about them. They are a secret brotherhood—trained assassins, all of them—and they guard the Great Emerald in their hidden temple." Q'enti looked at me. "Obviously Asto knew where the temple is, and he told you, didn't he?"

"I don't know what you're talking about, Q'enti."

"Oh, don't you, Qori dear? Well, I know how to help your memory. But first . . . ." She signaled Atoco who leapt to her side like a dog eager to please. "Separate them," she ordered with a wave at us, "and put them over by the hut. Then search these bodies."

Atoco gestured to four of his men who tied our hands at our backs, and marched us to opposite sides of the driftwood hut. Two of them shoved me to my knees and stood behind. A breeze brought Asto's stink seeping through the hut walls. I couldn't see Qhari, but I watched as the men pulled the feathered darts from Lizard-eyes and Nose-ring, and then set about stripping and searching them while Q'enti looked on. What does she expect to find, I wondered?

Q'enti knelt beside Lizard-eyes, and the men crowded around her blocking my view. A murmur rose, and a man quickly passed a knife into the center of the group. Silence followed. I shifted to see what it was they peered at so intently, but my guards cuffed me back into position.

The gathering broke up with Atoco ordering his men back into line. They went reluctantly, walking like those who have witnessed a miracle. Q'enti rose, clutching something. She held it in front of her, opening her fingers to stare into her cupped hand. The twinge in her left eye flickered uncontrollably. Atoco tried to say something but she waved him off. He bowed and backed away.

I watched impatiently. Whatever it was that fascinated Q'enti would not be good. She stood alone for some time and this also worried me.

At last Q'enti shook herself and smiled contentedly. Her hand slipped into her shoulder bag and came away empty. She gestured for Atoco, and the two whispered together. Atoco bobbed his head, then paused in surprise, and nodded vigorously again. He signaled our guards.

Qhari gave me a questioning look as we were hauled forth again. I shrugged in reply. He hadn't seen what transpired, and though I had I still couldn't guess what Q'enti planned for us. The guards jerked us to a halt in front of Atoco. He snickered while he checked our bindings to make sure they were tight, then with a flourish stepped aside and presented us to Q'enti. What worried me more than Atoco's snickering was Q'enti's friendly expression. She was as composed as if welcoming us to a reception.

"Now then, my dear," she said, "you were going to relate what Asto told you about the Great Emerald, and its temple."

I stalled. "You really believe the Eye of the Condor exists?"

Q'enti sighed and looked at me as if I was a petulant child. "You know about the cat's-eye emerald Asto brought, you fought two condor priests, and you've seen what condor dust can do. How can there be any doubt?"

"Condor dust?" Qhari said. "You mean the poison?"

"Of course," Q'enti replied, "what did you think Asto was dying from? He must have been poisoned when he stole the cat's-eye emerald. It's not a pleasant way to die, is it Qhari?"

Qhari tightened his lips and looked away.

That part of the legend was the worst—the insidious condor dust that only the condor priests knew how to make, and they alone had the antidote.

If the Great Emerald does exist, I thought, then Q'enti can chase after it if she wants. All I want is to get Qhari away from here.

"Now then," Q'enti said pleasantly, "I think we will place Qhari over there by the cliff and see if Atoco's men can hit a target at that range. No, Qori? That doesn't please you? Well then, what do you suggest?"

Qhari's mouth opened but I silenced him with a look. "If I tell you what Asto said, will you let us go?"

"Of course, my dear."

I knew she lied, but what could I do? I wished she would stop calling me 'my dear.' It made her appear the worldly elder, yet she was younger than me.

"Asto died before we could ask him about the Great Emerald and its temple, but he has a brother in Guayas named Pisar. He said Pisar knows."

In truth, I wasn't sure Pisar knew about the Great Emerald, it wasn't clear from Asto's ramblings, but it was what Q'enti wanted to hear.

Q'enti nodded at me, then stepped up to Qhari and peered into his face.

Qhari said, "It's true."

Q'enti studied him a moment longer, then, satisfied, she turned away.

I breathed a sigh of relief. "Can we go now?"

"Go?" Q'enti said. "Oh yes, I promised you could go, but I didn't say where. Qhari is going with Captain Atoco to a safe place, and you, Qori, are coming with me to . . . did you say Guayas? That's a hot land in the north, I believe. Well, it should be a delightful trip."

"What?" Qhari said for both of us.

Q'enti welcomed the shock on our faces. "I decided long ago you were the one, Qori dear, probably the only one who could find the Condor Temple. Don't look so sour, it is a compliment. Who else is so adept at this kind of work? All you needed was the proper motivation, and this man-woman brother of yours provided that. Don't worry, Qhari will be safe as long as you guide me to the temple, and return me to Cuzco with my prize, of course."

At last I understood. Indeed, how else could she lure me out of exile and force me to do her bidding? She used Qhari as bait and I was the catch floundering at her feet, helpless against her wishes.

Qhari said to her, "But coming after Asto was my idea. How did you know to follow me? And how did you know Qori would come?"

Q'enti smirked. "Some well placed information about emeralds was all it took to get you moving, and of course I had you watched."

Qhari lowered his head.

"Don't worry, Qhari," Q'enti said, "everyone in Cuzco knew about the cat's-eye emerald from Chincha, I just made sure you understood it was proof the Eye of the Condor exists, and with the Great Emerald you could have your sister pardoned. I admit you took the bait faster than I anticipated, but I caught up with you. As for your dear sister, I knew that spy Zapana would tell her about your adventures, and I let it be known that I too was bound for Chincha. Qori reached the right conclusion."

Qhari said nothing. He couldn't look at me.

Q'enti settled her gaze on me. "Don't blame your brother, Qori dear. I had some of my friends discuss the possibilities of the Great Emerald within his hearing." She grinned at Qhari. "Did you think you were eavesdropping on that conversation? It was arranged for your benefit."

Qhari looked miserable. I felt sorry for him but my mind already spun ahead. Take her to Guayas, I thought. There will be ample opportunity to lose her and double back to discover Qhari's whereabouts. Atoco isn't that clever. I'll find a way to free Qhari.

"Poor Qhari," Q'enti purred, "he's been made to look such a fool, but never mind, Qhari, I promise you your sister will be back within eight months to free you." Q'enti flashed wild eyes at me, and then stepped close to Qhari. "Here is a token of my promise," she said, "look at this." She withdrew Nose-ring's amulet from her shoulder bag and held it up to Qhari. "Look, isn't it beautiful?" Qhari glanced at the feathered amulet and turned his head to give me a puzzled frown. When he looked away Q'enti brushed the feathers aside to reveal a tiny packet, neatly cut open. She expelled a puff of breath. A fine powder gusted into Qhari's face. He jerked his head back and coughed. Q'enti snapped her hand closed and turned to me triumphantly.

"What have you done?" I demanded.

"Condor dust," she said prettily.

Qhari retched.

"Too late, Qhari," she said. "It's already in you."

"You're lying, Q'enti," I said for Qhari's sake. "That wasn't condor dust, it was just ashes."

Q'enti kept her hostess smile and gestured to the bodies of Lizard-eyes and Nose-ring. "And you think those two would carry ashes in their amulets? Well, in eight months you will know. It takes that long for the poison to kill. Qhari won't notice anything for a while, but then his insides will start to rot. Have you ever seen a person rotting from the inside out, my dear? Oh, yes you have, Asto." She turned to the hut where Asto's grotesque body lay and heaved a sigh. "That's what poor Qhari will look like if you don't bring him the antidote, and it can only be found at the Condor Temple. I doubt the condor priests will be happy to see us, but you will think of something, Qori dear, you always do."

Qhari turned frantic eyes on me and tried to speak, but there was nothing to say. He hung his head.

"How do you know about these things?" I said to Q'enti, using a tone that made it a challenge. I still couldn't believe any of it was true.

"You mean about the condor priests and their poison?" Q'enti couldn't resist sharing the tale. She thought it made her look terribly clever, but to me it only revealed the depths of her depravity. "Jungle savages killed a condor priest long ago. They found his tattoo and amulet, and passed on these discoveries before the condor brotherhood destroyed them. The amulet changed hands, and eventually a sorcerer smuggled it to me." She paused for a sly smile. "He traded everything he had for it, and he exchanged the amulet for one night with me. Foolish man. I wasn't certain the single dose of powder it contained was condor dust, so I tried it on him the next morning. Eight months later he looked like Asto. I knew then the legend was real, but how to track a wisp of smoke? That's when I thought of you, Qori dear. You should have accepted the quest when it was first offered. I planned to have you followed to the Condor Temple, but you were too stubborn to accept. I nearly lost you to the crowd.

"Anyway, you were tucked away safely in Wanaku, and when the cat's-eye emerald appeared in Cuzco I knew the first link to the temple had finally surfaced. The only question was how to motivate you." She smiled at Qhari, and glanced at the bodies of Lizard-eyes and Nose-ring. "But it turned out even better than I expected. These two brought more poison dust. Now you must reach the Condor Temple to find the antidote. And since there is no other way of saving your precious brother, I think I will come with you. I'm sure you will take good care of me while Captain Atoco entertains Qhari."

Q'enti burst into hysterical laughter. Atoco and his men, who stood back and heard none of this, looked at one another and grinned uneasily.

Q'enti waved Atoco forward. He came with four of his personal guards; they surrounded Qhari. "Qhari Puma is never to be out of your sight," Atoco said to his men, "and if anything happens to him your lives are forfeit." The guards nodded grimly. They looked more like cutthroats than soldiers.

"Where are you taking him?" I demanded.

Atoco stepped so close he pressed against me. He looked down with a sneer and stale breath. "Where you'll never find him. You better bring Lady Q'enti back safely, or Qhari is mine."

Q'enti spoke to Atoco but watched me out of the corners of her eyes: "If I don't return with the Great Emerald, Captain Atoco, or if I fail to return at all, let the poison do its work on Qhari Puma before you skin him." Then she said to me, "But don't worry, Qori dear, I'm sure we will be back with the antidote, and the emerald, even before the poison starts festering inside him. Won't we?"

Qhari and I had only moments alone before Atoco led him away. Qhari whispered, "Don't worry, I'll escape." He was serious, but I knew Atoco and his thugs wouldn't let that happen.

"I know you will try, Qhari, but Atoco is a bully so don't provoke him. It's more important for you to keep your strength up. I'll be back with the antidote before . . . ." My words trailed off but our eyes remained locked.

"You will find the Eye of the Condor," Qhari said, "and I know you will return with the antidote, if you can. But Qori, promise me that no matter what happens you won't let Q'enti use the Great

Emerald for her purposes. It's for you. Find the emerald and you'll find what you've lost."

"You, get moving," Atoco shouted, grabbing Qhari's arm and shoving him forward. Before the guards closed around him Qhari threw me a brave smile, but it was the love in my brother's eyes that stayed with me.

IX

Of a Voyage to Distant Shores, and of that which befell the Mariners in the great Ocean Seas.

The giant sail fluttered and snapped, then caught full. Sailors dashed to reset the daggerboards trailing beneath the raft, and the helmsman leaned into the steering oar. Our course steadied. The captain, until that moment shouting orders laced with obscenities, relaxed and exchanged a smile with his crew. I found myself grinning too, sharing the exaltation of gliding silently over the water propelled by wind and sail like a bird with outstretched wings. To the east a dark line separating sea from sky marked the coastline slipping by.

From inside the cabin Q'enti shouted, "Captain, we're too far from shore." She announced this several times a day since our voyage began. As always the captain called back, "Fear not, Lady, we need to be beyond the breakers, and out here we catch the fair winds, but I will steer closer-in soon." He exchanged a shake of the head with a nearby crewman. They hadn't wanted to bring us, and made Q'enti pay dearly for the passage.

"Choque," Q'enti shouted, using my assumed name, "fetch me some water." She traveled as Lady Orma, and I as her maid. The water jar stood beside her in the cabin, but she never missed an opportunity to have me wait on her. And since it was unseemly for a lady to consort with common sailors she stayed inside day and night, where she became bored with herself and found excuses to summon me. This time I ignored her and fastened my gaze on the sparkling water surging at the bow, luxuriating in the motion and fresh wind at my back. Qhari would love this, I thought.

Q'enti's shrill voice sounded again. "Choque! Where's my water? I'm still waiting."

The sailors shook their heads in sympathy as I rose to do my lady's bidding. They were all natives of the Chincha Valley, from where they took the coastal trade to the northern reaches of the Empire. We Incas are not sailors or traders, but we allow our subject peoples their customs, especially when the Empire benefits. The Chincha merchants were granted royal patronage when they joined the Empire, which worked to their advantage and ours. The men around me wore light cotton tunics, and bright turbans over shoulder-length hair.

"Where are we now?" Q'enti demanded as I entered. It was an oft-repeated question.

I knelt to dip a gourd of water for her. "The captain says we'll reach Tumbez tonight if this wind holds. That's as far north as he will take us."

Q'enti accepted the gourd, sipped, and handed it back with one of her practiced smiles. "I'm sure he will change his mind and take us all the way to Guayas. Have you seen the way he looks at me?"

Every man looked at her that way, they couldn't help themselves. "You haven't heard the men talking," I said. "Nothing will make them sail beyond Tumbez."

To the north of Tumbez lay hostile territory; the Island of Puná—stronghold of the feared pirates, and then the coastlands of the equally despised Wankavilcas with their capital at Guayas, where we hoped to find Asto's brother, Pisar. These coastal tribes had not been conquered yet, and for now remained outside the Empire. According to all reports their lowlands were not fit for civilized mountain people, and the natives, known for their ferocity, practiced barbarous customs. Our sailors amused themselves in the evenings horrifying one another with tales of these savage northern tribes.

"I don't have to convince the whole crew to sail to Guayas, only the captain," Q'enti said, "though there are some handsome ones among the crew, too . . . and you can look after the rest."

"Not me, Q'enti. If you want to whore for the crew you can, but leave me out of it."

Q'enti's eyes sparkled. "You are supposed to call me Lady Orma," she said. "Besides, if the lady handles the captain, it's only fair that her maid looks after the crew."

She enjoyed taunting me like this since we left Chincha, where she had negotiated our passage with emeralds found on the bodies of Lizard-eyes and Nose-ring. She still hadn't told me what she intended to do with the Eye of the Condor if we found it, but she didn't want anyone to know she was after it, and I certainly wasn't eager to have Inca officials know my whereabouts. So she became Lady Orma and announced I was her maid. It was a good plan, I admit, and I had often played a Qolla maid named Choque as one of my disguises, but I never served so demanding and degraded a mistress.

"No," I told her. "I will do what I have to for my brother, but I won't whore for you."

Her high-pitched laughter followed me back on deck.

The sailors were busy with the daggerboards again, lifting and lowering these planks to the captain's sharp commands. The wind stiffened keeping the great sail stretched full, but now it nudged us farther from shore. The daggerboards, reset and trailing beneath the raft, steadied our course northward.

A gull landed on the crossbar at the top of the mast, and others soon followed. I liked to think they were the same birds that joined us at Chincha, but they probably worked in relays with their cousins, each flock following us for a day or two before returning to their stretch of coast, yielding their place to new sentinels. Whenever the cooking brazier sent up smoke they landed searching for scraps. Now they rested on their perch facing the wind, allowing the swells to guide them into sleep under a warm sun. The wind chased away the clouds leaving the sun in a blue sky, and the water, now emerald green, broke white at the bow. I sat on the edge of the second deck and let the cold water tickle my feet.

Our raft was of medium size for the sea trade; it carried a crew of fourteen with Q'enti and me as the only passengers, but the big vessels transport fifty people and twice the cargo. The native Lord of Chincha kept a fleet of these ocean-going rafts built from long, sturdy canes tied securely in bundles as thick as timbers.

The main deck of our raft had nine cane timbers. The center bundle is the longest, and the others are cut back to form a wedge-shaped bow, but they are squared at the stern. On this sit smaller bundles like logs set across the length, which support a second deck of poles with a single, low cabin constructed of rush mats. Q'enti insisted on partitioning one corner for privacy. The cane timbers of the first deck are awash—hence this is called the wet deck—but the second level with its cabin is above the water—the dry deck. The single mast at the bow is fashioned from two poles that converge from the sides to a point, where a crossbar holds the top of the cotton sail.

Our cargo included bales of wool and cotton clothing, some bronze mirrors, and beads of turquoise and crystal, but the principal wealth was gold and silver diadems, pectorals, belts, bracelets, tweezers, tiny bells, and stacks of copper and tin ingots. All this would be traded for one main commodity—the sacred red shell of the thorny oyster, which only lives in deep northern waters. Thorny oyster shell is the favored nourishment of the gods, and required for all proper sacrifices and dedications. It is even powdered for medicines.

The captain noticed me sitting on the edge of the dry deck letting the water surge over my feet. He paused in his duties and went down on one knee beside me. I smiled up at him and remarked, "A fair wind, Captain." A good wind always had the sailors sharing quiet smiles, but his brow creased.

"A fair wind indeed," he replied, "but a bit strong." He sounded like a farmer who, no matter how fine the weather, always worried about too much or too little sun or rain. "Keep an eye on that for me," he said pointing to the southwest. It was a spot of gray surrounded by dark blue sky—another squall, but it would probably miss us, I decided. Still, the captain always worried. It pleased me that he found these lookout duties for me to pass the time.

We had become friends, in part because I spoke his coastal dialect, and because I trusted him with the raft, shared the rough food and accommodations, and never complained. I think he also felt sorry for me being Q'enti's maid. He was a short, thick man, with deep lines around his eyes from years of peering over the horizon, and streaks of gray in his hair. He wore a scraggly moustache and allowed long hairs to sprout on his chin. Inca men pluck their facial hair with tweezers, but among other nations those who can often grow whiskers. Aside from sailing and trading, the captain's conversation always included his wife and children back in Chincha. He spoke of them at great length in the evenings, so that by now, with the voyage almost complete, I felt I had known his family for years.

The captain had taken to carrying a bag of coca leaves at his hip. He now withdrew a few leaves, blew over them as an offering to the weather god, muttered a prayer, and then added them to the wad already bulging his cheek.

"How are those gums of yours today, Captain?" I inquired.

"Oh, much better, thank you Choque. They don't trouble me at all anymore. It's like having a new mouth. I've never felt better." I had recommended the leaves a few days earlier. He gave me a warm smile edged with green dribble, and returned his gaze to the horizon.

Soon after our voyage began I had noticed the captain constantly rubbing his cheeks. I knew he was in pain, and though I couldn't reveal myself as a healer, neither could I stand by and watch him suffer.

"Sore mouth, Captain?"

He had frowned at me. "Yes, it's come again, but nothing to worry about."

"Have you tried chewing coca leaves to ease your pain?" I asked.

"Coca? Only the nobles use it where I come from. Will it help with this confounded mouth of mine?"

"Most certainly, Captain. Lady Orma has a bag of coca. Would you care to try it?"

Q'enti was furious when I came to liberate her coca leaves. "I am saving that for an offering, or a bribe," she said. "I won't have it wasted on some raft captain."

"And what are you going to do about it? Have me thrown over the side? Who'd look after you then?"

I took the bag and left her fuming in the cabin.

The leaves of the coca bush have a numbing effect, and it pleased me to be able to relieve the captain's suffering. He was ever grateful. I looked at him now, kneeling beside me with eyes scanning the distance, the wind teasing his hair where it streamed from under his blue turban. He was content and in his element. I saw his wife bid him farewell on the beach at Chincha. She was a plain woman, short and plump. Why is the captain so devoted to her? I wondered.

"Captain," a sailor called from the bow. I looked to see the sail twisting, pushing us farther from shore, but the captain was already on his feet gesturing to the steersman.

"Thank you again for the coca, Choque," he said patting my shoulder, and then he hurried off shouting orders.

My thoughts wandered. When I first learned healing ways I was fascinated only with the herbs and their mixtures, but soon I came to savor the knowledge, knowing how to recognize ailments and administer cures. There is the power of knowing, I thought, and the hopeful looks of the patients when they place themselves in my hands, trusting me, and always so grateful for every small thing. But in truth, it is the patients themselves that draw me, not the medicines or the knowledge or the gratitude, but the people. How many times have I watched them face their agonies—the old ones with their pain-wracked joints, the fevered and wasted ones, the lame and mangled and blind—all those whom life has forsaken, yet they don't forsake life. They smile and jest, and in their eyes I see the spirit shine, even in sightless eyes. I was once physician to the Empress, but without that title, without that patient, am I any less a healer? Is there less satisfaction in relieving a Chincha sailor than an Inca noble?

My teacher said that when she took an interest in healing they tried to discourage her. They said she was too sensitive to treat the sick. But she came to understand this is the greatest asset of any healer. "It is the most important part of the knowing," she said, "for without it there is no compassion, and without compassion we are no more than the beasts of the fields."

"You'd best move into the cabin, Choque," a sailor called, "this one is starting to blow."

I realized I was sitting with my shawl drawn tight, and the wind blew strands of my hair straight out before my face. Water sloshed between the cane timbers of the wet deck, spurting up as the raft came down in the swells. I looked to the southwest; the spot of gray had grown to a black wall and the entire horizon was dark blue. The birds left their perch atop the mast, and the mariners struggled to lower the sail.

Q'enti yelled from the cabin, "Choque! Choque, come here."

Inside, the night watch lay rolled in their blankets trying to sleep. I stepped over them, and nodded to the old helmsman who sat with his back against the cabin wall; he was second in command—the captain's mate. He flashed the broad smile that frequented his weathered face, displaying all six of his teeth, then returned to carving a bone harpoon.

"What took you so long?" Q'enti said as I entered our room. It was a cubicle formed by hanging mats to block a corner at the back. Q'enti sat with a blanket draped over her shoulders, and her baskets and trunks piled at her elbows. There was barely space for the two of us to lie down at night.

Q'enti twitched her head at the cabin wall. "What's going on out there," she demanded. "It's too windy and a chill has come up. What's the captain going to do about it?" She sounded stern but there was apprehension in her eyes.

"Did you call me in here to complain about the wind and sea? Tell the weather gods what you want, the captain is only their minion like the rest of us mortals."

Q'enti flared. "Who are you to speak to me this way? You forget you are not 'Lady' anymore. You have no titles, no riches . . . no dignity."

I showed her my back, and returned to the main cabin.

"Your mistress is uneasy," the old mate remarked, setting his harpoon carving in his lap. "Mother Ocean is deep and sometimes She's angry, but Lady Orma should be praying to the Lord of the Wind now." He raised his eyes to the ceiling, and then smiled at me. "It's just a squall. Come, sit," he said patting the floor beside him, "and I will tell you of the strangest wedding I ever saw."

The wind whistled against the cabin, finding hollows and cracks unnoticed in fair weather. I pulled a blanket over my knees and bundled beside him. It was good to have something to take my mind off Q'enti and the storm.

"It was on the Island of Puná," he began. I gave him a puzzled look. "Yes indeed," he said, "the captain and I used to land there long ago. It was dangerous because when the Punáe aren't trading they're warring with their neighbors on the mainland, or pirating any raft unfortunate enough to be caught in their waters. But we had our own truce to trade directly for the shells of the thorny oyster, and they welcomed our cargo.

"You don't want to see any Punáe these days, let alone get near their island. Not since their new chief Tumbala decided to war on all foreigners, which for them is anyone who is not Punáe. Our rafts used to go even farther north, but that's a dangerous run now. The captain and I content ourselves with sailing to Tumbez, the last anchorage under Inca control.

"But in the days of which I speak the chances of leaving Puná Island with your life and a treasure of shells were good . . . well, at least reasonable; the Punáe are a savage and unpredictable people at the best of times, and I know of other peaceful traders who were invited to feasts, unaware that they themselves were the feast. But the captain and I were lucky."

The cabin lurched down, almost sending me sliding across the floor. Those sleeping around us rolled to the front wall, groaned, then pulled their blankets tighter and wiggled themselves into a row aligned with the rise and fall of the swells. I licked my lips tasting salt, and noticed the walls were damp. The old mate chuckled and patted my leg.

"Now it so happened," he continued, "that on one voyage we came ashore just when a chief's daughter was being married, and we were invited to the feast. Not wishing to offend them the captain and I attended, leaving orders for the raft to sail if we weren't back by morning. The Punáe have seven towns, each with its own chief under the great chief of the whole island. We were escorted to one of these where our hosts greeted us in all their barbarous splendor."

The raft tilted again, this time nearly dumping me in the mate's lap, and then the bow came down with a crash, pitching me the other way. The rigging creaked as if ropes were ready to snap, and the wind howled with such determination I thought it would blow our cabin off the deck. Net bags suspended from the ceiling swung wildly. The old mate chuckled. "A good ride, isn't it?" he said patting my leg again.

"Choque!" Q'enti shouted.

"There's nothing I can do for you, Lady Orma," I called back. "Try to get some sleep." I shared a nod with the mate. "And what happened at the wedding?" I said.

"The feast was lavish, though I've never been fond of lizard, but there were fish roasting, vats of maize gruel, platters of squash and beans, and every fruit of that land. There was also a cauldron of stew, but from their talk I couldn't tell whether a female captive made it, or she was in it, so I didn't have any. But their brew was good, a strange drink made from manioc, and potent."

"You speak Punáe?" I asked, raising my voice over the droning wind and leaning closer to him.

"A few polite phrases and some banter for trade. In truth, they are the same words we use with the Punáe's neighbors on the mainland, the Wankavilcas and Mantas. They claim to speak different languages but they all understand each other, and they have much the same customs. They trade with the Kañari in the mountains, so we use a few words of that language, too.

"Anyway, the bride was led out of her father's house and paraded before the important male guests, including the captain and me. She was a pretty thing for a Punáe, perhaps fifteen, dressed like the other women in a long gown that covered her from neck to ankle, and layered with strings of gold and silver beads. In spite of their savagery, or perhaps because of it, the Punáe are a wealthy people," he said turning to give me a meaningful look. "They wear gold nose pendants that cover their mouths. By the balls of Father Wind I say it's true! And gold and silver for their face studs, too."

Civilized people do not wear nose pendants or face studs, but savages often pierce their cheeks and chins to fasten adornments.

Again the bow crashed under, throwing me on my side, then tilted upward crowding me against the mate.

"Now this is the strangest part," he said, ignoring the pitch as if we sat under a tree. "The groom, the son of a chief from another town, took his bride by the hand and led her into a hut, and the rest of us were bid to follow. Once all the men were assembled inside, the groom bowed to her and the guests, and departed. The bride grinned at her audience, and then, quick as a clam fart, she dropped her clothes! She spread herself on a blanket and urged the groom's father to attend her.

"Well, you can imagine, the captain and I didn't know which way to look, but we were not allowed to leave. When the groom's father was done, his brothers and cousins took their turns, and then the principal men of the village."

My hands went to my mouth. "The poor thing. She was raped by all those men?"

"Not raped, she was laughing and encouraging them, though she did look a bit tired after awhile. It's their custom that all should enjoy the bride before her marriage. They say this is so everyone's curiosity is satisfied beforehand—hers and the men around her—so there's less cause for infidelity later."

"But you said she was only a girl." I had to repeat myself, shouting in his ear over the gale, before he nodded in understanding.

"She was young, but from the time they are old enough all their girls have many lovers, and they're encouraged to do so because it's considered natural. So I expect the bride was accomplished at such things, indeed, from the way she performed I can say it with certainty."

"But all those men?"

143

"The Punáe women have many ways of pleasing their men, and this bride was no different. Some she took in her mouth, and some mounted her on top, and others from behind, using both entrances."

"Say you so?"

"Indeed, the Punáe and their neighbors are much addicted to sodomy. The men not only do it with their women, but with each other. It's true, I've seen it. The Wankavilcas are even worse, if that's possible."

"But you didn't . . . I mean, with this Punáe bride?"

He smirked. "We were guests, and we didn't want to end up in their stew. The captain managed to get out of it, but only if I did the honors. I assure you I did us both proud."

The cabin floor slanted again and a net bag broke loose from the rafters, tumbling among the men. No one pretended to sleep now. They grumbled and rose, my storyteller with them. A blast of wind tore open a section of cabin wall and the raft lurched sending the men to their knees. "Stay here," the mate said to me sternly, then hurried on deck with the others.

"Choque!" Q'enti shouted. This time I made my way to the back corner, though I dared not stand so I crept on hands and knees. The cabin was thick with salty wetness and my clothes were damp. Q'enti knelt upright in the cramped quarters holding on to her belongings. When I entered she just stared at me, eyes wide and frantic. I crawled to her and she flung her arms around me.

"What's happening outside?" she whined. "Are we sinking?"

A wave crashed against the cabin sending cold water across the floor.

"My things will be ruined." Q'enti said. "Do something."

There was nothing to be done, and there the two of us sat for an endless time, soaked and thrown from side to side while the cabin creaked against the roar of wind and sea. The lashings on Q'enti's baskets came loose, and soon their finery spilled over us. Q'enti traveled with a wardrobe fit for court. A section of roof gave way, falling like an awning to press us against the wall. Q'enti shrieked and clung tighter. I managed to pull us out from behind the collapsed roof, only to find our partitions down and the main cabin awash. Bales of cloth also broke free and tumbled from one side of the cabin to the other, battering the sagging walls.

"Stay here," I shouted in Q'enti's ear, "I'll go for help."

"No, don't leave me," Q'enti cried.

"I must go," I said. "I can't retie the bales by myself, and they're going to destroy what is left of the cabin." I pried at the fingers clutching my shoulders.

A calm came over her. "Remember, Qori, if anything happens to me your brother is dead." She released her grip.

X

In which takes place a Terrible Misfortune, Creatures of the Deep appear, and a Perilous Situation becomes worse.

I made my way to the deck. Outside where it should have been light the sky crouched in angry blue without trace of cloud or sun. The mast poles had snapped, and men with ropes tied at their waists struggled in boiling water on the wet deck trying to cut them free. Others clung to the cabin on the second deck cinching cargo lashings. Everyone seemed to be waving for help. I glimpsed the captain with the old mate at his side, the two working frantically on the bindings holding the raft together.

Wind shrieked across the water hurling spray, and waves like snow-crested mountains towered in front and behind. The raft lifted and spun just before a wave crashed over us. I thought I would lose my grip and be washed away, but then I found myself sputtering and gasping for air once more. I raised my head and looked around—there were fewer sailors than before—and then I heard a scream from behind as the cabin collapsed.

I scrambled over the tangle of matting and poles, but before I could reach Q'enti another wave hit, washing the remains of the cabin over the side.

The raft swung broadside to the wind. With mast and daggerboards gone we drifted helpless before the storm. Another wall of foaming green lifted the raft on its side. I clung to the second deck and for an instant we pitched so steeply only naked sea lay below me. We crested and the vessel crashed to the other side, which had me clinging to the deck like an outstretched lizard, my legs above my head. The raft slid down the back of the wave against a churning wash that threatened to rip my fingers from their hold. When we slammed into the trough the bindings of the upper deck broke, and it slid half over the edge of the lower deck to hang precariously in the angry water.

With a moment's respite between waves I looked up, sputtering and wiping the salt sting from my eyes. Baskets and trunks littered the water. A few sailors still hugged the lower deck, having abandoned all thought of saving anything but themselves. The wind made a swarming, hissing sound above its base roar, drowning any calls for help. Close beside us floated a shapeless tangle of debris—the remains of the cabin. With a start I realized Q'enti was in the cabin when it washed over the side, and if I lost her I'd lose Qhari. Without further thought I dove into the sea.

I couldn't swim in my dress so I wiggled out of it. Coming up for breath I looked around, but then another wave came down sending me tumbling through its depths. Again I surfaced, this time not sure in which direction I faced, but then I saw the remains of the cabin and swam for it. "Q'enti," I shouted, but there was no reply over the howling wind. I thrashed in the debris of matting and poles, calling her name, and then my legs kicked something soft below the water. I dove, grasped the body, and pulled it to the surface. It was a drowned sailor. Trailing ropes entangled me as another wave drove my head beneath the surface. When I emerged the raft was no longer in sight. "Q'enti!" I screamed, "Q'enti, where are you?"

With the next wave the broken mass of the cabin came apart sending tangled clumps drifting in all directions. I swam frantically from one to another searching, but there was no sign of her. Then a swell lifted me high and I spied one more lone tangle. A log of bound canes floated by, and throwing one arm around it I kicked my feet and paddled with my free hand, gaining gradually on this last hope. If Q'enti wasn't clinging to it then she had already drowned.

Another giant wave lifted me, but my log kept me afloat—one of the smaller ones from between decks, which meant the upper level of the raft was now torn and scattered. I wondered if the captain and the old mate still clung to the lower deck, or whether it, too, had broken-up. But they were somewhere far behind me now; I couldn't help them, nor could they help me. If Q'enti isn't alive, I thought, I might as well join the others in their sleep with the fishes.

With the last of my strength I reached the floating mass—a few poles and some matting tangled in rope. "Q'enti," I yelled. No reply. Then I glimpsed an arm thrown over a spar and a mass of black hair billowing beside it. "Q'enti!" I dove and came up under her, pushing her head from the water. She was a limp, dead weight, still clad in her dress. "Q'enti," I shouted in her ear, but she made no response. I draped her over the matting, then retrieved my cane log and bound it to the debris. Swimming alongside, I shoved her legs on to this tiny platform so that she was out of the water and lying on her stomach. I pounded her back and screamed, "Q'enti, wake up, don't die on me!"

She made a faint cough. I pounded harder. Her body convulsed and she spewed seawater, then wretched and gasped. Her eyes didn't open, but she breathed.

Still bobbing beside this makeshift raft—there was only room on it for one—I grabbed a trailing rope and bound Q'enti's prostrate form to the wreckage.

Soon after I tied Q'enti to our raft the storm moved on, leaving us rocking gently on the swells, and alone beneath a hazy night sky. I couldn't see anything in the dark, and I had no strength to call out, so I draped my arms over a spar and rested my head while my body floated. Q'enti opened her eyes once, looked at herself stretched out on the tiny platform, then at me submerged to my shoulders, gave me a withering look, and pretended to sleep. She probably did sleep. I spent the night becoming increasingly waterlogged, and jerking my head each time I felt myself slipping.

Dawn presented an ocean as flat as a pond. When the morning haze burnt off I saw bits of wreckage scattered widely around us, but no sign of other survivors. Sea birds called overhead, occasionally landing on flotsam in the distance.

It was impossible to know where we were. The storm hit not far from Tumbez, but it had driven us away from the coast and northward for a long time before the raft broke apart, and after that Q'enti and I drifted all night.

At first I thought the distant movement in the water was another survivor and I called out, but then with a shiver I realized it was a fin. The shark nosed a basket floating on the morning calm, and then three smaller fins joined it. The basket vanished.

A breeze came up and the sharks, eager for more breakfast, cruised toward the next morsel—our raft. I watched their fins slicing the water.

Q'enti sat up and stretched. With her hair matted, dress tattered, and cosmetics washed away she looked miserable, but she still wore her wide belt, and she was dry. The scar on her cheek showed purple. "I'm hungry," she announced as if expecting me to produce her breakfast.

"So are they," I said.

"Who?"

I nodded over my shoulder at the advancing fins.

"What's that in the water?" Q'enti asked.

"They are called sharks."

"Sharks? The big fish that eat people? I heard the sailors speak of them."

"Indeed, very interesting, but I think it's time I joined you on the raft."

"There isn't space for two of us," Q'enti said flatly.

"There is now," I replied heaving myself up.

She swatted at me. "No, get back in the water."

The raft did sink lower with my weight so we were just at water level, but with both of us kneeling upright, pressed face to face clutching each others shoulders, at least no part of us dangled in the water. Still, it was a wobbly perch, and if either of us shifted we would both go over.

"This is no good," Q'enti said, "there isn't enough room. I can't move."

"Then why don't you go for a swim?"

"What? With those big fish—"

Her words ended in a gasp when the raft suddenly rocked. We clung to each other for balance. A fin rose to the surface, so close I could touch it. It was the big shark floating lazily beside us like a fat log, her gray body the length of our raft. A dull round eye studied us, and then she rolled on her side and vanished. Three more fins circled close by.

"Qori," Q'enti said with breath sucked in, "do something."

Another shark butted the raft, and from below two more bumps quickly followed. We rocked from side to side. I struggled for balance in our kneeling position, but Q'enti stayed glued to me and I found myself trying to shift both of us.

"Q'enti, move your knees apart to steady yourself."

"Why are they doing this to me?" she whined.

"Calm yourself. They don't know you are Lady Q'enti, or that you are rich, and they don't even care that you're beautiful. To them, you are just breakfast."

I shouldn't have taunted her for she let out a long wail and squeezed me tighter, if that was possible. She trembled, shaking us both, and making our perch even more unstable. But in this hopeless situation I found a wink of understanding, and it made me smile. The sharks didn't care; my flesh was the same as Q'enti's in spite of her wealth and honors. Stripped bare we are all equal.

"Oh no," Q'enti gasped, "the big one is coming again."

I glanced over my shoulder. A huge gray fin shot straight toward us. "Hold on, Q'enti," I urged. "Just keep your balance and stay on the raft."

"Oh . . . Oh . . . Oh!" she whimpered, each cry coming louder in anticipation of the crash. I braced myself.

This time the creature did not ram us; it put its head under the raft and jerked up lifting my end out of the water. Q'enti screamed and, finding herself tilted backward, tried to climb over me. "Stop, Q'enti, don't!"

When my end of the raft came down Q'enti had her knees around my waist and the rest of her over my shoulder, so we both continued backwards into the water.

I surfaced, and a gray body slipped by, pushing me to the side. It vanished with a swish of its tail. Q'enti thrashed wildly beside me, trying to scream but only swallowing seawater. She couldn't swim, and she was too terrified to think. I grabbed her and she pushed me away in terror. "Q'enti, hold on to me and I'll get you to the raft." Another long body glided past my legs. I turned my back to Q'enti and shouted, "Grasp my shoulders." She did, but she tried to climb on top of me again, forcing my head under water.

I managed to get my face to the surface, though Q'enti had her knees drawn up against my back and seemed to be trying to choke me and tear my head off at the same time. The raft moved away, and between it and us a fin sailed past.

There was no sense trying to calm Q'enti, even if I had the breath to speak, but my arms and legs were free so I paddled us toward the raft. The small sharks came by to examine us again. Their skin is like sand, so rough it can scrape off human skin and leave bloody wounds. If either of us bled the sharks would attack.

We reached the raft and I told Q'enti to climb on. She threw her upper body over the matting, pushing me under in the doing. When I surfaced free of her weight she still kicked her legs in the water. "Q'enti, pull yourself up," I shouted.

"I can't, I can't," she wailed.

Another close pass from a shark was all I needed to propel me on to the raft. I grabbed Q'enti to pull her legs from the water when I saw the great fin coming at her. I heaved with all my strength, and in that instant two massive jaws with ragged teeth in a pink cavern come out of the water.

Q'enti lay on top of me staring into my face. Neither of us moved. I couldn't tell from the look of shock whether she still had her legs. She blinked. I edged from under her and looked down. She was whole, but a piece of her dress was missing and a line of red welled on her calf. It was only a small gash, but it bled.

"Cover it quickly," I said. She didn't move, she just stared at me in a daze. I grabbed her hand and slapped it over the wound, then tore a strip from her dress to bind it. While I tied she stared blankly at the blood on her hand. Then with a look of disgust she swished her hand in the water to clean it.

I snatched her arm back just as another set of jaws broke the surface, clamped air where her hand had been, and vanished. They had the scent now.

There were no more lazy passes, the water boiled beside us while the four sharks lunged and twisted, snapping at one another. The raft trembled and swayed. I managed to get Q'enti kneeling upright again where she clung to me in terror.

In their frenzy one of the sharks dislodged a pole, and the raft sank low to the right. Water seeped around my knees, and I leaned to the left. It would take no more than a slap from a powerful tail to sink our perch.

Then, hugging Q'enti close and staring over her shoulder, I saw a great sail coming toward us. "Here," I shouted waving one arm high. "Over here, hurry!"

It must have spotted us earlier and been steadily approaching, though I didn't notice it until it was close enough to see figures on deck. "Hurry, here we are," I yelled. Q'enti only whimpered and kept her face buried in my shoulder.

Beside me a set of jaws burst from the water and snapped. The matting lifted as a long body dashed underneath. Another pole came lose, and drifted away.

The big shark lunged with head clear of the water and jaws wide. Q'enti grabbed a length of cane and whacked the shark on its snout. "Stop that. Get down," she ordered. The huge head vanished.

I looked at her in bewilderment. A moment earlier she whimpered and clung to me with eyes squeezed shut, and now she looked collected, and annoyed.

Q'enti glanced behind her. "Ah, a raft," she announced, aware of the approaching craft for the first time. "They better have fresh water and decent food on board." She said it as if it wasn't at all unusual for a raft to appear just then—indeed, anticipated as if she'd ordered it—and we were already safe on board confronting the captain.

Though the sharks still swirled around us I found myself grinning, thinking of her swatting a shark with a cane and telling it to get down. Q'enti looked at me as if I'd lost my mind. She sniffed and looked over her shoulder again. "Those men are strangely decorated," she said.

Sailors lined the bow, pointing at the sharks and jabbering excitedly, while ignoring us. It was a huge vessel of the same design as our Chincha raft, but constructed of balsa logs. It drew closer, and I saw that the sailors, clad only in loincloths, wore the nose pendants and face studs of Puná.

The Punáe raft coasted close enough for the sailors to throw us a rope, but no lifeline was offered. The men lining the deck hardly glanced at us, instead they hooted among themselves and gestured wildly at the sharks. One hefted a harpoon, but another shouldered him aside and cast a line with hook and bait. The frenzied sharks ignored the balsa raft and frothed the water around our floating perch, which was certain to capsize at any moment. I called to the men in the Chincha tongue, but they paid no attention. We were nothing more than live bait for their shark hunt.

The fisherman hooked one of the smaller sharks, and three of the crew joined him hauling on the taut line. But when they got the shark to the edge of the raft it twisted and thrashed, and the harpoon man gave it a jab. That was a mistake. The instant it bled the other sharks tore it apart, turning the water into bloody foam. The fisherman hooked another, but the other sharks sensed its distress and turned on it, too. Then the fins vanished and the red water went calm. The Punáe stamped their feet and pointed accusing fingers at the man with the harpoon, who cowered and protested. They seized him and made to throw him overboard. Then a chiefly looking man with a gold nose pendant intervened, and with sharp commands sent the sailors running to reset the sail and daggerboards.

I called to him but he looked through me, and was about to turn his back when Q'enti yelled, "Captain! You will take us aboard, now." He didn't understand a word she said but her tone caught him, and for the first time he looked directly at us. A slow smile spread across his face. "Captain," Q'enti persisted, "get me out of the water. Do it now." At the sound of Q'enti's command the captain's eyes opened wide and he beamed. He made some brutish sounds to a sailor, who looked from him to us in surprise, then shrugged and threw us a rope.

The sailor who dragged us aboard stared long and hard at Q'enti. I was naked and covered myself as best I could with my hands, expecting to be ravished, but he barely noticed me. In spite of our situation I felt a stab of jealousy. Q'enti pretended not to notice the stares. I tried to get his attention by thanking him and gesturing for something to cover myself—allowing him a full look at my breasts—but his eyes hardly flickered on me. He spoke not a word but tied us to the bow of the wet deck. When Q'enti demanded food and water he looked at her as if she was an exotic animal making strange sounds, and then departed with a shrug. No one approached us after that, and for the remainder of the day we lay on the balsa logs without a drop of sweet water, the huge square sail providing our only shade from the hot, blue sky.

We continued northward until a coastline emerged to the west, then veered toward it and followed low, bushy shores crowded by forests. The only word we understood from the sailor's jabber was, "Puná." Late in the afternoon we passed a cluster of dugout canoes on a long beach, and then rounded a point of sheer cliffs. From here the shore stretched westward, so I knew we had reached the north end of the island. A small bay bustling with sailing rafts and canoes came into view. On one side of this sheltered inlet a town poked from forested hills, while on the other side flat land sprinkled with fields and farmsteads traced the shores. The inhabitants ran to the oceanfront waving and calling, and our bow swung in.

"Q'enti, I am naked," I whispered. "Give me a piece of your dress, please." I had asked her several times but she refused to part with a thread. Q'enti turned up her nose and fussed with her dress, muttering about her need for make-up and proper apparel. I wasn't going to be paraded naked in front of an entire village, so I lunged.

"Stop," Q'enti said, "you're ripping my dress. Get away." She pushed and swatted at me. Just when I had a nice tear started strong hands clamped my arms and threw me aside. I came away with a tiny swatch. They undid our tethers, jerked us to our feet, and loaded us into a dugout bobbing alongside. The paddlers grinned and smacked their lips.

Like the men on the raft, our paddlers wore only loincloths with flaps at front and back decorated with carved shell pendants. Bands of tattoos encircled their arms and legs. They cut their hair just below the ear, and used strings of beads for headbands. The earspools dangling from their lobes were round and open at both ends, and the nose pendants covering their mouths were of many shapes: round, square, some long, others like half circles. They all wore shark-tooth necklaces.

Excited children splashed into the water around us, the older boys steadying the dugout and poking us in delight. With the bow of the canoe grounded we had to step out into a slimy bottom, sinking in the muck to our calves, and struggle to land. Once there, the Punáe washed their legs in a basin set out for the purpose, but refused us the dignity.

The piece of cloth I'd torn from the hem of Q'enti's dress wasn't big enough to cover my chest and middle, so I had to choose. I gave Q'enti a pleading look but of course she turned away. I held the swatch at my waist and placed my other arm across my chest, leaving my backside bare. It's impossible to appear dignified when you are naked. Q'enti smirked at me.

The path led up to the town. There was no grouping of buildings, let alone proper streets, only houses on stilts set far apart and scattered along the hills. We entered a broad, open area with a prosperous looking dwelling on the far side—the home of their chief, I assumed, and this was their plaza. Q'enti sniffed disdainfully. Women and children flocked to watch our arrival, and spit on us, while the men laughed and shoved us forward. As we passed a hollowed out log full of water Q'enti and I fell to our knees and gulped its sweetness, oblivious to the blows and shouts of our captors. They hauled us to our feet again. A woman shook her fist at us, and then tipped the log over as if its contents were spoiled. Without further welcome the

Punáe used their feet to stuff us into a tiny storage shed beside the big house, then secured the door from the outside.

The gray light of dawn poked through the cane walls of our tiny prison-shed, but it remained dark inside. The village stirred. A mother comforted her child, a dog barked, and wisps of smoke from the breakfast fires set my stomach rumbling.

There was just enough space for Q'enti and me to sit in front of the door with our knees drawn up, and lean back on the sloping pile of hard manioc roots. In this position we passed the night. Q'enti straightened and placed her hands at the small of her back, working her shoulders and groaning. "I will speak with their chief about these accommodations," she said.

"You may be sleeping more soundly than you'd care to by tonight," I replied.

"What do you mean?"

"Has it occurred to you that they've put us in a storage shed along with their food supplies?"

Q'enti lifted her chin. "They don't know who I am. As soon as I speak with their chief—"

"That would be unwise, Q'enti. If they learn we are Inca we'll be dead before you can blink. This island of Puná is outside Inca borders. The Punáe raid their neighbors and pirate every vessel caught in their waters, but they have a special hate for our people. They won't be impressed to know who we really are, and they don't fear the Empire."

Q'enti huffed, "Well, I won't be treated like a peasant."

"We better stop speaking our own language," I said, "just in case someone recognizes a few Inca words."

"What, these savages? They grunt like animals. They don't understand civilized speech."

"Perhaps they don't understand it, but some may recognize it. When the Punáe aren't raiding they're trading."

"Then what do you suggest?"

I ducked my head in surprise. Though she said it sarcastically, Q'enti had never asked my opinion on anything.

"Chincha rafts used to land here. Let's tell them we are from Chincha and we hate Incas."

"And how are we going to make them understand that?"

"The old mate told me Kañari is the language of trade in the north. Let's speak the Chincha dialect between ourselves in case someone overhears, and Kañari with them. You do speak Kañari don't you?"

Q'enti sniffed. "Of course," she said in Kañari, "all the best people do."

The Kañari are the most civilized of the mountain peoples in the north, and their province had been loyal to the Empire since Wayna Qhapaq's father conquered it. Like the Chincha, the Kañari traded widely and enjoyed a certain reputation among their neighbors. In Cuzco all the nobles spoke several languages, and Kañari was one of the favored northern dialects.

"Good," I said in the Chincha tongue, "then henceforth we speak Chincha and Kañari."

Q'enti nodded.

The sun illuminated the interior of the shed with a lattice of shadows and light. Q'enti still wore the remains of her dress with its wide belt. I hugged a scrap of cloth to me, suddenly aware of my nakedness.

"Do you think they're going to kill us?" Q'enti asked. There was no sarcasm, it was a genuine question and she said it in the Chincha tongue.

"That's what they are planning to do eventually," I said, "but if they were only going to kill us they could have done that at sea, or just left us in the water. I think they have something else in mind."

"Make a feast of us?"

"If that's all they are going to do it will be merciful," I said. Q'enti hadn't heard the sailors' stories of degraded Punáe customs, and since she now spoke to me as an equal—or at least an ally—I decided not to worry her. "We will know soon," I said, coming up on my knees and pressing my ear to the door, "I think I hear them coming."

The sound of an approaching crowd grew beyond the split cane walls of our prison. Drums pounded and bells jingled announcing the coming of some important personage. I knew our fate would be decided in the next moments, and Qhari's too if we didn't survive. My thoughts whirled. Escape? Not with Q'enti, she will be less than useless in a fight, besides, there are thousands of them and we are on an island. Be humble and beg mercy? The Punáe don't know mercy. To them we aren't human. Will the men attack us? No doubt all of them, and in front of the whole village. But no matter what happens I must endure . . . for Qhari I must endure.

I sat beside Q'enti and clutched my pitiful scrap of cloth—I'd never felt more vulnerable. The cold hand of danger settled on the back of my neck, and I gripped my knees to stop trembling. Q'enti stared tight-lipped at the door.

"Remember, we only speak Chincha and Kañari," I said to her, "and let me do the talking." Q'enti showed no sign of having heard me.

The sunlight piercing the cracks of the cane walls vanished. I could feel the throng outside pressing around the shed on all sides. The drums stopped with a final thud. In the silence someone untied the door lashings.

Brown hands dragged us into the sudden, blinding light. I found myself on my knees and sat back with thighs together, holding my tiny cloth to my chest and placing a hand over my eyes against the glare. Q'enti knelt beside me, also shielding her eyes. Savage voices rose around us.

I scanned the crowd, still blinking while my eyes adjusted to the sunlight. The entire village had gathered for the spectacle, a solid wall of curious faces with children squirming into the front row. Several stone-eyed men draped in finery stood in a line before us. They wore enormous gold nose pendants that hid their lower faces like masks. Among them I recognized the raft captain who plucked us from the sea. With a gesture and a stream of words he offered us to the giant beside him, a man twice the girth of the others who stood at the center wearing a tall gold crown. He raised his hand

and the crowd fell silent, though the nobles around him continued whispering.

"Lord, we wish you good health and humbly beg your mercy," I said to him in the Chincha tongue. There was a slight pause in the men's conversation when I spoke, but then they continued talking among themselves as if we were bales of goods. A warrior stepped forward, struck me, and pushed my head down.

Yes, I thought, how dare I look directly at their chief, but I must get them talking to us. With eyes on the ground I said in Kañari, "Long life to the great chief of Puná."

This time their conversation stopped and I sensed them looking at one another. After a pause one replied in accented Kañari, "You are of the Kañari people?"

"No, great Lord," I said, eyes still downcast and unsure to whom I spoke, "we are friends from Chincha."

They spoke among themselves again, and from the corners of my eyes I saw shoulders shrugging and heads shaking. "It doesn't matter," the translator said, "our gods will accept you anyway. They like Kañari, but it's long since they savored Chincha flesh." He said this with a smirk in his voice.

I glanced at Q'enti who, until this moment, had been studying her knees in white-lipped silence. To my horror she now raised her head.

"Q'enti, don't," I hissed. "Lower your eyes."

She ignored me.

"I bear greetings and a message for the great lord of this island," she said in a loud, firm voice. Her Kañari was excellent, but my jaw dropped at her words. What is she doing? She's going to get us both killed. "Be quiet," I whispered.

The warrior raised his hand to silence her, but she pushed him aside and jumped to her feet, hands planted on her hips.

We're dead, I thought.

"I will speak to the chief of chiefs and no other," she announced. "I am the sister of the Lord of Chincha."

I looked up at her in surprise. No one noticed me anymore; in what followed all eyes were on Q'enti. The men looked taken aback at this outrage but Q'enti kept them off balance with a flood of words. All the dignitaries understood her.

"My brother has rafts sinking under the weight of gold he wishes to send you. We don't want the Incas interfering with our trade anymore. They are weak. We seek strong allies, and we come in peace to trade directly with our brother the great lord of Puná. I will not waste my voice on mere chiefs. Show me the Great One. Only with he who is my equal will I speak."

There was a pause while the men looked at one another, and then the big man at the center replied in broken Kañari, "I don't see any gold, I only see two worthy sacrifices." The others chuckled. When he spoke his nose pendant moved, setting the disks of gold suspended from its borders jiggling, reflecting flashes of sunlight as if their beams were his words.

Q'enti stepped up to him, her head level with his chest, and jabbed his shoulder with a finger. "*Who* are *you* to speak to me thus? Where is the Great Lord? Is he afraid of me?"

The others tensed at Q'enti's sudden move and the chief stepped back in surprise. We're dead, I thought again.

The chief, disconcerted at having been startled in front of his lords, looked ready to have us gutted on the spot. But then, to hide his embarrassment, he pretended it was a jest and laughed, raising his hands in mock terror. "The Great Lord is indeed fearful of you, Lady," he said. Everyone chuckled. "I am he, Tumbala, Lord of the Punáe Lords, and this is my island. We catch many strange fish in these waters, but none as terrifying as you."

While the men around Tumbala laughed and mimicked his fear of Q'enti, I let out my breath. The danger was far from past—I still expected them to carry us off to their temple for sacrifice—but at least she had them talking to her.

Q'enti's hands returned to her hips. "Lord Tumbala? she said eyeing him up and down. There was a lot of him to look over. Q'enti nodded as if satisfied. "Very well, my Lord, you I will speak with. As you can see," she said spreading her arms, "I am not well attired, and my maid is naked." She nodded over her shoulder at me kneeling behind. I offered an uncertain smile and lowered my head quickly. "Our raft, which was laden with treasure for you, sank in a storm, but fortunately your captain saved us." She gestured to the raft captain who looked pleased to be noticed. "After you have provided suitable clothes and food, and private quarters, I'll deliver the message from my exalted brother, the Lord of Chincha."

An old man behind Tumbala said, "If Mother Water took their treasure and left them for us, then she wants us to share her bounty with the other gods. Our altars are hungry." The crowd inhaled in expectation.

Tumbala shrugged at Q'enti. "This has been most amusing," he said, "but as you have nothing to offer but bold words I must bow to the wishes of my priests." Tumbala signaled and warriors came forward.

"Wait, there's more," Q'enti shouted, shaking off the grip of the man at her elbow. My guard yanked me to my feet, but hers looked to Tumbala and hesitated.

"Besides the gold," Q'enti said, "which will be coming by the raft load if I am alive, my brother sends you a gift to seal the alliance."

We had one torn dress between us, and Q'enti wore it. What is she bargaining with, I wondered? I turned to her as expectantly as the others.

"A gift?" Tumbala said.

"The greatest gift of all," Q'enti replied. "Me . . . I am to be your wife."

XI

Of Debauchery and Licentiousness, Thievery and Mutilation, and the eating of Disgusting Things in the furtherance of Desperate Plans.

My mouth fell open when Q'enti announced she was to be Tumbala's bride. The line of dignitaries on either side of Tumbala turned to him for their response. He stood like a timber and stared down at Q'enti in surprise. The Punáe villagers did not understand what had been said, but they saw their chiefs' reaction and waited in hushed anticipation. Q'enti drew herself to full height—equal with Tumbala's chest, and dared him with her eyes, while I cringed on my knees behind.

She has no idea what she's saying, I thought. She doesn't know about Punáe wedding customs.

Tumbala regarded her in silence while the others waited for him to speak. Then the corners of his eyes crinkled and he laughed. His men joined him.

"You are to be my wife?" Tumbala replied in Kañari. "Thank you, great lady, but I already have a few wives." He gestured to a crowd of women who giggled behind their hands.

"Indeed you have many," Q'enti said, casting the women a condescending look, "and I suppose you cannot afford another?" Tumbala's face clouded while those around him murmured disapprovingly. "A pity," Q'enti continued, "because I am trained to please a man in ways unknown to your women."

Tumbala's eyes sparked interest and wandered over Q'enti. She straightened her shoulders and posed for him. When his gaze settled on her scarred cheek she flinched and turned her head, drawing a strand of hair over the left side of her face in a coy gesture, but I knew she burned inside. Tumbala snorted and listened to the men muttering around him.

"I have all the wives it pleases me to have," Tumbala said in a loud voice. Everyone fell silent. "But it also pleases me to taste exotic fruit. Therefore I have decided to spare the temple altar, for now, and marry you instead. Tumbala has spoken."

The Punáe moved us into the house of Tumbala's many wives. It was one large, open room strung with hammocks. Being new arrivals they gave us mats on the floor. The house consisted of split cane walls and a thatch roof, and it stood on posts higher than a man can reach. A log notched with stairs led up to the covered porch along the front. At first I thought the stilts odd as the house stood on a bluff well away from the ocean or any watercourse, but I soon realized the elevation helped catch the sea breezes, and kept insects and rodents at bay. The space under the house provided excellent storage, and a stout fence kept out prowling dogs.

Over the following days Tumbala's wives never ceased babbling and giggling at us, as did the villagers whenever we appeared. I couldn't tell whether any of them, Tumbala included, were serious about the coming marriage, or whether it was to be a mock wedding—mere entertainment and a good excuse for a feast. I wondered fearfully what they would consider the finale of such an event. But I didn't share these misgivings with Q'enti, who appeared her regal self in front of others, and complained bitterly to me in private. Nor did I mention the Punáe bride-sharing custom.

We dressed as Punáe women in cotton shifts that covered us from neck to wrist to ankle. These seemed overly modest for the hot days, but I was grateful to have a garment again. The only item Q'enti insisted on keeping was her wide belt, which she continued to wear day and night under her shift. Tumbala's wives presented Q'enti with a string of silver beads. When she demanded gold jewelry they laughed, and brought her a women's gold nose-ring. These are smaller than the nose pendants worn by men, but still hang to the upper lip. At first Q'enti tried to wear it on her finger, but I convinced her it was unwise to anger our hosts so the trinket had to be worn as intended. I almost talked her into having her nose pierced, but she discovered the tiny opening on the ring could be pinched to keep it in place without piercing. She knew I thought she looked ridiculous, and demanded a copper nose-ring for me.

Fortunately we weren't given face studs, a barbarous custom which Punáe men and women employ. They pierce their cheeks and under-lips to fasten gold and red shell adornments which, when tiny like those worn by the women are not unpleasing, but the men boast their wealth with elaborately carved birds and demons protruding from their faces.

Some of Tumbala's wives spoke a smattering of Kañari, and through them I swiftly mastered a small vocabulary of the Punáe language. Thus I discovered that many of Tumbala's wives were war captives, and others were peace offerings. The Punáe now kept an uneasy peace with their mainland neighbors, but previously they raided up and down the coast. I soon befriended a Wankavilca woman whose people occupy the mainland north and east of Puná. Their capital is Guayas, where Asto said his brother Pisar dwelled.

While the Punáe stockpiled food for the coming wedding feast, I used these days to learn about our surroundings and plan an escape. We had freedom of the town, which, being spread widely over the hills, allowed me to wander while Q'enti hid from sun and heat in our house. With the air so moist and hot during the day my face glistened even in the shade, and the effort of uphill paths soaked my cotton shift. But sea breezes provided some relief, and the early mornings and evenings were blissfully cool, though never chilly except just before dawn. On my walks I saw giant cieba trees with their swollen white trunks and writhing branches, and fields of maize and beans and manioc, berry bushes and fruit trees alive with twittering birds, and clearings full of the famous Puná sarsaparilla bush. The island abounded in everything necessary for its people, and their wealth increased many-fold through trade and piracy.

Looking north from the town I saw islands like stepping-stones to the mainland. One evening I found my Wankavilca friend sitting alone on the shores staring at them wistfully.

"Is your home far away?" I asked.

"No, just two days by dugout canoe," she said pointing over the waters.

I said, "You mean that island out there?"

"Oh no, beyond it. That's only one of many islands in the estuary of the Guayas River. But to the right of it there is a wide channel leading straight through the islands to the mainland. My home is near the port of Guayas. My father is chief of our village."

"Does your father know a man named Pisar?" I asked.

"Pisar? That is a Kañari name. No, I've never heard of him."

I leaned close and whispered, "He is a condor priest."

She stiffened and glanced over her shoulder, then said softly, "I've never heard of this Pisar, but it is said condor priests wander among my people. They are from many nations. Our priests give them sanctuary, but no one will speak of them. Let us say no more of this."

My next question delighted her. "Will you teach me your Wankavilca speech?"

"It starts tomorrow," I said to Q'enti.

"Are you sure? Good, then tomorrow I will be queen of these savages, and no one will deny their queen a raft."

"I said the ceremonies start tomorrow, but it may be a week before they end. Besides, Q'enti, you won't be a queen, you will be the most junior of twenty-three wives."

"Tumbala may be a savage, but even wild beasts can be tamed," she said smiling to herself.

"I don't like it," I said. "We have wasted enough time here. We must escape, and a chance comes soon."

"Are you in a hurry, Qori dear? Oh yes, that poor man-woman brother of yours; do you think the poison is eating him right now?"

"We are going to escape, Q'enti, so you had better be ready."

"We go when I say. Be patient, and within a month we will leave this island on our own balsa raft."

"I don't have a month to wait. When I give the signal we leave together, even if I have to drag you."

The Punáe moved us to a stilt-house of our own, saying that Q'enti wasn't to be seen before the marriage. Delegations from other villages arrived the next morning dressed in their finery. Q'enti spent the day preening and lamenting the lack of proper jewelry and cosmetics, though she managed to plaster over her scar again. I considered telling her about the sharing of the bride custom, but I was afraid that if forewarned she might refuse and upset my plans.

When the feasting began at midday I emerged to fetch platters of food. The plaza in front of Tumbala's house undulated with gold and feather headdresses, and the crowds spilled over the hills beyond. The women wore their finest shifts and jewelry: finger-rings, necklaces, earrings, bracelets and pendants of precious metals inlaid with crystals, blue stone, and the sacred red shell of the thorny oyster, leaving me open-mouthed at their wealth. The men of chiefly rank wore crowns and pectorals fashioned in silver and gold, and carved cylinders of red shell the length of my hand. The babble of Punáe voices was almost drowned under the thudding of drums, and nearby, somewhere beyond the crush, ankle-bells jingled calling the Punáe to dance. Catching the scent of kitchen smells I wedged myself between turned backs and pressed on.

When I reached the banquet I spied my friend, the Wankavilca woman, supervising the heaping of trays. "Greetings, sister," I said in her language. She smiled and motioned me to her side behind a line of blankets spread on the ground. These held mounds of manioc bread and fruit, and farther along maize gruel and fish stews bubbled in caldrons, smothering us in warm smells.

"Is your lady ready?" she asked with a twinkle.

"As much as she can be," I said. "I haven't informed her about the sharing of the bride yet. As I told you, it's not a custom among our people."

It had occurred to me earlier that Tumbala, being chief of chiefs, might be exempt from the bride sharing tradition. But when I asked my friend she only grinned and assured me Tumbala was generous with his women. The Wankavilca also practice this custom, she said, and it would be an insult to the bride if she wasn't allowed to sample her husband's relatives before the marriage. She showed surprise when I told her my people didn't have this practice, and she pitied our uncivilized ways.

"How long will the feast continue?" I asked. I spoke with a mixture of Punáe, Wankavilca, and Kañari words, but she understood me.

"Seven or eight days," she replied. "It depends on the food and drink, and the priests. They are going to make a special offering at the temple to end the festivities."

While we talked servers loaded my platters. "Will my lady be Tumbala's wife after today?"

"Oh no, not until the sixth day. Today she will have all the men she wishes—and perhaps tomorrow also, there are so many—and then we must finish the food and drain the urns of manioc brew. That will take a few more days. The priests will know when the time is right for the sacrifices."

"The sacrifices?"

She brightened. "Yes, Lord Tumbala has promised his people two men for the altar, and as a special mark of favor he will also offer one of his own wives to the gods. Isn't he generous?"

"Which wife?"

She looked at me as if I jested. "The new one, your lady, of course."

I almost dropped the wooden platters I held in either hand.

"Careful or you will spill the juice," she said helping me. "It's a great honor for your lady to be Tumbala's wife, but to be chosen as god feeder also . . . well, she must be very worthy. Here, take some sweet potatoes, and meat, you've forgotten the meat."

While I stood dumbly she unwrapped a steaming bundle of leaves, freshly lifted from where it had been cooking overnight beneath the coals, and extracted an iguana tail as long as my forearm. "No, please," she said, "I insist you take all of it. And do relay my congratulations to your lady."

The meat smelled delicious, but the presentation would have been enhanced by first removing the leathery, green lizard skin.

Tumbala's wives came for Q'enti that afternoon.

"You know you have to go through with this or we're both dead," I said to her at the door.

Q'enti smirked in reply.

"Take this," I whispered, pressing a packet of fat drippings into her palm.

Q'enti regarded the little bundle and smiled. "How thoughtful, my dear. Tumbala is a big man, but I'm sure I can manage him."

"He won't touch you for another six days, not until the end of the feast."

"The ceremonies last that long? How wearisome." She held up the packet. "Then what do I need this for?"

I looked on her with innocent eyes. "I thought you knew. The Punáe share their brides before the marriage. There are many eager men awaiting you. It's their custom, and if we offend them now . . . ." I drew a finger under my chin.

Q'enti stared at me with lips parted, but before she could speak Tumbala's wives bore her away.

For two days I worried, expecting to see Tumbala's priests coming for me at any moment. If Q'enti decided she'd had enough, or even demanded rest, the ceremonies would be ruined. I tried not to imagine what was taking place in that big hut packed with men, but my thoughts dwelled there. What was it like? I wondered. Were the men on her like a pack of dogs, or did Q'enti have them waiting in line while she indulged her passions?

To place my mind elsewhere I strolled the shores. The Punáe, being much preoccupied with their festivities, ignored me. I returned to the beach on the far side of the sea cliffs where several dugout canoes rested. Some required ten men to move, but there were also smaller craft that a woman alone could manage. I could have escaped, but without Q'enti I would never see Qhari again.

Is Qhari in pain now? I wondered. Has the poison begun to rot him? I must get Q'enti away from here soon. Will Pisar be at Guayas?

That is Wankavilca country, and they are said to be worse than the Punáe. Will they let us pass? Why should they? And even if Pisar is there, why would he help us find the Condor Temple? Enough, Inca Moon! These questions will be answered when you get there. Yes, getting to Guayas, think about getting to Guayas. What would Zapana do?

On a hill above the beach I chanced upon a low structure of logs built on the ground and encircled by a fence. Four guards lounged in the shade outside. As I watched from the trees two drunken chiefs came down the path, exchanged words with the guards, and vanished behind the wicker door. They emerged a short time later with small sacks and a net bag in which I caught the glint of gold. They staggered back to the village and the guards returned to dozing. Tumbala is distributing gifts from his treasury, I thought. When the time is right I'll return with plenty of strong manioc beer for these guards. After all, the poor fellows are missing the wedding feast.

Q'enti returned the next day. I sat in the shade under our house learning more Wankavilca from my friend when I saw her walking toward us. The plaza was not as crowded—many slept off the effects of the manioc beer in preparation for the evening drinking bouts—but lines of dancers still paraded to the thud of drums, and the big cauldrons bubbled their welcome to all bellies. We stood when we saw Q'enti approach, and my friend touched my arm. "Best let her rest for a few days," she said with a wink and departed.

Q'enti strode with chin up and back straight as she crossed the plaza, indifferent to the congratulations offered by those she passed. For a woman who had just spent two days satisfying the lusts of innumerable men she looked remarkably fresh, and unaffected by the experience. But when she drew closer I saw her lips were swollen, and her blinking eyes betrayed every painful step. She hardly glanced at me when she went up the stairs.

For two more days and nights she remained inside, saying not a word, but her movements told much of the story. At first she was unable to sit and only lay on her stomach. Her grimaces marked the effort of using her legs, and the redness of her swollen lips extended over cheeks and chin. I felt no pity for her—a lifetime of evil placed her beyond claim to sympathy—but I tended her because the chance of escape fast approached.

By the third day the salves and hot drinks of sarsaparilla root had their effect, and she began to sit up and converse. Of course, being Q'enti, she refused to acknowledge her discomfort, or refer to the experience as an ordeal. She knew I was curious but all she said was, "They were orderly and respectful for savages. The first two were delightful, and the next two amusing, but after that it was tiresome."

"We are leaving tonight," I told her.

"Tonight? No, we will do this my way," she said. "Tomorrow I wed Tumbala, and then soon I will have a proper raft for our journey."

"We don't need a proper raft," I said. "Guayas is not far from here. Besides, you will only be married to Tumbala for a day and then he is giving you to his gods."

I answered the surprise on her face with a full account of what the Wankavilca woman told me. Q'enti scowled. "That savage!" she said of Tumbala. "To make me go through all of this, only to turn me over to his priests!"

"It bought the time I needed," I said. "I haven't been idle. Everything is prepared and waiting for us, and I've learned enough of these tribal dialects to give us a chance with the Wankavilca."

Q'enti ignored my efforts. "Bought you time?" she said. "Time that I paid for!"

"You were the one who volunteered to marry Tumbala," I reminded her.

She fumed at me in silence.

The previous night I returned to Tumbala's treasury when festivities in the village reached a drunken peak. The night was dark, and not even Mother Moon pierced the canopy of vines arched over the path. With the drumming fading behind me, I hoisted the purloined jug of manioc beer to my shoulder, and grasped the roasted iguana tails. Thus I appeared when the guards saw me approaching.

"What's this?" one said, then remarked to his fellows, "Wake up, here is food and drink, and a woman for all of us."

"Food and drink, Lord," I replied, "but the woman must return to her master." Two of the guards continued to snore, an overturned jug between them, but a third sat up and rubbed his eyes. The man I addressed, the only one alert among them, said, "Your accent is strange, who are you?"

"A new-found servant of Lord Tumbala," I said, setting the jug and meat before him. "My Lord wishes me to return quickly, but he bids you enjoy this refreshment."

The man stiffened. "Lord Tumbala is your master? Forgive me. I meant no disrespect."

I bowed and retreated a distance up the path, then stepped into the dark forest and waited.

It wasn't long before a chorus of snores drew me back to the treasury. All four guards sat propped against the side of the building with heads on their chests. The drums in the village had ceased leaving the Punáe to their sodden dreams. Like a shadow I made my way to the wicker door.

Surrounded by ocean and feared by their neighbors, the Punáe felt safe on their island. Tumbala with his great raft fleets was undisputed master of these waters, and his numerous subjects rendered absolute devotion. It probably never occurred to him that anyone would dare rob his treasure house, and hence I found the sole entrance unbarred. The four guards, I decided, simply kept track of who came and went.

Inside the door a lamp of fish oil burned in the darkness, its dim glow showing torches piled nearby. I took one and ignited it from the lamp, then turned to survey the wealth of Puná. The building was long and low with mats covering the floor between thick log walls. Against these walls was so much treasure that only a narrow corridor lay open down the middle. I walked forward, my flickering light passing rolled jaguar and puma skins, bags of salt, bales of cloth, net sacks of thorny oyster shell, and bundles of parrot feathers—all too bulky for my purposes. But farther along I came upon urns brimming with trinkets of gold and silver: necklaces, bracelets, nose pendants and face studs of the finest workmanship. Here also were baskets of copper needles, awls, tweezers, fishhooks, and tiny bells. I knelt to examine a leather bag. It held copper ax-heads, valuable but heavy, and these I removed. Then, holding bag and torch in one hand, and glancing frequently over my shoulder like the thief in the night I was, I helped myself to the smaller valuables.

I filled the leather bag as much as I dared, then held it by its long shoulder strap to test the weight. The bag wasn't large, but loaded with gold and silver it was as much as I could carry and still run. These pieces won't be missed until the next inventory, I reasoned. They should be enough to buy our way through Wankavilca territory, and maybe even tempt Pisar when we find him.

I was about to leave when a basket full of small pouches caught my eye. I opened some and found they contained powdered dyes. An idea formed, and, smiling to myself, I slipped a pouch of red dye in with my loot.

Everything is ready, I thought. All I need do is steal away from here and hide my treasure near one of the smaller canoes. Tomorrow night, when the Punáe drink themselves into stupors, Q'enti and I will slip across the water. With luck we'll have a good start before they realize we're gone.

Then I heard a moan from the darkness. I froze and felt the familiar tingle on the back of my neck. My senses reached out, searching the blackness beyond the torchlight. The sound came from the rear of the building. I held my breath and waited, poised to flee or fight.

I heard nothing more and exhaled. The instinct to run gripped me, but I knew someone was there and must have seen my pilfering. Better to face this threat now, I decided. I walked to the back holding the torch in front of me like a weapon.

The rear space was empty, save for a post in the middle to which two men were firmly bound in sitting position. They were filthy and starved, each with his head slumped on his chest. One must have moaned in his sleep. Their hair was too long for Punáe men. Captives, I thought, taken in a raid and now awaiting the altar knife. These are the ones Tumbala promised to his people. He keeps them in his treasury to be counted along with his other goods. I pity them their fate, but my plans are set and they do not include taking unnecessary risks for strangers.

I began to back away when one of the men stirred and raised his head. Our eyes locked. It was my friend the Chincha raft captain.

Q'enti continued to fume long after I revealed Tumbala's plans for her. But once she understood that tomorrow was to be her last day, she grudgingly followed my instructions. Now, sitting alone in our house beside a flickering lamp, Q'enti watched me use a twig to mix water with the red dye I had stolen from Tumbala's treasury. "What are you doing?" she asked.

"The last preparation for our escape," I replied, stirring carefully to avoid getting any of the dye on my hands lest the stain be permanent. "Do you have the food and water ready?"

Q'enti patted the bundle at her side. "Enough for a few days."

Outside, the monotonous din of drums and feasting continued around the bonfires. It was the fifth evening of celebrations, and each night the Punáe seemed determined to out do their previous night's consumption. I lifted my head and listened, judging the clamor. Soon it would be time to slip into the dark.

I didn't tell Q'enti about my visit to Tumbala's treasure house, or whom I'd seen there. The less she knew the less there was for her to question. But I fought a long battle with my conscience. The Chincha captain knew the dangers, I thought, knew them better than we did. He took his chances as did we, and when the raft split apart I didn't see him trying to save us. Better if the sharks had eaten him. Sailors disappear at sea often. It is their fate. Surely that wife he always talked about knew she would lose him one day?

Again I saw that woman waving farewell from the landing at Chincha, her children gathered around. She was a chubby thing, not even pleasing of face, yet the captain's eyes glowed when he spoke of her. What could there be between those two? I wondered. Surely not lust or gain, at least not on his part. The captain can have many women, sailors often do, but he remains devoted to this one. Why? What is there between them that outlives passion? Was there more to Zapana and me than satisfying ourselves? We did that, but that isn't what makes me ache for him. Yes, I still ache for him, even more as time passes.

Will I return that fat little woman's sailor? I can try, but at what cost? Maybe forfeiting my life in the attempt, and Qhari with me. Foolish thoughts, Inca Moon. You will not jeopardize the mission by taking risks for people you hardly know. The captain's fate has nothing to do with you. Stick to the plan and slip away quietly.

The red dye was ready. Attaching a drop to the tip of the twig, I raised it and said to Q'enti, "Now, bare your shoulder."

"I won't let him put it in me," Q'enti said, hands on her hips.

I knew she was still too sore for that, though she wouldn't admit it. "Be quiet," I whispered, and motioned her on through the night. It was dark on the path under the forest bower, but Mother Moon shone bare faced from the heavens illuminating the fields in silvery sheen. Ahead of us the squat outline of Tumbala's treasury crouched in its clearing. Three of its guardians snored, but the fourth paced near the entrance to keep himself awake. I pointed to him and said, "He need not even touch you if you do this properly. Just lure him behind the building. I will be waiting there, and I'll deal with him."

"What are we doing here?" Q'enti said petulantly. "I thought you had a canoe ready?"

"I do, but there is something here I need. Now, go and seduce the guard." I pushed her forward and faded behind a tree. She looked at me over her shoulder, exhaled loudly, then set a resigned smile and strode forth. I scurried silently through the forest to take my position.

When the clamorous sounds of dancing and drinking began to subside in the village, Q'enti and I had slipped from our hut into the night forest. I fully intended to follow my own advice and go straight to the canoe beach, but my rebellious feet took us to Tumbala's treasure house. This is ridiculous, I thought, cursing myself. Inca Moon doesn't jeopardize an escape for the sake of two sailors. It's not only my life I gamble, Qhari's fate depends on my survival. Yet even as these thoughts assailed me I knew I'd go through with it, whatever the outcome, because it was what Qhari would do.

"Such a handsome man," I heard Q'enti coo. "Those in the village have drowned in their brew, but surely you can grant me the pleasure I seek." She spoke in Kañari. I don't know whether the man understood her words, but it didn't matter—Q'enti spoke clearly with her body to all men. This one proved no different. But before she could lead him behind the treasury, where I waited with a club, I heard one of his companions awake. There followed a low exchange between the men, followed by deep male laughter and Q'enti's giggles. Whatever her gestures were they worked, for she rounded the corner of the building a moment later hand in hand with the first guard, while the second waited his turn.

When Q'enti appeared with her man I leapt from the shadows and laid a mighty whack! to the back of his head. He went down instantly. Q'enti stepped aside, a wild look transforming her face. The guard's friend called out at the sound and hurried to investigate. I smashed my club into his forehead and he, too, crumpled. Q'enti watched, a feral smile spreading.

I dashed around to where the remaining two guards slept and found one of them rising drunkenly. He was slow, and a solid club blow to the top of his head returned him to unconsciousness. The fourth man, entirely overcome by drink, never stirred.

Q'enti had remained around the corner with the first two. I called to her in a low voice, "Q'enti, help me find something to tie them." There was no answer. "Q'enti?" I said again.

A pause followed, and then Q'enti stepped from behind the building. She stood perfectly still in the moonlight and looked through me. Her face held a look of rapture.

"Q'enti?"

As if called back from a dream she saw me, and then lowered her gaze to the prostrate men. I noticed she held a knife taken from one of the guards, and its blade dripped. I didn't need to look around the corner to know the first two now lay with throats slashed.

Q'enti glided forward with eyes still fixed on the two sentries at my feet. She didn't step or lurch, she glided through the night as if floating over the ground. I watched transfixed. The men lay face up with their legs toward the wall. Silently Q'enti knelt over the first man, her knees on either side of his head, and tilted his chin. The knife came around.

Qhari wouldn't allow this, I thought. But I was unable to move.

Unhurried, Q'enti knelt over her last victim. She moved slowly, precisely, as if preparing to devour a delicacy and savoring the anticipation. She lifted his chin and tightened her grip on his jaw. The cut was not a clean slice, but a wedge pressed deep and searching before being raggedly drawn through the neck, almost severing it from the trunk. Q'enti let the body twist away from her in its final agony. She lifted her face to the moon but saw it not, her eyes half lidded and a sigh of ecstasy escaping.

I left her and entered the treasury. The fish-oil lamp burned in its usual place. I lit a torch and made my way to the captives.

"I knew it was you, I knew you'd come back!" the captain said in hoarse greeting.

"Quiet," I whispered.

He nodded eagerly, eyes shining. I produced an obsidian blade and cut the bindings.

The other man croaked, "By the pendulous tits of Mother Sea, I didn't believe it when he told me. I thought he was dreaming."

"Shhh," I replied with a finger to my lips, and then smiled when I recognized the old mate. I had to help them to their feet for they had not stood or eaten in days.

I have to shepherd Q'enti, I thought, and now I'll have to carry these two as well. I supported them as they hobbled to the door, but when we emerged to the night air they stopped and turned their faces to the moon. They stood leaning against each other, drinking the soft breeze and moist scents of the forest.

"If you're ready . . . ?" I said gesturing toward the beach.

They looked at each other, these two old friends, and exchanged a grim nod. Then they parted, each standing on his own, flexing his muscles. "We're ready," the captain said.

I went to the side of the building and found Q'enti there. She stood over the corpses, her shift smeared with blood, arms crossed hugging herself, swaying gently and humming a lullaby.

"Q'enti," I said gently.

She didn't know I was there until I said her name again. When she focused on me she looked bewildered, as if she could not imagine what I was doing there. Her arms dropped, and I noticed the bodies at her feet were headless. She had placed the heads on the roof, after gouging out their eyes and tongues. If Tumbala caught us now there was no question about our fate.

Moving slowly I stepped closer and held out my hand. "It's time to go now, Q'enti."

When I touched her she shivered and shrank back. Then, just as suddenly, she stiffened and looked at me angrily. "Did you find what you needed?" she demanded. "Why are we standing here? Move, Qori, to the beach!" Without a backward glance at the devastation in her wake, she took my arm and hurried me to the front of the building.

"Who are they?" Q'enti said eyeing the two sailors. They stopped flexing and returned her surprise. "Lady Orma?" the captain said. The mate stared silently at the blood on her clothes.

XII

Of how the Escape was Thwarted, and a great many died in Fearsome and Savage Combat.

We stood in the trees behind the beach, our chests heaving after the run from Tumbala's treasure house. A scattering of canoes lay on the moonlit sand. The inshore waters were calm, but out in the bay a stiff wind drove swells northward. Contrary to my earlier visits, a line of balsa rafts now anchored in the bay.

"We'll take that one," the captain said pointing to the smallest vessel. There hadn't been time to exchange stories or tell him my plans, and he seemed to think he was in charge. He pointed to a dugout and said, "That will take us out to the raft. Ready?"

"Can the two of you sail a raft?" Q'enti asked.

"It won't be easy," the mate said, "but the captain and I have managed before. Besides, Lady, we are four. You and your maid can handle the daggerboards."

A raft was not in my plans, but then neither was the captain and mate. "Where are we headed?" I asked.

The captain looked exasperated. "Away from here, and quickly." I hesitated and he sighed, "Very well, this wind will speed us northward to the islands of Guayas. Once we round the first island we will be hidden from sight. We sail eastward to the mainland, and then south to Tumbez. If the gods are with us we won't meet any Punáe or Wankavilca vessels."

I exchanged a look with Q'enti. "We'll go with you as far as the first island," I said to him. "After that Lady Orma and I will take a canoe to Guayas."

The captain's mouth fell open. The mate said, "You're as mad as a one-legged crab! Guayas is the Wankavilca capital, and those puke-eating savages are worse than the Punáe."

Q'enti took over and elaborated the plan further than I dared. "No," she said lifting her chin in regal pose, "this is what we will do. You two will sail us straight to Guayas."

"They're both mad," the captain said to his mate, who shook his head in bewilderment. The captain turned to Q'enti. "Lady, I am in command. First we must take the canoe, and then seize the raft. Once we are underway you can explain yourself. But for now, we move."

That seemed wise to me and I nodded to Q'enti. She sniffed and shrugged.

"Ready the canoe," I told them, "and I'll meet you on the beach." All three turned to me in surprise, but there was no time to explain. I dashed into the forest.

The bushes folded over a hollow stump were as I left them after pilfering Tumbala's treasury. I swept them aside and retrieved the leather bag from inside the stump, slinging the long strap over my shoulder. The weight of precious metals caused me to list, but did not slow my pace on the return trip.

From the trees I saw our canoe pointed into the bay, with the two men standing beside it, and Q'enti on the sand nearby. I came to a halt. Something was wrong—the three stood perfectly still. Then I sighted movement approaching them from up the beach. The form of a man emerged. He held an arched bow with an arrow pointed at Q'enti. I hadn't examined the canoe landing at night, but I should have anticipated this guard.

"Move and she is dead," the guard said. He stopped ten paces from Q'enti. "Who are you and where are you taking that dugout?" He spoke Punáe. The three remained frozen, not knowing what he said, but understanding his tone—and the arrow.

For a moment I thought the sailors would leap into the canoe and leave Q'enti to her fate. It was the reasonable thing to do given that Q'enti, or Lady Orma, was of little use and no concern to them. But, while this must have occurred to them, they remained steadfast.

I slipped the leather strap from my shoulder and gripped it, hefted the bag's solid weight, then ran silently over the sand.

"Answer me or you will feel this arrow," the guard shouted at Q'enti.

I came up behind him at a run and leapt, swinging the leather bag by the strap and bringing it full circle. In that instant he heard me and turned. The bag smashed his face, crunching bone and teeth. He fell on his back with arms flung wide.

The captain helped me to my feet. No words were exchanged. I glanced at the prostrate guard. The mate stood over him with the arrow in both his hands, taking aim. He plunged, ramming it through the man's throat and into the sand beneath. I grabbed my treasure bag and we ran for the dugout.

They are narrow and low, these dugouts, and with four of us seated the water was only a hand span below the sides. Q'enti and I sat in the middle, the captain in the stern, and the mate at the bow, our paddles working furiously.

Q'enti had never paddled before. She splashed and knocked the side of the canoe until the mate turned with a scowl and snatched her paddle. As he laid it down quietly Q'enti straightened her back in noble indifference. I heard the captain breathe a sigh of relief behind me.

We made straight for the balsa rafts, gliding over the calm foreshore waters. Mother Moon saw our flight and took pity, hiding Her face behind a cloud and plunging the bay into darkness. A few lights twinkled ahead, reminding us that each raft would have its sentinels.

The captain steered us to the smallest vessel, though it still seemed enormous for the four of us to handle. In the dark I could see the outlines of larger crafts on either side, each with its protected hearth fire glowing in the night. The men held our dugout against the great balsa logs of the wet deck and waved for Q'enti and me to board. We did, though not very gracefully, and Q'enti almost upset the canoe, but I managed to get both of us and the treasure bag on board. I glanced around to make sure our arrival was undetected, and then helped the men on to the log deck. The captain was the last to step aboard, and as he set one foot firmly on the deck he pushed with the other, sending the empty canoe drifting into the darkness. Our eyes locked for an instant. With the dugout gone he would have to take us to Guayas, but this was not the time to argue. I lowered my gaze, allowing him to interpret my silence as acquiescence to his authority, for now.

Q'enti still had the dagger she used to butcher the treasury guards. The captain took it from her and ordered silence with a finger to his lips, then gestured for us to wait while he and the mate sought out the crew.

The two men stepped up to the dry deck, then parted, working their way along opposite sides of the cabin toward the stern. We waited, feet apart to the gentle roll as another swell passed, the creaking of taut lines the only sound in the night. If an alarm sounded now the big rafts could easily out run us.

A muffled cry came from the stern, followed by a splash. A moment later the captain and mate reappeared, nodded to us, and slipped into the cabin. Q'enti leaned forward listening in anticipation. There came a gurgling noise, and then a cry instantly choked into silence. Q'enti savored the sounds with eyes closed. The captain and mate emerged, each dragging a body. When these vanished over the side the captain cupped his hand to my ear and whispered, "That's the last of them. The rest of the crew must be at the village. We must cut the anchor rope and drift out of the bay before raising sail. Take Lady Orma into the cabin for now. I will tell you when to set the daggerboards."

The cabin interior was dark and I dared not light a lamp, but my eyes adjusted enough to see the dim outlines of bales and hanging net bags. I whispered the captain's instructions to Q'enti, who released a bored sigh and sat down to wait. Feeling my way along, I took stock of the cabin's contents. Whatever the main cargo had been was no longer on board, but there was food and fresh water, blankets, and a few bales of cloth. On closer inspection I found the bales contained alpaca garments traded down from the highlands—loincloths, tunics, cloaks, and dresses—so I selected liberally for the others and myself. The soft, light alpaca felt smooth against my skin.

When I handed a dress to Q'enti, thinking she would be glad to be out of her blood soaked Punáe shift, she eyed the dress with disdain and announced she was hungry.

"Put it on," I whispered, holding out the dress, "and then you'll find food and water in the back corner." I hefted the bundle of clothes in my arms. "I'm taking these out to the men." She complied with a deep sigh. As I left I noticed she still wore her wide Inca belt next to her skin.

The captain and mate were pleased with the clothing, and even more pleased with the food. Their cheeks bulged as they consumed whole fruits in two bites. They had cut the anchor rope, and under a stiff wind our vessel had already drifted far from the line of rafts in the darkened bay. But then moonlight sparkled the water. We turned our faces to the sky—the men still with food in their open mouths—and watched the shining face of Mother Moon reappear from behind the clouds. The other rafts did not seem so far away now. Indeed, I could see their cabins and masts, and then I saw movement.

A faint call came across the water. The mate touched the captain's shoulder and pointed. A figure on one of the big rafts waved his arms, shouting at us. In moments men appeared on the other vessels taking up the cry.

The captain turned grim-faced to the mate and said, "Raise sail."

The cotton sail snapped full. Water broke at the bow as our raft lunged over the swells. The captain and mate exchanged a grin. Having set the last of the daggerboards as directed I joined them on the dry deck. Mother Moon slipped behind a cloudbank when we cleared the bay, plunging the sea into darkness. Now there were no sounds or lights to our stern.

"A good wind," I observed.

"Couldn't be better," the captain said, then his face hardened. "At first they likely thought this vessel broke its moorings and drifted out, but by now they will know we escaped, and be after us. We won't know how far behind us they are until dawn. Those big rafts are slow to get underway, but once rigged and under sail they are fast—fast enough to take us."

"How far away are the islands?" I asked.

The mate peered into the darkness, and then raised a hand to his ear. "Listen," he said, "you can hear the waves rolling into shore."

I leaned forward, at first hearing nothing, but then I discerned a faint, tumbling roar ahead. The mate turned his head, listened again, and pointed across the bow.

The captain nodded. "No breakers in that direction," he explained. "As soon as we round this island we will be out of sight, and in Wankavilca territory. They control the Guayas islands. I've heard they have a treaty with the Punáe, but that doesn't include trespassing on each other's waters." He thought for a moment and added, "You better pray we don't meet any Wankavilca vessels."

I returned to the wet deck with the mate to reset the daggerboards. Q'enti remained in the cabin—sailing a raft was commoner's work, she said—but her presence on deck wasn't missed.

After clearing the bay there was time to exchange stories of our captures by the Punáe. "The wet deck remained intact," the mate said, referring to the wreck of our Chincha raft. "The captain and I clung to it along with three of the crew, but all the others were swept away. We thought you and Lady Orma drowned with them. We held on for two days without food or sweet water, and then a Punáe raft came upon us."

"Did the sharks trouble you?" I asked.

"Sharks? Well might you ask. No, not while we were alone, thank the Lord of Fishes for that, but later . . . ."

"What happened to the three who were with you?"

"That's what I was about to tell you. The Punáe rescued us, and then those slimy bottom-feeders used us as shark bait."

"Say you so?"

"May I eat farts if it's not true. Those muck-bathers took one of our men and tied a rope around him, slashed his legs, then trailed him behind the raft until the sharks came. When the fins appeared they pulled him close to the side and readied their harpoons. The bastards! Some of the sharks they hauled aboard still had pieces of him dangling from their jaws. When there was nothing left of the first man they seized another."

I took my hand from my mouth. "All three perished in this way?"

The mate nodded grimly. "It was only when the island of Puná came in sight that they ceased this fiendish sport, and busied themselves sailing to their harbor. By then only the captain and I were left."

"And you they kept for sacrifice," I said.

"It is so. We were for many days as you found us, bound and starved. I thought the captain had gone mad when he said you came to him. How did you know we were there?"

"A lucky guess," I heard myself say.

The mate studied the deck for a moment and then looked at me. "What is this about Guayas?" he frowned. "I thought Lady Orma wanted to join her husband in Tumbez."

That was the story I devised for Q'enti when we boarded the raft in Chincha. "A change of plan," I said and turned away.

He caught my arm. "You're not really a servant, are you? From whom are you hiding?"

"Let's just say we're not eager to meet any Inca officials."

"Very well, but why Guayas? The Wankavilca will flay you alive before you can shit, and then hang your skin in their temple. It's true," he said squeezing my arm tighter, "I've seen it."

I returned his stare. "We'll take our chances."

"The Wankavilca don't give chances," he said releasing my arm. "You can throw your life away if you choose, but don't expect the captain and me to follow. We are going to Tumbez—straight to Tumbez, and we don't give a shark's turd what Lady Orma says."

Red dawn found us entering a channel between low, swampy islands. The wind sank to a breeze and our sail slackened. The tide ran out revealing broad mud flats, and from the shores came early morning birdcalls and the screech of monkeys. With the daggerboards raised we took up poles to guide our craft through shallow waters. The channel narrowed, but ahead I could see open water. It seemed a safe, tranquil place, until the mate shouted, "Captain."

I joined them on the stern. A huge raft rounded the island, its crew rushing to change course into the channel.

"Wankavilca or Punáe?" the captain wondered.

The mate shaded his eyes and peered, then announced, "Punáe."

"I thought we lost them in the night," I said.

The captain sighed heavily. "They would have sent rafts in every direction, but I hoped they would stay out of Wankavilca waters."

"It's shallow here," I said hopefully, "and the channel narrows ahead. That raft is huge, perhaps it will ground on a mud bank."

The mate shook his head. "Not likely. They can go where we go, and from the look of it they have more than enough men manning the poles."

Our pursuer now looked like a giant water bug with a row of legs on either side rising and falling, as if crawling toward us. Shouted commands echoed across the water setting the birds and monkeys screeching again.

"We must do something," I said.

The captain gave me a weary smile. "We still might beat them through the narrows," he said, "and once in open water there may be a wind." He didn't look hopeful.

I dragged Q'enti from the cabin. "Poles?" she said. "Work the poles? Do I look like a peasant?"

Indeed she did not. The highland dress I gave her bore Kañari patterns, but was fashioned like Inca garments. She found a shawl to match, and dress pins to hold everything in place. Her hair was even combed and braided.

"Look," I said turning her toward the Punáe vessel. It was close enough now to see the faces of the crew.

Without a word Q'enti joined us at the poles.

The mud flats drew closer as the channel narrowed, but not enough to hinder our pursuer. The men with the long poles lining its sides dipped and pushed in rhythm, surging the great raft forward and plowing a wake. Our own efforts hardly disturbed the water though the four of us worked frantically. As in a nightmare when motion slows, we crawled toward the channel mouth while the terror behind us gained with each breath.

Arrows whistled past me. I glanced back at the Punáe raft to see archers crowding its bow. Among them stood others with coils of rope and grappling hooks in their hands. Soon they would be close enough to use them.

When we pushed through the channel mouth the Punáe shattered the morning calm with their war cries. The sound—like a crack of thunder—stopped our hearts and left us motionless. Grappling hooks flew, trailing their coils through the air. One caught our stern and its line went taut. The mate dashed for it, grabbing the hook and throwing it aside. A flight of arrows met him. He went down with a shriek, an arrow through his arm and another in his thigh. I leapt to his side intent on dragging him behind the cabin. As I grabbed him the Punáe archers took aim again. I lowered my head and pulled the mate, expecting to feel the rip of arrows in the next breath.

When the arrows didn't come I stopped and looked back. A silence so deep becalmed us that not even birds dared disturb its grip. On the Punáe raft the archers slackened their bows, and those at the poles stood idle.

With no hand raised against us I moved the mate along the outside of the cabin to the bow, where the captain and Q'enti stood gazing ahead. Before us lay a broad channel, and barely more than a sling throw away a raft coasted toward us.

"They altered course when they saw us," the captain said, still not moving.

The mate, propped against the cabin, said between clenched teeth, "Wankavilca." The raft approached without a sound, its bow crowded with warriors.

There came a sudden lurch as the Punáe raft butted our stern, almost knocking us from our feet. It had continued gliding forward even after the poling ceased. I looked back, but none of the Punáe attempted to board us. They spoke in whispers among themselves, eyes darting to the Wankavilca vessel.

The captain jabbed his pole in the water but found no bottom. "Only the sail can take us from here," he said as if making conversation, there being nothing to say about our predicament. We were in the hands of the gods now.

"Captain, help me with the mate," I said, "I must bind his wounds." It was good to have something to busy myself with while the Punáe and Wankavilca decided our fate.

The mate's wounds were simple to deal with because the arrows had penetrated through his limbs. While the captain held him I snapped off the points behind, and then with a quick jerk removed the shafts. The mate growled between clenched teeth at each move, but otherwise took it bravely. Q'enti watched with a look of amusement. I bound his wounds with strips torn from a cloak, only then noticing my hands were slippery with sweat.

Looking up I saw what the others were already aware of—the Punáe raft now floated beside us, its balsa logs touching ours, and the Wankavilca craft edged into the same position on our other side. The warriors on both vessels stood silently, weapons in hand, while a few knelt to secure lines. But no one boarded us. When joined, the three rafts made one floating platform.

"Welcome," I said to the Wankavilca in their language. Their eyes flashed on me in surprise, and then returned with steady gaze to the Punáe. "Save us," I said, but they ignored me.

The mate made to rise and I helped him. "Better to die on your feet," he whispered. "Do you see that Punáe captain? He's the one who found us on the ocean and fed our crew to the sharks."

I regarded the man, a short, thickset fellow wearing strands of shark teeth and a feathered headband, with a gold plaque fastened under his nose. His eyes flashed on Q'enti, then narrowed as he surveyed the Wankavilca. The two sides were evenly matched with about fifty men each.

A Wankavilca chieftain shouldered his men aside. Like them he wore only a loincloth with a narrow apron covering his privates, and a headband of jaguar pelt, but gold pendants dangled from his ears, nose, and lower lip, and more gold hung on his chest and wreathed his arms. The Wankavilca also cut their hair short, and wore nose pendants and face studs like their Punáe cousins, but instead of tattoos banding their arms and legs the Wankavilca men had a patch of designs over their left shoulders. The men around the chief kept their bows taut and spears leveled.

The silence ended when the two leaders conversed, each speaking his own tongue but understanding the other. I grasped enough of both languages to follow the exchange.

"You are in our waters," the Wankavilca chief said.

"Only taking what is ours," the Punáe captain replied. He nodded at Q'enti. "That woman belongs to Lord Tumbala, as do the others. They stole this raft, and shed Punáe blood in the doing."

The Wankavilca chief shrugged. "They may have committed crimes in your territory, but now they are in ours. Like the fish of the sea we take everything that comes from our waters."

"But we have a treaty."

"A treaty not to raid villages, or trespass on each others waterways."

The Punáe captain glanced at his men from the corners of his eyes. They strained to hold back, eager for the attack.

"We do not trespass," the Punáe captain said, "we only retrieve what is ours. Would you risk a war over a raft and a few fugitives?"

"Would you?" the Wankavilca chief replied.

I realized that neither man could retreat in front of his warriors. Each stood firm with dignity, and, I confess, a measure of truth on his side, but so it is at the outset of most wars. Yet it wasn't the fate of these two ancient rivals that concerned me. We stood between them, a thicket of arrows and spears leveled on either side of us. Whether we lived or died was no longer of concern to either party. Moving slowly, with hands open and away from my sides, I sat down, and urged my companions to do the same. They caught my look and hunched below the lines of arrows.

"In the name of peace," the Punáe captain said, "keep the raft but give us the foreigners."

It occurred to me he had few choices. He might replace the raft himself, but if he returned without us Tumbala would surely remove his head, or worse.

"You take the raft and we keep the foreigners," the Wankavilca chief suggested.

I saw that neither of them was serious about these negotiations. They only stalled while their men shifted for position.

The Punáe captain brought his hands to his hips. "What do you want with them?"

"They will be gifts for our temple altars," came the reply.

I felt like a llama with its feet bound while two priests argued over who would slit its throat.

The Punáe captain looked to his men with a shrug as if to say, 'I tried to reason with them,' and in so doing turned his body sideways to the Wankavilca. I recognized this as a defensive stance, making a smaller target for arrows. "Keep your head down," I whispered to Q'enti.

Then bowstrings sang and arrows zipped over our heads. Screams and the thud of bodies followed. The two sides recovered, pulling their wounded back, then war cries cut the air. They lunged. The four of us caught in the middle crouched together, and I found myself shielding Q'enti from the battle while the captain did the same for the wounded mate.

Feet stumbled into us and bodies fell above. The high-pitched shriek of war cries raised cold bumps on my skin. I glanced up to be certain no one threatened us. They fought in duals with spears and clubs and axes, howling in fury over the groans of the vanquished. None paid heed to our huddled group. Beside me a spear thrust left a Punáe holding his entrails, and an instant later his slayer went down with an ax sunk in his face. A fallen Wankavilca stretched to reach a club lying on the deck, but no sooner did he seize the handle than an ax came down leaving his severed hand still grasping the club. A Punáe screamed and went to his knees beside me, his arm twisted at an impossible angle, and then came the hollow sound of a ripe melon bursting as his attacker finished him with a club blow that caved in the top of his head.

Q'enti shivered beneath me while I held her flat to the deck. If she dies so does Qhari, I thought. Will I die defending Q'enti?

The fighters were now at each other's throats with bare hands, most having lost their weapons as they tumbled in pairs across the bloody deck. I saw a Punáe wrestle his opponent onto his back and sit on the man's chest, but both were so covered in gore the Punáe couldn't fasten his hands on the man's throat, so he used his thumbs to rip out his eyes. He held the orbs above his head, shrieking his victory to the sky while his victim howled in agony. Turning away with a shudder, I saw another Punáe leap on the back of a wounded Wankavilca, and seizing the man's hair smash his face on a timber again and again, until the Wankavilca had no face left. But still the Punáe continued yanking and smashing in blood frenzy, screeching like a demon.

When the battle began the two sides were evenly matched and the outcome uncertain. But the Punáe now pushed the Wankavilca back. The Wankavilca fought ferociously but less than half their number remained standing, and these stumbled backwards over fallen comrades. They snatched up weapons and retreated to their raft where their chief tried to organize a defense. But the Punáe, sensing victory, pursued vigorously and soon broke through, carrying the battle to the Wankavilca deck.

The captain looked at me and shook his head. "Prepare to meet Lord Tumbala again," he said, "if we live that long."

The sound of splashes swung my head to the Wankavilca vessel where the Punáe cast three more defenders over the side. The Wankavilca chief stood with his back to the water fending off two attackers with an ax, while his remaining men tried to fight their way to his rescue. One fell with a spear through his belly as I watched.

"We can slip over the side and swim to shore," I said to the captain.

"I'm not leaving my mate," he replied, jaw set.

It was a foolish idea—Q'enti couldn't swim either—but with the Wankavilca on the verge of defeat something had to be done. There was no question about our fate if the Punáe won.

Without further talk I rose and made for the Punáe raft. Behind me I heard the captain shout, "Wait, where are you . . . ?" I paid no heed. The deck was slippery with gore as I picked my way over the bodies. I gained the Punáe vessel without being noticed and ran to the stern. Here a helmsman grasped the great tiller oar, keeping the huge vessel steadied against our craft. He turned from the battle to look at me in surprise, unable to comprehend what I was doing. Resin-soaked torches lay piled near the pot holding the hearth coals. I snatched one up and, knocking the pot lid aside, ignited it. The helmsman dropped his oar and came at me, arms extended. I ducked inside his grasp and jabbed the flaming torch at his belly. He jumped back with a shriek. Taking the torch in both hands I swung hard, smashing the side of his head in a burst of sparks. He screamed, the flaming pitch sticking to his skin, and leapt into the water.

I kicked over the hearth pot spilling its coals on the other torches, and then dashed along the cabin side setting its roof thatch alight. Flames burst upwards. In moments thick white smoke churned into the morning sky. A wounded Punáe raised himself, shouting the alarm to his comrades still battling on the Wankavilca raft. All eyes turned and for an instant the struggles ceased. Then with a cry of desperation the Punáe turned as one and raced back to their flaming vessel. I dove over the side.

When I surfaced the battle had shifted to the Punáe raft, for the Wankavilca charged at the heels of their enemies. While some Punáe doused the flames others tried to hold back the Wankavilca. But there were not enough Punáe left to split their force, and in these moments of confusion the Wankavilca overwhelmed them. I saw our captain help the mate to his feet. They picked up weapons and, with the mate leaning on the captain and hopping at his side, the pair joined the slaughter.

I swam back and worked my way alongside the Punáe raft. The fire at the stern was extinguished but the cabin roof still smoldered. A Punáe body splashed into the water beside me. Another Punáe stood dueling on the edge with feet apart, his back to me. I reached up and grabbed his ankles from behind. Caught off balance, he hit the water with a spear in his chest.

I spied the captain and mate near the bow, each with an arm around the others shoulders. The captain held a spear in his free hand and the mate a club. They closed on the Punáe captain who stood alone with one hand on his bloody neck. His chest heaved and he held an ax weakly in front of him. "This is for my crew, you shark loving bastard," the captain shouted. He rammed his spear into the man's stomach. The Punáe captain dropped his ax and, grabbing the spear shaft in both hands, sank to his knees. The mate raised his club. "And from me, too, you puss-eating ass-stuffer." The weapon came down smashing the man's skull like an egg.

Q'enti! I thought. What's happened to her? I heaved myself from the water and knelt dripping on the deck, scanning the scene of devastation. The dead sprawled everywhere, in some places two deep, and the stink of blood and intestines and vomit wrapped the vessels like a shroud. Bodies floated alongside adding their own coloring to the water. The last Punáe stood huddled together, but defiantly waving their weapons and shouting hoarsely. None surrendered.

I scrambled across the Punáe vessel, stepping over bodies and slipping on gore. The deck of our raft, wedged between the Punáe and Wankavilca vessels, was littered with dead and dying. With a deep sigh of relief I found Q'enti where I left her, curled up like a turtle with her face buried in her knees and her hands covering her head. I knelt beside her. "Q'enti, it's over now," I said gently.

"Who won?" she said without lifting her head.

"The Wankavilca."

Q'enti sat up and looked around. "Is that good?"

XIII

In which Brazen Lies are told, a Heinous Crime is revealed and its Perpetrator Established, and the Fate of the Mariners is settled.

"Take your filthy hands off him!" the captain barked, shoving the warriors away from the mate. The old mate clung to the captain's side, waving his good arm and hopping on one leg. Blood seeped from his bandages. "Let me be, you stinking tidal slugs," he shouted, "I'll decide when it's time for me to go."

The Wankavilca were cleaning off the deck by dispatching the wounded and throwing them over the side. To them, the old mate looked ready for disposal. They didn't understand what was shouted at them in the Chincha language, but the refusal gestures were clear. They looked to their chief. I had already learned his name was Guayacan.

"Don't trouble yourselves," Guayacan said to us, and indicated the mate, "my men will look after him for you."

"Thank you, great Lord," I replied, "but we aren't ready to part with him." The four of us stood on the wet deck of our raft while Guayacan looked down from the cabin deck. A line of warriors stood behind us. The dead were already dumped over the side and floated in clumps nearby. The Punáe vessel, with half its cabin and dry deck in blackened ruin, drifted alongside.

Guayacan's eyes hardened on the old mate. "But he is wounded, and of no use to me." The mate edged against the captain who placed an arm around him.

"True, Lord Guayacan, but I can heal him," I said speaking in a mixture of Wankavilca and Kañari, which he seemed to understand.

Guayacan dismissed this with a wave. "He can't even walk up the temple ramp."

I didn't want to ask why he thought that necessary. The Wankavilca had not yet made clear what they planned to do with us, but I felt a cold hand on the back of my neck.

"Let them have him," Q'enti whispered. I ignored her.

"Surely, Lord Guayacan, you will show us mercy," I said. "Did we not fight for you? If I hadn't set the Punáe raft ablaze—"

"Enough!" he roared, causing me to shrink. "I attacked the Punáe, and I conquered them." His warriors exchanged glances. They didn't wish to be reminded of their near defeat, and their leader clearly intended to claim an unaided victory for himself.

"We have treasure," I said trying a new tack, "we can buy our wounded friend from you." My companions grasped enough to understand the direction of these negotiations, and at mention of treasure all three looked at me in surprise. "With your permission, Lord Guayacan . . . ?" I said edging toward the cabin. Guayacan looked indifferent. I returned with the bag of precious metals I stole from Tumbala's treasury.

The captain and mate exchanged a nod when I opened the bag, remembering my dash to retrieve it from the woods, but never knowing what it held. Q'enti eyed the gleaming gold and silver trinkets. They looked at me admiringly, but their faces fell when Guayacan snapped, "That's mine. This raft and everything on it, including you, belongs to me." The warriors at our backs grunted in agreement. Guayacan pointed at the mate and said to his men, "Dispose of that one."

They grabbed the mate and captain, trying to pull them apart, but the two clung to each other fiercely and a struggle ensued. One of the warriors raised his club.

"Wait," I shouted running to the mate's side. "I will give gold to every man if you leave him to me." The warriors looked to Guayacan while the mate and captain swallowed hard, gasping for breath.

"Please, take these," I said quickly, opening the bag and handing around gold nose pendants. "We took them from Tumbala. Wear them and shame that filthy Punáe."

Guayacan leapt to stop me. "Mine!" he said grabbing the bag away. But the warriors admired the gold pieces in their hands and none moved to return them to their chief. Guayacan swept them with a look but they stared back placidly, several already replacing their own ornaments with the prizes. "I was going to share this with you later anyway," Guayacan said to appease them.

"There is more for everyone," I said reaching for the bag. In his surprise Guayacan let go of it. The warriors crowded around and others who had been left out hurried over. Guayacan glared at me but didn't interfere. "Let my man live," I shouted, holding a clutch of silver above my head. The men bobbed their heads in agreement and converged grabbing at the silver.

Once everyone had something I slipped from the swirl and confronted Guayacan. "Your warriors agree my man should live, Lord."

"Then keep him for now," Guayacan huffed.

The old mate released a heavy breath, and the captain helped him to the bow. The two sat alone, nodding to me in gratitude. Q'enti rolled her eyes at this waste of treasure.

"You must have your share, Lord," I said offering Guayacan a handful of gold.

"It is all mine," he said stamping his foot.

"Pardon, Lord, but we intend to offer this at your temple. Surely your high priest won't be pleased if you take what is destined for the altar?"

Guayacan stiffened. "Everything I capture is mine by right, and it won't be the gold that's on the altar, but you."

The Wankavilca wasted no time returning to Guayas with their trophies. Three Punáe who had the misfortune to be knocked unconscious during the fight were tied to the wet deck of the Wankavilca raft, to prevent them from diving into the water or otherwise ending their own lives. We were forced to sit with them, though we weren't bound. Our party exchanged uneasy glances at being grouped with the prisoners destined for sacrifice. "At least we will reach Guayas alive," I told them. The captain and mate didn't look enthusiastic.

Guayacan sailed homeward in triumph with two Punáe rafts in tow and a knot of prisoners on deck. Every raft and village we passed sent up cheers, to which the victors replied with waves and shouts of their own.

I watched forests and mangrove swamps drift by, the shoreline low and hazy in the moist heat. The water went flat and brown when we entered the main channel of the Guayas, and the air settled like a sodden quilt. Though we sat quietly on the deck we all dripped in the heat. On the second day a mountain standing alone emerged on the eastern horizon, and then ahead of us hills rose behind the coastal plain. Other rafts joined our procession, so that we were a flotilla by the time the mooring lines were run out at Guayas. Hundreds crowded the banks to see our arrival, shouting victory salutes over pounding drums. Proud warriors jerked the Punáe captives to their feet for exhibition. Wailing followed when the names of the Wankavilca who did not return were called out, and then the Punáe were tossed to eager hands.

The four of us stayed huddled on deck during these proceedings, fearful that in the exaltation of the moment Guayacan would give us to the mob, also. They made us stand for display, but Guayacan kept us from grasping hands. Then, slinging my treasure bag over his shoulder, Guayacan led us in solemn procession to the temple.

The temple was a simple structure of poles and split cane, set atop the highest mound in the town of Guayas. When we arrived at the flat-topped summit, puffing and glistening from the steep climb, an attendant informed Guayacan that the high priest was at prayer in the holy of holies, but would emerge soon. Sullen guards ringed the patio where we waited. The captain and mate exchanged whispers, while Q'enti gazed off to the Guayas River where dugout canoes and log sailing rafts plied the channel. We sweated in the heat and thick air, which even a breeze moving over the plain could not dispel.

Guayacan stayed with us, not wanting to let his prizes out of his sight. He had remained adamant that we, and our treasure, were his to do with as he pleased, but he decided to march us to the temple as a prefatory gesture. The crowd that followed us from the landing waited at the foot of the mound in expectation.

Wooded hills rose behind the temple, and before us the town of Guayas stretched across a plain to the river's edge. Houses on stilts with thatch roofs stood between scattered trees, and wisps of hearth smoke curled into a hazy, white-gray sky void of cloud or sun. Somewhere a dog barked setting off others, and from the distance came the wail of an infant. The Wankavilcas didn't plan their towns with streets and compounds like civilized people, but scattered their dwellings on any convenient patch of ground. Here and there hand-built mounds like the one we stood on poked above the houses, their flat tops sprouting simple shrines. The dwellings continued along the river as far as I could see, so that it was impossible to tell where the town began or ended.

I wandered to the temple door and looked inside. The stench of charred flesh drifted on wisps of smoke through the interior. From the walls and roof dangled all manner of creatures, skinned and stuffed so they looked quite alive, which served as their gods. There were sharks and giant stingrays, toucans and eagles, jaguars and pumas, green lizards and black caimans, all with emeralds set in their eyes and looking frightful. But the most loathsome creature was an enormous serpent as thick as a man that stretched across the entire back wall above the altar. Its head turned outward to the viewer with jaws wide showing rows of needle teeth.

Q'enti came up behind me and peered over my shoulder at the horrors hanging from walls and roof. But when she saw the great serpent she shuddered and hid her eyes, then turned and fled. I hadn't known she was terrified of snakes, or indeed, of anything. Huge serpents from the eastern jungles are often brought to Cuzco where they are a source of great wonder and curiosity, but I'd never seen one this big.

From behind a skin cover in the back wall came the droning of prayers. A pair of tall, clay censors shaped like men with bowls on their heads framed the altar. The altar itself was no more than a wooden table covered with jaguar skins, on which rested three baskets brimming with emeralds. The stones were deserving of rings and necklaces, but topping each basket was an emerald as big as an egg. I remembered Zapana telling me of seeing such treasures. He said the people of the north revere emeralds, and deliver all they find to temples where they are worshipped as daughters of the Great Emerald—the Eye of the Condor. For the first time I felt a thread of truth in the tales, and envisioned the Eye of the Condor resting on a simple altar such as this, hidden deep within a secret temple.

A low bench sat in front of the altar before me. The bench, and the earthen floor around it, was encrusted with a thick, dark substance. With a shudder I realized it was the dried blood of sacrificial victims. It took little imagining to see the priests lay their victim on this bench, stretch his arms and legs wide, and raise a knife over his heart—or was it that quick? Among the creatures hanging from the roof were several complete human skins, flayed from their owners and stuffed with ashes. The old mate had warned me about this. Would we soon be joining these ghastly trophies?

I retreated to the patio where the mate sat with his injured leg stretched out while the captain fanned him with a cloak. "What's in there?" the captain asked with a nod to the temple. "Only a lot of heathen nonsense," I replied casually, and then knelt to fuss with the mate's bandages. The arrow wounds had not festered. Given time he would recover—if he survived the day.

The mate fixed his eyes on mine and said, "The puke-eaters are going to sacrifice us, aren't they?"

"Not yet," I replied cheerfully.

"But soon," he insisted, eyes downcast.

I joined Q'enti at the edge of the platform. Without turning she said, "Are you sure this will save us?" We hadn't discussed it but she knew what I had in mind.

"As long as you remember we are Kañari women, Q'enti, and you only speak that language." I spoke with more assurance than I felt. "Oh, and this time, be as haughty as you wish. Make them understand with whom they are dealing." She looked at me from the corners of her eyes as if to say, 'Of course.'

I knew we had only one chance. The ruse might work for Q'enti and me, I thought, if I just let Q'enti be Q'enti, but the captain and mate . . . ?

"Choque," the mate called. I turned to see the captain helping him to his feet. Two attendants emerged from the temple carrying a throne carved from a single block of dark stone. It had a rounded seat and up-curving arms, but no back, and the pedestal was a crouching feline. "For your high priest?" I said to Guayacan. He gave me a superior look. "She is a priestess, and I know her well. This won't take long. Your skin will be a fine addition to her temple."

The high priestess strode forth. It surprised me to find a woman ruling the temple, but what surprised me more were her clothes, or lack of clothes. She wore a wrap-around cotton skirt and a long-sleeved vest, but the vest was short leaving her midriff bare and open at the front revealing her breasts. On her head sat a high, domed crown of stiff cloth with side-flaps brushing her shoulders. A weight of gold jewelry flashed as she took her seat.

Guayacan bowed and sat cross-legged facing her, his back to us. The two held a friendly exchange in low voices, which appeared to contain boasting and congratulations, while the priestess glanced at us curiously. Spiral scars decorated her cheeks, her ears were rimmed with gold circlets, and she wore a large nose-ring, but she didn't look fierce. In truth, she looked quit regal on her throne, dry and unaffected by the heat while Q'enti and I sweated in our Kañari dresses. I could imagine Guayacan's version of events and decided it was time to intervene. I nodded to Q'enti and the two of us went forward. The temple guards stiffened and narrowed their eyes, but none moved.

"Greetings, Great One," I said in Kañari. They turned at this interruption, Guayacan looking annoyed. Q'enti pulled me back a step, placing herself in front. "Yes, greetings," she said lifting her chin. "Are you the supreme ruler of this temple? Because I'll speak with no other."

Guayacan scowled at us. "Kneel before Lady Goodgift," he ordered. I complied but Q'enti remained standing. Guayacan muttered in Wankavilca to Goodgift, "I told you they are impudent savages."

"Not so, great Lord," I replied in Kañari, "but we are most grateful to you for saving us, and trust you will be duly honored."

Goodgift looked impressed that I understood Wankavilca, and much to my relief she now spoke in passable Kañari. "Saved?" she said, eyes twinkling, "I thought you were captured?"

It was courteous of her to use this trade language for our benefit, though I didn't like the direction she took. Q'enti and I were fluent enough in Kañari to pass as native speakers to the untrained ear. Thereafter we all spoke Kañari. Goodgift seemed pleased to show off her knowledge, and Guayacan was forced to follow her lead.

"Not 'captured,'" Q'enti replied testily, "'saved,' as my assistant said." Once again she relegated me to lesser status, but this was not the time to complain. "The Punáe were trying to capture us," she explained, "to prevent us from reaching Guayas." She pointed at Guayacan. "But this chief saved us."

Guayacan worked his jaw. If he didn't capture us then he couldn't claim the booty and honors.

"We wish to reward his valor," I added quickly before Guayacan could protest. "Please give him the Punáe raft we brought, and allow him to keep the vessel he captured."

"But they are already mine," Guayacan said.

"Yes, and we want you to keep them," I said, "and some of the finer pieces in our bag." I gestured to the leather treasure bag beside him. Goodgift looked amused, and curious to see what was in the bag. She gave Guayacan a questioning look and with a sigh he opened it. When Goodgift saw the precious metals she raised her lower lip and nodded in admiration.

"Now where is the high priest?" Q'enti demanded. "I will only speak with my equal."

Goodgift looked indignant and exchanged a glance with Guayacan, who continued glowering at us. "I am Lady Goodgift, High Priestess of Guayas, and ruler of this temple," she announced coldly. "Who are you? And what are you doing with Punáe rafts and gold?"

"We took them from Tumbala," I said, "as gifts for you."

"*You* stole from Tumbala?" she said incredulously.

"Our raft sank on the way here," Q'enti said as if it was a small matter, "and so we stopped at Puná. Tumbala, that filthy savage, didn't want me to reach you, so I took what I needed."

Goodgift looked at her with new respect while I fumed silently, *She* took what *she* needed? Q'enti had nothing to do with the treasure or the raft! Behind me I heard the captain and mate clearing their throats. Be patient, I willed them, and stay out of this.

"As for who I am," Q'enti continued, "I am a condor priestess, and this is my assistant." She waved at me without taking her eyes off Goodgift.

Goodgift's mouth fell open. "But . . . but . . ." she stammered, "there are no priestesses. The condor priests are all men." She recovered and glared at us. "What jest is this? You think me a fool? How dare you speak of the sacred brotherhood!" Guayacan looked pleased.

"We are the first women," I said quickly. "Didn't they tell you? No matter, we are here now."

"Indeed we are," Q'enti said, "and if you don't treat us with proper respect our brothers will visit you and your temple. Do you know what condor dust is?"

Goodgift made a face at mention of the poison, but Guayacan looked blank. As I suspected he knew of condor priests from whispers, but only the highest understood their deadly secrets.

Goodgift rose suddenly and held up a hand. "No need for threats. There has been an unfortunate misunderstanding, but I sent for you and you are now my honored guests. I think we should speak privately," she said indicating the temple door.

Guayacan, still seated, looked as confused as I was. She sent for us? I wondered. Goodgift looked down at Guayacan with a frown. "You may rise," she said, including me with a wave. "And, Lord Guayacan, you will wait here," she added. "I want a word with you later." The veins on Guayacan's neck stood out but he lowered his head and backed away.

Once inside the sanctuary Q'enti kept her eyes off the huge snake hanging behind the altar. I couldn't blame her; its emerald eyes seemed to follow us.

Goodgift said, "The sign, please."

Q'enti produced a thin smile. I wanted to think it was because she admired my foresight and cunning, but in truth her lips pressed together in a tolerant grin for Goodgift's benefit, as if indulging a petty official. She nodded to me, and we each bared our right shoulder. Goodgift stepped closer, eyes bulging.

The red dye I took from Tumbala's treasury held true, and the six dots surrounding a circle I painted on Q'enti's shoulder showed clearly. I was careful to duplicate the size and position of the tattoos on Lizard-eyes and Nose-ring. Q'enti had given me the six dots like those on the novice Asto, but refused me the circle to keep me in my place. No matter, the tattoos had a greater effect on Goodgift than I dared hope.

We fastened our dresses again, not wanting Goodgift to study our handiwork too closely. She stood back with a hand to her brow and ran her eyes over our Kañari costumes, nodding to herself, and then bowed her head and showed open palms. "Why didn't you reveal the markings before?" she lamented. "Forgive me, and my people, and please spare this temple." She looked ready to burst into tears.

"Perhaps," Q'enti said, surveying our surroundings disdainfully, but pointedly avoiding the great serpent behind the altar. Goodgift lowered her chin and looked over her brows at Q'enti, pleading. Now is the moment to exact all we want, I thought.

"You will give the Punáe rafts to Guayacan," I said, "and honor him for aiding us, but the treasure bag stays with me." Goodgift nodded rapidly. "And you will have our two sailors transported to Tumbez," I said. Q'enti gave me a surprised look but shrugged, as did Goodgift. "And you will give them forty sacks of thorny oyster shell to compensate them for the raft they lost," I added. Goodgift looked at me askance, but then glanced at Q'enti and lowered her head again, nodding slowly.

Q'enti took charge. "We seek a man named Pisar. Where is he?" she demanded. My stomach tightened.

"That wretch!" Goodgift said, eyes burning. Q'enti and I exchanged a look. Goodgift lowered her voice. "Pisar is alive as I said in my message. We will not harm a condor priest, not even a novice like Pisar, but he must be punished. That is why I sent for you, though I didn't know you would be women." She gave us an admiring nod.

I locked eyes with Q'enti and we both took a deep breath, exhaling in unison. Clear enough, I thought.

I addressed Goodgift. "My Lady, we came as quickly as possible, but as we told you we had an unfortunate meeting with the Punáe. Tell us what Pisar has done and we will settle this immediately."

Goodgift looked relieved. "I'm glad you are women," she said. "We understand each other." I gave her an encouraging nod. Her face clouded and she said, "When our girls become women they can go with whom they please, providing they are never forced. Pisar likes the young ones, and their parents felt honored because he is from the Condor Temple." She leaned forward and confided, "I don't know why the young ones let him. Do you know him? He's such an ugly little man." We shook our heads and Goodgift continued. "As I said, Pisar likes the very young ones, those who have just reached womanhood. But before a girl reaches that stage she is a child and must be protected." Goodgift's voice lowered and she opened her hands. "You see, children don't understand these things, and they don't want it." What had been anger rising within me turned to disgust. Goodgift looked at the floor and said, "Pisar raped a child of nine years."

I felt ready to burst with fury. Q'enti nodded solemnly but I knew the deed meant nothing to her. She was incapable of compassion, and was only deciding how to turn this to her advantage.

"Pisar must be brought before me now," Q'enti said. "I shall return him to the Condor Temple where my brothers will punish him."

Goodgift hesitated. "But can't you do it here? My people must see justice."

As much as I wanted to avenge this hideous crime I knew Q'enti was right. We needed Pisar. I swallowed hard and said, "It's our law that justice must be done at our temple, but I swear to you that I will see him dead."

Goodgift stared at me and saw it was a promise I would keep. "Very well, if that is the law of the Condor, we are satisfied." She turned to Q'enti.

"I had to keep Pisar from my people so they wouldn't tear him apart before you arrived. Please wait." She offered a courteous bow and departed.

I said to Q'enti, "We must be gone from here today."

"Nonsense," she said. "I'm exhausted, and I need new clothes. How do you think I'll look in one of those vests? Besides, I'm famished. It's hot here, but a few days rest will do me good."

"Don't you realize there are real condor priests on their way to Guayas right now? They could arrive tomorrow, or today. They will denounce us at a glance, and then you won't find Goodgift so accommodating."

"You will think of something, my dear."

"We'll lose Pisar, and with him the temple."

Q'enti thought on this. "No," she announced, "I have changed my mind. We are leaving today."

Goodgift reappeared from behind a skin cover in the back wall. She held the flap aside while two men emerged bearing a cage suspended from a pole. The men set their burden down and left. Goodgift presented the cage with a wave. It was fitting accommodation for Pisar.

When I untied the latch the side fell open, and I stepped back holding my nose.

"No, no," came a whimper from inside. "It was a mistake, please, I didn't mean it. Don't. Please don't." It was a man's voice speaking Wankavilca.

"Come out," I said in Kañari.

A tangle of matted hair appeared, and two eyes blinked at me. I hoped he was quick enough to grasp our deception.

"Come out," I repeated sternly. "You won't be harmed, at least not today."

Pisar rolled from the cage, hands tied at his back. He groaned as he unbent his legs, and stared at us from the floor. He was a small, skinny man clad in a dirty loincloth. Ribs stuck out from a chest that was too broad for one his size, and though his head was huge his features were tiny and crowded. His eyes darted like an animal ready to bolt, until they settled on our Kañari dresses.

"Yes, we are of your people," I said.

Q'enti came and stood over him, her back to Goodgift. "We are condor priestesses come to take you back to the temple," she said giving him a wink. Pisar looked from Q'enti to me, and a cunning look spread across his features.

"Where you will be punished as you deserve," I added for Goodgift's benefit. "On your knees, filth."

Pisar gave Q'enti a shrewd look and dragged himself up.

I stood in front of him with hands on my hips. "A nine year old girl?" I said. Before he could reply I drove my knee into his face. I felt better, and Goodgift smiled. Pisar spit blood and glanced at Q'enti, who turned away with a bored expression. He gave me a sullen look. "I didn't know she was so young," Pisar said. "She looked older, and she wanted it."

"She wanted it?" Goodgift said. "Then why were there bruises all over her neck?"

Pisar cowered before Goodgift. "I thought she was just pretending to struggle," he whined. "Most women like it that way."

Goodgift and I exchanged an incredulous look. She said, "We're not talking about women, we are talking about a child."

Pisar sniffed and tears appeared. "But I told you I didn't know she wasn't a woman."

I slammed my knee into his face again.

"Stop! Don't hit me. I'm sorry. Please don't hurt me."

I was only getting started on him but Q'enti gripped my arm. She didn't care about Pisar, but we needed him in condition to travel. Privately I vowed to keep my promise to Goodgift and see Pisar dead.

"We shall take him now," Q'enti said.

Goodgift went to the door and signaled two guards. They dragged Pisar to his feet and marched him outside. We followed.

The captain and mate looked up expectantly, surprised to see this new prisoner. Guayacan still sulked across the patio.

"Oh, and one more thing," Q'enti said to Goodgift. "We need provisions, bearers, and a guide. Today."

"Certainly," Goodgift replied, "but where shall I tell the guide to take you?"

Q'enti stiffened and looked at Pisar. He growled at me through bloody lips, then sighed and muttered to Q'enti, "Eastward up the Kañar River and into the mountains."

"Up the Kañar River to the mountains," Q'enti announced.

"To the mountains?" Goodgift said. "The Incas rule there. My men can take you to the foot of the mountains, but not beyond."

The captain beamed and said with a look of amazement, "How did you do it?" The old mate, speechless with joy, simply threw his arms around me and held tight. When I finally escaped his embrace he had tears in his eyes, but still showed his six-tooth grin. Catching my breath I said, "It wasn't easy, but you'll be in Tumbez in a few days with a handsome profit to show for your toils." The old mate went limp with relief and had to sit down.

"But how . . . ?" the captain said again, shaking his head in disbelief.

Q'enti rolled her eyes. "Isn't it enough you are to live?" she snapped, and then gave me a hard look. It would have suited her if the Wankavilca had sacrificed them, removing the last witnesses to our journey north. She said to the captain, "When you reach Tumbez you're not to tell anyone about us."

"But Lady, you saved us," the captain said. The mate looked up and added, "I'll sing your praises for the rest of my life."

"No you won't," Q'enti said. "Tell them we drowned with the rest of your crew. Qori, silence these two or I'll give them back to the Wankavilca."

She called me 'Qori' in front of them, and they looked to me in bewilderment. They only knew me as the maid Choque, but the old mate had said they didn't really believe that story. I brought a finger to my lips and they held their tongues.

I felt daggers aimed at my back and turned to see Goodgift speaking with Guayacan, who stamped his foot and glared at us. Without looking down he dropped the treasure bag at his feet and marched past us in mute storm. Goodgift hurried over to us apologizing. "Forgive him," she said to Q'enti, "he's a warrior and doesn't understand diplomacy. But he will soon get over it. My temple will give a feast in his honor."

"As long as he stays out of our way," Q'enti said.

"Distribute these among the worthy," I said, giving Goodgift a double-handful of trinkets from my treasure bag. "Pick your best men for our escorts, and make sure there is sufficient food and comforts for this journey." Goodgift hurried away to make the arrangements.

"You are going up the Kañar River into the mountains?" the captain said from behind. I forgot he and the mate stood by when Q'enti announced our intent. Once in the mountains we would be in Kañar province, an Inca bastion. I knew our true destination must be elsewhere, but first we had to smuggle ourselves through Inca territory.

"Perhaps," I replied, "but you must forget about us."

The old mate clasped my shoulder. "I will never forget you Choque, or Qori?" he said slyly. "May the Lord of the Wind watch over you."

"And over you, my friend."

"I thank you, and my wife and children thank you," the captain said, taking my hands and holding them to his breast.

Yes, I thought, I'm giving him back to his wife after all. What is it those two share?

But before I could form words of farewell Goodgift returned and beckoned us. I squeezed the captain's hand, then went with Q'enti to see what she wanted.

"I've given the orders," Goodgift said, smiling broadly at her own efficiency. "The bearers are summoned, and for your guide you have a man of authority who speaks your language."

"Good," Q'enti said, "where is he?"

"Waiting for you there," Goodgift replied pointing to the bottom of the mound. We looked down and saw a man pacing back and forth. It was Guayacan.

XIV

Being an account of travels in the Nameless Land, of its Strange Inhabitants and the Terrors that dwell therein.

"Untie my hands," Pisar pleaded with Q'enti.

"I would like to, my friend, but you must remain bound as long as Guayacan is with us. Here, let me loosen the cords for you. Is that better?"

When we left Guayas they threw Pisar into the dugout with his wrists tied to his ankles. But by now, on the third day, Q'enti had convinced Guayacan to let Pisar travel with only his hands tied. Still, Pisar whined. Guayacan and his men were at the river negotiating our journey inland with a local chief, while Q'enti and I guarded Pisar in a clearing. This was the first chance we had to speak with Pisar in private. He sat between us on a log, his breath smelling like his armpits.

"Where are you taking us?" I said impatiently.

Pisar regarded me sullenly. He feared me, but Q'enti was his savior. "Where do you want to go?" he taunted.

"Now then, my handsome one, never mind her," Q'enti said leaning against him. "We want you to lead us to the condor temple, and we know you will, but we were just wondering about the route."

Q'enti had pleased the Wankavilcas by requesting the same clothes Goodgift wore, and in so doing pleased every man around, Guayacan and Pisar included. She still wore her wide Inca belt under the wrap-around skirt, but the open-fronted vest had a magical

209

effect. All she had to do was arch her back and look away innocently, and the men couldn't do enough for her. I confess she was more than well endowed, and perfectly shaped, and I hated her all the more. Being a modest woman I wore my Kañari dress, though I sweated underneath.

"You expect me to take you to the condor temple?" Pisar said. "Who are you, and what do you really want?"

His crooked teeth were so stained I couldn't bear to watch him speak. I looked away and let Q'enti converse.

"We wanted to save you from the Wankavilcas," Q'enti replied.

"Why?"

"Because we promised your brother Asto we would."

"You know Asto? He's still alive? Where is he?"

"Far to the south and gravely ill. He said you would take us to the condor temple to get the antidote."

Pisar chuckled. "I thought they would have tracked him down by now, or the condor dust would have killed him. Either way he will be dead before you return."

"You know about the condor dust?"

"Of course. Asto was poisoned when he stole the emeralds. I'm sure he told you about the emeralds?"

Q'enti gave an indifferent shrug. "Will you help us save your brother?"

"That piss-sucking fool?" Pisar balked. "It's because of him I was expelled from the brotherhood. Let him rot. I never liked him anyway."

"You're no longer a condor priest?"

"I was an acolyte like Asto, but when he stole the emeralds they banished me."

"What about the Wankavilcas?"

"They don't know I've been expelled. I had a good life in Guayas until that girl spoiled everything."

Q'enti reached out to stop me from hitting him. Pisar shrunk. "What's wrong with her?"

"It's her moon-time," Q'enti said. "Now, am I to understand the condor priests won't be pleased if you return?"

"They will kill me if they ever see me again."

"But you know the location of the condor temple?"

"Perhaps, but I can't believe you are doing this for that worm Asto. What are you really after?"

Q'enti nodded to herself and drew in her breath. "I want the Eye of the Condor."

Pisar laughed and shook his head, eyeing us up and down. "Two women? You wouldn't last a day in those jungles."

"Jungles?" I said.

"Yes, jungles." He spat the words. "Why? Did you think the secret temple is in the mountains? The Incas rule the highlands, but you know that. I can tell by your accents you're not Kañari. No, you are Incas, aren't you?"

Q'enti willed my silence with a stare, and then nodded. "Yes, you are very clever, we are Incas. But we have no wish to meet our people."

"Ah, so you're fugitives."

"Like you, yes," Q'enti said.

Pisar looked pleased with the answer. He liked Q'enti. "You're ambitious, I'll give you that. But the truth is that no one survives east of the mountains."

"You did," Q'enti said. "You have been to the condor temple."

"Yes, I lived there, but nothing could make me return."

"You can have this," I said spilling the contents of my treasure bag at his feet. The bag had never left my side.

Pisar eyed the baubles and snorted. "Ha! The treasures inside the condor temple would fill a hundred sacks, but what good is it if you're dead? No, you don't know the terrors lurking in those dark corridors. I will never go back, and if you are wise you'll return to wherever you came from." He sounded firm but his gaze lingered on the metal.

Q'enti sighed. "You are right, it is too dangerous." I opened my mouth but she gave me a cautionary glance and continued, "In a few days Guayacan will leave us and you shall be free. If your brother is still alive we will tell him we tried." Pisar nodded and relaxed. Q'enti said, "I suppose we owe you our lives. How can we repay you?" Pisar pursed his lips. His eyes wandered from the treasure to her breasts.

Q'enti pretended not to notice, and then brightened. "I know, please accept this." She slipped her fingers into the waist of her skirt, fumbling inside her Inca belt, and produced a tiny, oilskin packet.

Is this what she's been guarding all this time? I wondered.

Pisar looked curious, too, and leaned toward Q'enti as she undid the bindings. It held a thin pouch no bigger than a fingernail.

"Look," Q'enti said, opening the pouch and holding it up to his face. Pisar leaned closer.

Suddenly realizing what it was I drew back with a start. Q'enti expelled a puff of breath sending the dust into Pisar's face.

"What . . . ?" Pisar gasped.

Q'enti sat back with a smile. "You know perfectly well what it is," she said in a cold, flat voice. "And you know where the antidote is, so let's go there together."

Lizard-eyes and Nose-ring wore identical amulets, I remembered, and Q'enti used the contents of one on Qhari. I'd forgotten about the other amulet.

Pisar turned pale. "But where did you . . . ?"

Q'enti said, "From two friends of yours, who sought your brother Asto."

Pisar worked his tongue around his mouth and hung his head. "They always come in pairs," he said quietly.

Pisar didn't know that real condor priests had been called to Guayas, and were probably trailing us now. At least two of them, I thought, and nervously scanned the bushes.

"They found Asto," Pisar stated. "They always find their quarry."

"Yes," Q'enti said, "but we found them."

"It wouldn't have mattered to them," Pisar said. "They are pledged to fulfill their missions at any cost. Their own lives mean nothing."

Having faced Lizard-eyes and Nose-ring I knew he spoke the truth. The knowledge that his brother was dead troubled him not in the least, and he seemed to accept that he was now infected with condor dust, also. Pisar nodded to himself and gave Q'enti an admiring look—the admiration of one twisted mind for another. "You're very good," he said. Q'enti preened.

Guayacan and his men returned. "It's arranged," Guayacan said. "We have safe passage as far as the Nameless Land."

"The Nameless Land?" I said.

Guayacan tore his eyes from Q'enti's breasts and gave me his superior look. "The territory along the base of the mountains. It is called the Nameless Land because no chief rules there; a jungle full of outcasts, sorcerers, and thieves." I knew he smiled under the nose pendant covering his mouth. "You wanted to go up the Kañar River, and we are at its mouth now," he said. Then he pointed to the local chief and his men still waiting at the water. "Oh, and he must have a gift to let us pass. I told him you would see to that," he said gesturing to the gleaming pile at our feet. He seemed pleased to be disposing of it for me.

"But they are Wankavilcas, too," I said. "I thought you had the power to command them."

Guayacan shrugged. "They are like cousins, but they have their own chief and temple. A generous gift is required before crossing their land."

"And you will escort us through the Nameless Land?" I said.

Q'enti stood and arched her back. "I'm sure Lord Guayacan will protect us," she said, and licked her lips. Guayacan blushed.

Our journey from Guayas had taken us back down the Guayas River, but this time hugging the eastern channel until we reached the mouth of the Kañar River, which flows down from the mountains. Goodgift provided food and clothing, and cosmetics for Q'enti, in addition to a large dugout canoe which Guayacan and his five men paddled. The Kañar River is little more than a sling-throw wide, and over its brown waters hang moss-laden branches and woody vines. The coastal plain behind its muddy shores is low and lush, and in places swampy, disturbed only by the flight of parrots and chattering monkeys.

We continued upriver, and on the second morning I glimpsed a dark wall on the horizon ahead, looming above a line of clouds. "Yes, the mountains," Guayacan replied to the question on my face. "We are entering the Nameless Land." He shouted to his men, "Keep your eyes open." Pisar scanned the shores nervously. We passed a clearing baking under a relentless sun. Q'enti fidgeted and wanted to land, but Guayacan said it was too dangerous. The people and the forest in this unnamed territory were not to be trusted, he insisted, and we had to stay on the water. But when a plume of smoke up ahead announced a farm Q'enti could no longer contain herself. "Put into shore," she ordered.

"Why?" Guayacan said.

"Because I have to relieve myself, if you must know. Do as you're told."

Guayacan frowned. "Wait until we are past this farm."

"I said now, immediately," Q'enti shot back, turning to glare at him.

Guayacan shifted his steering paddle with a sigh and turned the bow toward shore. We landed with the farmstead still ahead, coasting in among snarled branches laden with drooping moss. The men at the bow examined the water before stepping out to pull the canoe, and while one steadied our craft another poked the bushes looking for snakes. He turned with a nod, and Q'enti and I disembarked. Pisar remained with the men. While I stood on firm ground with my hands in the small of my back, Q'enti walked into the bushes.

"Where are you going?" Guayacan shouted from the stern.

"I told you," Q'enti said without turning.

"Stay here by the water," he said. "It's dangerous in there."

Q'enti called over her shoulder, "I don't need an audience."

Guayacan shook his head and gestured to me. "You go with her, but don't go far."

Sunlight filtered in shafts through the canopy above, but the forest floor was shady and cool, full of shadows and dense underbrush. I walked behind Q'enti on a trail overhung with vines and leaning branches. "This is far enough," I said.

"Wait, I think there's a clearing up ahead." As Q'enti spoke she approached a moss-covered branch arched over the path with a vine hanging to one side. She stooped to pass under it and in the same motion brought her hand up to hold back her hair. The 'vine' sprung to life and Q'enti screamed, falling to her knees with her arm held high in the mouth of a snake! I ran up and the serpent released her, letting the limp arm fall on her crumpled form while it reared its head at me, fangs bared. The open mouth was like a hand stretched wide, and its sinuous body was as thick as a man's arm, covered with tan spots and diamond-shaped blotches. A goodly length of it dangled over the path, but much more coiled around the branch. Still hanging above Q'enti it stretched toward me, eyes glinting. "Come," I yelled to the men. "Come quickly!"

I snatched up a spongy length of wood—the only thing at hand—and approached the snake. It reared and I struck, but I only managed to anger it more. I stepped back, then gritted my teeth and leaned into another swing, this time smacking its head. It was enough to stun the serpent, but the soggy wood came apart in my hands leaving me weaponless. The creature hung head down, and then began uncoiling its body, descending on Q'enti.

The men came running from behind with their spears.

"Kill it," I shouted.

They drew back with a sharp intake of breath when they saw the snake, but then leapt forward stabbing. The serpent had just reached Q'enti when the attack began, and it reared again, jaws wide. Guayacan jabbed its coiled body above, while two others crossed their spears to lift its head away from Q'enti. The creature writhed and fell from the branch with a thud. We jumped back when it fell, and then the men circled, aiming for its head. Pisar arrived, not wanting to be left alone at the river, and hopped up and down urging the men on. The snake tried to slither into the bush but one man pinned it through the tail. Guayacan lunged driving his spear straight through its head.

I went down on my knees at Q'enti's side and brushed her hair from her face. She was unconscious, her face frozen in terror. I put my ear to her mouth—she breathed, but barely. I lifted her injured arm and saw two punctures, already purple. Pisar and Guayacan looked over my shoulder and shook their heads.

"She's alive," I said.

Pisar made a face. "For the moment perhaps, but look at the markings on that snake. They are the most deadly kind, more poisonous than any creature in the jungle."

I'm a healer, I thought, but what do I know about snakebites? We don't have serpents like this in the mountains, and I don't know the medicines of this jungle. "How long does she have," I asked quietly.

Guayacan shrugged. "Depends on how much poison got into her. Even if it was only a little she's not likely to last beyond sundown."

"This is a mistake," Guayacan whispered as we looked at the farmhouse. Pisar and the men waited nearby with Q'enti's limp form. "I told you, only outcasts and sorcerers live here, and outlaw bands."

"But they are farmers," I said indicating the house. "Surely they will know how to treat snakebite?"

Guayacan snorted. "They die from it too."

"Yes, but their sorcerers will know. We must find one."

"I don't want anything to do with them either. I will talk with these people to satisfy you, and then your charming friend can die under their roof."

After they killed the snake, I began dragging Q'enti up the path to the farm clearing. The men had protested, not wanting to leave the safety of the river, but I ignored them and finally they were shamed into helping me. Their eyes never left the bushes, and their spears remained gripped at alert.

The snake that bit Q'enti was as long as two men. One of Guayacan's paddlers, having removed its head, dragged the twitching body behind him. When I saw this I glanced at Guayacan, who shrugged and said, "Deadly, but very tasty."

There was only one house in the clearing, a large structure without walls under its thatched roof. When we entered the clearing we heard wailing. A family gathered inside, moaning and crying out, and though they must have been aware of our presence they showed no sign of it.

"What are they doing?" I asked Guayacan.

"Burying someone."

"In their home?"

"They always do that. Then they abandon the house and move elsewhere."

"I don't want to interrupt their funeral," I said, "but if we don't get help quickly there will be another."

We approached respectfully, entering the house and coming right up to them before a man turned. A bone awl pierced his nose, hanging crossways over a down-turned mouth. He folded his arms across his chest and stared at us. Guayacan spoke quietly to him in Wankavilca and he responded with grunts. A young woman wearing only a wrap-around skirt and strings of beads held a baby on her hip and sobbed quietly. Beside her an old woman with breasts pointed to her belly wailed over an open pit.

I peered down at the deceased, who lay on a cane bed. It was a man, but most of his face was ripped into a bloody pulp exposing bone and teeth, and deep claw marks trailed down his arms and legs.

Guayacan cleared his throat and extended an open hand to me. "It would be polite to offer a gift," he said. I handed over a gold face stud. The man examined it while he listened to Guayacan, but still hesitated. When I produced some tiny silver bells and a gold pendant the man's conversation increased. Guayacan thanked him and ushered me outside.

"The man they are burying must have been killed by a great cat," I remarked.

"Clearly. But they think he was murdered by a sorcerer, who turned himself into a jaguar and sought him out."

"Why?"

"Why did the sorcerer kill him? Because the man slighted him in some way. These sorcerers are jealous and vindictive, and greatly feared. Now the family thinks this one will kill them all unless they make amends with gifts. That's where your trinkets will go."

Guayacan's men rose from their haunches as we approached. They had skinned the snake and were cutting it into sections. Pisar looked on and licked his lips. I knelt to examine Q'enti. She hadn't recovered from the shock of the attack and remained unconscious, which was best for her. I touched her forehead. She sweated and shivered, and her gums bled. The poisoned arm lay outstretched, swollen and purple. I looked up at Guayacan. "What will they do to help us?"

"Who? Those people?" he said turning to look at the house. "Nothing."

"Nothing? What do they do when they are bitten?"

"They consult a sorcerer."

"Is there one near here?"

"Yes, somewhere out there," he said pointing off through the trees. "They call him Ceiba, and he is powerful."

"Good, then we must fetch him quickly."

"I think not. Ceiba is the same one who ripped apart that old man."

"Do you really believe he turned himself into a jaguar?" I chided.

Guayacan didn't smile. "Perhaps . . . and if he didn't then there's a jaguar out there with a taste for human flesh. Either way I'm not taking another step into this jungle. We must go back to the canoe and let the gods decide your friend's fate."

"If you go out there alone," Guayacan said, "I'll look for you in the next life, or wherever it is your people's souls dwell." I had tried threats and bribes—even offering him the remains of Tumbala's treasure—but he refused to go with me. Pisar looked at me as if I was mad. He had tried to talk me out of it, too, afraid that if I vanished and Q'enti died he'd be left alone with the Wankavilcas. Q'enti burned and shivered, and her purple arm swelled.

With only a tree poking above the canopy in the east to guide me I set off alone to find the sorcerer Ceiba. The path was no more than a game trail when I left the clearing, and it soon vanished in a confusion of possible routes, most ending a few steps away in the bushes. Alone, and surrounded by walls of green, I could only hope I was still headed in the right direction.

For a terrified instant I thought a snake had bitten me, but looking down I saw it was only a stick that jabbed my leg. Sunlight glinted through the dark canopy above, but few beams reached the forest floor. The under-story hung heavy with trailing moss and vines, and I waded through broad-leafed plants that hid the ground, never allowing me to see below my knees. What slithered there on the forest floor? I tried using a stick to turn the foliage before setting my foot down, but it slowed me to a halt, so I gritted my teeth and strode forward with false boldness. The ground cover rustled and I jumped back, only to glimpse an armadillo scuttling away. I held the stick upright in front of me now, trying to see every vine and twisted branch, fearful of walking into another horror like the one that felled Q'enti. I knew deadly creatures blend with the jungle and stillness is a trap, but the molted shadows tricked me into pauses I couldn't afford. "How far is Ceiba's house?" I had asked. "Not far if you don't get lost," Guayacan had answered.

I'm lost, I thought, and then shook myself. No, I can't be lost. I haven't time for this. Q'enti will be dead by sundown, if she isn't already, and I won't survive a night in this jungle alone. Qhari is depending on me. I must swallow my fears and push ahead. Where is that path?

My clothes clung to me in the sticky heat. I wiped sweat from my brow, and then struck out in a new direction. But I hadn't gone ten paces when my dress caught on a thorn bush, its needles leaving red lines across my arm. "Damn you," I shouted at the bush, and then kicked it. I jumped back with a cry and hopped on one foot, the other sprinkled with thorns. My shawl held fast to the spiny arms, keeping me in place, and in a fury I threw it off. "Then keep it," I shouted, leaving the torn shawl dangling on the plant.

I stooped to pick the thorns from my foot, and found I was standing in a mossy hollow with black water seeping over my toes. Balancing on one foot I brought the other to my knee and pinched at the spines, wishing my fingernails were longer. But a cloud of tiny flies buzzed around my head, and my hair kept falling in my face, and then an insect bit viciously and I swatted, which landed me on my bottom in the spongy moss. The flies buzzed into my nose and ears. "Enough!" I shouted jumping up. The back of my dress was soaked. I stomped through the bushes waving my hands at the pesky flies, and not caring in which direction I went as long as it was away from the sodden hollow.

"I hate you," I screamed at the forest. But the forest didn't care. It drowsed beneath its canopy, with only the shriek of a distant bird and the hum of insects to answer my challenge. Tears of frustration rolled down my cheeks.

"I don't care," I announced, wiping the tears and once more striding boldly through the undergrowth. Somehow it was reassuring to speak out loud to the jungle, as if convincing myself I wasn't afraid. "Qhari needs me and you can't stop me. Oh please, don't stop me." I found myself running—running and sobbing and tripping and running—with no thought of direction or what lay ahead. I crashed through the forest letting branches slap my face and spines tear my hands, blinded by tears that wouldn't stop. Then, charging through waist-high greenery, I cracked my shin on a hidden log and like a diver plunged face first into the dank forest floor.

Moments passed. I turned my head to spit out leaves and dirt, but remained stretched-out full on my stomach. The forest litter, churned where my face ploughed, was pungent and moist. I lay my cheek against its coolness and listened to my heart thudding. Though my leg felt numb below the knee I could still wiggle my toes. Nothing broken, I thought, but can I stand on it? Misery descended and I closed my eyes, burrowing my cheek further into the dirt. I'm lost, I admitted. I don't know which way to go, but it doesn't matter because I'll never find the sorcerer. Q'enti will die, and then Qhari will die. Qhari trusted me and I failed him. I can't do this anymore, dragging Q'enti along on this fool quest, pretending I'm brave when I'm not. Where is Inca Moon now? At least Q'enti will die as she deserves. But Qhari . . . sweet, innocent Qhari . . . he doesn't deserve to be eaten by poison. Zapana will never look at me again. I've already lost him because I thought I didn't need him, or anybody. And now there's nobody but me, and I wish there wasn't even me.

A low growl stirred the forest, a rumbling from deep in the throat of a great cat. I felt my hair prickling and the cold hand on my neck, and then a shivering took hold of me. The vision of the old man in his grave came to me, his face ripped off and body torn. The cat growled again, this time closer, and my shivering became a tremble until my hands vibrated and my heart pounded in my head. "Please don't," I whined, closing my eyes tight as if to make it go away. A twig snapped nearby with a sound that went through me like a blade of ice, and suddenly I found myself on my feet running in blind terror.

With arms flailing and feet barely touching the ground I raced through the forest, leaping bushes and ducking branches. I imagined the jaguar closing behind in great bounds, foam at its jaws and claws bared. Expecting to feel its teeth in the next instant I ran faster, flying over anthills and stumps and leaving the bushes swishing behind.

At last I slowed enough to realize I was alive and no spotted terror followed my trail. I fell to my knees, chest heaving. I knew the pain inside me wasn't just from lack of breath—it lodged deeper, tearing at my soul. Bile welled in my throat, yet my mouthed stayed parched as desert sand. A yellow orchid leaned toward me, but its scent couldn't hide the putrid smell of rotting death somewhere close by. I didn't want to know what it was but still my eyes searched the ground, settling on the fury ball of an anteater. Its stomach lay beside it, the entrails already crawling with worms. My approach must have interrupted some animal's feast. I cringed and tore my eyes away, wiping mosquitoes from my sweaty brow. The mosquitoes rose in a cloud, and then settled back down to feed.

A throaty feline sound came from the bushes. Cold sweat ran down my back. With a shudder I found my feet and dashed away. This time I staggered, gasping for breath and holding my sides in pain, but still I plunged ahead. What is it waiting for? I wondered. Why doesn't it finish me? I wiped tears from my eyes but they flowed so thick I couldn't see. It's playing with me, I thought, it's enjoying this!

I collapsed against a tree, whimpering between gulps of air, and hid my face in my hands. There was nothing left in me but a river of tears. I shook and wept, silently begging the cat to do what it must and be done with it. I don't know how long I huddled there, but long enough for the tears to cease, replaced by yawning emptiness.

The jaguar didn't appear. I scanned the bushes with a hollow stare, but nothing moved and no sound betrayed a presence. I rose weakly, holding on to the tree for support, and felt the pain shooting up my bruised leg. A parrot called, and far off a monkey sounded. There was no alarm in their chattering. I turned slowly and realized I stood on the edge of a clearing with a house.

I approached the house warily. It was a large structure framed by cane poles, open-sided but covered with a high, thatch roof. A man was the only occupant, though balsa-wood beds and other domestic needs indicated a family lived there. He sat cross-legged before a smoldering fire, a lean, long-faced young man with spiraling black lines drawn over his face and a blank expression. I was so exhausted I stood outside in silence, trying to think of a way to make him understand I sought the sorcerer Ceiba. Eventually he looked up and fixed his gaze on me. He stared for a long time, without surprise, looking through me more than at me, and finally gestured for me to join him at the fire.

"Show me your leg," he said. These were his first words, and to my relief he spoke them in Kañari—a courtesy to one who was obviously a stranger. I sat leaning back on my hands and offered my bruised limb. "Closer," he said motioning with his fingers. I lifted myself and shoved forward until my leg rested on his lap. He trailed his fingers over the welt on my shin, an angry blue and purple thing with torn skin and dried blood. I only felt a dull ache there, but the muscles were beginning to stiffen and I knew I'd be limping. He poked my toes and announced, "Nothing broken. It will heal in time."

"I know," I said.

He looked at me. "And do you know these scrapes will fester and rot your leg off? Look at those thorns in your foot. They, too, will grow angry with pus and eat your flesh unless treated. Shall I cleanse them, or do you intend to heal yourself?"

I felt too drained to explain that I was a healer. It didn't matter because I knew nothing about the plants in his jungle. I simply nodded. He dipped handfuls of water from a jar to wash the dirt away, and then sifted through a basket selecting his needs.

"Ouch!" I said, wincing as he applied a stinging brown resin over the welt. He grinned showing teeth painted black, and then wrapped long, pointed leaves around my leg. Words tried to form into questions inside me, but only swirled in emptiness. I watched in numb silence.

He glanced up at me and smiled to himself, then spoke to the questions he saw on my face. "You are not Wankavilca, and you were lost in the forest so you are not a lowlander. Kañari is the common language of foreigners, and I'm often called to tend the mountain people." As he spoke he produced a copper needle and pincers, and set to work on the thorns in my foot.

I finally managed to speak, though my voice came in a whisper. "I seek the sorcerer Ceiba."

"I know," he said without looking up. "He sits before you, and he prefers to be called 'shaman,' though he has the power of a sorcerer."

I had never met a sorcerer, or shaman, as young as this man, nor was there was anything imposing about him. He was slim and narrow chested, with thin arms and long, graceful hands. Yet he clearly knew healing ways, and he spoke with a quiet confidence that also infused his movements. I knew I spoke with the feared Ceiba, however youthful his appearance.

Thinking I should impress him I tried to speak forcefully, but something had left me and my words came in a jumble from the weary, hollow place inside. "I was lost, and a jaguar chased me. She will die soon. Her arm is purple and she sweats and shivers, and they say she won't last until sundown."

He stared in silence without blinking, but he seemed to be looking just above and around my head, as if studying a headdress. A light came into his eyes and twinkled like faraway stars. I had the strangest feeling he was not there, though he sat with my leg in his lap. At last he turned back to my foot and continued picking thorns. "The jaguar didn't chase you," he said quietly.

"But I heard it growling."

"Did it attack?"

"No."

"Did you see it?"

"No."

"If a jaguar chased you it would have caught you. But it wasn't chasing you. It was a spirit jaguar I sent to bring you here."

"To bring me here?"

"Yes, you were lost and it directed you to me."

He might have guessed what had happened from what I'd told him, and was taking credit for it as sorcerers often do, but at that moment there was no guile left in me and I was prepared to accept anything. I bowed my head. "Qhari will die," I said.

"Qhari is your sick friend?"

"No, he's my brother. Q'enti is the sick one, and she's not my friend."

Ceiba studied the air around my head again, then nodded to himself and returned to picking thorns. "You hate this Q'enti?"

"Yes."

"But if she dies from the serpent poison, your brother dies also?"

I hadn't told him it was snakebite but again he might have guessed. "Yes," I said. "Can you help her?"

Ceiba looked up from my foot. "Are you asking me to help you?"

"Me? No, it's Q'enti who needs you."

"Are you asking me to help *you*?" he repeated slowly.

Help me? I thought. I've never asked for anyone's help. People come to me for help, or they did, and they depended on my strength. I've always looked after myself no matter what happened. But now it's not there . . . whatever it was . . . pride? I'm empty, and I don't care anymore. Qhari is all that matters. "Please, help me," I whispered.

Ceiba spoke loudly. "What did you say?"

I lifted my head. "Please, help me," I said from deep inside.

"Do you trust me?"

"What?"

"You heard me," Ceiba said fixing his gaze on me again. "You asked me to help you, and now I'm asking if you trust me, completely?"

He stared into my eyes a moment longer as if looking inside me, and then returned his attention to my foot. He spoke again without looking up.

"People aren't to be trusted, are they? How many times have they turned on you with meanness? How many unfulfilled promises have you heard? How many slights and betrayals have you suffered from those you thought you could trust? You've seen the ambition and greed and pettiness in people, and long ago you gave up trusting anyone but yourself."

I knew he spoke the truth, though I had never allowed myself to think it, as if not putting it into words kept it from being true. Ceiba plucked a thorn triumphantly.

"There is weakness in every person, even in you," he said bending over my foot again. "You know your own thoughts, and they are not always worthy. Neither are your actions always blameless, though you try to tell yourself otherwise. This is true because you are human, like all those people whose tally of misdeeds you keep. You can't forgive them because you can't forgive yourself. Where there's no forgiveness, there's no trust. If you can't trust those around you, why would you trust a stranger?" Ceiba looked up at me, pincers suspended. "Are all people evil, or just weak? You have gloated on their weaknesses, but can you rejoice in their strengths?"

My mouth moved but no words came. I would have argued with him once, but there was no fight left in me. Instead I drank these thoughts like cool, clear water, and they began to fill the hollow inside.

Ceiba set down his pincers and applied resin to the punctures on my foot. It stung, but the healing power settled deep.

"There is good in most people," he said. "True, with some you must look closer, but it's there. When you find it, you can trust it."

"Do you trust everyone?" I asked. It was an honest question.

Ceiba smirked. "Some have sick souls. Trusting the good in most people doesn't mean being gullible with the few. The voice inside will tell you whom to trust. Listen to it."

"I trust you," I said, meaning it, wanting to say these words out loud to another human being.

He nodded. "You are forgiven."

This last remark sounds odd in the telling, and yet at that moment it seemed natural and exactly what I needed to hear. I felt as if an enormous weight lifted from my shoulders.

Ceiba finished dabbing resin on my foot. "We best go now," he said.

XV

In which Revolting Flesh is Consumed, the Sorcerer calls on his Demons, a pledge is made and honored in the manner of these Indians, and a Cruel Battle rages.

Ceiba led me straight back to Q'enti on a trail clear enough for a blind person to follow. I don't know how I missed it before, but paths are always easier when following someone who knows the way. I felt so fresh inside I hardly noticed my bruised leg.

When we arrived Guayacan and his men squatted by a fire toasting chunks of snake meat on the ends of long sticks. They kept a distance between themselves and the house with its newly deceased occupant. Guayacan stood and looked at me in wonder. "You?" he finally managed. "I was sure you were dead. We were getting ready to leave this cursed place. I can't believe you went into that jungle alone and came back alive." His men gawked at me.

There was a time I would have pretended indifference, claiming the praise of others as no less than my due, but that need had left me. "I was fortunate," I said. Ceiba nodded to himself.

"Fortunate?" Guayacan said. "You are as brave as any man I have ever met." From him it was high praise indeed.

Pisar lay nearby bound hand and foot. He looked up and whined, "They tied me like an animal again. Set me free, and make them give me something to eat." I ignored him.

"I brought Ceiba," I said, indicating the shaman at my side.

The men looked at this gangly young man with his spiral face paint and black teeth. "The sorcerer?" one said.

"The shaman," Ceiba replied turning his dark eyes on the man. A force seemed to come from Ceiba, as confident and powerful as it was invisible, and all the men shrank back.

Ceiba knelt over Q'enti, who now bled from her nose and eyes. "Has she vomited blood yet?" he asked.

"Yes," Guayacan replied, "she's beyond help now."

Ceiba gave Guayacan a look that said it was for him to decide, and Guayacan fumbled, "I mean, if you hadn't arrived she would die." Guayacan took a step back and bowed to Ceiba. "Pardon," he said. His men made the same gesture.

"Take her into the house," Ceiba said.

The men hesitated and looked to Guayacan who said, "Lord Healer, the family has left and there's a fresh grave inside."

Ceiba's expression said he knew this. "No dead soul can harm me," he stated, "and since you are strangers the man's spirit won't recognize you. Now, do as I say." The men leapt to do his bidding.

But once inside the house, with Q'enti stretched on a cane bed and Ceiba muttering over her purple arm, the men kept looking from the grave to Ceiba. Eventually one asked shyly, "Lord Healer, did you really become a jaguar to seek revenge?" Ceiba allowed a sly smile that could have meant anything, but didn't reply. The men's faces showed they took this as affirmation, and they kept a respectful distance.

Ceiba mixed powders in water and forced the concoction down Q'enti's throat. Then he had me boil sections of vine to produce a drink he called nepe, which would assist him in calling his spirit helpers. With all of us sitting in a circle around Q'enti he dribbled some of the nepe into her mouth, and then bid us consume the rest with him. Much to my relief it was not like Qhawachi's achuma brew, and I felt only a mild stupor. After wrapping Q'enti's swollen arm in a leaf poultice he settled down to shaking a turtle-shell rattle and chanting. I sank into a dreamless sleep that night listening to him.

The next morning Ceiba was gone. Q'enti finally opened her eyes, and with her first words demanded something to eat. It took a few days more for her to recover, during which she soundly cursed all of us for allowing the snake to bite her, though she trembled at the memory. I fretted at the delay, certain the condor priests had left Guayas and were not far behind. But Guayacan kept his men on alert against the perils of the Nameless Land, and there was nothing else to be done until Q'enti could travel. In the meantime the bruises on my leg turned blue and yellow, but eventually I was able to walk without limping. I left Pisar bound, telling him it was Guayacan's order and out of my hands, but privately I gave the men permission to throttle him if he complained.

Ceiba never reappeared, and I sensed I was not to visit him. He was a healer, and he had healed. There was no more to be said. Guayacan took me aside and confessed that after I fell asleep on the first night his men gave Ceiba some of Tumbala's treasure. That pleased me. I would have done it myself, but I knew a bond now existed between us that wouldn't let him accept it from me. The men, however, acted out of fear—hoping, no doubt, that he wouldn't come back as a jaguar—and so their gifts were accepted. On the morning we resumed our journey, just at dawn when mist still clung to the river, I spied a jaguar watching us from the riverbank.

We followed the river eastward for another day, the men bent to their paddles as the current increased. The mountains loomed ever closer until they seemed ready to fall on us. There are no foothills; the low coastal plain simply runs into steep, tree-shrouded slopes wreathed in clouds, above which dark ridges poke the sky. We made our last camp on the gravel bars where the Kañar River plunges from the heights.

The next morning, while the men extinguished the fire and readied the canoe, Guayacan approached carrying three bundles and dropped them at my feet. "That should be everything you need," he said. "The river will lead you up through the main pass into the mountains."

"Are there Inca outposts?" I asked.

Guayacan, still believing Q'enti and I were Kañari, gave me a strange look. "I suppose, but I've never been in the mountains. I'm told the Incas made your land another one of their provinces, and your Kañari lords do as they are told. They probably guard the passes for the Incas. Anyway, this is the main route followed by traders, so you will likely meet your people soon. But be careful. Outlaw bands roam the Nameless Land, and you can guess what they do to female captives. Stay on your guard."

I felt a tide of camaraderie for Guayacan even though he was never friendly. But I decided it was his warrior's pride, beyond which there was much good in the man. An air of respect developed between us after I returned from the jungle with Ceiba, and it infuriated Q'enti when he began to treat me as the leader. "You brought us far," I said.

"I fulfilled my duty to Goodgift. What becomes of you now is not my concern. I will take my men home . . . if Ceiba doesn't eat us." He said this last with a twinkle.

"Indeed, I hope you are spared," I said gravely. We shared a chuckle.

"One last favor?" I asked. He looked down at me, eager to be away. "My load would be considerably lightened if you'd be kind enough to relieve me of this." I held out Tumbala's treasure bag and his brows went up. I'd already removed a handful of trinkets for future needs, but the leather bag still swelled.

"You are welcome at my hearth," Guayacan said with an honest bow. For the Wankavilca these words are a pledge of friendship to the death, and are never spoken lightly. I returned his bow. "You are welcome at my hearth," I replied.

Q'enti came from behind. "What are you doing?" she demanded, eyeing the bag. She had donned her Kañari dress again.

"Lightening our load," I said.

"Don't give it to him. I might need it."

I handed the bag to Guayacan with a look that said it was time for him to depart. He bowed formally to me, nodded at Q'enti, and hurried to the waiting dugout. Pisar, lying on his side with wrists tied to his ankles, was glad to see Guayacan leave. He tugged at his bindings and showed his crooked teeth in a grin.

Suddenly bowstrings sang and arrows zipped around us. A cry turned my head to the canoe, where a man clutched an arrow stuck in his belly, and another fell face down in the water. Guayacan glanced to where arrows whistled from the trees, and then his eyes went to his dugout. He could have escaped, but then he looked at us, and snatched his bow from the canoe. "Bandits," he shouted to his men. "Get the women to the boat."

A wave of attackers charged from the forest. Guayacan went down on one knee, his bow arched, and two of his men joined him. Another ran for us beckoning frantically. An arrow ripped into his shoulder lifting and spinning him, and then he lay clawing at the gravel.

"Get down," I said to Q'enti, and ran to cut Pisar's bindings. Pisar lifted his head. "Hurry!" he yelled. I severed the cords and he jumped up. By the time I raised Q'enti to her feet Pisar was already half way to the canoe.

Guayacan thinned the attackers' ranks, but still they raced ahead in a ragged line shrieking like demons. His men dropped their bows and took up spears to meet the onslaught. I grabbed Q'enti's hand and we ran toward them, but two brigands cut off our escape. They came to a halt in front of us and leveled their spears. By their expressions they seemed to think we would simply surrender, and were more interested in what was happening behind them. My stride faltered when I recognized the amulet one wore at his neck—a condor priest.

I knew I had only one chance to stop him: he was still off guard as if we were already captured. Dragging Q'enti behind me, I continued straight at him. He seemed to think we were hurrying to surrender.

Without stopping I let go of Q'enti's hand and hurled myself at the condor priest, back handing his spear to the side and burying my foot in his groin. He bent double, grabbing his privates. I ripped the amulet from his neck and ploughed my knee into his face. The brigand beside him raised his spear, but I somersaulted at him and came up with my hand on his throat in a claw-grip. His tongue came out as I forced him to his knees. I let go, spun, and landed a sidekick to his head.

"Run, Q'enti," I shouted. She stood perfectly still, looking bewildered. "Where?" she said.

I looked to the canoe. Guayacan and Pisar stood alone dueling with a line of brigands. The last two of Guayacan's men lay prone, and renegades already plundered the dugout. Pisar had armed himself and accounted for two bodies. He was well trained as a fighter. Somewhere in the fray I knew there was another condor priest. They always come in pairs. These ones came with their own army.

"Kill them," came a strangled cry from behind. I whirled. The condor priest knelt with hands over his crotch rocking back and forth. I brandished his amulet and his eyes widened. Then I threw the cursed thing in the river. His eyes followed to where it plunked in the shallows. He turned in fury and yelled again, "Kill them, kill them," as he dragged himself to the river. His shouts alerted the men by the canoe. Two of them now turned and armed their bows.

I backed in front of Q'enti, not knowing what else to do, while the archers took aim. Guayacan saw them, and with a piercing cry he charged from the side. He leapt, piling into the first bowman and taking the second down with them. Before he could rise others surrounded him and hacked off his limbs.

Pisar skewered the man in front of him, gored a second, and then ran to the only open ground—where Q'enti and I stood. The brigands closed their circle around us.

Q'enti stood behind me with her hands on my shoulders, and pressed her forehead to my back. Pisar, still in a crouch and now armed with an axe, shifted back and forth scanning the ranks. The brigands were in no hurry to attack. Solemnly, several produced arrows and fitted their bows.

The condor priest limped into the circle. He studied Pisar, then shifted his gaze to Q'enti and me. His eyes settled on me and narrowed. He had retrieved his amulet and now made a deliberate show of tying it at his neck. In the silence a bird called from the forest, and the river lapped at its banks.

"That one is mine," the condor priest said pointing at Pisar. The brigands looked at one another and nodded. Pisar wove and bobbed as if inviting them to combat.

The priest turned cold eyes on me and announced, "After you're done with the women, skin them alive."

A flight of darts whistled from the forest, and in astonishment I saw the condor priest lifted from his feet by a shaft through his chest. All heads turned in surprise, and then a volley of sling stones hit with deadly force. A chorus of war cries followed, and Kañari warriors charged from the foliage with axes and maces held high. The brigands forgot us and, looking wildly from side to side, fell back to the river in a disorganized rush. Their archers paused to lose a few arrows, but the Kañari, armed with spear-throwers and slings, made short work of them.

Pisar straightened himself and frowned. He didn't look pleased to see the Kañari. Q'enti dropped her hands from my shoulders and wilted to the ground. She sat with a hand on her brow breathing heavily.

At the river the brigands splashed into the water, some already struggling waist deep and looking about frantically. The Kañari were professional soldiers and pressed on in formation, responding instantly to their captain's orders. In moments I saw renegades impaled on spears, hacked with axes, and smashed by maces. Surrender wasn't asked or offered. A tall man among the Kañari waded into the brigand ranks wielding a long maqana. He gripped the hilt in both hands, swinging the hardwood blade in a blur that dropped men around him like ripe seed.

In desperation a group of brigands dashed past the Kañari flank, running like deer into the forest. But the Kañari let them go and turned to finish the slaughter. That's when I realized Pisar was gone—vanished!

"Damn him!" I shouted. Q'enti looked up. "That shit-eating Pisar, he's run off," I told her. Q'enti turned to the forest and her arm shot out with finger pointed. "There," she said. I caught a glimpse of Pisar's back before the bushes swallowed him. Snatching up a fallen mace I raced after him.

The dense foliage fronting the river gave way to shady canopy, but sweat still bathed my face. I paused to look for paths. There were none. Then I spied a trail of broken limbs, the shrubbery beneath flattened where running feet set down. I followed at a trot, wary of shadows and woody vines. Pisar's sniveling and whining,

I realized, were cunning deception. Having seen him in battle I knew he could handle himself expertly, and with heartless efficiency. I had wondered what Pisar would do when Guayacan left us. He needed the antidote from the secret temple, but he didn't need us. Yet without him Qhari would die.

Voices ahead brought me to a halt. I peered from behind a tree and saw Pisar backed against a wall of thorn bushes, facing a half-circle of eight brigands. One of them, I now saw, was the second condor priest. He pointed at Pisar and spoke in a language I'd never heard before, but his tone made clear that Pisar was about to die. Pisar crouched in a fighting stance with battle-axe raised, shifting from foot to foot. The priest broke off and gestured to the brigands. They stood back and hefted their spears. I gripped my mace.

Pisar suddenly flipped his axe sending it blade over handle. The condor priest sidestepped and the axe sunk in a brigand's chest flinging him back. Pisar produced a knife and threw hard at the priest, but again the priest dodged. Grasping my mace in both hands I broke cover and dashed at the men from behind. I struck one on the head with a downward swing, and as the man beside him turned I swung back, smashing his face. Another swung at me with his axe. I parried the blow with my mace, but its handle snapped leaving me weaponless. Two brigands came at me. Behind them I saw the priest and two others leap on Pisar.

I somersaulted in front of the first attacker and came up with my knee in his crotch. But the instant he fell the second man jumped me. He seized my hair in one hand and, holding me at arm's length, raised his axe. I jerked hard in his grip, tearing my hair, but when the axe came down the swing was long and only the handle grazed my head. Still held fast by my hair, I saw the condor priest break away from Pisar and come at me with a club. The axe-man shrieked and released me when I plunged my fingers into his eyes, but at the same time the condor priest swung and a bolt of pain shot through my skull.

In the next moment I found myself on my back staring up through watery eyes. The priest stood over me with his club, calmly aiming the final blow. I looked to Pisar and saw he, too, lay prone. One man held him down while another hefted an axe.

Then a dark figure brandishing a maqana swooped across my vision like a bird of prey. His arms wove back and forth until the weapon zipped the air. The priest standing over me froze, and then his face burst in a splatter of red. The figure dashed out of my sight, but an instant later I heard two more bodies fall.

A gentle hand lifted my head. I tried to focus. A man knelt over me, his face pinched with concern. "Zapana?" I said weakly.

For the remainder of that day I slipped in and out of darkness, but during the conscious moments I realized they had put an ugly bandage around my head, and I refused to let Zapana see me. Q'enti's face appeared over me once, scowled, and retreated. At first light the next morning I lay staring up as a breeze stirred the branches above, and realized my senses had returned. We were still camped on the gravel bars where the Kañar River descends from the mountains. A Kañari soldier snored quietly beside me, and others slumbered nearby. I sat up and removed my bandage, then gently traced the egg-sized lump on the back of my head.

I had to bathe and clean my clothes before facing Zapana. I rose quietly and made my way up the riverbank seeking a private place. Kañari sentries eyed me silently but none interfered. I followed a green-walled path leading to the rapids, the air moist and blissfully cool at the dawn of a new day. How did Zapana get here, I wondered, and what am I going to say to him?

Zapana stepped from a side trail in front of me. He turned in surprise. We both stared. My hands went to my hair and then smoothed my dress, but these hopeless gestures were not foremost in my mind. I walked up to him and took his arm. He allowed me to turn him, and in silence we continued up the path together.

We stood arm in arm looking at the rapids. White water crashed against boulders raising mist, the first rays of sun painting a rainbow over the water.

"I thought I'd lost you," he said quietly, eyes on the water.

I didn't reply. He let the roar of the rapids drown my silence for a time, and then asked, "Where did you find the man Pisar?"

I wasn't ready to speak, still savoring the moment, but I wanted to hear his voice. "You first," I said smiling up at him. "How is it that Lord Zapana magically appears?"

Zapana grinned. "When we last met at Wanaku Pampa I was on my way north. As the reports claimed, I found the Otavalos and their neighbors uneasy under our rule, and there could be trouble, but not soon, I think. I intended to return to Cuzco, but when I reached Kañar province one of my agents met me. He had quite a story to tell about a woman named Qori at Guayas, who called herself Choque, and her companion Lady Orma, whose description matched Q'enti. He said you were traveling up the Kañar River to the mountains. Too many Kañari traders have vanished here in the Nameless Land of late, and the Kañari knew a gang of brigands was at work again. The Inca governor of the province had already given the Kañari permission to hunt down the butchers, and so I joined their expedition to this place. It seems we arrived just in time."

"You saved my life," I said.

Zapana looked surprised to hear me acknowledge this, then he shrugged. "I suppose it was my turn, but I don't keep score."

I had saved his neck more than once, but he was right, there was no need to keep score. Had he arrived moments sooner he might have saved Guayacan, too. The Wankavilca chief was a savage, but he had welcomed me to his hearth and died honoring that pledge. It was an example I would not forget.

I turned my thoughts elsewhere. "Your man learned of us in Guayas?"

"He wasn't in Guayas. He heard the tale from two Chincha sailors in Tumbez."

I smiled to myself. The old mate never could keep a good story to himself. "They arrived safely, then?"

"Apparently so. Delivered on a Wankavilca raft, no less, and with a cargo of thorny oyster shell. They traded for a new raft and crew as soon as they landed, the only smart thing they did in Tumbez."

I gave him a questioning look.

Zapana smirked. "Wait until you hear the rest of it. They dressed themselves like lords and ordered urns of beer, telling their tale to anyone who would drink with them. My agent was one of those. Then they turned to gambling day and night with Tumbez merchants, until they had nothing left but their loincloths and a crowd of angry creditors. They escaped to their raft and sailed away under cover of night. No one will see those two in the north again."

Those scoundrels, I thought warmly. Well, at least the captain's wife will have her man in home waters, and the old mate has stories to last a lifetime.

Zapana looked at me expectantly. He said, "Lady Q'enti won't tell me anything, so you must. Did you find Qhari?"

I sighed and took a deep breath, then with my eyes fixed on the churning waters the story tumbled out. Zapana took my hand when I told how Q'enti infected Qhari with condor dust before Atoco took him away, but he didn't interrupt. He only nodded in understanding of how I came to serve Q'enti, and the two of us went in search of Asto's brother, Pisar. His brows stayed raised when I spoke of our raft sinking in a storm, the shark attack, and our sojourn with Tumbala on Puná. Then I told him about our escape, and presenting ourselves as condor priests to the Wankavilca. When I finished we stood pondering the river together, his hand still clasping mine.

I wondered what Zapana was thinking. As lord of the Empire's secret forces he was sworn to uphold the law, and his loyalty to the Emperor was beyond question. Q'enti could go where she wished, but I had been banished by royal decree. Just knowing I broke my exile compromised Zapana. When I could bear the silence no longer I turned to him and said, "What should I do now?"

I wondered at the surprise on his face, and then realized I'd never spoken these words to him, or anyone. He knew I would abide by his answer. The eyes that were like stone in battle showed only tenderness. "We must continue, of course," he said.

"We?"

"The Eye of the Condor is the most powerful wak'a of the northern tribes. You have determined it exists, and you even found a guide to the secret temple. Lady Q'enti wants the Great Emerald for herself, but with it the Emperor could insure peace in our northern domains. It is my duty to deliver it to Him." He said this efficiently as if rehearsing his case for the royal council.

I pressed his hand. "Zapana, I'm a fugitive, and whether that's right or wrong doesn't matter. I broke Wayna Qhapaq's decree of exile. I can't drag you into this. Q'enti will see to it that you are stripped of everything, too."

Zapana's eyes danced. "Yes, you are a fugitive, and it's my duty to arrest you. Very well, consider yourself under arrest. As my prisoner you must do everything I say from now on."

"Zapana, be serious. I'm not going to let you ruin yourself."

"I am serious, and the prisoner will do as she's told." He said it firmly, and then bit his lip to keep from laughing. He put his hands on my shoulders. "You let me worry about Q'enti and Wayna Qhapaq . . . *and* Zapana. Right now we must find the antidote for Qhari. And we will, Qori. I swear it on my life."

A cold tingle on my neck made me shiver. "Zapana, don't say that."

"Very well, I swear it on my big toe."

"I don't want any piece of you harmed."

He grinned. "With Inca Moon at my side I fear nothing."

I wished the cold tingling would stop.

Zapana said, "Lady Q'enti will be pleased to hear you are recovered. She's been worried."

Worried because my death would deprive her of tormenting me, I thought. "She didn't tell you anything?"

"Nothing about your adventures, but she's certainly been charming. The Kañari captain is hoping her smiles will lead somewhere. And she prepared a fine meal for me last night."

"Q'enti cooked for you? I didn't think she knew how to cook. Well, you are still alive. You think she's charming, do you? Let me tell you some of the things 'charming' Lady Q'enti did."

Zapana held up a hand. "You already have. Don't worry, I know Q'enti's games."

Perhaps, I thought, but you're still just a man, Zapana.

238

"The Kañari know her as Lady Orma," Zapana said. "She's still using that name, and I agreed to go along until I spoke with you. I think we should let her keep it, and you should continue as Choque. Too many questions will be raised if our people learn the two of you are in the north."

"Then you're not going to tell the Inca officials?"

"It's best not to for now. One question will lead to another, and if the governor finds Qori Qoyllur in his province he will be duty bound to arrest you. Then I'd lose my prisoner." We laughed together.

Zapana became serious. "Besides, we stand a better chance of reaching the secret temple by ourselves. If the authorities knew about our destination they would insist on sending troops with us. You can't keep an expedition like that quiet, and the condor priests would vanish with the Great Emerald before we set out. What has Pisar told you about the temple?"

"Only that it's in the jungles to the east of the mountains."

"To the east, beyond the Empire's boundaries? That's the land of the Shuar people. None have been there and lived to tell about it. Are you sure Pisar is telling the truth?"

"No, I'm not. He said we must travel through the mountains, and after that he mentioned jungles to the east."

Zapana shifted uneasily. "Surely he can't mean the Shuar territory, but I suppose we have to follow him and find out." He thought for a moment and added, "First we must stop at the citadel of Hatun Kañar."

The place was famous as the ancient seat of Kañari chiefs, which our architects had embellished in Inca fashion to honor the Kañari and provide fitting accommodations for our administrators.

I said, "I thought you wanted to avoid Inca officials?"

"I do, but the Kañari recognized Pisar. He's wanted for an old crime, and they are determined to deliver him to their chief at Hatun Kañar."

"A crime?"

"They say he raped a child."

239

That explains why he wasn't pleased to see the Kañari soldiers, I thought. He's even wanted in his own land.

"Zapana, do the Kañari know who you are?" He wore Kañari garb and spoke the language fluently.

"They only know I'm an Inca lord. Even our governor in Kañar province doesn't know who I really am, and I prefer to keep it that way. But he understands I act with highest authority from Cuzco, and he doesn't question me. When we get to Hatun Kañar I'll have the governor speak with the native lord of the Kañari, their Great Lord, and arrange passage through the mountains. As for Pisar, I'll promise to return him to the Kañari after we're done with him."

There seemed to be a lot of people wanting to get their hands on Pisar. I told Zapana about the condor priests summoned to Guayas, and their appearance at yesterday's battle.

Zapana nodded grimly. "Even the condor priests want Pisar dead. Well, he won't be long in this world, but we must keep him alive until he leads us to the temple." He stared at the water and said, "That explains why there were so many brigands. They usually skulk in small bands looking for easy prey. Evidently the condor priests are able to summon them, and even make them fight. They battled well for common outlaws."

"Probably more terrified of the priests than simple death," I suggested.

"True. But if the condor brotherhood inspires that much fear in thieves and cutthroats, we can be sure their grip on the north has no limits. We must reach the temple before they learn two more of their brethren are dead." Zapana pressed my hand. "Don't worry, I'll get us through Kañar province."

Without Zapana it would have been impossible for me to take Q'enti and Pisar through the mountains undetected. Kañar had been an Inca province since the time of Wayna Qhapaq's father, and Wayna Qhapaq was born there. The Kañari were staunch allies and provided the finest provincial troops in our armies.

A heron glided low over the water seeking a tranquil pool for fishing. I turned to Zapana and took his hands, afraid to look up. I studied his long, slender fingers. "There's much between us," I said quietly.

He stepped closer and enfolded my hands to his breast. I knew he looked at me, but I could not meet his eyes. He waited for me to speak.

I swallowed hard. "Zapana, I admit I was willful and proud." I looked up to find him smiling at me.

"Well, you were Lady Qori Qoyllur, Royal Physician," he offered.

"I was, but I'm free of those burdens now."

Zapana squeezed my hands. "And you are still Qori."

XVI

In which Qori displays her skill in the Culinary Arts, Q'enti comments on the results, and Tenderness of a most Intimate Nature transpires in the night.

Late in the day our column crested a ridge overlooking a mountain valley. I paused to stare at the sweep of forests and meadows below, but my vision blurred again and I rocked unsteadily. Zapana gripped my elbow and whispered, "We will make camp down there."

I tried to smile. "We should go on while the light lasts. I'll be alright, and my head will be fine tomorrow."

The welt on the back of my head bloomed like a mushroom. Zapana had wanted me to recover at the camp on the gravel bars, but after our morning talk by the rapids I felt fit enough to climb mountains. The dead brigands were piled in the forest, but I insisted the Wankavilca be buried to keep animals from them. I prayed to the god of war over Guayacan's grave, and then our column began the steep climb up tree-shrouded slopes.

"I know you can go on," Zapana said, "but Pisar has wounds also, and Lady Q'enti is exhausted." I knew his concern was for me, but throughout the day he had gallantly blamed our frequent stops on others.

My head felt heavy. "Very well, we will camp," I conceded, "if only to save you from Q'enti's whining."

Zapana's lips parted in a smile. "I'll go ahead and see to the camp," he said indicating the valley below. "Come down when you're ready."

The thought of being in camp with Zapana had been in my mind all day. Would he say something about the sleeping arrangements, or just place our bedding together? Would he choose a place for us away from the others? What would happen under the blankets this night? I touched the egg-sized lump on my head and wished I were fit and clean.

Pisar limped along prodded by a Kañari spear, his hands tied at his back. He thought he would be free at the mountains, where he surely planned to abandon Q'enti and me, but he hadn't foreseen being captured by his own people. He turned pleading eyes to me. "I'm wounded, I can't go on," he said.

I knew he was damaged in the fight, but his injuries would heal. "Then we must make a pleasant camp for you," I said pointing below. Pisar rolled his eyes in relief. His guards shoved him on.

Q'enti straggled at the rear of our column surrounded by sympathetic soldiers eager to help. Previously she traveled by raft and dugout, and this was the first time she had to use her legs. When she came up to me she announced, "I've had enough. We will camp now."

"As you wish, Lady Orma," I said with a bow.

Q'enti smiled at the young man who carried her belongings. "Run ahead and gather grass for my pallet," she said. The man grinned and hurried away. Q'enti sighed and ran a hand through her hair. "Go and gather wood, Choque. Lord Zapana is hungry and I have something special in mind for him tonight."

I stepped close so the soldiers wouldn't overhear. "I'll pretend to be Lady Orma's maid as long as we are with these Kañari, but Q'enti, I'll not do your bidding."

"Oh, we've become feisty since Lord Zapana joined us, have we?"

"Call it what you will, but I'm not your servant. As for Zapana's supper, I already have that planned."

"You can't cook."

"I can so, and better than you. Leave Zapana to me."

"Oh, he's yours, is he? Well, we shall see about that."

Q'enti strode away with purpose to her step.

Men unpacked their loads in a meadow below, and the first wisps of wood smoke came to me on the breeze. It was sharp and pungent. The smells on the coast are muted by sodden heat, but in the mountains they drift fresh and far. I inhaled the cool air and felt color return to my cheeks.

The ascent up steep, bush-choked slopes that morning was hot work. Ferns like trees towered over us as we climbed single-file above the gorge of the Kañar River. Zapana insisted on walking just behind me, claiming he was admiring my backside, but his hands steadied me each time I stumbled. The undergrowth never thinned, but a cool mist enveloped us as we climbed through the clouds. At midday we reached a summit only to find higher mountains ahead of us, but the air was sweeter and highland shrubs poked from the greenery. I felt the mountains drawing me, and even Q'enti picked up her step.

We were still in low mountains when we stopped to camp, but the land opened to vistas of tree-clad valleys with tumbling streams. From my place on the ridge I looked down on the meadow in the forest, and beyond to higher, grass covered slopes in the distance. Flute music reached me, and I saw our Kañari escorts clustered in boisterous groups. The men were pleased to be home. With a sigh I started down, wondering what I was going to cook for Zapana's supper.

Q'enti tasted my maize gruel and made a face. "It needs more salt," she said.

"No it doesn't. That's the way I like it. Why don't you go and eat with the men."

"They have a deer," she said, brows raised. "Surely Lord Zapana would prefer a haunch of real meat." She looked disparagingly at the viscacha I roasted on a spit. I spotted this rabbit-like creature while coming down from the ridge and took it with a sling. It was a scrawny old animal, but with the ground maize the Kañari carried on their marches it would make Zapana's supper. I was pleased with myself until Q'enti came over to bother me.

"Lord Zapana likes viscacha," I said. "You go and eat the venison."

Q'enti ignored me and turned the viscacha on its spit.

"Stop that," I snapped. "That's my viscacha. You go and sit with the men."

"I was only helping. Besides, a lady doesn't eat with common soldiers. Why don't I bring some venison over here? I'll roast it."

"We don't need any venison, and we don't need your company. This hearth is for Zapana. You go elsewhere, Q'enti."

"Well, I think we should ask Lord Zapana about that. I will cook a haunch of venison for him, and he can choose." Before I could reply she hurried over to the men butchering the deer. I added more salt to the maize gruel.

I built our fire among the trees on the edge of the meadow, a private distance from the main camp but within view of it. Only the Kañari captain used a tent, which Q'enti had charmed him out of, and I waited until it was erected to choose my own ground. While I skinned my viscacha I had watched Q'enti talking to Zapana some distance away. She gestured at her tent and giggled like a girl. Zapana bowed to her and went out to place sentries. He's just being polite, I had told myself. He knows what she's like. Then I glanced at our rolled up blankets. I hadn't yet had the nerve to lay them out together.

Q'enti returned with a lump of bloody meat and, pushing my viscacha farther down the spit, fastened it over the coals.

"Stop," I said, "you're going to ruin my viscacha."

"There's room enough for both," Q'enti replied. "Here, I'll just add more wood to the fire."

"No, the fire is perfect. Go and start your own hearth."

"There's no need. We'll just make this one bigger."

Zapana strolled over. Q'enti leapt to her feet and arched her back. "Lord Zapana, would you care for some venison? It will be ready soon."

Zapana returned her smile and attempted not to stare at her chest. You can always tell when men are trying not to be obvious. "Ah, venison, exactly what I wanted," he said. Q'enti gave me a triumphant look.

"And viscacha," I said. "You do like viscacha." It was a statement.

Zapana eyed the scrawny carcass. "But of course, a favorite of mine. The two of you have prepared a feast for this humble soldier."

"I did the cooking," I said. "Q'enti was just leaving."

Q'enti made eyes at Zapana, and then gazed longingly at the roasting meat. To break the awkward pause Zapana said, "Well, perhaps Lady Q'enti would like to join us later." Q'enti brightened.

He doesn't have to be so gallant, I thought.

Zapana said, "I'll be back soon. There are still a few guards to post." After he left, Q'enti hummed to herself while she combed out her hair. I removed her wood from the fire.

Q'enti never left. She fussed with her venison, and several times I pointedly adjusted the spit to move my viscacha into the center. In silence she moved her venison back. There was enough for six people, and while the deer fat bubbled and hissed my viscacha cured to leather.

When Zapana returned I put his blanket by the fire and gestured for him to be seated. He sat cross-legged and rubbed his hands together. Q'enti retrieved my blanket and planted herself beside Zapana. "Here, dear, let me help," she said to me, passing two empty bowls but making no attempt to rise.

I scooped maize gruel into Zapana's bowl and added the blackened hindquarters of my viscacha. When I made to pass it to Zapana, Q'enti's hand shot out to intercept, and she handed the bowl to Zapana. "Qori cooked the viscacha," she explained to him. "But don't worry, my venison will be the main course."

Zapana put on a smile. "Ah, viscacha," he said lifting the meat in his fingers. He took a large bite, but his teeth stayed clamped and he struggled to pull the flesh away. Q'enti snickered. Zapana had to unfasten his teeth. "A strong old buck, just the way I like it," he chuckled. Then he growled like a dog and took a smaller bite. After more pulling a morsel came away in his mouth. "Excellent," he announced, chewing hard. I turned up my nose at Q'enti and filled her bowl. It wasn't my intent to wait on her, but I didn't want to upset Zapana with a scene.

"A bit too much salt in the maize gruel," Q'enti announced, "but then it is peasant's food. I suppose it's just the way you like it, Qori dear?"

Zapana, still chewing on his first bite of viscacha, said, "Oh, it's good, I like it too." He hadn't tried it yet.

"Water?" I offered Zapana.

Q'enti cut in. "But I have beer," she said holding up a skin bag. "That nice Kañari captain gave it to me. I suppose it's only a provincial brew, but a man needs beer, doesn't he, Lord Zapana? Here, let me fill your tumbler."

"Perhaps some beer, and a little water to wash it down," Zapana said. I handed him a cup of water at the same moment Q'enti turned with the tumbler. He held the vessels in each hand and sipped from both.

Q'enti said, "Now do try my venison, Lord Zapana. A man needs to keep up his strength, and there's a lot of you to nourish." She giggled behind her hand.

"I'm full, but a small piece would be good," Zapana said. He gave me an apologetic look. The viscacha stayed in his bowl with only a nibble gone.

Q'enti knelt over the spitted venison with a knife, moving the blade to indicate various cuts. Zapana nodded at a generous portion, then ducked his head when he saw me looking at him. Q'enti served him. "And for you, dear?" Q'enti said lifting her brows to me.

"I have more than enough," I said, holding up a shriveled viscacha leg. I clamped my teeth on it but the mouthful refused to tear away.

Q'enti held out her knife to me. "Try cutting it, dear. If that doesn't work, I'm sure the nice Kañari captain will lend you his battle-axe." Her high-pitched laughter filled the night. Zapana stifled a chuckle, glanced at me, and continued shaking in silence with head down.

"It's been an excellent meal," Zapana said at last, "but now I must get back to my duties." He stood. "I'll see you both in the morning."

I shook my head in disbelief. "Where are you going? Q'enti was just leaving. Your blanket is here."

"Ah, yes, my blanket, good," he said picking it up. "It will be cool tonight." He stopped when he saw the look on my face. "Didn't Lady Q'enti tell you? I'm sleeping up on the ridge with the guards."

I looked at Q'enti. The two of them had been talking earlier. Q'enti made a show of remembering. "Oh, yes, Lord Zapana did ask me to tell you, but I forgot."

Zapana gave her a friendly shrug as if it was of no importance. "In the morning, then," he said cheerfully, and strode off.

I gave Q'enti a burning look. She glared back.

"You can't let them take me to Hatun Kañar. You must not!" Pisar raised his bound hands imploringly.

"It's not my choice," I told him. "The Kañari insist on presenting you to their Great Lord. But Lord Zapana will prevail on the Inca governor to have you released."

We were a day from the citadel of Hatun Kañar, and Pisar had been begging to see me. I stood alone with him while the men set up camp. He wore a dirty tunic from a dead brigand, his hair hung past his shoulders in matted tangle, whiskers sprouted on his chin, and his bare feet were filthy.

Pisar hopped from foot to foot. "You don't understand, I can't go there. He will kill me."

"Who?"

"The Kañari Great Lord. If he sees me I'm dead."

"Lord Zapana will arrange your release."

"The Great Lord won't listen to the Incas, not when he sees me. He will murder me on the spot. It's true." Pisar stopped fidgeting. "Remember, Choque, or Qori, whatever your name is, if anything happens to me you'll never find the condor temple."

"I heard that you raped a child in these mountains."

"It was a misunderstanding, nothing more. I didn't know she was so young."

I held back the urge to strike him. "It seems you have a lot of 'misunderstandings' with children."

"Oh, she wanted it. She just changed her mind later."

I slapped him so hard his chin hit his shoulder.

"What did you do that for?" Pisar whined. He straightened himself and eyed me warily. "That girl was years ago. It doesn't matter now. But if you let them take me to the Great Lord I'm dead. Do you understand? You'll never reach the condor temple."

I turned from his fetid breath and wondered how many other children he had savaged. "If it was years ago why are you so certain the Kañari Great Lord will ignore the Inca governor and execute you?"

Pisar looked down. "Because she was his daughter."

A father would be justified, I thought. I wish I could deliver Pisar myself and watch him receive his due. How is it I'm forced to protect such filth? I promised Goodgift I would see you dead, Pisar, and I shall.

"Our Kañari escort is determined to deliver you, but I'll see what can be done," I said. Pisar looked relieved.

"Can you feel the condor dust inside you yet?" I asked.

Pisar snorted. "It takes months to work."

"If a man was poisoned four months ago, would he suffer now?"

"Why? Do you know someone?"

"My brother," I said in a whisper.

Pisar widened his eyes. "Your brother? Was it Lady Q'enti?"

I nodded.

"Now I see. Lady Q'enti wants the Eye of the Condor, and you want the antidote. I suppose she's holding your brother somewhere?"

It amazed me how their minds worked the same. Pisar saw the answer on my face and bobbed his head in understanding. He seemed pleased with this new knowledge.

When Pisar spoke again his eyes were distant. "The victim feels little for the first six months. The real pain begins in the seventh month, and soon after the body grows distended and leaks blood. Death comes in agony at the end of the eighth month."

I thought of Asto lying in his driftwood hut, his body like a bloated seal and blood seeping from eyes and nose. He wasn't coherent at the end. The thought of Qhari in the same condition brought a pain to my throat. He asked me to kill him swiftly if he was ever infected with condor dust. Almost four months had passed since Q'enti poisoned him. We had yet to find the temple, and the return south would take a month of hard travel.

"But just a pinch of antidote taken daily for a week stops the poison," Pisar said. He saw the hope in my eyes and added, "The elder condor priests take some every day, but it's forbidden to all others. They guard the antidote even more jealously than the condor dust."

"Where did this evil dust and its cure come from?" I asked.

Pisar shrugged. "I was an acolyte and they withheld much from me. The elders know, but only the high priest can make the potions. It's a secret that came with the Eye of the Condor in ancient times."

"Then the antidote is kept with the Eye of the Condor?"

Pisar looked vague. "Well, it's somewhere in the temple."

Pisar needed the cure, too, but did he need us to find it?

"I will lead you to the antidote," he said, "but only if you keep me from Hatun Kañar."

He spoke as if he was doing me an immense favor. I didn't trust him but I needed him and, whatever his reasons, he was offering to take us to the temple. "If I must," I said.

Pisar showed his crooked teeth.

"Are you really taking us east of the mountains to Shuar country?" I asked.

Pisar chuckled. "You heard about those savages? It's all true. They really do cut off people's heads and shrink them to the size of a fist." His tiny eyes sparkled. "And they use blow tubes with poison darts. No one leaves their jungles alive, unless . . . ."

"Unless?"

Pisar blurted something in an incomprehensible tongue. I recognized it as the same language the condor priest used when he confronted Pisar in the forest. "You speak Shuar?" I said.

"Don't you? A pity. But if the Shuar are in a good mood I'll get us through their lands."

Relying on Pisar was not a comforting thought.

As the evening cooled I sat by the hearth combing out my hair. The river was shivering cold, but my clothes were at last clean and my skin tingled with freshness. The comb felt good on my scalp. It slid easily through my hair. Q'enti strolled over and watched me dabbing berry juice on my lips.

She sniffed at a pot. "You are boiling root for skin lotion," she remarked. I didn't reply. Q'enti looked behind me to the low bower I'd fashioned in the bushes. Inside, blankets covered a nest for two.

Q'enti remarked, "I'm glad you're finally making some attempt with your appearance, dear. You looked like a diseased guinea pig." When I ignored her she said, "I see that bruise on your leg is still ugly." I moved the fold of my dress over the leg. The bruise I suffered when seeking Ceiba was now a hand-sized blotch, but at least it wasn't yellow and blue anymore, and it didn't hurt.

Q'enti stood over me. "And how is that poor head of yours? Is the wound oozing puss?" She tried to stroke my head but I slapped her hand away.

"It's fine, Q'enti, and no concern of yours. Why don't you go somewhere else?"

Q'enti poked her nose into my bower. On a pallet of fresh grass lay two blankets, one spread over the other. "Expecting company tonight? Lord Zapana, perhaps?"

"Zapana? He told me he was sleeping with the men again."

Thus far Zapana had stayed with the Kañari soldiers. He said he needed to ensure they remained on their guard. We were in their territory, but there was a chance more condor priests were on our trail. I accepted this, but suspected he was really waiting for me to recover. In truth I was glad of it. I wanted to be fresh for him, and my head wound was now healed.

Q'enti looked at me quizzically. "If not Lord Zapana, then who?"

"Never mind, Q'enti. Go away."

"Do you have a secret lover?"

"Go away."

"Who would sleep with you?"

"If you must know, Q'enti, I'm expecting the Kañari captain. Now go away."

"My captain? We shall see about that." Q'enti stormed off.

The root I boiled for skin lotion simmered in a clay pot. I skimmed off the salve and set it aside to cool, then rose to check my bower. Another branch needed folding over the roof before I entered its snug confines. Greenery kept the interior safe from rain and prying eyes. There was enough height for him to undress when kneeling. I smoothed the blankets again and fluffed the grass, its sweetness mingled with fresh forest smells. A skin bag of water and a cup lay at the head of our bed, where he could reach it if he was thirsty, and I'd hidden a few maize cakes in case he got hungry. My shawl will make his pillow, I decided.

Satisfied that my bower was ready—I couldn't help but think of it as our nest—I returned to the hearth and added a few more sticks to the coals. The fire should be inviting, I thought, but not too bright. I prepared a tiny bowl of fat with a wick to light his way into the bower.

The lotion had cooled enough. I worked some over my hands, feeling the suppleness return. Poor skin, I thought, too many days in the sun and wind and rain. I took a smear and rubbed it into my arms, savoring the slippery wetness, then raised my hands to my neck. The rest of me needed attention also. I looked around to see if anyone was watching. My hearth was a private distance from the others, and dusk fell thick, but still I turned my back before opening my dress. The evening air felt cool on my naked chest. Placing the last of the salve in my palms I cupped my breasts and worked the slick moisture.

A birdcall penetrated the forest, quickly answered by another. It was the sentries announcing they were in position. I pinned up my dress.

Kañari soldiers unrolled their blankets by fires as I strolled through the camp. Q'enti's tent stood in the trees nearby. She had a lamp burning inside. I saw two shadows on the tent wall. Good, I thought, she took the bait and lured the Kañari captain. That will keep them both out of the way.

It was a cloudy night, and dark. Firelight flickered on the faces of seated men, but those who stood outside the glow were only shadows. The crisp air carried the scent of evergreens. From another hearth came a familiar laugh. It was deep male chortling, full and honest. I smiled and thought, "It is so like Zapana to hold back nothing in everything he does. He gives himself to each moment, surrendering to the joy of what is. My stride turned instantly in his direction.

We had been lovers, but years had passed since I'd felt his touch. In truth, I'd never stopped wanting him, even when I pushed him away. The morning he took my hand at the rapids I knew all was forgiven, but in the days since then he had been busy with the column and our meetings were public. I wondered if he thought we were just old friends now? Did he still want to bed me, or did he think that was behind us? He might be shocked if he knew what I wanted. Would he turn from me as I had from him? I deserve that, I thought, but everything inside me is begging him to take me in his arms. I feel like a girl fretting over her first kiss.

I had rehearsed what I was going to say to him but now I hesitated. What if he said 'no'? I decided I wouldn't let him decline. I would walk up to him and state, 'It's time for bed.' No, that's too obvious. Perhaps, 'Come with me now,' and make it an order. Too demanding. 'Take me to bed.' Too direct. I stopped walking. What am I going to say to him?

I didn't see him approach. He stood in front of me, so close I could have leaned against his chest. I glanced up at warm eyes, then quickly lowered my head. His tunic was clean and he didn't have the man smell of the others. He said nothing, and I couldn't speak. With eyes cast down I brushed his hand, afraid he might pull away. His long, slender fingers opened, entwining mine. Hand in hand, and without either of us saying a word, we walked urgently to my bower.

My hearth had died to glowing coals, the soft light shrinking the world to a tiny, private place of our own in the dark forest. I lit the lamp and handed it to him, gesturing to my bower. He smiled when he saw the little green cave with its nest inside. With lamp extended he bent low and entered. Lamplight winked through the leafy dome. I remained standing by the fire, suddenly afraid, not knowing what to do next.

After an endless pause Zapana emerged and joined me, leaving the lamp inside. He spoke softly. "You made all this for us?"

I couldn't look at him. "It's hardly a palace at Tipón, but I made it for you."

"It's a palace to me, my Lady."

"I'm not 'Lady' anymore, Zapana."

He took my hands. "You are to me."

I rested my head on his chest and his strong arms enfolded me. The urgency that brought us here remained, but he sensed my hesitation. Holding me close he stroked my hair. The rising lump of his manhood pressed my belly.

I put my arms around him and boldly let my hands rest on the curve of his siki. I stirred against him rubbing my breasts on his chest and pressing his hardness. He was so tall; he had to lean down to rest his chin on my head.

He brushed back my hair exposing an ear. My breath caught when his feather kisses tingled my neck. I moaned and rose on tiptoes to fill his embrace, leaning my head aside to expose more for him. His tongue traced my ear, filling my head with moist, slippery sounds. Next he wetted my lips. Then, taking me in a full embrace, he pressed his lips to mine and gently turned his mouth from side to side, searing me. I sank back in his arms, my legs no longer holding me.

Still locked together I guided his hand to my breast. He groaned and opened his lips to me, massaging my breast in his huge hand.

I pulled back, taking his hands in both of mine and holding them between us. Our gaze locked. The hearth light glowed on his copper skin, his eyes huge with passion and breath hot. I drew him to the bower.

We knelt beside the pallet, facing one another, our eyes adjusting to the lamp's flicker. With fluid motion he removed his tunic and flung it aside, revealing a muscled, hard body clad only in a loincloth. His skin shone like warm honey. He waited patiently, offering himself with humility. Humility is truth, and it was truth I saw in Zapana's eyes. Overhead the branches moved, but I couldn't tell whether the sigh I heard came from the wind or me.

I dropped my shawl, then, forcing myself to move slowly, I pulled the pin from the left side of my dress, baring a shoulder. His eyes fixed there, widening. I pulled down the dress fold, exposing one naked breast. Zapana leaned forward. He licked his lips and quivered, holding himself back. I raised my hand to my right shoulder, slipped the dress pin, then curled my fingers around the fabric and paused. Zapana drew in his breath. I let the cloth slide from me and sat before him naked to the waist. We both trembled. His lips tightened and he swallowed hard, then he raised open hands to my breasts. I watched his hands coming toward me and threw back my shoulders. He lifted my breasts, feeling their pliant firmness. Zapana watched me, his face flushed and curious to see the passion this touch aroused.

I could wait no longer. Pushing him down on the blankets I tugged at his loincloth. He lay back with dreamy eyes half closed, surrendering to my whims.

When the world returned I lay in the crook of Zapana's arm staring at the green arch above. The lamp still flickered softly, and blackness shrouded the forest beyond. A blanket covered our entwined legs, but the heat of our union rendered the night chill a cooling touch. Outside the wind sighed through the trees. The leaves stirred overhead, but in my mind I gazed on gentle hills where grasses swayed in the breeze. I snuggled closer to Zapana. He stroked my hair absently.

"Are you here?" I asked.

He chuckled and his chest shook. "You caught me. I was at Tipón."

"Thinking of duty again?"

"No, thinking I didn't want to be there."

"It was your dream to be Lord of Tipón."

"Yes, and it came true. But now . . . ."

"Where would you rather be?"

"Where I am now. Here with you listening to the wind."

I lifted my head. "What will happen . . . after we find the temple, I mean?"

"We will free Qhari."

"Yes, but after that?"

He pulled my head back to his shoulder. "Does it matter? Only the gods can see tomorrows. We have this night, and if my ancestors call me at dawn I'll die a contented man."

"Don't talk that way."

A smile traced his lips.

"Aren't you afraid of anything, Zapana?"

He squeezed me again. "I was afraid I'd lost you."

"I was afraid you had also," I whispered.

Zapana raised himself on an elbow and searched my face. "What is it you are afraid of now, my love?" I ducked my head. He hadn't called me 'love' in years. I hadn't let him. "Tell me," he said earnestly, "trust me."

Yes, the voice inside me said, if there is one soul in this world you can trust it's him. Share your secret fears with those you love, holding nothing back, and trust them to know what's best. Was it Qhawachi or Ceiba who said that? Or was it me?

I reached out my hand and he took it.

"It was long ago, Zapana, but when they whispered about you and Q'enti I was hurt, and furious. In truth, I needed to believe it, because I wanted an excuse to be angry with you. No, please don't say anything, let me finish. I was afraid. I'm not pretty like Q'enti, and I convinced myself another woman would steal you from me. I told myself you just felt sorry for me, or you were in love with the mystic of Inca Moon, but you'd tire of the real me. I didn't trust you, because I didn't trust myself."

"It's Qori Qoyllur I want," he said softly.

"I know, and I feared that. I was afraid to become one with you because I thought it meant losing myself. I was a free woman in Cuzco, Zapana, free to do as I pleased, and free to chose any man I wanted."

"And you are still free," he said. "I wouldn't want you any other way."

These words startled me. Then I understood that he bared himself, demanded no promises, allowed all choices, and trusted me. He only asked me to be me. Could there be a more perfect love?

XVII

Of that which came to pass at the Great Citadel of Hatun Kañar, and of how Love Found was soon Shattered by Intentions most Vicious.

The next morning I emerged from our bower and stood stretching luxuriously. Zapana had already eaten and left to rouse the men. My breath steamed in the gray dawn. I blinked and gazed around contentedly, noticing a fine, white dust covering the foliage. In the Kañari camp men knelt in rows, their outstretched hands beseeching the north.

"The mountain lords," a Kañari soldier said when I asked about the white dust. "One of the big ones that spews fire. Someone has angered it."

I looked to the horizon but saw nothing.

The soldier snorted. "You can't see it. It may be up near Quito, but the dust reaches us down here."

Q'enti came out of her tent and stretched. The Kañari captain followed her, smirking at his men. They snickered as he swaggered over to them. Q'enti noticed me. "Good morning," she called. "Did you sleep well?"

"Extremely well," I said. Her smile faded in puzzlement.

Zapana returned from inspecting the sentries. He came straight to me and bowed in courtly fashion. "My Lady," he said in greeting. I returned his bow. "My Lord." We stood grinning at each other. Q'enti smacked her forehead and vanished in her tent.

Zapana was busy with the men thereafter, but I was content to watch him and send a quiet smile his way whenever I caught his eye. With reluctance I bid farewell to our bower, but knew I would return there in my dreams. The column saluted the rising sun, and then marched toward it. Q'enti trailed sullenly at the rear.

We would reach the citadel of Hatun Kañar this day. Our journey from the coast had taken us above the tree line, to rolling meadows of hard grass and scrub, rock faces painted orange with lichens, tiny lakes, waterfalls, gushing streams, and cold drizzle from mists swirling low over the land. From there we descended through evergreen forests to our present surroundings, where fields checker hillsides and rivers charge through ravines. Herds of deer watched us from the distance, lifting their heads to sniff in our direction. Here, the air is still cool and thin, and the bean plants grow taller than the maize, but the land is rich and sprinkled with farms.

During the morning march we passed a town. The Kañari chiefs live in stone houses, but the peasants dwell in round huts of wattle-and-daub with high, conical roofs of grass. The men and women wear their hair long and coiled on top of their heads. In Cuzco we called the Kañari 'gourd-heads,' because that is what the commoners use to cover their coiffures, but the lords sport bonnets like cone-shaped sieves replete with colored streamers. The men wear tunics in the Inca manner—a knee-length, upside-down sack with openings for arms and neck. The women favor two fashions; some wear a wrap-around dress like a blanket in the Inca style, while others prefer their traditional brocaded blouses and ankle-length skirts. They all wear sandals made from the tough fiber of spiny agave plants, and they decorate themselves with macaw feathers because they believe their ancestors were macaws.

Zapana wore his maqana on his back fastened by a strap across his chest. The hilt protruded in easy reach behind his right shoulder. He could draw the two-handed weapon in one motion, and even throw it blade over handle with great accuracy. Of course, a maqana is not for piercing or cutting; the hardwood is shaped like a pointed blade but it has the weight and strength of a club. When Zapana threw it the target shattered. The Kañari soldiers pestered him for demonstrations and, pitting their own against him, wagered voraciously. Zapana always won.

From up ahead I heard Zapana's laughter. He jested with the men again. One didn't have to hear what he said—the sound of his deep, honest laugh made everyone chuckle. Men followed him regardless of their nation. They knew he was firm but fair, and his judgment sound. I never heard him give an order, but his suggestions elicited immediate action.

Even if we weren't bedding I'd still want to be near him, I thought. I care for this man with a love that sets no conditions. I can be content just sitting at his side, sharing the small things. I thought of the raft captain and his plump wife, and understood.

Zapana fell in beside the Kañari captain. The captain playfully jabbed Zapana's shoulder in welcome. It's just as well they get along, I reflected, and the captain is relaxed after a night with Q'enti. He won't like what Zapana is about to ask him.

I told Zapana about Pisar's fears, and Zapana agreed that under the circumstances it would be unwise to parade Pisar at Hatun Kañar. "If I was this Kañari Great Lord—this father," Zapana had said, "I'd personally saw off Pisar's head, after I skinned him." We both knew it would be hard to convince the Kañari captain not to present his captive in person, and receive the reward.

Zapana hurried back toward Q'enti at the rear of the column. He gave me a faint smile as he passed to let me know the negotiations were still in progress. As much as we despised Pisar we couldn't risk losing him. Zapana went by again on his way back to the front of the column, and this time he winked at me. Still, it was almost midday before he returned with the verdict.

"I'll go with the captain this afternoon to face his Great Lord at Hatun Kañar," Zapana said. "I need to speak with our governor there, anyway. There's a village not far from the citadel where you can wait with Pisar. I'll join you there tomorrow."

"And the captain has agreed to all this?"

"Yes, for certain considerations."

"Such as?"

"Lady Q'enti has agreed to spend another night with him. I explained it to her. She sees what must be done."

"The harlot!"

Zapana looked at me. "Whatever else you may think of Lady Q'enti, she's doing what she must—for all of us."

"I suppose. And that will keep the captain happy?"

"That and your gold."

"My gold?" I had given it to Guayacan, but when he died I decided to keep it for emergencies. "All of it?"

Zapana shrugged. "The Kañari have been lugging it for you since we met. Besides, what do you need it for?"

"Only to smooth our passage, but I think we should keep a few pieces for the Shuar."

Zapana made a face at mention of the Shuar. "Very well, but if Pisar really intends to take us east into Shuar country we'll need more than a few nose-rings, or a sack full. Those savages are only known from legend. They keep traders out, even the Kañari, and no one who has gone there has ever returned."

"None but the condor priests," I replied.

Zapana nodded grimly.

Our path joined a flagstone road branching from the Kañar River, which led through green hills studded with fields and farmhouses under a blue sky. Late in the day we gained a view of another high valley. It was wide and gentle, the grassy slopes merging below with broad bench lands, and a deep, narrow ravine slicing down the middle where fast water flowed. Farmsteads and a village dotted the distance, and at one end of the valley a hill rose crowned with the citadel of Hatun Kañar.

The citadel showed the blending of our peoples. It was the ancient seat of Kañari lords, now adorned with fine Inca masonry and temples where Kañari and Inca worshipped together. A single, high-peaked structure stood atop an oval platform of perfectly fitted stone blocks, below which stood a small House of Chosen Women. A discrete distance away was another assembly of stone buildings with high, thatched roofs where the Kañari held court. As in all civilized provinces the Kañari lords commanded their people as they always had, while our Inca governor advised in private.

"That's your road," Zapana said, pointing beyond a fork below. The other branch ran straight to Hatun Kañar. "You'll reach a village before sundown. Wait for me there. I'll join you tomorrow after I've spoken with our governor and the Kañari Great Lord."

I nodded. It would have been sweet to pass the night with him again, but there would be other nights. As if hearing my thoughts he squeezed my arm. "Watch Pisar closely," he said, "and I'll see you tomorrow night."

The Kañari captain assigned ten men to help me guard Pisar, then set off with Zapana for the citadel. They had hardly begun when Q'enti raced after them. "Lord Zapana, wait for me. I'm coming too."

Q'enti slowed as she passed me, her bearer hurrying behind. "You stay in the peasant village, dear. I'm sure Lord Zapana needs my help with these officials, and besides, I want a proper bath." I stood open mouthed as she dashed after the men.

Pisar studied the evening sky. We stood outside our round hut, one of several scattered along the roadside, the pungent smoke of supper hearths still lingering in the crisp air. Our Kañari guards lounged nearby, never taking their eyes off Pisar. For the moment Pisar was free of his bonds, but on my orders they would tie him hand and foot for the night.

A thousand twinkling lights looked down from the black bowl overhead, and Mother Moon covered the land in ghostly shadows. A dog I petted earlier slunk by in silence, its tail between its legs. I reached out a hand but it skittered away from me. Odd, I thought.

"What are you staring at?" I asked Pisar. He hadn't taken his eyes from the heavens.

"The time fast approaches," he said without looking at me.

"What time?"

"The time for us to arrive at the condor temple."

"What do you mean?"

Pisar gave me a sly look. "You will know when we get there, but we'd best not linger in these mountains."

We would be in unknown lands when we left Kañari territory, and completely dependent on Pisar. He will try to escape, I thought, unless he needs us for something. But I can't guess what that 'something' might be.

I became aware the night was too still. Another cur slunk by with its tail lowered submissively, and even the guinea pigs behind the mud hearths stopped squeaking. Suddenly the earth trembled and a rolling shudder passed under my feet. I looked about. The Kañari soldiers stood wide-eyed, no one moving. Another tremor like a gentle wave shook the land, and then all was still again. The men looked about in relief.

Earthquakes are not uncommon in Cuzco where they can strike with great force, but I didn't know the mountain lords in the north flexed their muscles this way also. Pisar looked at me and shrugged, then returned his gaze to the sky. The Kañari quickly assembled an offering to bury.

I wondered if Zapana had felt the tremor. I imagined him reclined on a bearskin drinking sweet beer with the governor, and idly picking at trays of delicacies while listening to flute music. He would have bathed and donned a fresh tunic. But another thought marred that warm image. Q'enti would be at the gathering, too, no doubt devouring Zapana with her eyes. She knew I'd tricked her into sleeping with the Kañari captain. What revenge did she have planned?

Q'enti answered that question when she arrived the next day leading three bearers straining under their loads. "A few clothes and necessities for our journey," she said when I eyed the porters. "The Inca governor was very kind." I knew the bales were for her personal use.

"Lord Zapana isn't with you?"

"He's been delayed," she said breezily.

I raised my brows.

She explained, "It's taking Lord Zapana a bit longer than he expected to secure Pisar's release, but he's confident it will be granted. He will join us tonight, or tomorrow. You've kept Pisar safe, I trust?"

"He's bound to a pole in the next hut with four men standing guard."

"Poor Pisar, he's been tied since we met him."

"If he wasn't do you think he'd stay with us?"

Q'enti shrugged. "He also needs the antidote from the condor temple."

We stood in front of the hut the Kañari had assigned me. Q'enti directed the bearers to place her things inside, and when they left she entered sniffing and looking around. There wasn't much to see aside from two low sleeping platforms and a clay oven on the dirt floor. Q'enti looked up at the thatch roof and sighed, "Well, I suppose it's better than a tent." Her eyes shifted to me. "Are you still in that old traveling dress? Poor thing, I should have brought something better for you. Still, I suppose you are more comfortable in peasant clothes."

My dress was frayed, but clean. Q'enti had sampled the luxuries of Hatun Kañar. She wore a new dress and shawl of alpaca, woven fine and soft in bright yellow with red and purple trimmings. Her dress pins and bracelets were gold, and her sandals were soft leather with plush wool bindings. Cosmetics touched her eyes and mouth, hiding the scar on her cheek, and she wore her hair in braids piled atop her head. The governor had indeed been generous. I had to admit she was breathtaking when dressed for court, but we weren't headed there.

"Perhaps you have clothes to share with me," I suggested impishly.

"What? Oh no, dear, these are my things," she said gesturing to the bales. "Besides, they would never fit you. You're not full enough."

Q'enti started sorting through one of her bales, and I was about to leave when she said over her shoulder, "I wore my Wankavilca clothes at the banquet last night. You should have seen the men's eyes popping."

"You didn't!" The long-sleeved, open-fronted vest Goodgift had given her hid nothing.

Q'enti turned, beaming, eager to tell the story. "At first I was attired like a lady, of course. But later, after the servants left and the beer flowed, well . . . the governor was curious to see how Wankavilca women dress, and so was Lord Zapana." I imagined her titillating them with descriptions all evening, and then giggling when she agreed to model.

"You wore that vest in front of Zapana?"

"Why not? Lord Zapana appreciates a full bosomed woman as much as the next man." I stood rooted with my heart in my throat. Q'enti's eyes narrowed, glinting cold sparks. She continued, "Indeed, our Lord Zapana can be quite greedy when he's aroused, and he gets so big."

I stared at her, my mouth open but no words forming. She's lying, I thought, and then felt myself wilting with the certainty that no man could resist Q'enti.

Q'enti pursed her lips. "Come, dear, don't be upset with him. He's only a man, and we had drunk so much beer. I promised him I would never tell, so you're not supposed to know. It just slipped out."

I lifted my head. "You cruel bitch," I said, emphasizing each word. Q'enti tried to keep an even face but her eye twitched, and then she exploded in maniacal laughter. I retreated outside but her high-pitched hysterics followed.

Zapana didn't come that night. I stayed away from Q'enti, pacing up and down the road. When dusk fell I left my hut to Q'enti, and withdrew to a solitary shed. The Kañari soldiers watched all this in puzzlement, but one look from me was enough to silence them.

Huddled alone in my shed with a blanket over my head I pretended to sleep, but my mind never stopped dwelling. Q'enti's words repeated over and over like a song I couldn't banish. It was all so easy to imagine. Yes, Zapana was just a man, and I'd caught him looking at Q'enti as all men do. With his head full of beer and Q'enti offering herself in that vest . . . . But how could he do this to me? And with Q'enti? If it was anyone but Q'enti! He held me so tenderly only the night before, and asked me to trust him. I gave him my very soul. I even dreamed of a future together.

What was it Zapana had said? "You're still free to be yourself and make your own choices." It sounded so loving at the time, but it would also apply to him. Did he mean he was free to take any woman he wanted when it suited him? Did he expect me to live that way? I didn't want to believe it, and then another thought occurred to me. Zapana had looked at me sternly when I said Q'enti was a harlot for agreeing to sleep with the Kañari captain again. He said she was only doing what was necessary to save Pisar. It was true, but Q'enti never missed an advantage. Had Q'enti agreed to it only if Zapana slept with her? Q'enti would do that just to get back at me for tricking her with the captain. And Zapana? If he felt he had no choice he would do what he must. He would do it for Qhari and for me, because without Pisar we were lost. Yes, I decided, she forced him, and he hoped I would never learn of it.

My mind whirled again. Q'enti forced him? What man wouldn't want to be so used? Did he do with her what he did with me? Those same things I thought were ours alone? I couldn't bear it if he did. But what do any man and woman do? He probably laughed with her—laughed at me. I remembered the rumors about them in Cuzco. Zapana always denied it, but I knew that if I were in his place I'd deny it, too. Perhaps this wasn't their first time, or even their second or third. Maybe they were secret lovers all these years?

Thus I passed the night with my knees drawn up and the blanket soaked with tears. Each time I reached the end of my manufactured story I started over, unable to stop tormenting myself, elaborating the possibilities and witnessing them in my mind. I wondered how I could ever face Zapana again. How should I act now that I knew? What would he say, if anything?

Then, just before dawn, I settled on a version I thought I could live with. Q'enti forced him. It's done, and there's nothing that can change that now. Zapana saved Pisar, and he did it for me. It doesn't matter exactly what happened between him and Q'enti, though it would have been a rough coupling and not the tenderness we shared. Will I cast him from my life because of one night? No, somehow he's found me again, and I'll never let him go. You can get over this.

A mature soul sees beyond bedding. There's so much more between us. And if I don't let it eat me then Q'enti doesn't win.

"The governor was most obliging, as always," Zapana said. "He knew Lady Q'enti, for he, too, is from Lower Cuzco, and he was honored to have her in his province. But he won't be mentioning her, or us, in his dispatches."

A quiet look from Zapana was enough to seal the lips of most officials. Even if they didn't know he was head of the imperial spy web they sensed the power behind him. I stood with my arm around Zapana's waist outside Q'enti's hut. It was midmorning and he had just arrived. Q'enti watched nearby.

When I saw Zapana coming up the road I straightened my clothes and took a deep breath. I wasn't supposed to know what happened between him and Q'enti, and I told myself it didn't matter anyway. I was determined it wouldn't come between us, and everything would continue as before. Better if nothing is said, I thought.

"The Kañari Great Lord was difficult?" I inquired.

Zapana put his arm around my shoulders. This was the first time we showed affection in front of others. "Yes, the Kañari lord was another matter. Can't blame him. He wanted Pisar dragged before him immediately."

Up the road Q'enti pretended to organize her porters, but glanced our way frequently. I pulled Zapana closer.

"But you finally convinced him?" I said.

"Yes," Zapana said slowly, "after I promised to return Pisar to him, or compensate the loss."

"Compensate?"

"He demanded the contents of the imperial storehouses at Hatun Kañar as security."

I looked up at him. He seemed pleased when I met him on the road with a kiss—a public statement we both wanted—but I knew he sensed something different about me, a hesitation I tried to hide. "And our governor agreed to such a condition?" I asked. "All the storehouses of Hatun Kañar?"

"Yes, well . . . if Pisar doesn't return with us I promised the governor I would reimburse him from my stores at Tipón."

"All your wealth? You'll lose everything."

Zapana looked unconcerned. "All that matters is that we have Pisar now, and the Kañari will guide us to the passes above the eastern forests. After that we're on our own."

The same Kañari captain arrived just then, and went straight to Q'enti. He must have set out with Zapana, but Zapana had rushed ahead. Was Zapana eager to see me, or feeling guilty? I tried to brush the thought aside. The captain opened his arms to Q'enti. She greeted him with a scowl and his arms fell, but still he grinned at her, anticipating the night ahead. Q'enti shot a cold look at me, which then changed to cautious study. She still sought my reaction to Zapana, unconvinced by my show of affection.

The Kañari led Pisar outside. He blinked at the sky and then questioned Zapana with a look. "We march," Zapana called to him. Pisar smirked and straightened himself.

In the days that followed we traveled east to the valley of the Paute River, this being the only destination Pisar would reveal. The route took us from the cool heights of Hatun Kañar to lush, sunny valleys cloaked in fruit trees, where the effort of our march raised sweat in the midday heat. We passed plantations of tree tomatoes and, as Zapana had said, I saw fields of maize towering like forests. Though he estimated the stalks to be the height of three men they seemed much taller to me; I felt like a bird flittering around the base of trees. The ever-present mountains remained rounded and green. They separated valleys but stood singly, never crowding one another, leaving the vistas open and rolling. Again we ascended to cool pastures, and then above the tree line to a wet, misty land of tiny lakes where streams rushed through meadows of tough grass and scrub. Farmers provided sheds for our lodging, and higher up we sheltered with herders. For the first time Pisar was in a hurry. He fretted over our daily advance, always urging us onward, and each night he studied the sky.

There is little privacy in a column. When we followed the Kañar River into the mountains there were few dwellings, and at night our camp spread out among the trees. But now, taking advantage of a more populated route, we found ourselves crowded at night into one-room structures with snoring soldiers. These arrangements were dry and warm after a long day's march, but hardly secluded enough for lovers. At night, Zapana pulled the blankets over us and held me, but all we could do was exchange frustrated looks.

Secretly I was glad. I worried at the thought of intimacy. One part of me wanted it, and another feared I would be cold to his touch. He had been with another woman. Did he stroke her in the same way? I kept telling myself it didn't matter, but I couldn't get over the feeling that something private had been taken from me. During the day I tried hard to reassure him and myself with looks and touches, but I tried too hard. I knew he sensed something was wrong, yet I couldn't answer the question in his eyes.

Q'enti watched all this. When she started smiling at me again I knew she saw through my façade. My attentions to Zapana became even more forced, and his responses embarrassed. The more determined I was the more awkward I became, but I couldn't stop myself. I clung to him by day and turned from him at night.

Zapana remained cordial toward Q'enti—that was his way with everyone—but coldness seized me each time I saw them speaking. I hated it, I hated what I could not stop myself from thinking, and I hated Q'enti most of all.

On our last evening in the mountains, while the men arranged the camp around a peasant's hovel, I wandered to a view looking down on the cloud forest. The sun had slipped from the sky but the light still held in afterglow. We had come down to forests again, which dropped in a dense tangle to the clouds below. I didn't know what dangers lurked beneath that floor of white, nor did I care. My agony consumed me as I sat on a boulder staring blindly at the mists.

I felt a hand cover mine and turned with a start. Zapana gave me an uncertain smile, and sat quietly beside me. I withdrew my hand and shifted away, pretending I was making room for him. He didn't try to fill the space between us. We sat in silence.

"I heard news from Cuzco at Hatun Kañar," he said at last.

He knew I wanted to be alone, but he was trying. "What news?" I said without interest.

"It seems there have been some promotions and demotions."

It was an invitation to gossip—an easy conversation about others, but Cuzco was a distant world, no longer part of mine. "As always," I said.

Zapana laughed but it was a hollow sound. "Well, some interesting news about old acquaintances of yours," he persisted. He was determined, so I let him prattle on about priests bungling ceremonies, administrators strutting for notice, pending marriages between royal houses, and new estates awarded to the worthy. I nodded and said, "hmmm," while my thoughts strayed elsewhere. Then he said, "And some bad news for Lady Q'enti. I haven't told her yet. I think I'll let her discover it for herself when she gets back to Cuzco."

"Yes?" I said turning to him.

Zapana looked pleased to have my attention. "It isn't much. It's just that her consignment for the House of Beasts killed its guards and escaped. Lady Q'enti will have to wait for her sport."

"What does Q'enti have to do with the House of Beasts?"

"I thought you knew. Soon after you left Cuzco she became mistress of the House of Beasts. It's the first time a woman has held the post, but nobody else wanted it. They should put her in there. No, maybe not, she'd terrify the other creatures." The laugh that followed was honest, and I joined him.

"When did you hear about this?" I asked, pleased with anything that might upset Q'enti.

"The governor told me when I came back through Hatun Kañar. A runner arrived with the usual reports, but he passed along the gossip, too."

I shifted my seat on the boulder and looked at him intently. "When you came back through Hatun Kañar? I thought that was the only place you'd been."

Zapana hunched his shoulders. "Didn't Lady Q'enti tell you?"

"Tell me what?"

"When we arrived at the citadel the Kañari Great Lord wasn't there. He was out at a hunting camp. The governor told me where to find him, so I left Q'enti and set off. That's why I was a day late getting back."

I held up my hands. "Stop. Are you saying you didn't spend the night at Hatun Kañar with Q'enti?"

Zapana made a sour face. "I wish I had. The governor ordered a banquet to honor her that night, but all I got was tough venison and a wet tent at the hunting camp. When I returned to the citadel the next day Q'enti had already left, and the governor couldn't look at another tumbler of beer. I had a warm bed that night, but I ate alone."

I placed my palms on his chest. "Zapana, are you telling me that you and Q'enti didn't feast together?"

Zapana looked confused. "I just told you. On that first day I wasn't at Hatun Kañar longer than it takes to boil a pot of potatoes. I had to find the Kañari lord. When I reached his camp I sent a runner to tell Q'enti I would return to the citadel the next night. When I arrived she was gone. I thought she went ahead to tell you. Do you mean to say you knew none of this?"

I shook my head numbly.

"Lady Q'enti didn't tell you anything?" he asked.

I threw my arms around him. "Nothing worth remembering."

XVIII

Concerning those who are surely the most Insolent and Barbaric Savages ever encountered, of their Heathen Customs, Outlandish Beliefs, and Brutal Ferocity, and of how Inca Moon vanished when she was most needed.

Pisar held out his bound wrists. Zapana's bronze knife flashed, severing the cords with a single stroke. Pisar flung the bindings aside and stretched, working his fingers. He showed crooked, stained teeth.

"I told you I'd set you free," Q'enti said as if it was her doing.

"And I'm most grateful," Pisar replied without sincerity. He rubbed his forearms and studied the three of us with amusement.

We stood on the edge of a plunging valley cloaked in dense bush and forest, a pampa of white cloud hiding the Paute River far below. From the pass above came a shout. We turned to see the Kañari captain raise his spear in farewell. He called something to Q'enti, who ignored him, and then our guardians passed from sight.

"Are we really headed down there?" Zapana said indicating the valley below. Pisar nodded, enjoying himself.

"Can we slip by the Shuar?" I asked.

"Slip by them?" Pisar laughed. "They will know we are in their land long before they let us see them."

"Can you get us through?" Zapana wondered.

Pisar's eyes went cold. "I think they will let me pass, and perhaps you, too, if I ask them, but they don't like strangers. They fear the condor brotherhood enough to concede a treaty, but it only applies to priests."

I turned and bared my shoulder exposing the condor tattoo. "Q'enti and I have the mark."

"Very clever," Pisar said. "That worked with the Wankavilca, but the Shuar know all the priests by name, and they know women aren't admitted to the temple."

"Do they know you've been expelled?" Zapana asked.

"Probably, and I wouldn't chance going back if I didn't have to, but I might be able to talk my way through. As for you . . . ." His words ended with a shrug.

Q'enti said, "I'm sure all will be well." She arched her back and made eyes at Pisar. "You will look after me, won't you Lord Pisar?"

Pisar's head went back in laughter. "It's 'Lord' Pisar now, is it? And after you poisoned me with condor dust?" He grinned at Q'enti. "I like you because I can trust you to serve your own interests first and always." Pisar turned his gaze on Zapana and me. "But you two . . . well, we shall see how useful you are."

The path beneath the shadowy canopy was a slash of red earth crowded by tangled greenery, so narrow we had to walk single file, and so twisting that I couldn't see farther than a few paces. Even I had to bend low where it snaked under bowers of thorn bush and woody vines, continuing down and down always, disturbed only by the distant call of birds. Pisar walked in the lead and Zapana took the rear position. We carried bundles of food and cloths, except Pisar who refused to burden himself. Q'enti had assumed we would lug her bales for her when the Kañari left, but when she mentioned it no one bothered responding. In a huff she cached her things at the last peasant hut and, forced to carry her own needs, tried to pretend her burden was a large purse suspended from a shoulder strap.

In silence we continued down through the pampa of clouds where mist keeps the slopes wet and cool, giant ferns tower, and moss drapes the gnarled trees. I glanced over my shoulder at Zapana frequently. His presence was comforting in this mysterious land, but mostly I just wanted to look at him.

How could I have doubted Zapana? I wondered. I misjudged him completely. I was so certain Q'enti spoke the truth, but I was so wrong, so terribly wrong.

"Be careful," Pisar called back to us.

I looked up and saw a section of path washed out, spilling red mud down the mountainside. Pisar had already crossed and now directed Q'enti to handholds of leaning bush and vines. The slope below fell away into mist.

I couldn't move my feet. I stared at the washed out section of trail. It was no more than ten paces long, but it seemed an impossible barrier.

Zapana came up behind me. "Take hold of that vine," he said.

I didn't reply.

"Qori?" he said gently, leaning over my shoulder.

I said nothing, wondering which vine I should grasp and whether it would hold my weight. Zapana extended my arm toward a thick creeper. "Take hold," he whispered. He nudged me forward. I leaned from the waist but my feet wouldn't follow.

"Qori, what's wrong?"

"I don't know. I'm not sure."

Zapana stepped in front of me. "Here, take my hand. Good. Now put your other hand on this vine and step forward. Come on, I'm holding you."

It was a shaky step, but I made it. Thus he led me from one handhold to the next, though it was a slow crossing. I couldn't catch my breath, and was sure my feet would slip from under me at any moment. Pisar and Q'enti watched from the other side. Zapana said to them, "We're fine. You go on now." They exchanged a puzzled look and set out.

Zapana held my shoulders, his face pinched with concern. "Qori, are you all right?"

I couldn't look up so I spoke to his chest. "Yes, I'm fine. I just . . . . It looked dangerous, that's all."

Zapana turned me to the trail and patted my shoulder. "I'm right behind you," he said.

We came out beneath the clouds into a gentler landscape. The path still continued down, but a break in the forest showed the mountains were behind us. Below, the Paute River wound eastward in a broad valley between rounded hills of dense green. But we soon found the hills only look gentle from above. Their forested slopes are steep, and the bush too thick to step from the trail. It's high jungle—a rolling land of canopy trees, towering stands of cane, and tangled growth. The air isn't as fresh as it is above the clouds, but neither is it oppressive like the swampy plains of the coast. By nightfall we reached the surging brown waters of the Paute River.

"What are you doing?" Zapana demanded of Pisar.

"Lighting a fire."

"And the Shuar?"

"They know we are here. They will be deciding what to do about us right now. This fire will show them we are not trying to hide."

Zapana said, "If they know we come in peace will they welcome us?"

"Welcome us? They will never do that." Pisar chuckled and looked over his shoulder at Zapana. "If you wake up in the morning then you will know they have decided to let us live another day, but if you feel stings in the night it will be poison darts from their blow tubes, and you will never wake again." He turned back to his fire. Q'enti put on a brave face and huddled close to him.

Zapana and I spread our blankets on a bed of moss outside the fire's glow. I lay my head on his shoulder and listened to the rustling forest. Jungles come alive at night, and I knew all manner of creatures slunk and slithered around us, but my thoughts dwelled elsewhere. As if hearing them Zapana whispered, "What happened on the trail today?" Ever since I hesitated at the washout I knew he'd been wondering. So had I.

"I don't know. When I saw the path fallen away I didn't know what to do."

"Are you sick?"

"No."

After a silence I said, "Zapana, I'm worried. That's never happened to me before."

"I know. Perhaps it's nothing. You'll be better tomorrow."

"I hope so, but I keep wondering where Inca Moon was. She wouldn't have hesitated."

He enfolded me. "Don't worry. You will be yourself again tomorrow."

Yes, I thought, perhaps tomorrow. But I was so wrong about you, Zapana, how can I trust myself anymore?

The Shuar appeared to us on the morning we reached the juncture of the Paute and Upano rivers, where tumbling brown waters race through gorges overhung with vines and tangle. A misty rain fell. At first the trail ahead looked vacant, but when I wiped the rain from my eyes warriors materialized as if by magic. Zapana placed a hand on my shoulder as we stood staring, his maqana gripped and ready. Pisar gestured for us to wait while he went forward. Human shadows moved in the forest around us.

When the exchange began I was certain our end had come. A Shuar stomped up to Pisar and menaced him with his lance, then bellowed in his face. Pisar, unarmed, didn't flinch. The warrior began a shouting chant, stamping back and forth shaking his lance to the rhythm, and threatening Pisar in a tone that needed no translation. Pisar stood calmly, and when the man finished Pisar launched into his own shouting chant, repeating the dance and waving his fists. He ended by screaming in the man's face. The warrior looked at him placidly, and then an exchange in calmer words followed.

"What was all that shouting about?" Q'enti asked when Pisar returned.

"We were just exchanging greetings," Pisar said casually. "He was telling me who he is, who his relatives are, how fierce he is, and how the forest spirits love him. I replied in the same manner. He knows me, but the ritual is always the same."

"Will they let us pass?" Zapana asked.

"Even better. They will escort us to the house of their Big Man, Quirruba. I know him, and two of his sons-in-law are with this hunting party."

Q'enti sighed heavily. "Then we are safe."

"Well, I am," Pisar said, "at least until Quirruba's house. As for the rest of you, they don't think you are human."

"Not human?" I said.

"You don't look like them, and they think your speech sounds like animal grunts. They have been listening to us for two days."

"That's ridiculous," Q'enti said raising her nose, "they are the savages."

Pisar grinned. "Perhaps you should explain that to them."

I looked at the Shuar who returned sullen, sideway glances. Their only garments were wrap-around cotton skirts tied at the waist with a string. They were barefoot, had long sticks through their earlobes, and wore their hair wound around their heads with a tuft of red and yellow toucan feathers at the front. Each man held a small, round shield and palm-wood thrusting lance, and some had spear-throwers. Several carried a long, round section of palm slung in a bag over their shoulders, which I took to be the deadly blow tubes Pisar warned us about.

Others emerged from the forest around us, and the whole party headed north following the Upano River at a pace just short of a run.

The path took us up and down hill, past waterfalls and streams hidden by stands of cane. Parrots squawked in the canopy and distant monkeys howled, but the tree-sized ferns along the trail blocked all view of the forest creatures. When we came to an abandoned clearing on top of a hill I saw in the east a range of forested mountains rising to meet low clouds. Pisar paused and stared also. "The Cutucú Mountains," he announced. "Aside from condor priests, no outsider has ever seen them." I knew from his look these mountains were our destination.

When a monkey sounded close by I watched a man stalk it with his blow tube. These are made from a section of palm longer than a man is tall. While the others waited the man stepped off the trail and moved silently among the trees, pausing to listen and scan the canopy before moving to the next cover. When he sighted the quarry he raised his blow tube, slipped a dart into the mouthpiece, bulged his cheeks, and expelled a sharp puff. I didn't see the dart leave the tube, but moments later a monkey fell from the trees.

After a days' journey north we turned east, camping that night on the shores of the Upano River. Where the Upano is not surging between cliffs it is broad, and shallow enough to ford. We crossed at dawn when fog blankets the river and layers the hills, a silent, brooding land shrouded in green where ghostly shadows rise behind the mists. The forest dripped after its nightly rain, keeping our legs and arms damp as we followed the narrow path, and the air, heavy with green smells, felt warm and moist. Behind a dense, gray-white sky the sun appeared in a fuzzy glow, but by midday patches of blue opened, and the exertion of the march raised sweat on our brows.

Pisar told us the Shuar call themselves the 'Numerous People,' but even though we were now deep in Shuar territory we had seen little evidence of people aside from the trails. Eventually we encountered clearings where manioc and maize grew, along with gourds, tobacco, and cotton, but our guides kept us angling away from these before any houses appeared. I suspected the wild plants edging these plots were also useful, though I didn't recognize them. "Some are fish poisons," Pisar said when I asked him. "Those ones over there are for medicine, though the Shuar don't use them often because they think all illness is caused by magic and evil spirits, which their shamans suck out of them." The one plant I did recognize was ayawaska, which transports its users to supernatural realms. When I remarked on this Pisar said, "The Shuar say this world we live in is a lie. The true world is the world of spirits, which the ayawaska helps them see."

The next day the trail led us directly to a house, where a man and his two wives lived in the middle of their fields. The lead warrior paused at the edge of the clearing and shouted at the house. Pisar said this was to let them know we weren't enemies. He listened to the conversation with the house owner and came back with a worried look. "A raiding party is in the area," he said.

"Another tribe?" Q'enti asked.

"No, Shuar from a distant neighborhood, probably bent on revenge killing, so they are after certain people. But if they see you, who aren't even human, they might seize the opportunity to take fresh heads."

I grimaced. "They are headhunters?"

Pisar grinned. "Oh, most certainly, yes. A Shuar man hasn't lived until he's taken a head, or several. They pride themselves on their ferocity, and their Big Men are also the most accomplished killers. But they only take heads from enemy tribes, or foreigners like you. Among themselves assassinations are common by ambush or poison or magic, though sometimes they wait years to take revenge. The feuds go on for generations. A man has to be very careful about his friends, and know the friends of his friends and their relatives."

Zapana looked at the house. "Are we on the edge of a village?"

"A village?" Pisar chuckled. "The Shuar don't have villages. Each man builds his house far from his neighbors, and moves whenever the garden soil turns poor. They know the other men in their district, and sometimes they visit and hunt together, but the cautious man trusts no one. Those who came for us were sent by Quirruba."

"Quirruba is their chief?" Q'enti said. "Good. I will meet this Quirruba and let him know with whom he is dealing."

"I think not," Pisar replied. "Unless you want to be another trophy gracing the walls of his house you had best keep silent. They're not sure I'm human either, but I speak their language and I'm a condor priest. They may decide to kill you just because they like the shape of your head."

Q'enti looked down in silence. Pisar raised a finger to Zapana, "And you must remember never to look a Shuar woman in the eyes, or they'll think you're flirting, and her husband will kill you. If you stare at a man he'll think you're challenging him."

"Will the warriors obey this chief Quirruba?" I asked.

"The Shuar don't have chiefs. Every man makes his own decisions, and they only act together when a Big Man persuades them. These are the kakaram, the 'powerful ones,' who have taken heads and given feasts. But they can't give orders. Quirruba is a ti kakaram, a 'very powerful one.' He led many raids and is the most feared killer in this district. He's also generous to friends, a fine hunter, an expert weaver, has six wives, and lived long enough to have grandchildren.

All this is proof to the Shuar that he controls potent magic. Still, the moment he shows weakness other kakaram will try to kill him for the honor."

After we passed the house most of our Shuar escort departed for their own dwellings to protect their families from the raiders. But the two young men Pisar identified as Quirruba's sons-in-law stayed with us. The news that a killing party lurked nearby made them move cautiously. We soon learned they feared more than ambush. With the region on high alert mantraps had been set. They discovered one, though it was so well hidden no one but a Shuar would have guessed it was there. A freshly cut sapling was bent and tied sideways in the bush beside the trail, so that the slightest touch to a cord stretched across the path would release it, catching the unwary in the stomach. The cane spikes fastened to the sapling were honed to needle points.

Quirruba's house stood on a rise surrounded by gardens. It was a long structure with doors at its rounded ends, a gabled roof of palm thatch, and a watchtower. The walls were staves set upright with gaps between to let in light and air. The first thing I noticed when we entered was a woman sitting just inside holding an infant to one breast and a puppy to the other. Both suckled greedily. Pisar glanced at the animal and remarked, "It must have lost its mother, but the Shuar are a practical people. Why waste a good hunting dog?"

Center posts for the roof also supported platforms keeping urns and baskets out of the reach of children, and other goods dangled in net bags. Counting children there must have been twenty people in the house, but it was large enough for three times that number. Dogs tied to palm-slat beds along the walls snarled and strained at their leashes.

"This way," Pisar said. "Quirruba awaits us at the other end." Q'enti walked behind Pisar, her head bowed. He had already warned her this was not the place for one of her haughty outbursts, and for once she seemed to agree. Zapana put a hand on my shoulder and smiled wanly. We followed.

By silent agreement Zapana and I had not discussed the possible outcomes of this audience. We were in Pisar's hands. At first it was a relief to wake each morning and find that Pisar had not run off in the night. Then I began to wonder if he needed us—but for what?

For all that Pisar had told us about the great Quirruba, I found him an unimposing figure at first sight. He was a man of years sitting on a stool with a back-strap loom tied about his waist, weaving a length of cloth. The Shuar don't have metal so Quirruba wore no gold or silver, nor any other adornment to set him apart from other Shuar men. But he had lived long enough for his hair to turn silver, a feat, Pisar assured us, which proved the spirits were with him. Quirruba faced the wall and didn't bother turning when we approached.

Pisar sat on the earth floor behind Quirruba and motioned us to do the same, then spoke in a stream of incomprehensible babble. A silence followed during which Quirruba seemed more interested in his weaving than us, but at last he glanced over his shoulder and shouted at Pisar. Much to my surprise Pisar shouted back. After several sharp exchanges their conversation settled down, though both continued to speak forcefully. Quirruba finally untied his loom and turned to face us. He gestured to a woman, who produced stools for us, and others appeared with bowls of manioc beer. The women dipped their hands in the bowls before serving and licked their fingers. Q'enti questioned Pisar with a look.

"To show us the brew isn't poisoned," Pisar replied.

"How charming," Q'enti said.

Pisar and Quirruba continued their conversation while Zapana and I kept watch from the corners of our eyes. The women stayed in their end of the house with the children, returning only to fill our beer bowls at frequent intervals. Two sons-in-law lounged nearby. Everyone appeared to ignore us, but not a word or gesture went unobserved. Zapana looked relaxed, yet I knew he was ready if a fight erupted. But what will I do? I wondered. I don't feel like Inca Moon. I don't feel like anything at all.

Zapana caught my attention and nodded to the women's door. A man we hadn't seen before entered with a clutch of birds. The women stirred but none rose. Quirruba and the two sons-in-law glanced in his direction. I became aware that everyone watched the man without staring. He walked over to one of Quirruba's daughters and held out the birds. The girl hesitated and the house fell silent. The man stood patiently with the birds extended, and then the girl rose and took them from him. The women sighed and the house breathed again.

Two more bowls of manioc beer followed before Pisar and Quirruba finally stood. It was a heady brew, but not wanting to offend them I kept pace and now found myself pleasantly unsteady. Q'enti rose awkwardly and giggled, bringing the first smiles from Quirruba's wives. Even Quirruba allowed himself a smirk, and the house relaxed. Pisar showed Quirruba's half-finished cloth panel to Zapana, and Zapana nodded admiringly while fingering the textile. Quirruba said something and indicated all the people in the house with a sweep of his arm.

"He is telling you he makes all the cloth," Pisar said, "and a man with six wives and many children needs nimble fingers at the loom." We all nodded at Quirruba in admiration. Quirruba chuckled contentedly.

Q'enti gestured to the loom. "What is he making?"

"A wrap-around skirt, of course," Pisar said. "That is all the Shuar make, and only in one size. They sew two of them together for a woman's dress."

The women wear their dresses wrapped around and pinned with a bone needle at the right shoulder, leaving the left shoulder bare, and tie the waist with a cotton belt. They have few adornments, though some had ornamental sticks through their lower lips, and all wore tiny bundles of sweet-smelling seeds at their breasts, and toucan feather earrings. They cut their hair straight across their foreheads and let it hang over their shoulders. The women and children are exceptionally clean like the men, and I admired their glossy black hair. The dirt floor of the house was well swept, and all belongings carefully stored.

When Quirruba left we gathered around Pisar. "Will Quirruba let us pass?" Zapana asked.

"He won't stop us," Pisar said.

Q'enti looked impatient. "What does that mean?"

"It means he won't accompany me to the condor boundary as he usually does. He heard I was banished from the brotherhood, but he doesn't know why. He also told me the earth moved a few days ago. He thinks it's a bad omen. Then, I appear with three strangers. Quirruba isn't sure what all this means, though he won't admit it, and he decided the wisest course is to neither help nor hinder us."

I said, "Can you lead us to the temple?"

"Certainly."

"Then we are safe for now."

"We are safe inside Quirruba's house because he is honor bound not to attack anyone visiting him peacefully, but once outside his door other Shuar may be tempted, and then there's the raiding party. Quirruba said they killed a man not far from here."

Q'enti looked up. "You said Shuar don't take heads from other Shuar. Why was this man killed?"

"Revenge. Their shaman divined that this man's sister poisoned a relative of theirs at a feast some years ago. The woman lives far from here, and a woman's life is a poor exchange for a man's anyway, so they waited and murdered her brother instead. This raiding party may have others to visit before they're done."

"But they have no reason to harm us," Q'enti said.

"None, except they might want your head. You're not Shuar." Pisar looked at Zapana. "Have you noticed them watching you? They admire that beak nose of yours. I wouldn't trust Quirruba's sons-in-law either. They've been whispering about you since we met. Once we leave this house any man who wishes can attack you."

"I can look after myself," Zapana said.

"I know you can, but can you look after these women at the same time?"

Zapana glanced at me as if he was about to boast on my behalf, then looked away in silence. I wilted, knowing what he was thinking but unable to find words of my own. I hadn't been able to decide anything for days, and I even shrieked with Q'enti when a snake crossed our path. Without Zapana to guide me I was useless.

To spare me the embarrassed silence Zapana pointed to the trophies hung at the men's entrance. "What are those things?" he asked. They looked like blackened monkey heads, except they had long, human hair.

"Quirruba won't mind you admiring these," Pisar grinned, and beckoned us with a wave.

They hung from cords through the tops of the heads, their lips sewn shut. Long cotton strings dangled from the mouths, and some had feather tufts tied in the hair. The distorted features almost looked human, except the skin was black and the largest was not much bigger than a cupped hand.

"Tsantsa," Pisar said with a flourish, "shrunken heads. I told you the Shuar are headhunters."

"Those things are human?" Q'enti said, her hand at her mouth.

Pisar grinned and nodded.

"But they can't be, they're too small."

"As I said, they are shrunken heads. This is how the Shuar prepare their trophies."

Zapana peered closely at one and felt its hair. "They are human," he announced in astonishment. "But how do they make them so small?"

"The Shuar have no use for the skull," Pisar replied. "They slice the back of the head to skin it, then they boil the skin and dry it with hot stones and sand inside. After some days of treatments it shrinks to this size, with the hair intact. The smaller ones are women and children. The Shuar believe the dead person's avenging soul is still contained in the head, so they blacken the skin with charcoal to prevent the soul from seeing. The power of these heads helps Quirruba's wives prosper in their gardens." Pisar looked at us wickedly. "If you aren't careful you'll be joining these fine things."

Zapana grunted in dismissal and turned away. I tried to imitate him but the sound came out like a moan. Just then Quirruba came back through the door and saw us examining his trophies. He grinned smugly.

Warm smells drew us to the women's end of the house, Quirruba leading the way. Each wife had her own hearth consisting of three logs in a circle, their smoldering ends joined at the center. Liquids bubbled in clay pots. The girl who prepared the visitor's birds presented them to him in a gourd bowl. Again I felt the whole house watching, the wives holding their breaths, but no one showed outward signs of interest. When the girl squatted beside the visitor and picked food from his bowl Quirruba smiled broadly, and his wives giggled. Then everyone returned to other concerns. Quirruba said something to Pisar and chuckled.

"He says this daughter refused to cook for four other suitors," Pisar explained, "but she's finally made her choice. Now Quirruba has a new son-in-law."

"When is the marriage?" I asked.

"They are married," Pisar replied. "You have just witnessed a Shuar wedding ceremony, such as it is. Tonight they will sleep together, and the man will stay in this house to help his father-in-law. At the end of a year the couple will move away and build their own house."

Quirruba motioned us to another hearth. His wives fetched our stools and handed us more bowls of manioc beer, congenially dipping and sucking their fingers with each serving. The beer was well strained and had a strong, refreshing taste. I saw one of the wives brewing a new batch earlier, and noticed they prepare it in the same way as our maize beer, by stirring the mash while chewing handfuls and spitting it back into the urn.

Peanuts and pineapples were set out along with boiled manioc and sweet potatoes, but before I could reach them a wife proudly handed me a steaming bowl. I looked down at a gray-blue lump beside a handful of plump, white things. The others also stared at their bowls. Pisar received his last. He sniffed it with relish and licked his lips. "We are honored," he said, "they brought out the delicacies—monkey brains and grubs."

We stood on the edge of the garden in the night air. Q'enti doubled over and spewed the contents of her stomach again. This time I joined her, heaving out all the Shuar 'delicacies.' Zapana turned away looking pale, but controlled himself. Pisar came over. Behind him the doorway filled with curious Shuar.

"I assured them you don't think they poisoned you," Pisar said. He looked disgusted with us. "I told Quirruba that since you're not human you're not accustomed to human food, and spewing is your way of showing pleasure."

Pisar turned his back and studied the sky. Stars shone between the clouds, and the moon approached fullness. Zapana joined him.

"When we reach the temple," Zapana said, "how will we deal with the condor priests? Are there many?"

Pisar kept his eyes on the night sky but replied, "Too many for us to handle, but if we arrive at the right time they won't be there."

I spit and wiped my mouth, then retreated to Zapana's side as Q'enti heaved again. "When is the right time?" I asked.

"One night each month the brotherhood goes to a sacred lake for worship. All attend, and they return before dawn. That's when my brother Asto stole the emeralds and fled. Curse him! I was with the others at the lake, but still they banished me."

"On which night are they absent?" Zapana inquired.

Pisar turned from his sky gazing and fixed his eyes on us. "Only the condor priests know about the sacred lake, and what I'm about to tell you is another of their closely guarded secrets. The ceremonies are always held on the night of the full moon."

We looked at the sky. "That's tomorrow night," I said.

"Precisely. Now you understand why I hurried us here. If we leave before dawn and journey into the mountains without rest we should reach the condor temple at the mid point of night. The priests will be at the sacred lake then, but when we arrive we must move fast because they're never gone long." Pisar studied us for a moment and added, "Remember, if you fall behind on the trail I won't wait for you. We must arrive at midnight. If not, the opportunity won't come again for another month, and by then the Shuar will have told the brotherhood about us. We only have this one chance."

When Pisar and Q'enti returned to the house I said to Zapana, "Tomorrow you should go with Pisar while I wait here with Q'enti. We will only slow you down, and you don't need us."

Zapana shook his head. "There's no stopping Lady Q'enti. I don't know why she insists on seeking the Great Emerald herself, but she is determined to reach the condor temple. Besides, it's dangerous staying alone with the Shuar. I don't want to come back and find your head on display with Quirruba's trophies."

I leaned against his chest and he enfolded me. "I'm not worried about Q'enti," I said. "Zapana, I'm not myself anymore."

"I know. What happened?"

"I don't know. I can't seem to make up my mind about anything. I'm afraid I'll be wrong. I don't trust myself."

Zapana sighed. "That's not Inca Moon talking."

"I don't know who Inca Moon is anymore, but I'm not her, and if I go to the temple I'll only burden you."

"You won't do it for Qhari?"

I imagined Qhari bound and huddled in the corner of a cold, dark room, the condor dust rotting his insides, and Atoco gloating over him.

"I will do anything for Qhari, you know that, but I won't be any use at the temple. I'll only put you in greater danger."

We stood in silence for a time, and then Zapana said, "I know why Qhari went after the Eye of the Condor."

"Did he say something to you?"

"No, not before he vanished from my grandfather's estate, but he knew I'd hear about it and tell you, and you would come after him. I think he did it to stir you out of your bitterness."

It was true. Qhari told me he wanted to save me from self-pity, and after meeting Qhawachi and Ceiba that burden was lifted. But whatever clarity I gained now lay hidden under a cloud of indecision. "What should I do?" I said in a whisper.

"Do you trust me?"

That was the one question I didn't have to think about. "Yes," I said, "completely."

Zapana rested his chin on my head and held me close. "I can live without Inca Moon, but not without Qori Qoyllur. If you stop now, before doing all you can for your brother, I will lose Qori also. You're coming to the temple, even if I have to carry you."

XIX

In which is given an account of the Condor Temple, where Diabolical Devices of Lethal Cunning await the unwary, and the Earth Groans.

Sun broke through the clouds at mid morning promising a hot day, but we already sweated under Pisar's determined pace. The Shuar awaken long before dawn and so had we, setting out in the cool gray mist and rain. Now the forest lay moist and pungent, still dripping as if it, too, sweated in the heat. Pisar took the lead—keeping us on the main path where mantraps were less likely—followed closely by Q'enti who for once kept up without complaint. I hurried behind her, and Zapana guarded the rear.

The Cutucú Mountains rose around us, their steep slopes shrouded in tangled green beneath canopy trees, but when the trail crested ridges we caught glimpses of sheer cliffs and waterfalls hidden in the jungle below. Zapana stared down through an opening in the trees. "We are being followed," he said.

Pisar frowned. "How many?"

"Several, I can't be sure of numbers. They are far behind but moving fast."

Pisar said, "It might be the raiding party, if it is not up ahead waiting for us, or perhaps it's Quirruba's sons-in-law after our heads. Keep an eye on them."

Pisar had armed himself at Quirruba's house with a lance and bamboo knife. They cost me the last of Tumbala's treasure. The sons-in-law showed great interest in Zapana's bronze knife, and Pisar said that if they asked for it as a gift Zapana had to comply. So Pisar offered gifts first, using our extra clothing and Tumbala's trinkets. Quirruba had little interest in the garments—they were the clothes of non-humans, and inferior to his work—nor did he know what to do with the silver and gold nose pendants, but a copper fishhook and bronze needle caused murmurs of amazement. While these passed from hand to hand Pisar chose his weapons. Q'enti and I also received bamboo knives, and though the sons-in-law glanced longingly at Zapana's knife none dared ask for it.

As we continued into the Cutucú Mountains Zapana kept close watch on the men following us. At mid afternoon he announced they were uncomfortably close. We paused at the base of a cliff where the trail disappeared behind a waterfall. Pisar looked worried. "Whoever they are they want us," he said. "But we can't afford to lay in wait for them. The condor boundary isn't far now, and they will never cross it. If we move fast we might out run them."

Zapana held my hand, leading me a step at a time along the slippery ledge behind the cascade. I pressed my face against the wet moss on the cliff face, a plunging torrent of crystal roaring at my back. Unsure of my footing, I might have clung there forever but Zapana pulled me on until we emerged in sunshine. I paused gasping for breath, comforted by the soft earth beneath my feet. Pisar shook his head at my timidity, and even Q'enti rolled her eyes. We stood in a long clearing, beyond which the trail looked like a rabbit hole disappearing into the bush. "Let's get moving," Pisar barked.

With the waterfall behind us we were about to re-enter the forest when Zapana arched his back in pain. A tufted sliver of cane appeared between his shoulders, and a spear zipped past. "Ambush!" Pisar shouted, and spun with lance pointed as two warriors charged from the path ahead. Four more leapt from cover and came at Zapana. Q'enti screamed and threw her arms around me. Zapana ignored his wound and drew his maqana.

Pisar threw his lance, felling one attacker before the other collided with him, knocking them both flat. They wrestled on the ground with knives drawn. I turned to watch Zapana, whose maqana wove back and forth in a blur before the surprised Shuar. With a sudden strike Zapana split a Shuar head, and the other warriors backed off warily, circling around him. "Zapana, behind you," I shouted. Zapana bent low and spun, the heavy maqana shattering his attacker's thigh, then an equally deft blow snapped the man's neck. Without pause Zapana whirled to the fore just as two men piled into him.

I should jump one of them, I thought. But Q'enti had her head pressed to my shoulder and I realized I held her as firmly as she held me. Zapana threw off his attackers and brandished his weapon again. I saw Pisar still wrestling on the ground. With a wet thud Zapana's maqana opened another head. The remaining warrior ran to the waterfall, then turned and armed his spear-thrower. Zapana didn't hesitate. His maqana flew blade over hilt, smashing into the man's chest and knocking him backwards over the waterfall.

Zapana turned just as Pisar finished his attacker. Pisar looked up heaving for breath, and yanked his knife from the man's neck. Q'enti raised her head and looked about. Shuar sprawled everywhere. Her grip on me slackened, and she sank to her knees.

"Qori, look out," Zapana shouted.

A lone warrior with lance extended charged at me from the trees. I watched him coming, but stood rooted like a tree. From the corner of my vision Zapana leapt, shoving me to the ground. I heard a groan, and then a sharp crack. Looking up, I saw Zapana release the man's head, having turned it backwards between his powerful hands. The body slumped away revealing the lance rammed through Zapana.

"He's finished," Pisar said. "Let's be on our way."

Q'enti shook her head sympathetically. "Poor Lord Zapana, and you were such a good fighter." She turned away eager to leave.

The shock of what had happened left me outside myself, unwilling to comprehend. Though my mind was numb, the healer in me still acted by instinct, mercifully keeping my hands busy and my thoughts focused on the task.

The serrated blade of the lance went clean through his side, which allowed me to break it off behind and withdraw the shaft. Fortunately the blow tube dart in his back hadn't broken, and this

I pulled straight out. Zapana bit down on a stick while I performed these operations and bandaged his wounds, cutting strips from my dress. He now sat propped against a tree with my shawl folded behind to keep the pressure off his back. Six Shuar lay dead around us, the seventh having vanished over the waterfall along with Zapana's maqana.

"We are not leaving him," I said.

Pisar balked. "We've lost enough time, and the Shuar following us will be here any moment." He sneered at me. "I suppose *you're* going to stop them?" I ducked my head. Pisar sighed, and went down on one knee beside Zapana, looking him in the eye. Zapana held his gaze.

"That blow dart was poisoned but it won't kill you," Pisar said. "It takes many of those to stop a man. The poison will make you groggy, and in your condition that's probably best. Given time you might even recover from the lance wound, but we don't have time." He looked into Zapana's eyes. "You don't want to know what happens to Shuar prisoners. They will be here soon. Shall I end it for you?"

Zapana studied him calmly. "Give me weapons and place me by the waterfall. I'll hold them off as long as I can."

Pisar nodded and lifted Zapana.

"No!" I screamed, throwing my arms around Zapana.

Pisar groaned and pushed me away. "Come along," he said gripping Zapana roughly. Weeping, I clung to Zapana as Pisar half-carried him back to the waterfall, and propped him against the cliff. While Pisar went for the weapons I held Zapana close, pressing my cheek to his breast.

Zapana stroked my hair. "Leave now," he whispered.

"No," I sobbed, "I'm staying with you."

"You must go. And I must do alone what needs to be done here."

"No, Zapana. I'm not leaving you, ever."

"You are not leaving me, my love, we are only parting for a time. There are things you must do, and things I must do, but we will always be together in our hearts."

"No, I can't go. I love you."

Zapana released a sigh and held me closer. "Do you know how long I've waited to hear you say that?"

Pisar returned and held out a clutch of Shuar spears. "They will come through the waterfall one at a time," Pisar said. "You should be able to stop a few, and the others will hesitate, at least for a time. Farewell, Lord Zapana. I'll see you in the underworld."

"Qori, are you coming?" Q'enti called. "Remember, your brother Qhari needs the antidote."

Zapana said, "She's right, Qori. Do it for Qhari. Go now."

I held Zapana closer, refusing to release him.

Zapana looked at Pisar and said, "She will be along soon."

"Then she'd better be quick," Pisar said. Q'enti and Pisar hurried off, leaving us alone with the roar of the waterfall.

Zapana continued stroking my hair. After a silence he said, "Do you remember that last night at Tipón when we sat with Qhari by the brazier under the stars? That is the only part of the evening I chose to remember, the three of us together."

I thought of Qhari sitting across from us, looking quietly pleased at having brought us together again. He loved Zapana too, and with a love no less pure than mine. Zapana knew Qhari's feelings, and he loved Qhari in his own way, but he waited for me. It seemed the three of us had lived lifetimes together, and Qhari lived only to sacrifice his happiness for ours.

"I remember," I said in a whisper, listening to Zapana's heart beating slow and steady.

"I go there when I'm trying to sleep," Zapana said. "I know that no matter what happens, if I keep that image before me I will always be there with you. When you want to see me, Qori, see me there with Qhari, the three of us together always."

My shoulders shook with sobs. Zapana took my head in his hands and turned my face to his. "I am content," he said. "I know you love me, and I love you, Lady Qori Qoyllur. Carry me in your heart and I will never leave you."

I couldn't speak for the pain in my throat, and I hardly saw his face for the tears that fell like the waterfall.

"Listen to me," he said wiping the tears from my cheeks. "Stop crying now, that's my girl. Look into my eyes. Look deep into me. There is nothing else, just our souls. When I stop speaking you will turn and follow Pisar. You mustn't look back, not once, nor falter in your steps."

He saw my fear rise but steadied me, fixing me with his piercing eyes until I stopped trembling. His voice came with soothing confidence. "You will do what must be done. Always, from this moment on, you will do what is right. There is nothing you can't do. You will not worry or hesitate. I trained you. I coaxed the talents out of you that were always there. You have the gift, now trust it. Trust yourself. We may err, but with true hearts we always win in the end."

I felt a surge of strength glowing within, and then his lips pressed mine with a heat that branded my soul.

"Go now," he whispered.

Pisar turned to us with a crafty grin. "The River of Jaguars," he said, presenting the watercourse with a flourish. It was little more than a shady jungle stream, shallow and overhung with vine-covered trees. "It marks the condor boundary, and no Shuar will cross it. We are safe until we get to the temple."

Q'enti glanced around. "Is this the path the condor priests take?"

"Yes, it's the one trail leading in and out, but only those sent on missions leave. Right now all of them will be preparing for the vigil at the sacred lake."

Dusk fell fast, thickening the shadows around us. "How far is the temple?" I asked.

"Close enough for us to rest here until full night, but we should cross first."

We splashed through the river, the water no more than knee deep, while a noisy flock of parrots cawed their displeasure and darted to other trees. Their calls faded with the light like echoes in the still forest.

Where the path continued a strange sight greeted us. I pointed. "What's that?"

Pisar grinned. "Come and see."

It was a staff sunk into the middle of the path with a dried condor head perched on top, looking black and evil. Below it the shaft went through a human skull, and below that dangled a jaguar pelt. I looked at Pisar. He chuckled.

"The Shuar are terrified of it," he said. "When the priests first brought Asto and me through Shuar territory they carried one like it. We wouldn't have seen a Shuar if the priests hadn't insisted old Quirruba accompany us to this boundary. The Shuar think this condor staff is full of magic, and they will die if they even look at it."

I turned away from the frightful thing. "Are you sure we won't meet any condor priests on the trail?"

"No, I told you, on the night of the full moon they are all at the sacred lake. The path is unguarded, at least by men."

I raised my brows at him.

"You'll see soon enough. Even if you had somehow gotten this far without me you would never make it to the temple, even in daylight."

Exhausted, Q'enti heaved a sigh and leaned against a tree. She had looked surprised when I caught up with them, but Pisar set such a pace it was all she could do to stay with him, and no words were exchanged. Both of them sensed something different about me. Now Q'enti studied me with a spark of amusement.

"You poor thing," she cooed. "It must have been hard for you abandoning Lord Zapana to the savages."

I whirled and pinned her neck to the tree with my forearm, while pressing my knife to her right cheek. "If you ever mention his name to me again I'll give you a matching scar," I hissed. Q'enti's eyes bulged. I released her just as suddenly, drawing the butt of my knife across her face. She shrieked and held her cheek, then searched her hands for blood. Finding none she sat down heavily.

"Have you wet your dress, dear?" I enquired pleasantly.

Pisar made a whistling sound and shook his head. He turned away knowing this was between Q'enti and me. Q'enti looked up, her left eye twitching.

We rested in silence as night fell. The forest, so quiet in the day, came alive under the full moon. Howler monkeys sounded nearby and a night bird gave its high-pitched whistle in response. The bushes rustled, and high above, branches stirred in a breeze. Insects scurried over the forest litter, making strange clicking and twilling sounds. Pisar said they called it the River of Jaguars because there were so many of the great cats here, undisturbed by hunters in this forbidden zone. Were jaguars watching us now? I wondered.

I struggled to keep Zapana from my mind, pushing the thoughts away before they formed into words. I told myself he waited for me at the waterfall, knowing that if for one instant I allowed myself to imagine his last stand I would fall into blackness forever. In my mind I saw only his eyes, and heard his calm voice admonish me to do what was right. Inca Moon will not let you die in vain, I promised him.

I sensed Zapana sitting to one side of me, and Qhari on the other. Together the three of us will see this through, I thought, and then Inca Moon will rid the earth of Lady Q'enti.

Pisar stood and stretched. "It's time," he announced. "Now we go to the condor temple." He gave us a measuring look. "I'm sure you will be useful in your own ways, but if you hope to survive you better do exactly as I say." I wondered what he had planned for us—why he bothered bringing us this far—but without worrying over it I knew I was ready for whatever lay ahead.

An owl hooted as we started through tendrils of mist on the night trail, the forest bright with silvery shadows. There were few clouds and for once it didn't rain, though the air felt fresh and alive. We were three more creatures seeking and hiding in this immense jungle, alert to every snap and rustle.

It wasn't long before Pisar showed us the first mantrap. I wouldn't have seen it in the day let alone at night, but he knew where it was and approached carefully. Q'enti and I waited while he heaved a moldering log onto the path and stood it upright, holding it before him. "Now watch," he said, and let the log fall forward. I heard a snap and a swish as a bent sapling sprang across the trail, its bamboo spikes quivering as if straining to gut us. Pisar wiggled his eyebrows at me.

Thereafter Pisar set a frantic pace, and with him in the lead I only heeded the ground at my feet. Once I had to leap over a fat snake slithering across the path, and farther on I glimpsed two shining eyes watching from the underbrush, but these went by in a blur. When Pisar held up his hand again I collided with Q'enti. She jumped away as if I struck her, then gave me a look telling me to keep my distance. We watched Pisar go down on his knees and creep up the trail a distance, then flatten and reach an arm forward. I heard a snap, and suddenly from the canopy above a timber swooshed down the path butt first. We ducked as it arched over our heads and swung back. When the rocking stopped it came to rest over Pisar's prostrate form. He rolled from beneath and jumped up wiping his hands. He was right, I realized, we never would have survived this passage without him.

Twice Pisar set off snares—these being loops hidden on the path that could seize a foot, and fling the victim against a tree with branches trimmed to spikes. Farther along he showed us a section of trail that looked like any other, but was a thin cover over a pit full of sharpened stakes. He said he sprang these traps so they wouldn't slow 'him' on 'his' return journey, as if Q'enti and I weren't part of the escape plan.

The last device almost caught us. It was a boulder perched above the path on a sheer slope, levered and strung to a trip-cord. Pisar stood with his feet on either side of the cord showing us the fatal rock above, when suddenly the earth trembled. It lasted only a heartbeat but the bindings snapped and the boulder fell. Pisar dove away and I grabbed Q'enti, pulling her back just as the rock crashed where we'd stood.

"Enough games," Pisar said picking himself up. "Anyway, that's the last one." He looked around and added, "Unless the gods have something more in store for us. We must hurry. Come, the temple is here."

He led us around a turn where a valley opened to view. Far below in the moonlight a river snaked through the dark jungle like a swath of silver, and an enormous white cliff shot straight up from the forest floor. The river looped against the base of the cliff, where I could just discern a jumble of slabs fallen from above in ancient times. From this distance I realized the stones must be the size of houses, but they were dwarfed by the immensity of the vertical wall above.

Pisar examined the moon and nodded to himself, then pointed to the rock-fall at the base of the cliff. "No one but the brotherhood has ever seen it," he said. "You are looking at the condor temple."

Moonlight sparkled on the river. A floating branch rushed by and vanished in the undertow. Pisar pointed to a lone boulder set upright on the far bank, then placed himself directly opposite and boldly stepped into the river. The stepping-stones beneath the surface were invisible. Q'enti gripped Pisar's shoulders, and I set my feet in her steps. When we reached the other side I looked up at the white cliff, arching my head back to my shoulders until the jungle-draped rim was silhouetted against the night sky. Even Q'enti looked awed as we stood like insects staring up. "This way," Pisar said. He took us along a well-worn path through the underbrush and up a slope. The trees stopped where the rock-fall began; the slabs now covered with thick moss and shrubs. Halfway up Pisar moved some bushes aside to reveal a dark hole that plunged downward at an angle. It might have been the entry to an animal den, but Pisar's excitement told me it was the hidden portal to the condor temple. "Are you ready?" he said.

Q'enti looked at me. "Remember, Qori, if I don't come out of there alive your brother is dead."

I took one last look at the full moon looming in a starry sky, then crouched and followed Q'enti's broad siki into the earth. The tunnel sloped down. Blackness enfolded me and my shoulders brushed the walls, but after a distance the floor leveled and we stood upright. When Q'enti moved aside I saw the soft glow of a brazier. We stood on paving stones in a small chamber, the walls and roof composed of jumbled boulders chinked with mud and stones. I followed Pisar in selecting a torch from a pile and igniting it on the brazier. The room burst open in brilliance. Pisar motioned us to the rear of the chamber and held his torch high, revealing a stone staircase continuing down to darkness. He gave Q'enti an eager look and said, "The Eye of the Condor awaits. Would you like to go first?" Q'enti's eyes went wide, but I held her back and said, "You know the way, Pisar, so you go first." Pisar scowled back, and then with brand extended he began the descent.

The torches caste our shadows on plastered walls as the steps led down and down, the air surprisingly fresh and dry. At the bottom a vertical wall of smooth stone confronted us, and the passage turned sharply to the right following the cliff face. The opposite wall had fresh cracks in the plaster, and the floor, now level, lay under fiber mats. Tiny bowls of fat with lighted wicks twinkled from niches down the corridor like a dreamscape. I caught a sniff of fresh air and saw a fist-sized hole in the ceiling leading to the surface. It reminded me that beyond the smooth plaster lay ancient rock-fall, naked slabs of stone wedged at odd angles. The cracks in the plaster were not reassuring.

Pisar led the way. An alcove opened on our right but he wasn't interested. "The vestment chamber," he said over his shoulder, hurrying on. Then the walls came alive with color in a mural of fantastic demons. Fanged and grimacing, they swirled over the walls and ceiling grasping human heads. Some held trumpets and flutes as if playing for this mad orgy, while others shredded tiny humans with their talons. Pisar stopped and watched Q'enti and me staring at the demons in fascination and horror. "They are meant to make the unwary look up," he said. He lowered his torch to a line of round eyes spaced along the base of the mural just above the matting. "As these condor eyes watch you, so must you watch them," he said. Then he knelt and lifted the matting. A yawning chasm stretched from wall to wall. Timbers set one long stride apart extended across the abyss below each condor eye, but the spaces between fell away to blackness. Pisar replaced the matting and stood.

"How far does this pit continue?" I asked.

"Ten steps to the other side of the paintings," Pisar said. Q'enti swallowed hard and Pisar added, "It's too far to jump, but set your feet in front of the condor eyes and they will guide you." He gave me a hard look. "Shall I lead?" he said. I returned a nod. Q'enti sighed and braced herself, then took a deep breath and followed Pisar.

With relief I felt my foot arch over the first timber beneath the matting. Reassured, I swung my step to the next solid footing. I would have skipped across like Pisar, but Q'enti took one shaky step at a time, resting both feet on each timber before attempting the next. Suddenly she tottered and fell backwards, frantically waving her arms for balance. Pisar, already across, turned with outstretched hands but was too far away. I leapt to the next perch and grabbed, catching one arm as she fell through the matting. Struggling to keep my balance, I held tight while she swung helplessly over the black void below. For an instant I thought of dropping her—a fitting end for one so evil—but if she didn't return . . . Atoco would kill Qhari. I set my knees and pulled. Q'enti managed to get an arm and leg over the timber, but once secure she froze there, whimpering.

"Come on, Q'enti," I said gently. She sniffed and shook her head, clinging to the timber with eyes sealed. "You look ridiculous," I said. "If they could only see Lady Q'enti now with her dress hiked-up, hanging like a peasant." Q'enti forgot her terror and glared at me, then set her face and heaved herself onto the log. She finished the last three strides to safety with head up and back straight.

Where the mural ended so too did the concealed pit. The floor mats continued, and in spite of Pisar's assurances I stepped warily. With so many cunning traps behind us I didn't trust this place, and when I cast my senses ahead I felt the familiar cold hand on my neck.

"The shrine room," Pisar said excitedly, gesturing to an opening on the right. He rushed in with Q'enti at his heels while I waited by the entrance, scanning walls and ceiling for more fiendish devices. Pisar moved with confidence to the altars lining the walls. Jaguar skins draped the shrines, and behind each hung a stuffed creature with emerald eyes like those at Guayas. Smoke from bowls of smoldering sweet wood found its way through a hole in the roof; it seemed as if the condor priests had just stepped from the room. Q'enti studied the baskets of emeralds on the altars, her eyes wide; she took a handful and let them tumble through her fingers. A huge condor with outstretched wings hung in a back corner, keeping watch over open sacks of emeralds. Pisar ignored the jewels, becoming more frantic as he searched from altar to altar. Finally he said, "It's not here." He sounded desperate.

"What isn't here?" Q'enti said dreamily, holding up an emerald the size of a tomato. Flashes of cool green reflected on her face.

"The antidote," Pisar huffed. "It's usually kept here in a feathered bag, but sometimes the elders put it on the altar in the sanctum with the condor dust."

"The sanctum?" I said.

"Yes, where the Eye of the Condor lives."

"Which is where?"

"Farther along the corridor."

I invited him with a sweep of my arm. "Shall we?"

Pisar hesitated, looked around in frustration, and then stomped over. "Are you coming?" he called to Q'enti. Q'enti looked up from stuffing emeralds into her shoulder bag. "What? Oh, the Great Emerald. Yes!" She hurried to join us.

The passageway followed the cliff face as before, but beyond the shrine room the floor covering changed from matting to maize husks. I felt the hair on my neck stiffen. Pisar bowed graciously to Q'enti, waving her to the lead. I pulled her back. "You go first," I told him. Pisar folded his arms and shook his head.

We stared at each other in silence, and then I understood. "You've never been to the sanctum, have you?" I said.

Pisar shrugged. "The novices aren't allowed beyond the shrine room."

"And you're not going to lead us farther, are you?"

"No," he smirked, "but I'll be right behind you."

"This is why you brought us, isn't it?"

"I'm sure you will be careful."

Q'enti reminded Pisar, "You need the antidote, also."

"Yes," Pisar conceded, then looked straight at me, "as does she." He showed his crooked teeth. "I knew you would be useful."

Before I could answer the floor vibrated with a deep rumble, and then came the groan of stone grinding stone. I reached out to steady myself. Cracks shot across the wall and plaster fell, filling the passageway with dust. The rumbling stopped, leaving us breathless and wide-eyed.

Pisar straightened himself. "The strongest one yet," he said. "When they hit with that force there are usually more to follow. The priests will be racing back right now to check the damage. We must move quickly." He turned to Q'enti and pointed down the dust filled corridor. "After you." Q'enti looked at me and repeated the gesture. "For your brother," she said.

The floor beneath the husks felt solid, but I edged forward a step at a time, uncovering it with my foot before putting my weight down. Q'enti and Pisar waited behind, urging me to make haste. I moved in a crouch ready to jump or dodge, my eyes darting over ceiling and walls, my senses reaching out to the unseen. When I paused to wipe the sheen from my brow I felt the cold hand tighten on my neck.

Q'enti called, "Hurry, go faster. It's just ahead."

The lamps lining the passage were extinguished by the quake. My torch burned low but gave enough light to see through the settling dust. I crept on, gently turning the maize husks to search for trip-cords. On the plastered wall high above my head a demon face protruded, and farther along, where the corridor ended, a doorway opened to the right. With the sanctum only steps away I straightened and breathed in relief.

"Hurry," Q'enti called from behind.

I took half a step when something held me back. It's too easy, I thought, and looked around cautiously.

"Can you see the Great Emerald yet?" Pisar called. "Is the antidote with it?"

The sculptured demon face stared at the blank wall opposite, its lips pursed as if whistling. An oracle? I wondered. Why is it set so high?

"Hurry, Qori," I heard Q'enti say from close behind. She and Pisar had advanced, both eagerly straining forward.

I knelt and reached ahead, brushing the husks aside beneath the demon face to reveal flagstone paving. The stones appeared firm, but I pressed down on them with my hand to be sure. One yielded to the pressure, sinking slightly, and then I heard a puff like an exhaled breath above. I shot backwards as the dust expelled from the demon's mouth drifted downward in the torchlight.

"That's how Asto was poisoned," Pisar said triumphantly. "It must be the last device, because Asto entered the sanctum and escaped." The condor dust remained suspended in the air below the demon head. Pisar and Q'enti pressed themselves against the opposite wall and edged past. I followed, and then the three of us stood at the entrance to the sanctum looking in.

The Eye of the Condor sat on its pedestal in the center of the stone altar, illuminated by a shaft of moonlight from a vent above. We stood transfixed, Q'enti with her hand at her mouth and Pisar gaping. The legends were all true. The emerald was pure as crystal and as big as a squash. Its fiery green depths demanded attention, seizing us as if by a spell.

When my breath returned I looked about. Except for the altar in the center of the flagstone floor the chamber was empty. The floor stones were expertly cut and fitted, and a large, six-sided slab occupied the space in front of the altar. On the altar five cat's-eye emeralds surrounded the Eye of the Condor, with a sixth place vacant marking Asto's theft. Pisar pointed to a black leather pouch beside the Great Emerald. "Condor dust, enough to kill an army. But where's the antidote?"

Q'enti gazed at the black pouch, her left eye fluttering. The three of us remained on the threshold staring into the chamber.

Pisar's thoughts twisted his lips in a snarl. "If the feather bag with the antidote isn't here, they may have left it in the vestment chamber, or taken it with them." His eyes settled on the Great Emerald again, and he spoke bitterly to it. "I served you, and you cast me out. But now your power is mine." With greedy hands extended he pushed ahead of us through the door. I heard the snap of a trip-cord and pulled Q'enti back. Pisar remained in the doorway standing perfectly still, a row of stakes pointing through his back.

Q'enti spoke with icy calm. "Good. That saves me having to get rid of him later." She ducked and squeezed past Pisar. The spiked bar that skewered him was a bent sapling of Shuar design, evidently added after Asto's theft.

"Q'enti, be careful," I said. "There may be other traps."

"There's nothing here," she replied, striding across the flagstones, "only what I came for." She approached the altar from the side.

I edged past Pisar. When he saw me standing before him he blinked and his mouth worked like a fish, but no sound came. I watched his agony with satisfaction. "In Guayas I promised Goodgift I would see you die, and now that pledge is fulfilled." Pisar blinked again, his life dripping away at his feet. "Can you see all the little girls you destroyed, Pisar? Hold their faces before you as you die." Pisar managed a long wail, and then his eyes went blank.

Q'enti stood at the altar clutching the black bag of condor dust, her look far away. Holding the pouch low she opened it and peered inside. A feral smile spread, then she sealed the bag and held it aloft in triumph. "The power of death," she shouted at the roof. "They will all fear me now."

I saw everything clearly then, and stood ridged with horror. Q'enti never really wanted the Great Emerald—it was the condor dust she sought all along. With such a quantity she could threaten multitudes. Even the Emperor would be forced to concede her will. And I had delivered this to her—the ultimate evil in the hands of evil.

I stood just inside the door, for the cold hand remained on my neck and my feet refused to advance. Frantically I looked about for the feathered bag containing the antidote, but there was no sign of it. The vestment chamber, I thought, it must be there. "Q'enti, bring the Eye of the Condor, we're leaving."

Q'enti tied the black pouch around her neck and arranged it under her dress, then stared at the Great Emerald. "It may be useful, too," she said to herself, as if it was an afterthought. "Perhaps I'll start my own cult." Reluctantly she dumped the smaller emeralds from her bag and hefted the Eye of the Condor with both hands. She turned the stone, holding it up to the shaft of moonlight bathing the altar. It cast a green glow over her.

"Q'enti, hurry. We must search the vestment chamber for the antidote."

Q'enti cast me a look of contempt. She had everything she wanted. She fitted the Great Emerald into her shoulder bag, where it bulged as if there was a head inside, and turned her back on the altar. She had approached the altar from the side, but now on the return she stepped on the six-sided flagstone directly in front of it. The instant she did so the slab yielded slightly, and I heard a heavy puff of expelled air like that which came from the demon head in the corridor.

"Q'enti, look out!" I shouted.

It was the wrong thing to say because Q'enti, who froze staring down at the depressed stone when she heard the sound, now looked about her with frantic eyes, and seeing nothing she looked up at the ceiling . . . just as the dust expelled from the roof overhead settled in her face.

It was too late to do anything. Q'enti knew she had inhaled condor dust. Calmly, she walked over to me and said; "Now you *must* find the antidote. I am not leaving without it."

The click of sliding rocks turned our eyes back to the roof, and then another trembling began, showering us with plaster. "Hurry," I shouted, slipping by Pisar's impaled body. Q'enti dashed for the door. I grabbed her hand and pulled her through. The corridor shook like a living thing. The poison-spouting demon head crashed to the floor behind us.

My torch wavered as the tremor rumbled louder. Whole sections of plaster fell from walls and ceiling choking us, and a naked boulder burst through the wall. We scrambled around it but other slabs thrust from the roof and wedged precariously over the passage.

We reached the pit and found the matting had fallen through leaving the bridging timbers exposed. They shook and groaned as if unable to hold the walls apart. A rock fell from the roof snapping one.

I shouted in Q'enti's ear, "Don't think. Just leap from one log to the next without stopping."

Though every instinct screamed at me to fly across the timbers I waited for Q'enti to go first. Her feet sprouted wings. I moved a step behind her ready to grab if she fell. The timbers vibrated but without hesitation I jumped from one to another. Q'enti reached the broken log and leapt over the gap. She managed one foot on the next timber and slipped, falling straight down but flinging her arms over the perch. In the same instant I jumped the chasm and landed with knees bent, waving my arms for balance. The torch fell from my hand into the void below, receding like a pinprick into endless darkness. I sat with the log between my legs and grabbed Q'enti, pulling her up. She struggled on to the timber just as one end broke from the wall and slumped. I dragged her to the other end, certain it would break with each frantic breath. When my back pressed the wall Q'enti sprang to her feet and, using me for support, leapt to the last timber and then to safety. I drew myself up in a crouch, the broken log now swinging from side to side, and jumped. My foot hardly touched the last timber and then I landed beside Q'enti. A great roar shook us to our knees. In the dust-choked dimness I saw the log we had clung to fall away, and then an enormous slab fell from the roof taking three more timbers with it. The trembling stopped.

I pulled Q'enti to her feet, both of us coughing and spitting dust. "The vestment chamber is just ahead," I said. "The antidote must be there."

We turned and froze. Lights appeared through the dust before us. They grew stronger and carried voices. We stood with our backs to the pit and stared at the condor priests.

XX

Of how that which came to pass did so.

Condor priests filled the passageway holding their torches high in the filtering dust. With nothing behind us but the yawning pit we stood motionless watching them come on. An elder raised his arm for silence. Hard eyes bore through us.

The elder spoke, trying two languages before repeating himself in Kañari. "How did you find our temple?" He looked genuinely puzzled.

Q'enti stepped forward and straightened herself. "I am Lady Q'enti of Cuzco, and I will not leave this place without the antidote to the condor dust. You have it here in this temple, now give it to me."

The elder chuckled. "Incas," he said over his shoulder, raising a grumble from the men. They were huge brutes with hairstyles of the northern tribes. Several gripped axes. "We came here a generation ago to avoid your people," the elder said. "How is it you find us now, and how did you pass the Shuar and survive our traps?"

"Where is the antidote?" Q'enti demanded.

"It doesn't matter because you are not leaving our precincts alive. I am only curious to know—" His words ended as a tremor shook the corridor. A man called out, "Master, the Eye of the Condor?"

The elder looked around wildly. "Quickly, to the sanctum. Throw these thieves in the pit."

I snatched Q'enti's shoulder bag and held it up. "Destroy us and you destroy the Great Emerald."

The elder spread his arms holding the men back. I pulled the emerald from the bag and held it in both hands above my head. Instantly the priests fell to their knees, heads bowed. But the elder remained standing, his face pinched in agitation. "You shouldn't touch that, what are you doing?"

I stepped back to the edge of the pit and held the emerald over the void. "Give us the antidote and let us leave in peace," I said.

The kneeling priests moaned, raising their arms as the elder shifted uneasily, eyes darting. A stronger tremor came, this time removing the last of the plaster and shaking us to our knees. On the far side of the pit slabs fell from the roof. Still clutching the Eye of the Condor I stayed on the brink. The elder crept to me on hands and knees. "Give it to me," he begged.

"The antidote first," I replied, "and your promise of safe passage."

"Here, take it!" He lifted a feathered bag from around his neck and held it out.

A boulder slid through the wall and stones rained from above. "Qori!" Q'enti wailed.

The rumbling forced me to shout, "And your oath we leave here alive."

"Yes, yes!" the elder cried, eyes frantic. He dropped the feathered pouch in front of me and held out trembling hands.

I placed the Eye of the Condor in his grasp and hung the pouch at my breast. The corridor reverberated with the force of a new shock, slamming my face to the floor. Then slabs fell from the roof and a crushing weight pinned my leg.

"We've got to get out!" Q'enti screamed. She struggled to her feet and turned to leave.

"Q'enti, my leg is caught," I shouted. "I can't move."

She paused only an instant. "Then look after yourself. I'm getting out."

"I have the antidote," I said. "Without it you're dead."

"Give it to me," she shrieked, falling to her knees and tearing at my breast.

I seized her throat in a claw-grip. She went limp, her mouth open and tongue extended. "Listen to me, Q'enti, you are going to lift this boulder off my leg."

I released her and she sat back gasping. "Do it now," I yelled. We both strained, but the slab hardly moved. On the next attempt a jagged edge beneath the rock tore my flesh, but I gritted my teeth and pulled until the leg came free. A ragged gash ran from knee to ankle, but nothing was broken. I ignored the pain and came up on my knees.

The rumbling stopped as suddenly as it began leaving the shattered passageway thick with dust. During my struggle the elder remained curled around the Great Emerald, but now he stood and held up the stone in triumph. Those kneeling before him pressed their foreheads to the floor.

Q'enti looked dazed. I took her hand and raised her. "Come along, Q'enti," I said pulling her forward. The elder had his eyes closed in prayer, and the priests, heads bowed but torches held upright, barely noticed our passing. I snatched a priest's torch, but its owner never lifted his head. We continued through the hunched bodies clogging the corridor, passing the vestment room and reaching the stairs. I glanced back once. There must have been thirty priests kneeling in the passageway. I wondered at the devotion that placed their idol before their own lives.

Part way up the staircase the rumbling came again with new violence. The stones shook and cracked under our feet, sliding away behind us. I seized Q'enti's arm and dragged her two steps at a time up the crumbling stairs. We staggered into the brazier antechamber just as the stairway collapsed. A mighty shudder knocked us to our knees and the walls twisted. Behind us the shaft leading downward gave way, sealing the priests in their temple forever.

I pushed Q'enti to the exit as the walls fell around us. "Hurry, Q'enti. Move!" On all fours we scrambled up the dark tunnel, and then came a blast of dust from behind as the antechamber caved in. I shoved Q'enti's broad siki and piled ahead. Earth rained down but the fear of being buried alive kept me fighting. We must have shot from that hole in the earth like arrows, for suddenly I found myself lying beside Q'enti in the fresh air staring up at the moon. Behind us the tunnel slumped shut.

Dawn found us at the River of Jaguars. Q'enti let her legs collapse and sat with a thud, but her eyes were clear and her back straight. My limbs felt like twigs, yet my mind leapt with visions of the night's events. Before us the River of Jaguars lay hidden under mist like a path of white winding through the forest stillness.

"Give me the antidote," Q'enti said.

"In exchange for what?" I said, feeling the feathered bag safe at my breast.

"Just give it to me."

"That wasn't the bargain, Q'enti. I delivered the Eye of the Condor into your hands. The antidote is mine."

"You gave away the Great Emerald. I don't have it now."

"True, but you have the condor dust, and that's what you were really after."

Q'enti's hand went to the black pouch secured at her neck. "Then give me enough antidote to cure myself."

"Are you afraid, Q'enti? Imagine how Qhari feels."

"I will let him go. As of this moment he is free, you have my solemn word. Now give me the antidote."

She looked so intent I had to smile. "Your solemn word, Q'enti? What's that worth? Perhaps I'll give you the antidote when I see Qhari, but not before."

I went to the riverbank and bathed my injured leg. The gash down my calf was a swollen, angry red, but it wasn't deep. Ragged patches of dried skin and blood kept it sealed. If only it doesn't fester, I thought, at least not until we get out of here. Ceiba had said that in the jungle even bramble scratches could rot off a limb.

Q'enti watched me. "How are you going to get me through the Shuar lands?" she said. "Remember, unless I return safely your brother is dead."

"You never let me forget that, Q'enti, as if I need reminding. I'll get you through—you've always known that. As for the Shuar, this will stop them." I went to the condor staff and pulled it from the ground. The black condor head, white skull, and jaguar pelt looked as menacing in the dawn light as they had the night before. "Pisar said the Shuar are afraid to look at it."

The mist lifted and though the morning sun remained hidden in a gray-white sky its heat filtered to the dozing tangle below. Having crossed the River of Jaguars we continued on the main path into Shuar lands, the jungle now quiet save for the hum of insects and bird song. Q'enti walked behind me, her silence gathering like a cloud. What's she planning now? I wondered. The game has shifted—I have something she needs, but she has months before the poison takes effect, and Qhari doesn't have much time.

When we approached the waterfall I hardened myself against what I might see. It was only yesterday, I reminded myself, but it seems like a lifetime ago. We left six dead Shuar here, and Zapana. Have animals been at them in the night? Will Zapana's headless body lie across the path?

The grass in the clearing was trampled and smeared red, but the Shuar bodies had vanished. Quirruba's sons-in-law must have removed them. At the waterfall I tried to keep my gaze on my feet to avoid seeing the savaged remains of the man I loved, but my eyes wandered. I stopped and looked about. His body was gone, also. The roaring cascade disappeared in a handful of mist far below on the jungle floor. That's how I would have gone, I thought. When Zapana could hold out no longer, he would have deprived them of their trophy in a last, defiant act of heroism.

Q'enti watched me, saying nothing. She knew I would make good my promise to give her a matching scar if she mentioned Zapana's name, and she stayed back with eyes averted. I wished she would taunt me.

I carried the condor staff over my shoulder as we followed the winding trail through the mountains, a vein of red in a tumbling sea of green. With the fearsome condor emblems to guard us the Shuar kept their distance—indeed, we saw no trace of people—but I felt eyes watching us from the forest depths.

It was full night when we reached Quirruba's house, walking like the dead with no feeling in our exhausted limbs. The place stood empty, yet hearths smoldered in the moonlight. A dog barked revealing that its owners huddled nearby in the bushes, hoping, no doubt, that the dreaded condor staff would pass them by.

"Quirruba," I shouted from the door of the house. When no response came I yelled again. Silently Q'enti made her way to a cane bed and curled up.

"Quirruba," I bellowed, "I command you to show yourself." I knew he wouldn't understand my words, but he would understand my tone.

A faint voice from the darkness answered, "Qori?" My heart stopped. I hastened forward searching the night. "Qori?" the voice came again, leading me to a tiny bower on the edge of the garden. I went to my knees and peered inside. Zapana stared back at me.

My hands went to my mouth. Zapana lay on his back, but held out his arms to me. I threw myself into his embrace.

We held each other in silence until our heartbeats slowed, content to know we were both alive and together again. I faced it, I thought, I faced the fear of losing him, and I survived. He gave me the strength to do so. Now, by whatever miracle, I have him back, and nothing will stop me from loving this man to the end of my days.

I whispered, "I love you."

"I love you, too," he said. In the dark I felt his tears on my cheek sealing the truth of his words.

Zapana stiffened. "The antidote?" he asked.

"I have it here." He relaxed against me.

"And Pisar?" he inquired.

I told him about the temple and Pisar's end. "A fitting death," he remarked.

"Indeed," I said, "but the Kañari Great Lord will demand compensation. You promised him the contents of the storehouses at Hatun Kañar if Pisar didn't return to face his justice. What will the Inca governor say?"

Zapana dismissed the consequences. "The governor will pay the Great Lord, and I'll reimburse the governor from my storehouses at Tipón."

"That will cost all your wealth."

"I have everything I need right here," he said drawing me close. "You brought Lady Q'enti back? Good. Did you see the Eye of the Condor?"

I told him the full story. When I described the Great Emerald and what became of it he sighed contentedly. "I told you the legend was true," he teased. "And now the Eye of the Condor lies buried with all its priests."

"You taught Inca Moon to be thorough," I said.

Zapana began to laugh, then sucked in his breath and held his side.

"Zapana, how did you come to be here? What happened at the waterfall?"

"Pisar was right, it was Quirruba's sons-in-law following us, and a few of their friends. I don't know what they planned, but when they saw the dead raiding party they backed away from me. There was a lot of jabbering, and then they made a litter and carried me here. Quirruba wouldn't let them put me in his house, I suppose he didn't want to be responsible, so they built this bower and left me."

"I thought you were dead."

"So did I, but it didn't trouble me, not after you told me you loved me. Tell me again."

"I love you."

In reply he nuzzled me.

"How is your wound?" I asked.

"I think it's still clean, no pus yet. But it may be a while before I can walk."

The lance had gone through his side leaving a gaping hole. As a healer I would have ordered three weeks bed rest, providing the wound didn't fester. But I had no medicines and I didn't know the healing plants of the Shuar lands. From what I'd seen of the Shuar they were more interested in magic than medicines anyway.

Zapana stirred. "Why does Quirruba fear you?"

I told him about the condor staff.

"Excellent, then we must leave tomorrow."

"You can't travel."

"The Shuar carried me this far. With that staff I'm sure you can convince them to carry me out of here." His tone became serious. "Qhari doesn't have much time left, Qori. He needs us."

The Kañari herder and his family fled their hut when they saw the Shuar coming. The Shuar were just as anxious to be away from the high, cool pasturelands. They set our litters beside the hut and ran back down the mountainside, vanishing in the clouds below.

Q'enti jumped off her litter and went inside to see if her bales of clothing were still as she left them, while I limped to Zapana's side and helped him rise. We exchanged a grin, feeling the crisp air welcoming us home to the mountains.

It had taken patience to coax Quirruba from the bushes, and even more to convince him with gestures to provide the men and litters. In the end it was the sons-in-law who assembled others to help. Still, they wanted to abandon us on the edge of their territory at the Paute River, and only agreed to carry us into the mountains when Zapana promised them his bronze dagger.

The journey took many days. At first only Zapana rode, but when my leg turned ugly I required a litter, also. Then Q'enti announced she would not walk like a peasant while others had litters, and refused to go farther unless the Shuar carried her, too. Her bearers seemed to fear her sharp tongue as much as they feared the condor staff, and when we reached the herder's hut they dropped her litter and ran.

I helped Zapana to a boulder in the sun, and sat beside him. Behind us Q'enti muttered to herself in the hut. Zapana saw me wince as I stretched my leg. I made little of it on the journey while I tended his wound—which remained miraculously free of corruption—but each day my leg grew worse. He now pulled back the fold of my dress exposing it for the first time, and gasped. Below my knee the limb was grossly swollen, greenish-purple, and oozing pus. Zapana looked at me sternly. "You never told me," he said.

"What was there to tell?"

"Can it be saved?"

"With the right medicine, perhaps."

Zapana exhaled heavily and sat back. "We are in civilized lands again where my commands are obeyed. I will send for a healer immediately."

Q'enti emerged from the hut attired in a clean dress and shawl. "Well, at least these peasants didn't steal everything," she said.

Zapana spoke to her forcefully. "Lady Q'enti, you will summon the owner of this hut and order him to make haste to the nearest outpost. He is to report that Lord Zapana is here and requires a healer and escort immediately. Do it."

Zapana had never spoken to Q'enti this way, and for a moment she stood blinking at him. But then, seeing the look on his face, she set out calling the herder.

Zapana watched me glaring at Q'enti's retreating back. I carried her over oceans and mountains and jungles, putting up with her petty demands and taunting, and saving her miserable life at every turn. Being forced to serve her filled me with helpless frustration, but what burned more was the obvious enjoyment she took in holding this power over me. Yet I reminded myself it was nothing compared to the terror she would unleash on the world with the condor dust. She had to be stopped, just as soon as Qhari was safe.

Zapana said, "Has Lady Q'enti told you where Qhari is being held?"

"No, not a hint, but wherever it is her henchman Atoco will be close by."

"Ah yes, Captain Atoco, an ambitious worm, but clever in his own way." I raised my brows and Zapana explained, "He knows how to curry favor at court and guard his own interests. Right now those interests are tied to Lady Q'enti." Zapana leaned against me and lowered his voice. "You said Lady Q'enti has a bag of condor dust. What does she have planned?"

"You can guess. For the sake of the Empire she must be stopped."

"But Qhari?"

"After I free Qhari I'll deal with her."

Zapana sat upright with a start. "What do you mean? Qori, you're not intending—"

"Why not? You know about her intrigues, and the families she ruined. Everyone who stands in her way dies. True, it's never been proven she murdered the victims herself, but everyone knows. She's a blight on the Empire, and now she has the condor dust."

"Would you do this for the Empire, or for your own revenge?"

"Does it matter?"

"Qori, she's the daughter of a royal house, the oldest and most respected house of Lower Cuzco. You married into Upper Cuzco, and Q'enti's kinsmen will demand revenge. Anyway, you forget that you and Lady Q'enti are forbidden to harm one another by royal decree. If you kill her it will be your death also."

Yes, I thought, Q'enti's father arranged that years ago in exchange for settling a dispute between Upper and Lower Cuzco, but it never stopped Q'enti from harming me through others. It was her plotting that cost me everything and sent me into exile, yet she appeared to beg mercy for poor Lady Qori. That's how Q'enti operates, and she's brilliant at it. Even after this affair is settled she will find ways to torment me, and she will do it through my loved ones. Zapana and Qhari will never be safe.

Zapana heard my silence and saw my face set in determination. He took my hand. "Qori, for my sake please don't kill her. I don't want to live without you."

I said nothing but thought, For your sake I will kill her, Zapana. Q'enti can threaten me, but not those I love.

Zapana squeezed my hand and forced me to look at him. "Leave this to me and I will find a way to destroy the condor dust and deal with her."

He was serious, and I knew he would try, but he didn't know Q'enti as I did. Deal with Q'enti? I thought. There's only one way to deal with her.

"I'll think about your offer," I said.

Zapana stared at me intently. "It's not an offer, it is a promise."

"I know," I said, "now let's not speak of it further."

Four days later the herder returned with an escort of a hundred Kañari soldiers. The physician they brought agreed that Zapana's wound healed well, but she wanted to cut off my leg.

"Nonsense," I said, "it only needs draining and a poultice. What manner of healer are you to go about chopping off people's limbs?"

"I *am* a healer," she flared, "and personal physician to the Lord of Hatun Kañar. How dare you question my judgment."

Zapana came between us. "Our apologies, Great Healer." He cast a look at me cautioning silence. "This poor lady is overwrought with pain, but she, too, is a healer of renown, and was once personal physician to the Empress. Perhaps, as a courtesy to me, you will allow her to confer with you?"

The woman looked at me in surprise. We hadn't been introduced and she assumed I was a servant, but she knew Zapana was an Inca lord. "Very well, my Lord, if that pleases you," she said lowering her eyes. Zapana gave me a stern look. I made a face and returned a resigned nod. "Then I shall leave you two masters to your arts," Zapana said.

Zapana departed while the healer clucked and tittered at his gallantry. It was good to see Zapana walking again.

I placed a sweet smile on my face. "Now then, sister, would you please enlighten me on the contents of your healing bag?"

She had the usual assortment of herbs, and among these I found a supply of pepper tree resin—an effective plaster for wounds, and coca leaves to draw out the pain. When I examined a tiny pot containing pungent brown resin she smiled to herself and waited to see if I would recognize it. I took a dab on my fingertip and felt a sting.

"From the Nameless Land?" I ventured.

The woman regarded me with new respect. "Yes, I obtained that from the great sorcerer Ceiba." She sat back and nodded smugly, expecting me to be impressed. I was, but not with her. "He likes to be called 'shaman,'" I told her. Her face fell.

Relief swept over me. This was the same mysterious resin Ceiba had used on me before, and the healing was immediate. I imagined Ceiba sitting before me again, that skinny young man with spirals on his face and blackened teeth, looking through me and hearing my thoughts. He had healed more than my body. For an instant I felt his presence. He would say he gave the resin to this woman

316

knowing she would bring it to me in my time of need. Ceiba sees far like Qhawachi, I thought. Silently I thanked Ceiba for watching over me. I was sure I heard him laugh.

The healer spoke to Zapana at the door, waving her hands in exasperation. "The evil in her leg won't depart. Unless the limb is severed she will die. Try to reason with her, my Lord." She left in a flutter.

Zapana sat beside me, his face drawn with concern. He knew few survived the removal of a limb. I shook my head reassuringly. "Don't listen to her. She doesn't understand the power of what she carries. I found everything I need in her healing bag."

Zapana sighed with relief. "I thought I'd lost you."

"I'm not so easily gotten rid of, Lord Zapana. You should know that."

"Indeed not, my Lady," he said lifting my hands to his lips. He looked at me seriously. "How long will it take?"

When we told Q'enti she howled, "Twenty days! I need a bath and decent food. No, this won't do. You must stay here while Lord Zapana and I go to Cuzco."

Cuzco? I wondered. This was the first hint she had given of our destination, and Qhari would be close by.

"I won't leave without Lady Qori," Zapana said.

"She is not a 'Lady,'" Q'enti sniffed. "The Emperor banished her to Wanaku, and she broke her exile. She is a criminal, and so is anyone who helps her." Q'enti turned jeering eyes on Zapana. "Did you think the three of us would stroll back to Cuzco together? If they find her with us we will be executed, too. Not even you can change that, Lord Zapana."

So much had happened I almost forgot I was a hunted woman among my own people. Death would be swift if they caught me away from Wanaku, and, as much as it galled me, Q'enti was right— anyone with me faced the same penalty. Q'enti could probably wiggle out of it, but she would make sure Zapana suffered.

Zapana worked his mouth as if swallowing something bitter. "Then you go to Cuzco, Lady Q'enti, and we will meet you there."

"That doesn't suit me," Q'enti shot back. "When I left Cuzco I explained my journey was a pilgrimage. Now I shall return in the company of none other than Lord Zapana, who will verify my story. We met at a shrine in Kañar Province, isn't that what happened, Lord Zapana?"

Zapana hung his head.

"Besides," Q'enti continued, "I expect to travel the royal road in luxury and honor, and I am sure Lord Zapana can arrange that with a nod."

"Zapana can't travel," I said. "His wound needs more time to heal."

"Then he can journey like me in a hammock. You didn't think I'd walk, did you?"

I followed Zapana's stare to his clasped hands. They trembled and his fingers whitened. He'd heard of how Q'enti manipulated people, but he never guessed she would dare threaten him. Poor Zapana, I thought, now you're seeing the real Q'enti.

Zapana lifted his head. "And if I refuse?"

"Then I will tell every sentry between here and the holy city that Qori Qoyllur has left her exile and is headed for Cuzco. That should make traveling very interesting for both of you."

I said, "What about the antidote, Q'enti? You need it and I have it. If I'm captured—"

Q'enti cut me off. "Lord Zapana will carry the antidote. If you fail to arrive he can trade the cure for Qhari, so your precious brother will live. As for me, my dear, the poison will not affect me for months. I have plenty of time to make the exchange, but Qhari doesn't. Poor Qhari will be suffering long before we enter Cuzco."

"You don't need to wait for me to reach Cuzco," I said. "If Zapana has the antidote with him, he can exchange it for Qhari as soon as the two of you arrive." Q'enti didn't know, but I had already prepared for this possibility days earlier when I gave Zapana half of the antidote as a precaution.

Q'enti smiled without warmth. "And you could just slip straight back to Wanaku, my dear? Wouldn't that be convenient? But, alas, we have a bargain, you and I. You must be present when the exchange is made—Qhari for the antidote. Don't worry; I shall wait for you. I shall wait until the last possible moment when Qhari is bloated and drowning in his own bile. You remember what Asto looked like? That poor man must have been in terrible agony."

Zapana looked at Q'enti in disbelief. "Why are you doing this?"

Q'enti smiled sweetly. "Because it pleases me." She departed leaving her high-pitched laughter ringing in our ears. Zapana watched her go, and then turned to me open-handed.

I sighed. There was no way of explaining this to him, except with the truth. "Did you ever wonder why I don't have children, Zapana? I never told you, but Q'enti stole that from me years ago, because I revealed something she did not want known. She knew I was pregnant, though not yet showing, and with one savage kick she murdered my unborn child and left me barren. That child was yours, Zapana."

Zapana's face drained. He took three wobbly steps and sat down hard.

I placed my hand on his, wishing I could make it easier for him, and drew a deep breath. "So with a flick of my knife I took what she loved most—her perfection. The scar on her face matches the scar in my heart, and she hates me as much as I hate her. But she doesn't want me dead, not yet . . . she wants to watch me suffer. She knows I'll do anything to spare Qhari, and this plan of hers amuses her. She doesn't need any other reason."

Zapana stared at me. "Our child?"

"Yes. It was long ago, soon after our first bedding. Before I could tell you, Q'enti stole it, and afterward . . . I didn't want you to know I was barren."

Zapana thought back and nodded. "And then her father agreed to end a court dispute if Q'enti was declared untouchable."

"Yes, and she was ordered not to harm me, though she finds ways to get at me through others."

Zapana sat in silence absorbing this, then said, "And now she thinks she has both of us doing her bidding." He raised his head.

"Qori, she can't force me to go to Cuzco with her. I am not leaving you here alone."

"If you don't go with her she will tell them I broke my exile, and they will search for both of us. There isn't time to evade patrols on the back trails; I must travel swiftly on the main road. I can do that in disguise, providing they aren't watching for me. Besides, it's a comfort knowing that if anything happens to me you will still be able to save Qhari."

"But, my love, I can't abandon you."

"You're not abandoning me. Remember what you said at the waterfall? We are only parting for a time. Do this for me and for Qhari, and I'll never leave you."

Before he left, Zapana ordered cloth for me to fashion disguises, and in the lonely days that followed sewing kept my hands busy even if my mind wandered. When my leg healed it would still take two months to reach Cuzco, providing I advanced unhindered, and by then the condor dust would be eating Qhari. Q'enti would try to make Zapana give her the antidote long before they reached Cuzco, using everything from seduction to threat, but Zapana knew that once she had the cure none of us were of any use to her. Still, she would goad him with constant reminders of Qhari's pain, and my perilous journey alone through the heart of the Empire.

Zapana said that whatever disguise I appeared in, I was to wear a yellow feather on my left wrist. He would station his agents along the road watching for this feather, and they would pass on messages from him. One of his men would wait for me at the first guard station outside Cuzco. Zapana would join me, and together we'd face Q'enti. At least that's what Zapana thought, and I agreed to it in order to set him on his way. But when it came time to settle with Q'enti I didn't want Zapana anywhere near. The long road to Cuzco awaited my step, and at journeys end lay Qhari suffering in some dark prison. I wanted to set out now, today. I felt like a fox with its leg in a snare, desperate to be gone but tethered. Still, as the days of forced idleness slipped by Ceiba's resin healed at a marvelous rate.

The swelling went down and healthy color returned to my leg. Soon I was able to walk short distances with the aid of a staff.

It was odd that after so many years I'd only now confessed to Zapana that we once had a child, but Q'enti murdered that innocent babe before it was born. At the time I was waiting for the right moment to tell Zapana he was to be a father, but I delayed too long, and then later we quarreled and it didn't seem to matter anymore. I was sure I'd never have a child again, and I didn't want Zapana to know I was barren. What was truly strange was that now, after years of bitter silence, I confess all this to him, and then only days after he departs I feel the stirrings of new life within me again.

After we reaffirmed our love in that bower I built in the mountains, my moon time didn't come. I thought it was only late because of the exertions of the journey, but as the days passed a knowing came upon me. It was too much to hope for—I had been so certain I was barren—and I tried to push it from my mind. But I knew. Now, with another moon come and gone, there was no doubt. I would finally be a mother, and Zapana a father, but Q'enti had no place in the world of our child.

XXI

Concerning travels on the Royal Road, where Qori sees a Fine Lady and listens to a Pichiko Bird, soldiers and spies mark the way, and the Rewards of Compassion and Humility are manifest in a most satisfactory manner.

From up the road I watched sentries swarm a group of travelers. There were more soldiers at this station than usual, and it was the women they questioned most thoroughly. I felt a tingle on the back of my neck. But the guards saw me approaching, and I didn't want to rouse suspicions by turning away.

The first part of my journey had gone well. My leg healed without scars, and I was able to cover good distances each day striding from early morning until dusk. The sentries along the royal road paid little attention to a Qolla widow returning south after losing her soldier husband on the frontiers.

The royal road traverses the length of the Empire; one arm goes through the mountains, and another stretches along the coast, with side branches connecting coast and mountains. It runs straight wherever possible, and its bridges and rest stations are always kept in repair. But only royalty, the army, and those on imperial errands are allowed to use the Emperor's highway. Commoners walk on an unpaved trail beside the royal road, which still offers the most direct route through the mountains. This was my path, but now up ahead a guard with hands on his hips watched me through narrowed eyes.

"Sister!" came an excited voice. I turned to the man who stepped from the side of the road. He raised a hand to the waiting guard and shouted, "She's my sister-in-law. We waited long for this joyous reunion. Come later and join our feast." The guard waved and turned away.

The stranger placed his arm around my shoulders and drew me aside. He whispered, "I serve the Lord of Tipón," then gestured to the yellow feather tied at my left wrist. Zapana had said his agents would recognize it. I allowed myself to be led into a stand of trees.

As soon as we were alone the man straightened himself and, fixing his gaze on the distance, recited in formal tones, "My Lord Zapana sends greetings and speaks thus: The person has broken her vow and announced your absence. All guard stations and patrols are on alert. May Illap'a watch over you." He relaxed and looked at me.

I had thought Q'enti wouldn't be able to resist spreading the word, and with troops now searching everywhere I would need the god of war watching over me. Any hope of reaching Qhari in time depended on following the royal road directly to Cuzco, and Q'enti wouldn't miss an opportunity to make this as difficult as possible.

I returned the messenger's stare. "Is that all?"

He hesitated, then cleared his throat and assumed formal posture again. "I love you," he blurted. The poor man looked so embarrassed I snickered. "That's the whole message and he made me say it," he added quickly, cheeks flushed and eyes down caste.

To spare him I said, "Those are code words." He looked relieved.

I tilted my chin toward the waiting guards. "How thorough are they?"

"Very. No one gets past without having their story checked. It's the same at the stations south of here. They keep people waiting for days."

I sighed. Q'enti not only made this journey difficult, she made it impossible. "I must pass," I said, "but I can't reveal my identity. Do you have any suggestions?"

"No, Lady. My task was to wait for the yellow feather, and pass on the message. Now I must be off to other duties."

Zapana was loyal to his agents and would never place their lives in danger over personal matters. Collusion with me was treason. The man had done enough. "Lord Zapana and I thank you," I said releasing him with a nod.

He exhaled in relief, but then he stepped closer and confided, "Lady, I cannot help you, but there are friends of yours waiting nearby. Lord Zapana said they might come. I promised I would tell them when you arrived. Shall I fetch them?"

"Friends? Who?"

He pointed. "Over there, on the other side of the trees."

I looked around in puzzlement while the man fidgeted. "You may go," I said absently. He bowed and hurried off.

Friends? I wondered. I didn't know I had any.

When I reached the far side of the copse my mouth fell open. "Mistress!" they shouted in chorus and ran to kneel before me. I stood in bewilderment while they reached to kiss my hands, trying not to react to the overpowering stench of urine. When they rose one left a fresh puddle, but no one remarked. I left three Filthy Ones at my hut in Wanaku, and four now crowded around, but the more puzzling question was how they came to be so far north. "Girls, what are you doing here?" I finally managed.

"We came to take you to Cuzco, Mistress," the Chupaychu girl said.

"To Cuzco? But how did you know—"

"A man named Lord Zapana sent a messenger to us—yes, a messenger just for us. He said you are in trouble and need to reach Cuzco with all haste, but the road is blocked."

"Lord Zapana sent you to meet me?"

"No, that was Two's idea, but we all agreed. When we arrived at this place a friend of Lord Zapana's was also waiting for you, and he seemed to recognize us. Lord Zapana must have told him. Who is Lord Zapana?"

"The man I love," I said without hesitation, drawing a sigh from the girls. "But who is 'Two'?"

"I am," the Wamali girl said. "We decided that since our people cast us out we should all have new names."

The Chachapoya girl added, "But we all wanted to be named Qori, and we couldn't decide, so we call ourselves Qori One, Qori Two, Qori Three, and Qori Four. You haven't met Qori Four." She ushered the new girl forward who fell to her knees and kissed my feet. "Mistress," she uttered, "it is an honor. I have heard so much about you, and I am yours to command."

"She's another Wamali," Two said proudly.

Flustered, I pulled the girl to her feet and said, "Stop that. I'm not your mistress."

"Yes you are," four determined voices chimed.

"I see, well, we can talk about that later. You all speak Runasimi now?" They spoke with thick accents and confused some words, but when they first came to me they all spoke different languages.

"We are trying, Mistress," Three said. "We couldn't talk very well with each other anyway. We needed one speech, and so we adopted yours."

"Very well. Now, how is it the imperial guards let you pass? Who gave you permission to travel?"

They grinned at one another. Two said, "We don't need permission. We are outcasts, without lord or nation. Since we've been removed from the counts we don't exist. But we try to report to the sentries anyway."

"Oh, yes," One giggled, "you should see us. We go to every guard station wailing and begging food. They throw stones and chase us away. They're afraid of us! We eat from the fields along the road, and no farmer will dare come near."

I had been wondering how these four thought they could help me reach Cuzco, but now the answer shone like a beacon.

Three tipped a dipper of water down the back of my dress. The girls laughed at the shock on my face, and then danced around me chanting, "Filthy One. Filthy One." Four shoved One, and a game of chase broke out as they pelted each other, and me, with sticks and leaves. I surrendered and joined the Filthy Ones.

On a clear morning we looked down on the golden roofs of Wanaku Pampa. From our distant vantage on a grassy hill overlooking the high plain on which the city stands, we watched a llama train file past the royal viewing platform in the great plaza, where work gangs assembled for their orders. Smoke from breakfast fires drifted over the city, and the bark of a dog came faintly on the breeze. Under a bright sun Wanaku Pampa yawned and stretched, content in the work of empire.

"They won't let us walk through the city," One said, "but let the guards refuse us anyway. There is a path around the outskirts. The boys will run out to pelt us, and we shall howl for them, but soon Wanaku Pampa will be behind us."

It was the same at all the stations we passed. The girls would splash water on my dress and place me in their midst, then approach wailing and wringing their hands. When stones and curses flew we would hurry on, much to the relief of our tormentors.

The girls were excited when they told me of all that happened after I left. As Zapana promised, Wanaku received a new governor who decreed the Filthy Ones were to be left in peace at Warapa, and even granted them a small field. They traded crops for yarn and guinea pigs, and built huts, creating their own community with chores assigned to each. The Chupaychu girl called One seemed to be their unofficial leader, but that didn't stop them discussing all matters until everyone was satisfied. They were all talkers, and even now as we traveled southward they kept up a constant banter of conflicting opinions on things great and small. But no one ever lost her temper; it was their way of passing the time. When I spoke they obeyed instantly, but when they asked me to settle their disagreements I refused. How could I favor one over another? Depending on the situation, I gave them general advice from my own experience, and they reached satisfactory conclusions on their own.

Three told me how they explained my absence from Warapa. "When the soldiers came looking for you we said you went into the mountains to pray. The chief of Pachacoto was with them, and he was most upset."

The image of that officious little man came to mind. He lorded his position over the other colonies, and when I didn't grant him a sympathetic ear he called me 'witch.' He probably still wore the snot-stained cloak the old governor gave him.

"And what did the great chief of Pachacoto have to say?" I asked.

"Oh, he had a great deal to say about many things," Two said, "especially concerning you. He said he warned the officials about you, and they should have listened. He swore on the souls of his ancestors that if you were still in the province he would find you, and deliver you to the governor."

"So, the chief of Pachacoto is looking for me," I mused.

Two's face lit up. "Yes, and now more diligently than ever. The Inca commander grew so weary of listening to the man's bluster, he said that if the chief didn't find you, he would be replaced."

"Then we have to make sure he doesn't find me."

Two hunched her shoulders and grinned. "That would please the people of Warapa."

After Q'enti reported that I broke my exile, they sought me everywhere. But, if I suddenly reappeared within the boundaries of Wanaku, I could explain my absence as a pilgrimage to the nearby mountain gods like the girls claimed. It would appear the chief's search for me wasn't thorough.

As One predicted, a gang of boys spied us skirting Wanaku Pampa and gave chase. We kept our shawls over our heads so we wouldn't be recognized, though onlookers probably thought we did so out of shame. I had changed to a ragged, stained dress like the others, and imitated their pitiful wailing. The wailing had become a contest with each trying to dramatically outdo her sisters, and much discussion afterward on who had been the best. The boys conveniently hurried us past the city, while their parents watched from a distance and made signs to ward off evil.

Beyond Wanaku Pampa we continued on the commoner's path beside the royal road, stepping aside only when meeting other travelers. Traffic on the royal road was always busy with trains of tribute-laden llamas, army contingents, administrators, and noble entourages. We stopped and held deep bows when nobles passed, but even nobles had to move aside when the Emperor's messengers dashed by.

A royal banner came in sight leading a small caravan. Imperial guards marched four abreast followed by a lady reclining in a hammock. Then came formations of relief bearers in bright livery, followed by the lady's steward and servants, and her baggage train. I recognized the woman from Cuzco—a minor daughter of a minor house, but nonetheless a royal princess. She was one of those whose life revolved around entertaining and being entertained, and she probably headed north to join her husband in some new posting. If so, she didn't look happy about it. While her bearers sweated and her servants stumbled behind, she sat with chin in hand staring through us.

Head bowed, I watched her passing. Those who carry you, princess, are beneath your notice, I thought. I can't begrudge you your life of ease for you were born to it and know no other, but I can pity you. You have everything, so you can't blame life's woes on lack of wealth. Your title owns you, forcing you to meet the expectations of others—those who judge every garment you wear, every word and gesture—yet without title where is your place in life? I know your kind, and I know your fears. Your only defense is pride, a vulnerable pride easily pricked, but it's all you have.

I imagined Qhawachi, Seer of the Lines, sitting before me with his huge belly on display, eyes oddly slanted in that round face, and his hair tied like a tusk on his forehead. He is content to be himself, I thought. He told me to be like Qhari and care not what others think. Did I lose my wealth and titles, he asked, or was their burden lifted from me? Ceiba taught me that when one faces the world with humility people come to your aid, but when you face it with pride you make yourself a target. This proud lady in her hammock thinks humility is weakness, but with it the world is your ally.

That morning I wakened just as dawn touched the sky and found my girls already seated at the fire, a mush of boiled maize their only food. They sat in silence with far away smiles listening to a gray and black pichiko bird perched on a nearby rock. The bird fluffed its red collar and whistled, 'pichi, pichi,' to the new day. I thought of it now as the noblewoman's entourage receded up the road. Would she take pleasure in the song of a bird at dawn? Even if she rose that early she wouldn't notice, already preoccupied with plans for her banquet that evening.

In the days that followed the road to Cuzco passed quickly. I didn't tell the girls about the child I carried. It was still too new and precious for sharing. I knew it was a boy.

The sentries eyed the line of supplicants in which I stood, waiting to question those entering Cuzco. Their guard station was beside the shrine where those coming from the north catch their first glimpse of the holy city. The man in front of me hurried forward and laid maize cobs on the altar stone, while a priest nodded and asked if he wished to cleanse his heart before entering sacred Cuzco. The line moved quickly. Soon it would be my turn at the altar, and afterwards I would face the guard's questions. If Zapana's man is close by he better hurry, I thought.

When the shrine came in sight One had said, "We can take you no farther, Mistress. They will never let a Filthy One enter holy Cuzco. It is time for you to become as other women. We'll wait here for you."

"Take the girls back to Wanaku, One. I don't know how long I'll be, and there's nothing more you can do."

"But how will you get home, Mistress? No, we shall wait. Whether you are gone days or weeks we'll watch for you. The girls have already decided, and you don't want to argue with them."

I glanced at the others and saw their chins set. "Very well, One, but I don't deserve this devotion."

One said playfully, "No, Mistress, you don't, but we'll think of a way for you to make it up to us."

I changed to simple but less ragged clothes, and shared teary hugs with the girls, wondering if I would ever see them again.

"Next, move along," the priest said, waving me forward with cupped hand while the man ahead of me went to give confession. I laid my bouquet of wild flowers on the flat stone and bowed to Cuzco. Far below in the Huatanay Valley the city basked under a blue sky, its massive thatch roofs framing the great plaza. I used to call You 'my city,' I thought. I longed for You, and believed I could never be happy elsewhere. You're as beautiful as I remember, but now I'm content to drink of You and move on without regret.

The priest leaned close. "Confession, my daughter?"

I looked around. If I didn't accept confession my next stop was the guard station, where all those entering the city are questioned and counted. Then a young man wearing a frown came striding toward me. "There you are you shirking slug! I have been waiting half the day for you." He grabbed my shawl and pulled me to my feet. The priest protested, but the young man silenced him by laying a fine cloak upon the altar. "For holy Cuzco," he said with a bow, and then roughly pushed me away. "You lazy llama," he cursed me. "You people have no sense of duty. You were supposed to meet me here at dawn. What will they say when we're late? Hoist that sack and let's be on our way." The priest shook his head and waved the next traveler to the altar.

The guards listened with respect when the young man explained he was delivering tribute from his family's estate—a huge sack of alpaca wool on the back of a small serving woman bent double under the load. The captain nodded and ushered us forth while his counter added more knots to the day's tally.

I struggled along behind the young man until, having passed beyond sight of the guard station, he turned and said, "I am sorry, Lady, but the Lord of Tipón ordered me to be convincing. Here, let me help you with that sack."

I placed my hands in the small of my back and stretched. "What are Lord Zapana's instructions?"

"There is a compound on the outskirts of the city where you will be safe. Lord Zapana is at Tipón, but as soon as he hears from me he will come to you."

Zapana will come after he's seen Q'enti and arranged the exchange, I thought. At last we will learn where Atoco has been keeping Qhari.

"Very well," I said, "but I shall wait for word from Lord Zapana at the House of Chosen Women."

"Lady?" came the startled reply. The House of Chosen Women was in the heart of the city, and its interior forbidden ground to men.

"You heard me. Tell Lord Zapana to contact me through the Most Esteemed Mother, Sumaq T'ika."

"But, Lady, my orders were . . . ." His voice trailed off when my hands went to my hips.

The young man departed shaking his head. I loaded the wool on my back and continued into the city, peering from beneath the shawl drawn over my head. The mud-brick compounds of the outer districts gave way to fitted stone walls and paved streets, where soldiers and servants rushed by under the eaves of thatched roofs. No one paid attention to a servant bent under her load. Keeping my head down, I crossed a stone bridge over the Huatanay River and entered the great plaza.

The great plaza of Cuzco always made me pause in wonder, even when I lived in the city. The royal viewing platform near the center, and a round tower in one corner, were all that interrupted this vast expanse. It was the favored place for pilgrims and nobles from the provinces—the center of the world. Visitors were banned from the plaza during Inca rites, but on this day hundreds strolled its pebble pavement in tribal costumes and outlandish hairstyles, gawking at the massive temples and palaces fronting the square. I hurried through their midst toward the towering walls of the House of Chosen Women.

"But there are no deliveries scheduled for today," the ancient gatekeeper said with a frown. He stood in the plaza guarding the sole entrance to a world he had never seen. Even so, only old men were allowed this close to the girls sequestered within.

"True, grandfather, but this wool is a special gift for the Most Esteemed Mother. She will be angry if it's delayed."

The old man huffed and drew down the corners of his mouth, then grudgingly tapped his staff on the door. "If this is a mistake I'll see you punished," he admonished me. The door opened a crack, and while the gatekeeper averted his eyes an Esteemed Mother peered out questioningly.

"Alpaca for the Most Esteemed Mother," I said. "My mistress wishes me to deliver it personally."

"You may set it in here," the woman replied, sliding the door open just enough to let me pass. I raised my brows at the old guard, who sniffed and turned his back.

The greeting courtyard was vacant except for sacks of alpaca wool along one wall, and bales of new clothing along another. The Esteemed Mother closed the door and gestured for me to place my burden with the wool destined for spinning. "Mother, I must speak with Lady Sumaq T'ika," I said to her.

She gave me a look of disdain. "That isn't necessary. I will inform her of this gift. What is your mistress's name?"

"Mother, please tell Lady Sumaq that it is from a woman who slept beside her when they were both girls in this House, and that the bearer has a message for her ears only."

The woman looked into my eyes. The House of Chosen Women, though shut off from the outside world, was not unaccustomed to intrigue, and neither was this priestess. She nodded. "Very well, I shall inform Lady Sumaq. Wait here." She hurried through a door in the high wall to the complex beyond.

Memories came flooding back to me. How many years did I spend within these walls? Was it only four? It seemed like a lifetime, and it was a lifetime ago. I hated it, and loved it, and the Esteemed Mothers taught me everything a proper Inca woman should know, whether or not I wanted to learn.

The priestess returned to the courtyard and beckoned me with a smile. "The Most Esteemed Mother will see you in private immediately, sister. Please come with me."

I followed her through the maze of storehouses and dormitories, past the brewery, past the spinning and weaving stations, and through the teaching patio where a language class was in progress, my passage studied by big, curious eyes, and young heads bent together in whispers. From my own time here, I knew the girls would make up a fantastic story to account for this strange old serving woman being escorted to the Most Esteemed Mother. What they didn't know was that this time no imaginings of theirs could match the truth.

When we arrived at the shrine of Mother Moon the priestess gestured to the entrance, bowed to me, and departed. Inside, Mother Moon stood in Her niche, a figurine half gold and half silver dressed in tiny garments of finest weave. The brazier before the idol cast soft light on Sumaq T'ika, who stared at me with hands at her mouth. A sob escaped her and she ran to my arms.

We clung together stroking each other's hair, uttering sounds of delight and comfort, and then we laughed and dried each other's tears. Sumaq led me to a bench against the wall where we sat pressed together and clasped each other's hands. What touched me most was finding that she still welcomed me. I wouldn't have blamed her had she been cold. Like all those around me I'd treated this old friend badly.

"I'm so sorry I couldn't help more when Captain Atoco made that ridiculous accusation," she said earnestly.

It was Sumaq who arranged for me to meet the warlord Chalcochima in the temple of Illap'a before my sentence was passed. I had thought Chalcochima would save me, but . . . . "It wasn't your fault," I said. "Q'enti learned of the plan and poisoned Chalcochima. Did he recover?"

"A week later, yes. He was supposed to lead the Emperor's entourage, but when he couldn't travel they replaced him. The poor man came to me afterwards. He was most distraught."

"Because he lost his position, or because of what happened to me?"

Sumaq looked down. "Well, both, but mostly because I suggested Illap'a would frown on him if he didn't help you."

I never knew Sumaq had forced him to meet me. In those days the efforts of my friends meant nothing if they didn't produce the results I wanted. I remembered thinking that Sumaq owed me that favor. How did I come to use those around me and take them for granted?

"Did Illap'a forgive him?" I wondered.

"Oh yes, and he was so relieved. Lord Chalcochima is now supreme commander of the imperial troops in Cuzco." Sumaq looked at me and squeezed my hands. "Qori, what happened to you was so wrong. You were the best agent in the Empire."

"I was an agent, and I did my best," I said quietly.

Sumaq's brows went up. "That doesn't sound like Inca Moon." "Perhaps not," I responded, "but it's Qori Qoyllur speaking now."

Sumaq patted my hands and beamed.

"I'm supposed to be in exile," I said. "You haven't asked me what I'm doing here."

"I've been waiting for you to tell me," she said leaning back and arranging her dress.

The story poured out of me, beginning with Zapana's arrival at Wanaku Pampa with news of Qhari's journey to the coast. Sumaq nodded solemnly. "I heard your brother Qhari vanished from his post without permission. If they catch him now he will be punished."

"I know, but that's the least of his worries. Sumaq, Qhari's life is ebbing away at this very moment." She listened in silence while I recounted the tale, and she made a face each time I mentioned Q'enti. When I finished she said, "Qhari has to be saved, and the condor dust must be taken away from Lady Q'enti. But remember, Qori, Lady Q'enti is untouchable. As much as we all want to be rid of her, she must not be harmed." I looked away "Sumaq, I'm a fugitive, and anyone who aids me could be executed. I have no right to ask this, but . . . will you help me?" Sumaq turned startled eyes on me. "*You* are *asking* for help? This is indeed a new Qori." She shook her head in wonderment. When her gaze settled on the statue of Mother Moon she smiled and whispered a prayer of gratitude. "Of course I will help you," she said turning back to me. "The cause is just, and you are my dearest friend." I explained my plan, and though she protested that Zapana would be angry she finally agreed. Then she took my hands again and stared into my eyes. "Qori, I see something in you I've only seen once before. Are you with child?"

Sumaq had guessed my first pregnancy, and she was still one of the few who knew about it. I couldn't keep the grin from my face. "Zapana," I confided.

"Oh, Qori, I prayed for this!"

"But it must be our secret a little longer," I said. "Zapana doesn't know yet, and if he did he would never let me do what must be done."

Sumaq frowned. "I still don't like this, Qori. You need his help, too."

"Sumaq, I love Zapana. I don't want him harmed. He's done so much for me, but I must face Q'enti alone."

The next afternoon, when Sumaq returned from her deity-husband's temple, she found me pacing in her quarters. I stopped in mid stride and looked up. "It's settled," she said, not looking pleased about it. "But I didn't like deceiving Lord Zapana."

"What did Zapana say?"

"He came to the temple in person—at least I think it was him, he was disguised as an old man—and he asked about you at great length before he said anything else. He wants to see you, and he wants to know why you are staying at the House of Chosen Women."

"What did you tell him?"

"I told him you are well, and you appeared at my door so I gave you sanctuary. But he looked troubled, and I think he suspects you're going to attempt something on your own. Qori, the poor man is frantic for your safety."

"As I am for his. Is the meeting with Q'enti arranged?"

"Yes. When Lord Zapana heard you reached Cuzco he went to see Lady Q'enti. She agreed to exchange Qhari for the antidote tomorrow at mid afternoon."

"Then Qhari is in Cuzco. Where is the meeting taking place?"

"At the House of Beasts."

"The House of Beasts?"

"That's what Lord Zapana said. Lady Q'enti was appointed steward of that dreadful place not long after you were exiled. Nobody else wanted the position. She built a new compound outside the city, and she had Captain Atoco restock the menagerie."

I remembered Zapana mentioning this. We laughed because some of her creatures had escaped. Still, there had been ample time for Atoco to find replacements.

Sumaq said, "You are expected to arrive at the House of Beasts alone, but Lord Zapana plans to make a surprise appearance." She drew her face in disgust. "I hope they haven't been keeping Qhari in that place all this time."

"If they have it's a wonder he's alive," I said. "But then, we only have Q'enti's word on that. Did you see Atoco?"

"Yes, after Lord Zapana left I summoned Captain Atoco to the temple as you requested. He chose to interpret this invitation to mean that my divine husband was going to bestow an honor on him. I don't know how he got that impression," she said with a conspiratorial lifting of her brows. Then Sumaq twisted her mouth. "He's such a slimy little man." Seeing my impatience she hurried on. "Captain Atoco said he and Lady Q'enti would be delighted to change the meeting time to ensure privacy with you. They will greet you at the House of Beasts soon after dawn tomorrow."

At last the place and time are set, I thought. Zapana thinks the meeting is not until the afternoon, so he will be late—much too late to be implicated in whatever happens. I should have guessed Q'enti would use the House of Beasts as her dungeon. Poor Qhari.

Sumaq studied me. I knew she wanted to ask if I could handle this alone, and tell me how worried she was, but being a true friend she didn't voice these obvious fears. Instead she said quietly, "Qori, you mustn't harm Lady Q'enti, or it will be the end of you, too."

XXII

In which are trod the Halls of Horror.

Gray dawn struggled over the walls of the House of Chosen Women. The Esteemed Mothers rubbed their hands and drew their shawls closer, some coughing gently, their breath steaming in the sharp mountain air. Sumaq handed me the bag from the kitchen, and I arranged its long strap so the bag hung at my back beneath my shawl, out of the way and out of sight. The feathered pouch containing the antidote hung at my breast. I gave Sumaq a reassuring look while patting the outline of the dagger tucked inside my wide belt. Sumaq didn't smile. She hugged me quickly, then placed me in the middle of the line and stepped back, her hand at her mouth. She had wanted to come but I refused saying her presence would attract attention. In truth, I didn't want her connected with today's events. If the worst came to pass she could say she had given sanctuary to a former chosen woman, but had no knowledge of where the woman had gone. The Esteemed Mothers nodded to me, then drew their shawls over their heads when the door slid open. Outside in the great square the old gatekeeper held a deep bow as we passed.

The city still lingered indoors around breakfast hearths, but a night patrol paused in its rounds to bow. A dog cocked its head watching this silent line of covered women, then came forward with tail wagging to lick our fingers. It didn't know it was being disrespectful, and its innocence was rewarded with covert pats. But we kept our backs straight and eyes forward as expected of priestesses when they walk among the people. When we reached the checkpoint where all those entering or departing the city are questioned and counted, the guards bent at the waist while their captain made obeisance. He wouldn't dare question us, but as a courtesy our leader informed him, "We go to make offerings to the daughters of Mama Qocha, and shall return this evening." The captain muttered, "Of course, Mother. May the great ocean Mama Qocha, source of all water, allow the springs of the mountains to refresh our fields forever." Without looking up he waved us on.

The sun, now poking over the mountains, watched the farmers of the Huatanay Valley yawn and amble to their fields. Green slopes with bare outcrops frame the valley bottom, where the Huatanay River is directed through its masonry channel past copse and village. The air, still crisp, carried the smells of animals and greenery, fresh earth and wood smoke. Our party halted on a rise and the senior Mother took me aside. "Over there," she said pointing to a stand of trees crowding the valley side. Peering closely I discerned the walls of a mud brick compound sequestered among the trees.

"Thank you, Mother," I said. "If they should ask later, do you remember what I told you?"

The priestess nodded and rehearsed, "I didn't know she was the same woman who took sanctuary with us. That morning she dressed like the other priestesses, and when we left the House of Chosen Women she must have slipped into line without anyone noticing. Then, when we came in sight of the House of Beasts, she left us without a word. That's all I know."

The women around us bobbed their heads. They didn't know who I was or what I intended at the House of Beasts, but they trusted Sumaq, and Sumaq had placed the House of Chosen Women at my service. I thanked each with a smile and left them in peace.

A foreboding silence cloaked the woods as I approached the House of Beasts. No birds flittered or called, no tiny creatures rustled the leaves, and no stray dogs watched my passage. The plastered walls loomed before me. There were no guards. All lay still and quiet. Part of me wanted to run from this place, yet I knew that somewhere within Qhari lay in agony—if he was still alive. The gate was left open a crack. I gritted my teeth and slipped inside.

The entrance court was a small space enclosed by high partitions. On either side of me stairs led up to walkways tracing the inside walls like battlements. The wall in front of me had a single door at ground level, now sealed by a log gate. The entrance to the underworld, I thought.

"It's been long since we met," a churlish male voice said.

Startled, I looked up to see Atoco standing at the top of the stairs on my right, his guards clustered behind. Atoco looked down with the thin-lipped grimace that passed for his smile, his hands on his hips. "Lady Q'enti is pleased you honored the bargain and came alone," he said. "Do you have the antidote?"

"Do you have my brother?"

"Of course."

"Alive?"

"More or less. He groaned when I kicked him this morning." Atoco allowed his men to share a harsh laugh, then his face became stern and he barked at them, "Seal the door." Two men instantly clattered down the steps and secured the gate behind me. Atoco beckoned, "Come up here, and Lady Q'enti will show you where your brother abides."

When I reached the top Atoco led me along the walkway, his men following close at my heels. From the outside the structure looked like any rectangular compound with high, blank walls, but the inside was like nothing I'd ever seen. From the walkway above I looked down on a maze of rooms, courtyards, and passageways, many with walls cloaked in vines, but all of them open to the sky. I glimpsed movement in shaded corners. The stench of dung and death wafted upward, causing me to blanch and turn my head. Atoco chuckled.

Q'enti waited half way along the wall. She turned with the practiced sincerity of a hostess greeting an unimportant guest. "Qori dear, I'm so glad you could come."

"You did everything in your power to stop me, Q'enti."

"What? Oh, you mean the soldiers looking for you along the road? I didn't want to tell them you left your exile, it just slipped out. But it doesn't matter, you're here now."

She said it so smoothly I half expected her to offer beer like a good hostess. And, as usual, she dressed splendidly in soft alpaca of the finest weave, rich in color and draped to accent her generous curves. She wore her hair in braids wound around her head, which made her slender neck seem longer and her eyes even larger.

"Where's Qhari?" I demanded.

Q'enti sniffed as if I was being rude. "Close by. Where is the antidote?"

"Here," I said opening my shawl to reveal the feathered pouch. Q'enti's eyes fastened on the bag with triumph. I'd given half the antidote to Zapana, left more with Sumaq, and tucked a packet in my belt for Qhari, but there was still plenty in the bag to cure Q'enti. It was a waste because she wasn't going to survive the morning anyway, but I had to go through the motions to secure Qhari's release.

Q'enti reached eager hands. "Give it to me."

I slipped the bag from my neck but held it away from her. "And Qhari?"

"Captain Atoco will show you," she said. She gestured to Atoco who said, "I have your brother, but first I'm curious to know how you evaded every patrol and guard station between here and Hatun Kañar."

I didn't want to endanger all those who helped me so I said, "Humility and compassion made it possible, Atoco." Atoco stared back in puzzlement.

My answer was lost on Q'enti, also. "Yes, well, whatever," she said. "Now give me the bag." I let her grab it from my hand. She ripped open the drawstring and turned her back, quickly shoved some of the precious powder into her mouth, and sipped from a flask. When she faced us again her look was feral.

"There, Q'enti, you've won," I said. "You made me serve you, and you made me deliver the antidote, on your terms. Now I'll collect my brother and leave in peace."

I had already decided that if Qhari were dead I would slit her throat before she could gasp. Atoco would be next, and as for his men it would suit me to spill their blood until I was stopped. But that rage had to wait until I was certain about Qhari.

Q'enti smiled. "You probably think I planned to trick you, Qori dear, but I assure you I can't wait to see you reunited with that man-woman brother of yours." Q'enti nodded to Atoco. "Show her where her brother is . . . and let her go to him."

Atoco smirked. "Look over there," he said pointing to the far end of compound. I stepped to the edge of the walkway and peered over the maze below. Atoco indicated a shed against the back wall.

"Qhari is there?" I said.

"Yes, and waiting for you. All you need do is go to him."

I looked closely. There were no stairs leading down, nor any doors through the outer wall. Unless a rope was lowered from above, the shed could only be approached at ground level from the far end of the maze. Q'enti watched in delight as this dawned on me.

"The House of Beasts has only one entrance," she chirped. "But you may go down and walk through the maze. Captain Atoco and I will wait up here and guide you."

Atoco added, "But be careful, it's long since the beasts were fed."

"Is it?" Q'enti said innocently. "Then we must feed the poor creatures. Captain Atoco, show Qori how you look after the animals."

Atoco snickered and waved to one of his henchmen, who came forward with a sack dripping blood. The man extracted a handful of entrails. I didn't want to see this spectacle, which was obviously arranged for my benefit, but, I thought, at least I'll know what to expect.

The rooms and corridors below had appeared empty, but when the man flung the entrails into the center of a courtyard the maze came alive. A puma appeared instantly and fought over the scraps with a snarling jaguar. They were huge beasts, snapping and growling at one another. Q'enti watched in fascination, her left eye twitching.

Atoco directed the man to cast a handful into a patio near the entrance. A bear dashed from a corner and devoured the morsel. Starvation had only quickened its attack.

A guard hefted a basket. He dumped live mice into another enclosure. To my horror the ground came alive with slithering vipers of all lengths and colors, including some like the one that bit Q'enti in the Nameless Land. They hissed at one another and closed on their hapless prey. Q'enti shuddered and looked away.

The men now brought out a live monkey in a tiny cage. The poor creature was muzzled and frantic. Atoco was telling the men not to drop it near the cats when Q'enti interceded. "Leave it," she said.

"But, my Lady," Atoco protested, "it's for Squeezer. She hasn't been fed for a month."

Q'enti stamped her foot. "I said leave it! I don't want to see that thing." She spoke with eyes sealed as if trying to banish an image. Atoco shrugged and the men returned the monkey to its cage.

Q'enti regained her composure. "Now then, my dear, you see that we do feed the beasts, though I'm afraid these tidbits only sharpened their appetites. You may go down and enter the maze—Qhari awaits you at the far end—while Captain Atoco and I watch from up here."

It was the old emperor Pachakuti, founder of the Empire, who ordered the first menagerie. Fearsome animals brought to Cuzco from the eastern forests were kept in caverns where war captives and those convicted of treason were thrown. If a man survived three days he was granted freedom. Later it became a penalty for various crimes, and the place of captivity moved as the menagerie grew. But only Q'enti, the self-proclaimed Mistress of the House of Beasts, ever conceived of a compound with a maze and viewing walkways above. Who else would want to witness such horror? And she had stocked it with the deadliest creatures ever encountered.

Left alone, I would have used a rope to lower myself onto the roof of Qhari's shed, but I wasn't alone, and Atoco's men would make sure I ran the maze for Q'enti's amusement. Even if I reached Qhari I knew Q'enti would never let us leave.

But while Q'enti proudly showed me this evil place from above, I studied the layout with its blind turns and dead ends, and saw the route to Qhari's prison.

Atoco's men escorted me back down to the entrance court. Four of them stood with spears leveled, while the other two untied the log gate to the maze. Atoco and Q'enti watched from above, and at Atoco's signal the men pried the gate open a crack and began stuffing me through. They were in a hurry. As I wedged between gate and jamb, half in and half out of the maze, I yanked a spear from an unsuspecting hand and squeezed through beyond their reach.

Q'enti stamped her foot. "She can't do that. No weapons allowed."

The men had already sealed the gate and I knew they wouldn't be coming after me. I stood in a small courtyard covered in old straw and feces, and glanced up to see Atoco trying to calm Q'enti. Then I heard a deep growl from behind.

The bear charged in fury. They are usually lumbering hulks, and the swiftness of the attack and horrid bellowing rooted me. I saw black fur and a white face with jaws wide trailing spittle from yellow fangs. It was only two paces away when I raised my spear—a defense of instinct more than plan—and then it sprang from its hind legs with front paws spread wide. I fell on my back watching the sheer bulk of it crash down, pinning me under a black weight. But instead of ripping off my head the beast turned its eyes to the sky in a wail of agony. The butt of my spear sank in the ground at my side, and the shaft disappeared deep in the creature's chest. It whined like a child, then slumped to the side snapping the shaft, and slowly dragged itself away.

I lay stretched on my back with heart pounding, stunned by the suddenness of events and their outcome. It all happened in a gasp, and the upward pointing spear on which the bear fell was more good fortune than design. The bear staggered to a corner with the broken spear still lodged in its chest, its legs failing, whimpering like a human. I now saw that its eyes were encrusted, its claws twisted, and every bone in its emaciated body visible beneath loose folds. Diseased and starved, the poor creature raised it head for one last defiant bellow before collapsing in death.

"My bear," Q'enti cried. "She killed my bear. Captain Atoco, stop her!"

I glanced up. Atoco stood in front of Q'enti with his back to me, arms flapping wildly. I couldn't hear his words, but his gestures said he wouldn't enter the maze, where so many other deadly creatures still lurked.

The bear's courtyard had three doors in one wall, but having observed them from above I knew they led nowhere. There was also a tunnel through the wall at ground level that one could scurry through on hands and knees, but it led to a snake pit. A small window set high in the wall offered the only route to the corridor behind. Its sill was above my head, so I would have to pull myself up and squeeze through.

Staring up at the window, I felt the familiar sensation on the back of my neck. This window had separated the bear from the great cats waiting ahead, but the serpents in the compound could slither anywhere. From above I'd seen entrances to dens where animals waited out the chill mountain nights. No doubt the reptiles also had their warm hideaways, but with the sun they were free to dangle from leafy bowers and curl on ledges. That's what made me hesitate; if I pulled myself up to the window, what would be waiting there?

I knew if I pondered too long I would never move. There were too many such possibilities and unknowns ahead. Move cautiously, I thought, but move.

The bag Sumaq had given me that morning still hung at my back. I undid my shawl and removed it. The bag rested on the ground when I held the shoulder strap at waist level. I gripped the strap firmly, then jumped up and swung the bag at the window overhead. It passed through, but did not dangle on the other side. An interior ledge? I wondered. I pulled the bag back, then tossed it again. The result was the same, but when I jerked it back there came a tug. I yanked hard, and the bag came down on my head with a fat snake attached! I leapt away. The serpent lifted its head, flickered a black tongue at me, and then retreated in the opposite direction leaving its fangs caught in the fabric of the bag. I released an enormous sigh. Q'enti's high-pitched laughter drifted over the maze.

Reaching up, I grasped the sill and pulled myself into the window, finding it just large enough to crouch on my knees. As I suspected there was a ledge below the sill on the inside, now happily vacant. The walls of the room before me were covered with trellised vines. I cared not to think of what curled among them, but snakes attack only when disturbed, so I dropped to open ground and stayed away from the foliage. Two doors confronted me. When I stood on the walkway with Q'enti there wasn't time to memorize the entire route through the maze, but my impression had been to stay to the left. The left exit was partially covered in greenery, and looking closely I saw a snake wrapped around a vine at eye level, which an unwary hand would try to brush aside. I scurried beneath the serpent on hands and knees.

I found myself in a narrow corridor with rooms opening on either side. Farther ahead the passage ended in a blank wall, so I reasoned the last room on the left would allow access to the rear of the compound. Stout gates fashioned from crossed poles leaned beside the entrances to some rooms, ready to be slid into place. This is how they pen the animals, I decided, but such sturdy barriers must mean the great cats are close. As if hearing my thoughts the growl of a feline came from somewhere ahead. I glimpsed movement on the walkway, where Q'enti hurried for a better view.

Clutching Sumaq's bag in front of me I advanced down the corridor with slow, unsteady steps. A few paces ahead a door opened on the right. A gate leaned against the wall beside it. I envisioned a cat poised to leap from inside. Suddenly a jaguar bounded from a room at the end of the passage and came straight at me with teeth and claws bared. I ripped open the bag and seized a handful of meat, throwing it in front of the beast. The cat paused to snap up the morsel, which vanished in a gulp, then laid its ears flat and showed its fangs in a throaty snarl. It looked as sick and starved as the bear, but its eyes burned and it tensed to spring as my hand went to the bag again. This time I threw the meat at the entrance to the room on my right. The cat leapt on it, only three paces away. In terror I threw the bag into the room, and when the jaguar followed I raced to the gate, shoving it into place. My hands shook as I struggled with the bindings. From inside the cat leapt at the gate, its huge paws plunging through the lattice of poles to swipe at me. I cried out and jumped back, but then with trembling fingers I managed to secure the last knot.

I leaned against the wall fighting for breath. From above I heard Q'enti bark at Atoco, "Where did she get the meat? That's not fair."

With the jaguar penned I walked on unsteady feet to the end of the corridor, and peered into the last room on the left. It was a small space enclosed by high, vine-covered walls like the others, but the floor was piled with fresh straw. A curled viper basked on the straw in a patch of sunlight. Detecting movement at the door it lifted its head and flicked its tongue, then slithered under the straw. I wondered how many other serpents moved unseen in this nest? I spied two more among the vines, but they were not a worry as long as I could see them and keep my distance.

There were no other doors in this room, only a tunnel through the back wall at ground level. Qhari's prison should be on the other side, I reasoned, but if I wiggle through on my knees I'll be vulnerable to whatever else lies in wait. More snakes? Probably, but there's also a puma somewhere in this maze.

I cursed myself for having thrown the entire bag of meat to the jaguar. It was done in a moment of frenzy, and now the only defence I had left was my dagger. I slipped the blade from my belt. It was sharp enough to shave a man, but of little use against serpents and great cats. I stared at the straw I had to cross to reach the tunnel, and imagined needle-fanged terrors beneath each step.

There must be an easier way through, I thought. Perhaps there are passages to the rear courtyard from other rooms? If I work back through the maze . . . ? No, Q'enti wouldn't make it easy for anyone. You're stalling, Inca Moon, and if you hesitate any longer you'll lose your nerve. Trust yourself. You know what to do.

I fastened my eyes on the tunnel entrance, banished all thoughts, and dashed forward. My feet sunk in the soft straw, but I covered the distance to the tunnel in three quick bounds and stuffed myself into the opening, squirmed through and shot from the other side. I leapt to my feet, frantically brushing my hands over my body to rid myself of snakes. There were none, nor did anything slither after me. I'd been lucky, but my hands shook and I gasped for breath.

Q'enti's jeering laughter came from close by. I looked up and saw her with Atoco and his men standing above. They had followed every step of my progress, hurrying from station to station to get a better view. Now I stood in the last courtyard at the rear of the compound with Qhari's shed in sight. But even though I survived the maze Q'enti didn't look worried. She nibbled her bottom lip in excitement.

I scanned the courtyard, a much larger enclosure than the others I passed through. The mud-brick shed that held Qhari jutted from the back wall in one corner, its thatch roof sloping against the wall, well below the walkway. The shed was windowless, and the stout door lashed tight. Two stunted trees grew beside the shed, their writhing branches offering a patch of shade over ground sprinkled with straw and dung. Greenery burst in profusion from the corner opposite the shed, almost hiding a ledge, but the remainder of the courtyard was bare. At least there are no snakes, I thought.

Arching my head back, I stared up the blank walls to where Q'enti stood far above. She leaned forward eagerly, rubbing her hands in anticipation. What does she know? I wondered. Then I followed her gaze to the green-shrouded corner, and froze.

The puma must have been watching me from its ledge behind the vines since I entered the courtyard. It now appeared in full view swishing its tail, an enormous, tawny beast with ears alert, and staring at me. It leapt from its perch and landed lightly, then bared white fangs in a growl.

I remained motionless, though my mind raced. Lock myself in the shed with Qhari, or climb on the roof? The beast will be on me before I take three steps. Charge and frighten it away? No, that might startle the creature but it won't be frightened. Perhaps if I wait for it to leap and slash its throat . . . ? I looked at the pitifully small knife in my hand and, in spite of the situation, smiled at this ridiculous notion.

The puma's eyes never left me, its tail twitching. Then its ears went flat and it lowered its head with a snarl. It paced farther to the left, stopped to sniff in my direction, and edged closer. I sensed that any move on my part would loose a charge. This animal must have been a recent catch for it wasn't starved or diseased. Hungry, perhaps, but it looked more annoyed at my presence, and it continued stalking me without haste.

A commotion erupted above. Turning my head slightly I glanced up from the corners of my eyes. From outside the compound a figure clambered over the wall and dashed along the walkway. He carried a spear, and had a maqana strapped to his back. "Stop him," Q'enti shouted. The man met the rush of guards head on, slamming the butt of his spear into one man's face and then swinging the point upward to slash another. Before those behind could reach him he dove off the walkway, landed on his back on the roof of the shed, and slide down to the courtyard where he arrived in a crouch, spear held crossways. The show-off, I thought. I returned my gaze to the puma.

The cat was also distracted by this new arrival, and backed off. But it turned with a roar and pawed the air in front of it, then began pacing and snarling over its shoulder.

"It's about time you got here," I said without turning.

"I thought you could use some help," Zapana said. He came to my side but kept his eyes on the puma. The wound he received in the north had healed well.

"I was doing fine," I said breezily. "How did you know I was here?"

"I had the House of Chosen Women watched, of course," he said. "Besides, you're always early for your appointments." He gave me a quick glance. "Have you seen Qhari?"

"Q'enti says he's in that shed behind us. Aren't you a little old to be jumping off roofs?"

Zapana shrugged. "A moment of exuberance. How do we get out of here?"

"You're so adept at getting in, I thought you might have a plan."

Zapana pursed his lips. "Not yet, but I will."

The puma became more agitated. It slunk low to the ground with tail down and ears flattened, eyes fixed on us, its fangs bared in a feline hiss. Those on the walls above waited in silence, and without looking up I knew Q'enti had her hand at her mouth, willing the great cat to charge. Zapana adjusted the maqana strapped to his back so it hung out of the way, and lowered his spear. He knew he had one chance to end this quickly. If he missed we'd have a furious puma on us, and one swipe of its claws could rip off a face.

Zapana's eyes never left the cat. He edged close beside me and went into a fighting crouch, muscles tensed, the blade of his spear pointed at the animal. I took the same stance, but with only a dagger to defend myself. The puma was now just ten paces away.

I had tried to keep Zapana safely away from this final encounter, but he came on his own, and I loved him all the more. Now, staring fanged death in the face, I felt a contentment knowing that if these were to be our last moments, we shared them together. But if this is to be our end, I thought, he should at least know about our child. My pregnancy was three months advanced but still not showing. "Zapana," I said softly, "there's something I must tell you."

"I love you, too," he said quickly without taking his eyes from the cat.

"That, too, but what I mean is—"

Without warning the puma sprang at me. I saw only its gray eyes and a whiskered, white muzzle drawn over paired fangs the size of thumbs, and two huge paws with claws bared as it leapt. There wasn't even time to run. Zapana came up from his crouch and lunged as the cat left the ground. A piercing scream filled my ears when the great beast came down, knocking me flat on my back. I thought the scream came from me, but then I felt the animal's weight withdraw and heard a pitiful whine.

The cat clawed the ground, trying to drag itself away on its front legs. Zapana's spear stuck clean through its belly. Growls of defiance ended in howls of pain.

Above on the walkway Q'enti hopped up and down. "My puma! He killed my puma. He's not supposed to be here. This isn't fair!"

Zapana helped me to my feet. We stared at the cat's agony. "You should have pierced it through the heart," I said.

Zapana hung his head. "I tried but missed. It's a magnificent creature." In silence he untied his maqana, and gripped the handle in both hands. He approached the puma. The animal snarled at him, and then turned its head away in resignation. A single blow ended its suffering.

We shared a look, and then as one turned to the prison holding Qhari. Windowless, and with a stout door bound in place, it kept the animals and serpents at bay while trapping Qhari inside. Seven months had passed since Atoco took him, and the poison would now be entering its final stages. I remembered Asto's bloated and ravaged body, and shuddered.

I cut the door bindings and Zapana shoved it aside. The smell within made us duck our heads. I took a deep breath and stepped into the dark, fetid room. As my eyes adjusted I saw the space was no more than two paces wide by six long, and bare except for a water jug by the door and a shape stretched beneath a rag of blanket against the wall. I ran forward and knelt. Zapana peered over my shoulder.

Qhari's eyes were shut and he breathed raggedly, but he breathed. "He's alive," I said. Zapana exhaled loudly. Qhari's eyelids twitched, but remained closed. A rope bound his wrists to a wooden pin set in the wall. I cut his hands free and gasped at the sores encircling his wrists. Atoco hadn't taken any chances. Qhari's face was puffy, but the bleeding from eyes and nose hadn't begun, and his body was emaciated rather than swollen. The condor dust had yet to take its full toll.

I ran my fingertips over his dear face whispering, "Qhari, oh, Qhari." He looked as innocent and peaceful as when we were children sleeping side-by-side. With eyes closed he stirred and smiled, muttering, "Qori, I knew you'd come again. Stay longer this time."

"Qhari," I said louder, taking him by the shoulders, "this isn't a dream. I'm here. Wake up."

"Qhari, you're safe," Zapana said.

Qhari stiffened and blinked, raising his lids slightly, then his eyes opened wide. "Qori? Zapana?"

"We're here old friend," Zapana said leaning forward to pat Qhari's limp hand.

My tears spilled on Qhari's face, and then I seized him in a hug. "Oh Qhari, I thought you were dead," I wailed. Qhari struggled to speak. "Yes, Qhari," I said holding him closer, "what is it?"

Qhari swallowed with effort. "You . . ." he began with labored breath.

"Yes, Qhari?" I urged.

"You're squeezing me to death."

Zapana chuckled and I sat bolt upright. This was an old jest between us, and I responded in the manner expected. "Well fine, Qhari Puma. You just lie there and have a nap while sister makes a fool of herself, or would you like to go for a stroll in the maze?"

Qhari smiled weakly. "I'm glad you are here," he managed.

"Are you, Qhari Puma? Well, a fine greeting for your sister, and after all I've been through. You're as dumb as a slug, Qhari Puma. Did I ever tell you that?"

"Often," Qhari grinned. He raised a feeble hand and I pressed it to my face.

Zapana still snickered. I gave him an indignant look, which made him hold his lips together as his shoulders shook. Then he said, "Did you bring it?"

"Of course." I produced a packet of antidote. "Get the water."

Zapana retrieved the jug by the door, and then lifted Qhari's head while I placed a large dose on Qhari's tongue. Zapana said, "Here, old soldier, this will fix you," and then trickled a few drops of putrid water into Qhari's mouth. Qhari swallowed and coughed.

"A few more doses like that and you'll be fine," I told Qhari, patting his hand.

"Not if I have to swallow it with that filth," Qhari muttered.

"Oh, and I suppose only Cuzco beer is good enough to save your life, Qhari Puma?"

"You don't happen to have any?" Qhari said. Zapana laughed, earning my most disapproving frown. He raised his hands in silent defense and backed away.

Qhari pressed my arm. "Did you find the Eye of the Condor?"

"Yes, and you were right, it exists, but we can speak of that later. Right now we must get you out of here." Qhari relaxed with a faraway smile.

Qhari was too weak to stand so Zapana lifted him in his arms. Qhari draped an arm around Zapana's neck and snuggled against his shoulder. He looked peaceful. Zapana said, "Come on, old friend, we'll get you out of here."

"I'm not 'old,'" Qhari replied peevishly without opening his eyes. Zapana's shoulders shook with mirth as he carried Qhari into the sunshine.

We left the shed to find Atoco and six guards before us in the courtyard, spears leveled. Q'enti stood to one side with arms folded, her eyes casting daggers. They had lowered her from above in a basket, and ropes dangled from the walkway where the men had scrambled down.

Q'enti said, "You should not have come, Lord Zapana. You weren't invited."

"But I did come, Lady Q'enti," he said evenly, still holding Qhari's thin form.

"Yes, and Captain Atoco informs me you came alone, but you killed my puma."

"It was the cat or us," Zapana replied.

I stepped forward. "I fulfilled the bargain, Q'enti. You have your antidote, and I have Qhari."

"But I don't have the Eye of the Condor," Q'enti said, eyes twinkling.

"You did. You had it in your hands, but it was lost," I reminded her.

"You gave it away."

"To save your life, yes, and now I've saved your life again with the antidote. I even ran the maze for your amusement, Q'enti. You had your revenge on me, now let us go."

Q'enti's hands went to her hips. "You cheated. You were supposed to come alone and without weapons."

"Lady Q'enti," Zapana said in a commanding voice, "we are leaving now. Don't try to stop us."

Q'enti stared at Zapana curiously. "You are my one regret, Zapana. Such a big, handsome man. Why didn't you come to me?"

I knew she would have tried often on their journey back to Cuzco, but I never doubted Zapana. He was probably the only man who ever turned her down.

"Come to you?" Zapana said incredulously. "You disgust me."

"What?" Q'enti flared. "You can't speak to me like that, I'm beautiful."

"No, you are ugly," Zapana said flatly, shaking his head.

Q'enti reddened and stared at him in open-mouth fury, her left eye fluttering as if it was about to fly away. In spite of her make-up the scar on her cheek stood out like a welt. Atoco knew what was coming and signaled his men to be ready. Besides thrusting spears and shields, two carried clubs and the other four had battle-axes. Atoco hefted his mace, waving the spiked head at us. Zapana could handle any two of them, I knew, and so could I, but seven?

Q'enti found her voice. "Captain Atoco," she bellowed, "kill them."

XXIII

Being the Conclusion of this Tale, in which is revealed Those Who Died and the manner of their deaths, and how Fate dealt with the living.

Atoco leapt forward in fighting stance. The men behind him set their jaws and advanced, spears leveled. Q'enti backed off to the side, eager to watch the final combat.

Ignoring Atoco with studied calm, Zapana propped Qhari in a sitting position against the shed and said to him, "Watch our backs." Qhari was too weak to stand, but his eyes opened and he replied, "I'll cover you." He said it earnestly, and we nodded as if taking him seriously.

Zapana hefted his maqana, and I gripped my tiny blade. "Seven of them against you and me," Zapana said.

"I know," I replied, "not very good odds for them."

Zapana grinned. "Well, old girl, we've had a good run. No one can say we led boring lives."

"I'm not 'old,'" I said.

"You and your brother," Zapana chuckled, shaking his head. "No, you're not old, and you're still as beautiful as the first day I saw you. You were only eighteen then, on the terraces of Tipón, do you remember?"

"Yes, and you were holding a maqana on that occasion, also."

Atoco paused to watch this exchange, for he couldn't believe we were ignoring him. In truth, we weren't. While we appeared to be chatting we studied Atoco's warriors from the corners of our eyes, seeking the weak and hesitant. There were none. They were well armed and well trained brutes, and their scars showed they were not strangers to combat. Yet their confidence was their weakness. I had already seen Atoco nod to the two men farthest on his right. They would come at me while Atoco and four others surrounded Zapana. I saw the look in Zapana's eyes. He was determined to kill Atoco before the others dragged him down. The warriors tensed and Atoco raised his mace to signal the charge.

"I'm carrying your child," I said suddenly.

Zapana's head jerked around. "What?"

"I am sure it's a son," I said keeping my eyes on the warriors.

Zapana gulped. "My son?" He stared at Q'enti who waited safely off to the side. "You bitch," he thundered. "You will not steal another child of mine." Q'enti looked confused. With a piercing war cry Zapana raised his maqana and bolted at the men. They scattered in surprise and even Atoco was caught off guard. A soldier held his spear crossways in defense, but Zapana's first blow snapped the shaft, and then his maqana swished back smashing the man's face.

The warrior in front of me was distracted by Zapana's attack. I somersaulted at his feet and came up inside his grasp, opening his throat with a flick of my blade. Dropping spear and shield, he covered his neck with his hands and fell back. I whirled as the man on my left attacked, backhanding his spear aside and plunging my dagger into his eye. Without pause I turned to help Zapana.

Zapana had accounted for a second body while I was busy, but the surprise of the attack was over and they now surrounded him. While Atoco and another man harried Zapana from either side, a third rushed him from behind with spear lowered. From where I stood there wasn't time for me to intercept this assailant, so I threw my knife. It pierced his arm an instant before he collided, deflecting but not stopping the spear from slashing Zapana's back. Zapana staggered forward while fending a blow from a battle-axe. Then, from the other side, Atoco's spike-head mace smashed his ribs.

Q'enti hopped up and down waving clenched fists. "Kill him! Kill him!" she shrieked.

I ran forward as Zapana staggered and parried another blow from Atoco, but the axe-wielder swung again sending Zapana to his knees. The man I wounded yanked my blade from his arm and, taking his club in one hand, turned to meet me. I leapt high and ploughed both feet into his chest before he could swing, knocking him flat. Scrambling to my feet I sprang at the axe-man, struggling to get a claw-grip on his throat. When he broke my hold I fastened my legs around his waist and tore at his eyes.

Zapana still tottered on his knees holding his huge maqana in his right hand, his left arm hanging useless. Atoco danced around him delivering a rain of vicious blows that Zapana deflected with failing strength. Q'enti, still hopping up and down, moved under the trees beside the shed for a better view. "Kill her!" she screamed at the man I struggled with. He dropped his axe, for with me glued to his chest he couldn't use it, and lifted me with both hands. I flew through the air and landed on my back, the breath knocked out of me. The axe-man rearmed himself and came at me. His face was a welter of scratches, but his eyes burned like coals. The wounded man with the club picked himself up and closed from the other side.

I struggled to my feet and backed up to where Qhari lay propped against the shed. My only thought was to reach Zapana. The two attackers edged forward, now more cautious. Q'enti urged them on. "Slash her face! Skin her alive!" Zapana fended another blow from Atoco, but reeled trying to keep himself kneeling upright. He didn't seem to have the strength to raise his maqana again. Atoco darted away, posed with his mace, and danced forward to strike from another angle.

The two stalking me charged from opposite sides. There wasn't time to meet both. I crouched and leapt as the axe-man raised his blade above his head. Coming up inside his swing I fastened my fingers on his throat and dug deep, expecting the club-wielder to strike from behind. But the blow didn't come, and with my victim on his knees choking I glanced behind. None of us had heeded Qhari's limp form, though this struggle took place almost on top of him. When the man at my back stepped over Qhari's legs, Qhari tripped him, and then with strength from some hidden place Qhari rolled on top of him and seized his club. The man looked up with terrified eyes to see Qhari raising the weapon.

"Leave . . . my . . . sister . . . alone," Qhari shouted, each word spoken with a blow that splattered the man's brains. Qhari cast me a wan smile, then his eyes rolled into his head and he fainted.

The man I struggled with worked his thumbs into my wrists and broke the hold. I drove my knee into his face. He fell back but his fingers found the butt of his axe. I ran to a fallen spear and snatched it up. When I turned he was already on his feet spitting blood and teeth, but armed and ready to charge. I threw hard. He tried to dodge but the spear caught him in the thigh. He screamed and went down heavily. The shaft remained firmly lodged, and from the way he writhed I knew the blade was sunk in the bone. He would give no more trouble.

Atoco ceased posturing and swooped on Zapana. It happened only paces in front of me, but even that distance was too far for me to help. Atoco's mace landed on Zapana's back with a hollow thud, causing him to slump on his face. Light of foot, Atoco twirled in place to show his victory, and then poised for the killing blow. In that breath I dashed at him, knowing I was already too late. Suddenly Zapana's head came up, and with the last fiber of his strength he swung his maqana sideways catching Atoco on the shin with a sharp crack! Atoco howled and collapsed. As I knelt at Zapan's side, Atoco scuttled away backwards on his hands, dragging his broken leg.

"You are alive," Zapana gasped in relief.

"Oh my darling man," I cried throwing my arms around him. His breath caught in pain and I released him. With a smashed shoulder and broken ribs this was no time for embraces. "Help me to my feet," he said through his teeth.

I placed his good arm around my shoulders and we stood. The courtyard was a scene of devastation washed in blood. The bodies of five men and a puma lay sprawled in death, while Atoco and the man with the spear in his leg dragged themselves to the side. Qhari lay where he fainted, half covering the warrior whose brains he spilled while protecting me. Zapana whistled at the carnage. "You are a dangerous woman to be around," he said to me.

Q'enti stood by the trees trembling with rage. "No!" she shouted. "Captain Atoco, get more men and stop them. I am ordering you." Atoco, now as far away as he could get from us, didn't look inclined to jump up.

Zapana tried to hold me back when I turned to Q'enti. "This is between me and her," I said to him. He released me reluctantly. I retrieved my knife and walked over to Q'enti.

Q'enti backed farther under the trees. She pointed a trembling finger. "You stay away from me."

"You stole my first child, Q'enti, but this one will live in a world without you."

The question on her face changed to understanding. "You are with child? Zapana again?" She saw the answer in my eyes and looked past me to Zapana. "That's why you wouldn't come to me?" she said.

Zapana replied, "Even if it wasn't for our child, you are still the most disgusting creature I ever met."

"You can't talk to me that way," Q'enti shouted. Her eyes narrowed in a malicious glare. "You forget I still have the condor dust."

"Where is it?" Zapana demanded.

"Where no one but me will ever find it. So beware, Lord Zapana."

"There's no time for that, Q'enti," I said. "You've claimed your last victim." I took a step toward her and she backed off.

"Captain Atoco," she bellowed. Atoco turned his head away in silence. Q'enti gave him a look which said she would deal with him later, then turned laughing eyes on me. "You can't touch me. I am Lady Q'enti, daughter of the oldest and most respected house of Lower Cuzco, and I am untouchable by royal decree."

"I don't care, Q'enti. Shall we make this quick, or should I cut your pretty nose off before I slit your throat?"

Q'enti stamped her foot and waved fists over her head. "No, no, no! If you touch me you're dead, you idiot!"

Suddenly a set of jaws shot from the branch above and seized her wrist. Long coils as thick as a man's thigh fell on her shoulders, instantly encircling her body. I jumped back in horror as Q'enti's shrill scream filled the courtyard.

"Help her. Help Lady Q'enti," Atoco shouted frantically, trying to rise.

Zapana came to my side. He looked around as if to seize a weapon, but then caught himself. He relaxed and put his arm around my shoulders. So this is Atoco's 'Squeezer,' I thought.

The great serpent released Q'enti's hand now that it had its coils around her. Its full length slipped from above, and though it circled her four times, still half its sinuous body slithered on the ground. Q'enti's arms were free, and she beat at the cable of muscle constricting her chest. But she struck wildly with little effect, for she didn't want to touch the creature anymore than she wanted it touching her. Her mouth stayed open in a continuous ear-splitting scream.

"Kill it," Atoco called, now standing on one leg.

From the other side of the courtyard the man with the spear in his leg shouted, "Save Lady Q'enti." But he couldn't stand, and only waved a feeble arm.

Zapana and I watched while Squeezer wrapped Q'enti's arms and legs. It didn't care that she was Lady Q'enti, or that she was beautiful. Q'enti's scar gleamed white on her purple face. Her eyes bulged. The stench of voided bowels filled our nostrils. Q'enti stopped screaming long enough to rasp, "Help me, I beg you, please!" Red bubbles formed on her lips. Her voice choked off and her tongue came out. The weight of the creature made her fall on her back. Now prone, her head was the only part showing as Squeezer finished wrapping her in thick, crushing coils. Its head came up and hovered over her face, jaws wide showing needle teeth like the stuffed serpent we saw at the temple in Guayas. Q'enti stared with eyes bursting, a cold, silent scream in her open mouth. Her most terrifying nightmare had come to life, and it was as horrible and pitiless as her soul. The creature clamped its jaws across her face. Next came the sound of bones snapping like dead branches.

A commotion at the far end of the maze made us turn. Imperial guards ran along the walkways above. I recognized the commander of the Cuzco garrison, the warlord Chalcochima. "He's early," Zapana remarked.

Chalcochima peered down. "What's going on here?" he demanded. Some of his men lowered themselves by ropes to the courtyard.

Zapana looked up. "I told you to come at mid-afternoon. Did the messenger mistake my words?"

Chalcochima frowned. "No, he did not. But if there's mischief afoot in my jurisdiction I don't wait to be summoned, not even by you, Lord Zapana. You should have reported this earlier. The House of Beasts is Lady Q'enti's domain. Where is she, and who are these men?" he demanded, gesturing at the bodies. "Did you kill them?" Zapana whispered to me, "I thought we'd be gone by the time he arrived to clean up." Four of Chalcochima's guards surrounded us, but stood at attention with spears upright, unsure what to do. "Lady Q'enti is there," Atoco shouted, hopping on his good leg and pointing to Squeezer. Squeezer had given up trying to swallow Q'enti but was reluctant to leave, remaining wrapped around her lifeless form.

Chalcochima leaned forward studying Squeezer, his officers crowding around. "Kill it," he ordered his men on the ground. They approached warily, and then one jumped forward driving his spear through the serpent's head. Squeezer writhed, withdrawing coils and trying to slither away, but soon stopped and moved no more. Enough of Q'enti's crushed body lay uncovered for everyone to see who it was. The officers with Chalcochima gasped, and joined the warlord lowering themselves by ropes to the courtyard for a closer examination. Some wore collars of rounded feathers, the mark of Q'enti's lineage.

Qhari stirred and I went to him, rolling him on his back and placing his head in my lap. "What?" he said when he saw the new arrivals.

"Hush, Qhari," I whispered. "Q'enti is dead, and Chalcochima is here." Qhari sucked in his breath. Regardless of what was decided concerning Q'enti, Qhari and I were still fugitives and Chalcochima was pledged to enforce the law. We stayed quietly off to the side while Chalcochima questioned Zapana.

"What happened?" Chalcochima asked Zapana, giving him a hard look. I knew they were friends, but only in private. When Chalcochima spoke in front of his men he favored no one.

Before Zapana could answer Atoco shouted, "He murdered Lady Q'enti."

Chalcochima seemed to recognize Atoco for the first time. "It appears the serpent killed her, Captain Atoco."

"It did," Atoco said, "but he stood and watched. He could have saved Lady Q'enti."

"It is true," the man with the spear in his leg called. "I saw it. He and that woman fed Lady Q'enti to the snake."

Chalcochima glanced my way for the first time, but Zapana grabbed his arm. "That's not what happened," Zapana said. "Lady Q'enti lured me here and was killed by one of her own creatures."

Zapana was trying to divert attention from Qhari and me, and Chalcochima appeared willing to let him. He knew me instantly, of course, but when he glanced my way he looked through me without recognition. The officers with him, all younger men, didn't know who I was, but one of them recognized Qhari. He blurted, "It's Qhari Puma, the Steward of K'allachaka. Lord, this man is absent from his post without leave. He was a fugitive for months." The young man looked pleased with himself.

Qhari raised himself on his elbow and spoke in a loud, firm voice. "I am Qhari Puma of K'allachaka, and Captain Atoco took me hostage. Lord Zapana came to rescue me."

Atoco arrived from across the courtyard carried between two guards. Like many of the men present these soldiers were his Lower Cuzco kinsmen. Atoco looked frantic. He was Q'enti's minion, and if the full truth came out his part wouldn't go unnoticed.

"Qhari Puma fled his duties and hid here without my knowledge," Atoco said. "He's a man-woman—I can produce witnesses, and Lord Zapana is his lover."

A buzz came from the men, but Chalcochima held up a hand for silence. "Enough, Captain Atoco. There are serious charges pending here, and various accounts of events. What's clear is that many have died, including Lady Q'enti of Lower Cuzco." He raised his voice for everyone to hear. "I swear to Lady Q'enti's kinsmen there will be justice." Heads nodded and whispering began.

Chalcochima held up his hand again. "Until my investigation is complete Captain Atoco will remain in Cuzco, while the fugitive Qhari Puma is to be held at Tipón along with Lord Zapana and his maid."

"She's not a maid," Atoco said. "She is—"

Chalcochima cut him off. "Enough! I will decide whom she is and what's to be done with her. You will hold your tongue, Captain Atoco, and hope I don't find that you're involved in this."

From the door of my cottage I watched Qhari directing the Tipón servants. He had them laying blankets around a pile of kindling at the edge of the terrace. The sun dipped behind the mountains. Two weeks had passed since we rescued him from the House of Beasts. Each day the antidote worked marvels, and now the old Qhari strutted about searching for ways to keep busy, annoying the servants with meddling suggestions and then making them laugh. He knew he was a pest, but Qhari never could sit still. The venture he now directed was to be a surprise for Zapana and me.

"What's he up to now?" Zapana asked from his bed.

I went to him. "I think Qhari is going to surprise us again."

"Again?" Zapana said with a grin. "Last night it was a troop of acrobats, and the night before flutists playing outside our door. I'm going to have to send him back to K'allachaka just to get some peace around here."

I tucked the blanket at his neck. "You just lay there and be good."

"I've been 'good' for ages. A man can't lay in bed forever. It's time for me to rise."

"I am your physician, and you can rise when I tell you, not before. If you're good I may let you go out this evening."

I had reset his shoulder using chilca herb, and kept a plaster of pepper tree resin on his cuts. They were now almost healed, but

Atoco's spike-head mace smashed ribs, and there is nothing more painful or slower to heal than broken ribs. Still, in spite of his playful laments, he lay quietly most of the time and the ribs mended well. I knew he enjoyed the role of complaining patient as much as I savored being the scolding healer.

When we arrived at Tipón with Qhari and Zapana on litters, our escorts sought to put us in the palace. That didn't suit me. The palace seemed cold and formal, and my men needed to recover in a home. I had them taken to the little complex of cottages Zapana built for me. With Qhari installed in one, and Zapana and I next door in the largest structure, I shooed away the maids and set about arranging comforts. Zapana watched me fussing with lamps and hangings and flowers. He smiled. The Tipón storehouses had been emptied compensating the Kañari for Pisar's death, but there was nothing in them I needed anyway.

My belly blossomed, perhaps not enough for those who didn't know me to notice, but it seemed huge to me. I felt my son growing inside. When he kicked I placed Zapana's hand there. Zapana stared in wonder, then lay back and gloated at the ceiling.

"My son isn't going to be a spy," I warned Zapana.

"Certainly not," Zapana agreed, "my son is going to be a warlord."

One day, when Qhari's health was restored enough for him to get into mischief, he dashed into our cottage and tied Zapana to his bed. With his helpless captive before him, Qhari solemnly recited bawdy jests until poor Zapana shook with laughter. I charged to the rescue, beating Qhari with a pillow. The wretch turned into my sister and announced 'she' knew better than me how to care for a man, and threatened me with a pacae fruit. She left only when I agreed to let her have one of my dresses, which she wore when she came to visit the next day.

But in whatever garb Qhari appeared he had an endless fund of questions for me about sailing rafts. "How do they know which winds to follow? How do they change course? What's it like standing on the deck under full sail?" When we were children we stood hand-in-hand on the beach watching the great sails pass far out to sea, and we told each other stories about where they were bound. I had forgotten this childhood fascination, but it never left Qhari. He still dreamed of a life on the water.

I fretted daily while tending my men, expecting Chalcochima's soldiers to arrive any moment with a summons to the royal council. Regardless of later circumstances, Qhari had abandoned his duties and traveled without leave, and I broke my banishment. But I worried most for Zapana. Aiding me was a lesser crime compared with being blamed for Q'enti's death. I knew Atoco was busily covering his tracks by raising support for that charge among his Lower Cuzco kinsmen. To save Zapana I resolved to claim all responsibility, and at the same time make up a suitable story to cover Qhari's actions, too.

Messengers from Chalcochima arrived often, but they insisted on speaking in private with Zapana, and Zapana was frustratingly vague about these communications. "Routine matters," he would say. I feared he was bargaining his life away to save mine. Once, I even spied Qhari speaking earnestly with Chalcochima's messenger. When I confronted Qhari he claimed he was ordering tern eggs for the kitchen. He never could tell a convincing lie.

"Chalcochima won't let his men talk to you because that would be acknowledging your presence here," Zapana said when I complained to him. "You don't know him like I do, Qori. He is always cold about official matters, but he's risking a great deal trying to keep you out of this."

"Perhaps I don't want to be kept out."

"No, I'm sure you don't," Zapana said, "but that's the way of things. Don't look at me like that, I know you're planning to shoulder all the blame." I balked, none too convincingly, and Zapana smiled. "I know you," he said, "but believe me, Chalcochima won't let you speak. He thinks your banishment was his fault, and he's determined to make it up to you whether you like it or not."

"But you and Qhari . . . you did it for me."

"Yes, but we make our own decisions in this life, and good or bad we stand by the consequences. Qhari and I only did what was right, and if we can live with that so must you."

I replied glumly, "After the royal council meets none of us may have long to live."

"Perhaps, but that time hasn't come," Zapana observed. "We have today, so let's not spoil it by worrying about tomorrow. Come here you pretty thing, I need a kiss."

That night I took Zapana outside where Qhari waited on the blankets. Zapana insisted on walking unaided, but grimaced when he lowered himself to sit cross-legged. Qhari sat grinning at us from across the fire.

The servants wouldn't leave Zapana alone. "A pillow, Lord?" his chamberlain asked.

"Thank you, I have three already," Zapana said. "But Lady Qori has none." The chamberlain turned to me. "Pillows?" he inquired hopefully. Before I could answer Qhari cut in. "No pillows for her, or me, thank you."

The furnishings were sparse indeed. Qhari even had us sitting on old blankets. Zapana's chamberlain was not impressed with these arrangements and lifted his nose. "I have a jar of fine Cuzco beer, Lord. Shall I pour?"

"Not necessary," Qhari interjected. He produced a skin bag from behind his back, pulled the stopper, and took a mouthful. The chamberlain winced. "And take away the drinking cups," Qhari ordered.

"But, Lord . . . ?" the chamberlain protested to Zapana.

Zapana chuckled. "Do as he says, please."

The chamberlain persisted, still addressing Zapana. "Perhaps a brazier, Lord, instead of this smoky fire?"

"It's good enough for us," Qhari said with a swagger. "Now drop that pot of mush and be gone."

Zapana held his ribs and chuckled again. To placate the chamberlain, who was quite put out when Zapana settled in my cottage, he said, "It is my wish that we humor Lord Qhari tonight. Please withdraw and take your people with you. Thank you for your service." The chamberlain cast a deadly look at Qhari and me, then clapped his hands and the servants reluctantly followed him away.

"Lord Qhari?" I said when we were alone.

"I just promoted him," Zapana said.

Qhari sat up with eyes shining. Zapana couldn't really promote him to nobility, but the fiction pleased them both, and soon it wouldn't matter anyway. Qhari saluted him with the skin bag, took a deep swallow and coughed, then passed the skin.

Zapana hefted the bag and asked, "What is it?"

"Fire," Qhari announced, wiping his mouth on the back of his hand. "Some call it happy brew, and others call it llama piss, but it will knock you flat on your—"

"Alright, Qhari," I said, "what's this all about?"

Qhari glanced at me indignantly. "It's obvious, we're on the trail."

I shared a look with Zapana. "What trail?" I said.

"Any trail," he said sweeping his arms wide.

Zapana laughed and saluted him with the bag, then took a swig. He coughed and handed the bag to me. "Llama piss," he said in a hoarse voice.

"Now tell me about those Puná pirates again," Qhari said. "What kind of rafts did they sail?"

I lifted the bag and felt the liquid burn my throat, but with effort I didn't cough. The men looked impressed. With a thousand stars twinkling in the blackness overhead, and our world reduced to the glow of the fire, I began, "It happened like this . . . ."

The three of us waited in a courtyard attached to a private audience chamber in Wayna Qhapaq's palace. Outside, the streets of Cuzco bustled under a blue sky. On the way to the palace we passed llama trains and imperial guards, nobles carried in hammocks, ambassadorial entourages, pilgrims, administrators, messengers, and priests. The business of empire ground on in spite of, and oblivious to, the small drama about to unfold behind closed doors.

The summons made no mention of me, but Zapana finally relented and allowed me to attend in the guise of Choque the Qolla maid. There was a price for this—his agents had contacted my girls, the Filthy Ones, who still waited patiently outside the city, and I had to agree to join them for the journey back to Wanaku immediately after the judgments. To avoid street gossip, Qhari and Zapana covered their heads until we entered the palace, but once inside there was no need to shield their identities. They wore their finest knee-length tunics, with stylish bands of colored fringes dangling at their calves and ankles. They looked handsome, but resigned. Chalcochima entered the courtyard in conversation with Atoco, who limped with a staff. The guards snapped to attention. We remained seated on a bench against the wall. "You should have broken both his legs," I whispered to Zapana.

A moon had come and gone while we waited at Tipón. Zapana said the delay was a good sign. Negotiations continued relentlessly, though Zapana refused to tell me what was being said. He only mentioned that Q'enti's condor dust was never found. The Emperor Wayna Qhapaq, who still journeyed deep in the south of the Empire, was informed that His chief spy was on trial, and kept abreast of developments by messenger as the bargaining progressed. But Zapana could not keep Atoco's intrigue from me, for even the servants at Tipón knew the gossip of Cuzco. Lower Cuzco was outraged at Lady Q'enti's death, and a serious split developed with the royal families of Upper Cuzco, to which Zapana belonged. It was hypocrisy, for even Q'enti's kinsmen had feared her, and no one liked Atoco, but as always the shrewd saw leverage for concessions and fanned the flames. The Empire could not survive without unity—unity at any price.

At the last moment Chalcochima managed a concession of his own. Because Zapana was head of the imperial spy web and privy to the Emperor's secrets, security was best served by holding the trial in private, and not in front of the royal council. This was good news. Atoco would have had his supporters crowding the great hall. But, the change of venue also meant the verdict would rest with a few judges, and their decision was final. Atoco chose not to notice the three of us when he entered the courtyard with Chalcochima. He smiled when the warlord patted his back, and directed him down a corridor to the audience room. "I'll bring them along in a moment," Chalcochima called after Atoco. Atoco returned a friendly wave.

We stood. Chalcochima refused to look at me but said to Zapana, "I see you brought your maid. She waits out here." It was an order. Zapana nodded and gave me a look. I rolled my eyes and stepped back.

Chalcochima turned to Qhari. "My messenger relayed your version of events." I remembered Qhari speaking intently to the man at Tipón. Chalcochima shook his head in disbelief, and Qhari's shoulders sagged. "That's the most ridiculous tale I ever heard," Chalcochima said. "Do you really expect us to believe that you made Lord Zapana do your bidding, and you are responsible for Lady Q'enti's death?" Chalcochima snorted. Zapana and I exchanged a grin. "As for your sister," Chalcochima continued, "as far as I'm concerned she's still in Wanaku, so you needn't make up stories about forcing her to leave her exile. You may wish to lose your head, Qhari Puma, and before this day is over it may happen, but not on these counts. I didn't tell the judges what you told me, and I advise you not to anger them with such foolishness."

Qhari hung his head. I should have guessed he would try to exchange his life for ours. Zapana placed a hand on Qhari's shoulder. "Thank you, old friend," he said. Qhari looked crestfallen but still managed to mutter, "I'm not old."

Chalcochima studied Zapana. "As for your story, Lord Zapana, I think we've negotiated it into acceptable form. Does your offer still stand?"

Zapana nodded grimly. "Who are the judges?" he asked.

"The Emperor's brother is still He Who Speaks For The Lord. He awaits you inside with the leader of Lower Cuzco. These two will pass judgment on you. I don't know what they might decide, and right now I don't think they know either. They want to hear from you first."

"Will you be present?" Zapana wondered.

"Yes, as guard and councilor, but aside from Qhari Puma and Captain Atoco there won't be anyone else in the room."

"Atoco looked pleased just now," Zapana observed.

"The worm," Chalcochima said with disgust. "Oh yes, Captain Atoco and I are 'friends,' but he doesn't trust me anymore than I trust him. In spite of your offer he may yet drag your 'maid' into this if it goes badly for him."

A guard came from the corridor and snapped to attention in front of Chalcochima. "Lord, they are waiting for you."

Chalcochima gestured for Qhari and Zapana to follow him.

I grabbed Zapana's hand. "What did you offer Atoco?" Zapana smiled and brushed back my hair. "There were many offers and demands in the negotiations, and then counter offers and counter demands. I don't know how far Atoco will go, or what the judges will find acceptable. Just remember this, Lady Qori Qoyllur, I love you."

Tears welled in my eyes, but before I could speak Qhari drew me away. "Don't worry, sister, I'll do my best for him." I watched their backs retreating down the hallway, and then Zapana stopped and called to me, "When the boy is old enough, give him my maqana."

I can't say how long I sat in the courtyard twisting the corner of my shawl, but it seemed an eternity. At last the chamber door opened and Atoco came limping down the corridor. I jumped to my feet. Atoco held his head high, smiling to himself. The guards and servants lining the courtyard stood formally, but all watched Atoco with eager eyes. Atoco looked at me, and his lipless mouth curved in a cruel grin. I stood rigid, silently begging news, but he passed by without a word.

Moments later a maid rushed back through the door Atoco had exited. Atoco hadn't remained silent long. The woman spoke to the guards. "It's settled," she gushed to a row of heads bent forward. "Captain Atoco has been promoted to commander, and he is taking over the Cuzco garrison from Lord Chalcochima." A buzz erupted. Pleased at being the first with the news the woman waved for silence. "And there's more. Commander Atoco has been given a new estate with twenty thousand llamas!"

I collapsed on the bench and buried my head in my hands. It's over, I thought, and Q'enti has her final revenge on all of us.

The chamber door opened again and Chalcochima emerged, head bowed. He saw me waiting at the end of the hall and his steps faltered. When he came up to me he swallowed hard and whispered,

"I did what I could, but Atoco has arrayed all of Lower Cuzco against us. The judges are deciding the men's punishment now. But, I can tell you this, they made Atoco leave you out of it."

Though my thoughts dwelled with Zapana and Qhari, I knew Chalcochima had suffered for me, too, and for the first time he seemed willing to talk. "They took the Cuzco garrison away from you?"

Chalcochima shrugged. "Atoco doesn't waste time spreading the news. No, they didn't take it from me, I offered it to Atoco."

"In exchange for what?"

Chalcochima's expression went vague. "It was part of the arrangement. Besides, I'm a field officer, not a court jester. I belong on the frontiers with my men."

We both turned when Zapana appeared. My heart quickened, and then fell. Zapana walked slowly down the hall with eyes downcast. My knees weakened and I clutched Chalcochima's arm for support. Zapana reached us before he lifted his head. I saw love and resignation in his eyes. But before he could speak Qhari came from the audience room. He strutted over with chin up, and looked from one questioning face to another.

"Well, do you want to know?" he said.

The three of us nodded. Qhari drew himself up and imitated the judges. "Qhari Puma, for abandoning your duties and traveling without permission we strip you of your position, confiscate any wealth a mere steward may have, and sentence you to banishment." Qhari grinned at us. "At least I get to keep my head."

I touched his arm. "Oh Qhari, you're no longer Steward of K'allachaka?"

Qhari shrugged. "No, but I was tired of it anyway."

"Where are you being exiled?" Zapana asked.

Qhari's face lit up. "They have banished me to Chincha. I'm going to be a sailor!"

Zapana looked down smiling. Even if Qhari didn't realize who was responsible for this, I did. I said, "Isn't there a temple in Chincha where a certain young 'lady' of your acquaintance resides?" Qhari actually blushed. "Never mind," I said, sparing him, "I happen to know a raft captain and mate in Chincha who will be glad to welcome you aboard."

Qhari beamed, and then he saw me looking at Zapana expectantly. "Haven't you told her yet?" he said to Zapana.

"I was about to," Zapana said.

"Then get it over with," Qhari said, moving to Chalcochima's side. Chalcochima leaned forward intently.

Zapana fastened his eyes on me. "They decided I was responsible for Q'enti's death."

"And I suppose you agreed with them?"

Zapana looked away. "They had to blame someone." Turning back he saw the impatience on my face and continued. "They took what's left of my wealth, including Tipón. They also revoked my noble status, and my position in the Emperor's service. And, like Qhari, I've been banished."

Chalcochima gripped Zapana's arm. "No death sentence?"

"No, my friend, they took everything but spared me that."

I couldn't move my hand from my mouth. Relief washed over me, replaced an instant later with the realization he was destroyed. He would never see Tipón again. "You've lost everything," I said in a whisper.

Zapana grinned. "Lost everything? No, I'm free of all those burdens."

Chalcochima nodded vigorously at this. "Where are you being exiled?"

Zapana put his arms around me. "To heaven," he said. "They banished me to Wanaku."

THE END

SOURCES

EYE OF THE CONDOR was inspired by the 16th and 17th century chronicles of:

Juan de Betánzos
Pedro de Cieza de León
Bernabè Cobo
Garcilaso de la Vega
Pedro Pizarro
Pedro Sarmiento de Gamboa
Agustín de Zárate

and the modern works of:

Catherine Allen
Brian Bauer
David Blower
Michael Harner
Regina Harrison
John Hyslop
Bruce Mannheim
Julia Meyerson
Craig Morris
John Murra
Susan Niles
María Rostworoski de Diez Canseco
John Rowe
Frank Salomon
Douglas Sharon
Irene Silverblatt
Margaret Towle
Gary Urton

Author's Note

Fact and Fiction in Eye of the Condor

Tawantinsuyu was the largest native empire of the Americas, a rugged land of mountains, deserts, and jungles stretching from Ecuador to Chile. Within this vast territory the Incas ruled millions. The empire was a mosaic of ethnicities, each group maintaining its own language, dress, and customs, yet inextricably bound to the Inca state through reciprocity, contrived mythology, fear, and the ambitions of its native rulers. The provinces were once independent nations, later caught in the Inca juggernaut of diplomacy and overwhelming military superiority. Those embedded in the state matrix, surrounded by Inca loyalists or barriers of geography, and long accustomed to imperial rule, gave less trouble. But newly conquered lands on the frontiers were volatile, and beyond them lay fiercely independent chiefdoms and big man societies.

The Inca expansion began less than a century before the Spanish arrived, so the empire was still a work in progress. Nonetheless, the Incas maintained over 40,000 kilometers of roads replete with bridges, rest stations, forests of storehouses, and an efficient messenger service rivaling that of the Roman Empire. Their splendid terrace systems rippling down mountainsides are marvels, and their megalithic walls fashioned from multi-angle stone blocks weighing up to 50 tons must be counted among the wonders of the ancient world. These are the monuments of culture, but it was the Inca genius for organization, adaptive management, and diplomacy based on reciprocity—envisioned on an imperial scale—that made the empire.

At best there were never more than a few hundred thousand Incas—Incas by blood and those in the Cuzco area made Incas by privilege. They believed they ruled the Andean world by divine right, chosen at creation to civilize and bring light to a world of chaos. Their conquered subjects were never more than 'provincials,' and beyond them lurked the savage hordes. If you detected snobbery in Qori Qoyllur toward non-Inca peoples, it is because Qori was as much a product of her time and place as you are of yours.

The Incas live on. Today, millions of Andean natives carry the blood and beliefs of their ancestors, and speak the Inca tongue. Foreigners have labeled this language Quechua, but its speakers call it Runasimi—Human Speech, and refer to themselves as Runa— The Real Human Beings.

Archaeology and ethnography continue to teach us much about the Incas, but every study begins with the Spanish chroniclers who wrote in the first century after the conquest. They were priests, bureaucrats, and soldier-adventurers, each with biases, and they often contradict one another on details. But the broad outlines of Inca culture and events are reasonably secure, while questionable points are fertile ground for the storyteller.

What is related about Inca culture in this novel is derived from the chroniclers, and informed by the work of archaeologists and ethnographers. All of the places mentioned (except the Condor Temple) are real and can be visited today. Wayna Qhapaq, Chalcochima, and Tumbala are historical figures; all other characters are fictitious.

The Incas often used spies, yet we have no evidence of a formalized 'secret service' like that operated by Lord Zapana at Tipón, or female agents like Qori specializing in disguise. But it was fun to write.

All the principal chroniclers mention the fabulous emeralds of Ecuador. In 1609 Garcilaso de la Vega (the younger) published the fullest account:

"All the inhabitants of this coast [Ecuador], even quite far north, observed the same customs and worshipped the same idols: the sea and

fish, tigers, lions, big snakes, and all sorts of other wild animals, according to their whims. In the Manta valley, which was the metropolis of this country, they also worshipped a giant emerald, which was said to be as big as an ostrich egg. On important feast days it was taken from the temple and shown to the people, among whom were throngs of Indians, who had come from a great distance to worship it and offer up sacrifices of emeralds that were smaller in size; because the priests and the cacique of Manta had persuaded these poor people that small emeralds were the daughters of the big one and that, therefore, no other offering would be so well received. This selfish reasoning had permitted them to accumulate in Manta an incomparable treasure of emeralds, which was discovered by Pedro de Alvarado and his companions—among whom was my father, Garcilaso de la Vega—at the time of the Peruvian conquest. However, since these conquistadors knew more about war than they did about precious stones, they broke the greater part of this treasure, being unable to believe that it was composed of real jewels, and not bits of glass, since the stones were not resistant to shock. As for the giant emerald, it had disappeared well before they arrived. Indeed, the persons who hid it, did it so successfully that it has never been found since, no more than have many other treasures that were buried in this same earth."

This quote inspired our Eye of the Condor, yet it contains all that is known about the giant emerald. The condor priests with their hidden temple and poison dust are fictions of this story.

The Filthy Ones are another fiction, though women in the ancient Andes, like women in the developing world today, undoubtedly knew this distress. Obstructed labor can result in a tiny hole called a fistula being torn in the bladder and rectum causing incontinence. From what is known about Inca beliefs it is plausible that such unfortunates would have been treated much as described here.

The use of the word "wool" in this novel is a misnomer. Technically, sheep produce wool, and alpacas produce camelid hair.

Little is known about homosexuality in Tawantinsuyu except that the Incas had strict laws against it, yet tolerated the practice when it was part of religious rites among their subject peoples. Cieza de León (1553) mentions the 'transvestite' temple in Chincha that our heroes visited, but Qhari's secret gatherings at K'allachaka are imagined.

The strange paths in the desert that Qori walked upon are the famous Nazca Lines, giant ground drawings etched on the plains in antiquity, and the great ceremonial center of Qhawachi (Cahuachi) is also well known to archaeologists. Both predate the Incas by a thousand years. While the Nazca Lines continue to defy a single interpretation, Qori's spirit flight may not be too farfetched; the hallucinogenic San Pedro cactus was used by the ancient inhabitants of this desert.

The chroniclers make clear the Chincha Valley was one of the most important and wealthiest provinces of the Inca realm. Early documents claim it was the center of sea trade, and archaeologists speculate metal and alpaca cloth were shipped north to Ecuador in exchange for spondylus shell (thorny oyster—found in Ecuadorian waters but sacred to all Andean peoples). The seagoing rafts in this novel are based on early Spanish reports, and the well-documented balsas of Ecuador.

The Punáe, Wankavilca, and Kañari are portrayed as they are known from ethnohistoric and archaeological sources. Near the end of Wayna Qhapaq's reign, after our story takes place, the Incas subdued Guayas and the island of Puná, though never invested them with the infrastructure of empire.

The Shuar people, popularly known by the Spanish name Jívaro (uncivilized), still live in the Cutucú Mountains of eastern Ecuador. Their description is based on ethnographic accounts.

Finally, the House of Beasts was real according to the chroniclers, though the Incas never called it by this name. The old emperor Pachakuti is credited with founding a menagerie of great cats (pumas, jaguars, and ocelots), bears (the Andean spectacled bear) and serpents (giant constrictors and poisonous varieties). The animals were kept in a house or houses referred to as a prison. War captives and criminals were locked inside, but if they survived three days they went free. This prison was in or near Cuzco, but we do not know precisely where, what it looked like, or whether it changed locations under later rulers. However, no one but the deranged Lady Q'enti could have devised the House of Beasts found in this novel.

There is a covenant between readers and writers of historical fiction. The reader trusts the author to convey the flavor of time and place within a plausible tale, and the author trusts the reader not to confuse novels with history books.

P.H. Carmichael